Broken Bones

A Jack Troop
Adventure

Daniel Oliver Betz III

Owl Publishing, LLC.
150 Parkview Heights Road,
Ephrata PA 17522

717-925-7511
www.owlpublishinghouse.com

ISBN: 9781949929034

Library of Congress Control Number: In Process

Editing by Kate Matson

Cover Design by Owl Publishing, LLC.

DEDICATION

This book is dedicated to my wife, Patricia C. Betz.

CONTENTS

ACKNOWLEDGMENTS

My sister, Jane E. McLain in no uncertain terms, she told me to start writing after I retired. My brother, James P. Betz was very interested in this story and encouraged me to finish the project. I had additional support from my sons, David O. Betz and Jonathan D. Betz. My mother, Janet W. Betz has supported me her entire life. She will be 97 in January 2019.

CHAPTER 1:
The First Broken Bone

The 'Roonies' was a low-income housing project in Chester City that was championed by Mayor Patrick Rooney in the late 1950's and completed in 1962. The boarded-up, graffiti-scarred, unoccupied old building that the two young black men had chosen to meet in was located on Hope St. Residents now snickered at the name and referred to it as 'no hope' street.

The building reeked of human fecal matter, urine, and vomit. These odors were mixed with the scents of dead rodents, old rotten food, the smell of marijuana, and the distinct smell of dank stale air. Used needles littered the stained concrete floor.

Darnell Ducette was one of these young men. He was accompanied by Marcus Wayne. Both were eighteen years old and had known each other since grade school and had also played football for the Stannard High School Stallions in Chester City. The team had won the state championship in each of the last two seasons.

Darnell was a six-foot-two-inch 215-pound quarterback. He was one of those lucky young men born with five percent body fat that left him with the chiseled body like a statue of a Greek god. He had perfect teeth that endowed him with a perfect smile that he flashed freely. His dark eyes were so piercing they were like two lasers with a glare and fire that could penetrate cold steel.

Darnell was actively recruited by major college football powers 1 across the nation along with lesser known programs like Chester City State University. Amazingly enough, Chester City State succeeded in signing Darnell. No one understood why, but Darnell wanted to play football in his hometown where he was adored. He loved the idea of being the big fish in a small pond. He had been offered and accepted a full scholarship and would get columns upon columns of newspaper publicity and hundreds upon hundreds of live interviews.

Marcus was three inches taller and fifty pounds heavier than Darnell. He was mule strong but not very fleet of foot. Major universities did not actively recruit him, so he accepted a partial scholarship to Chester City State. Unlike Darnell, Marcus' hair was long and unkempt. Marcus lived in the Roonies with his single mother and several siblings. Money for haircuts was not in the family budget. When his hair needed cutting, his Mom cut it with scissors. The quality of the haircut depended on just how high his mother was at the time of the cutting.

Darnell was not only a gifted athlete he was also very intelligent. Marcus was not a great athlete and was hardly the sharpest tool in the shed.

Neither of the young men was in the old rotting building for the ambiance. They were finalizing a plan, a plan that would come to fruition in the death of a seventeen-year-old girl.

"Marcus, you understand how this is goin' to work out now?"

"Yeah, man. You goin' to pick me and Bobbie up at six tomorrow night. We both get in the back seat and," Marcus trailed off.

Darnell cut in, "Where you sittin' man?"

"Backseat, Darnell. I said that."

"Right side, man. With Bobbie sittin' behind me and you sittin' behind Tawney," Darnell barked.

"I know that," Marcus grumbled.

"Then say it! This has got to be done right!"

Marcus just nodded.

"Alright. So what happens next?"

"We drive over to Tawney's and pick her up." Marcus stared at Darnell expectantly, hopeful he got that right.

"Good man. Then what?"

"Ah, I guess we drive out of town toward Morrisville. Uh, we kind of just chit chat on the way."

"Fine," said Darnell. "Now we get maybe three miles outta town when there's that big right bend in the road. You remember?"

"Yeah, I remember. I gotta keep my eyes open."

Darnell replied harshly, "Damn right you do. So I start turnin' at the bend and then I yell, 'Watch out!' Then what?"

"I duck down. Cover my head."

"Yeah. And I do the same. The girls don't see this comin' and I turn the wheel hard and run the car into the ditch. Shake up the girls."

"Yeah, I know," Marcus replied without expression.

"Now this is the important part. Either you or me. Whoever moves the fastest and man, you gotta move fast. You reach over from behind or I get her from the front. Right? Grab her head with two hands and twist it. Twist it real hard. Listen for the neck to snap. You'll hear it. Then lay low in the seat. Tawney will be dead. Got it?"

"Sure Darnell."

"Can you do it, Marcus? You're not afraid?"

"Aw, hell no. Jus' like trying to break the neck of some fat-assed offensive lineman. Piece o' cake."

"Okay. That's it exactly. No fuck ups. I can't have this bitch hanging around me no more. I got a future to protect. See you at six o'clock tomorrow."

The two young men left the old stinking building and went their separate ways.

The next day was Saturday, February the eighth. A light coating of sleet and rain was falling in the Chester City area. Darnell thought this would make it easier to get the car to accidentally skid. He pulled the car to a stop and picked up Marcus and his girlfriend Roberta Green, known to her friends as Bobbie.

Bobbie was a tall black young woman with mocha skin and long straight black hair with auburn highlights. She was obviously the offspring of more than one generation of black and white interracial couplings. Marcus led Bobbie around the old sedan and opened the rear door. She sat down behind Darnell. Marcus walked back around the car and sat behind the empty passenger seat.

Great, thought Darnell. He had remembered.

Darnell drove to the home where Tawney Johnson lived with her mother Lucille. Tawney was looking for Darnell through the front window as Darnell pulled up curbside. He didn't go in to pick her up since Lucille hated the sight of him. As Lucille yelled at her daughter, Tawney hurried down the sidewalk without a glance back at her mother. She entered the car and Darnell smiled at her as he pulled away from the curb.

Tawney smiled brightly and said, "Hey Darnell. I didn't know we were double dating."

Darnell grinned. "It's a surprise. We're goin' up to Morrisville for a little party."

"Oh Darnell, you know how I love parties," Tawny said. In the back seat, Marcus smiled while looking at Bobbie. She smiled back.

Some idle chatter among the four then ensued as Darnell carefully guided the vehicle over the slickening road to Morrisville. Darnell was tense as he got closer to the big bend to the right. He had to do this perfectly. He could feel the tension throughout his body as he focused on what was about to happen. But was Marcus truly ready to do this? Too late to worry. Marcus was watching as the bend came into sight. He gripped the edge of the seat preparing to brace himself. He had started to sweat. His insides tightened, and he thought to himself that now was not the time to lose his nerve. The two girls were chatting with each other, neither of the girls aware of the coming crash. Both were thinking about a good party tonight. Lots of laughs. Lots of beer. Maybe even some weed.

Here it comes.

"WATCH OUT!"

Darnell hit the brakes and turned the wheel, sending the car into a skid. It slid off the road and over a hump that was the beginning of a ditch. The car hopped the bump and followed down into the ditch, slamming grill first into the far side.

Both Darnell and Marcus ducked down with their hands over their faces. Bobbie's face slammed nose first into the top of the driver's seat, breaking her nose and knocking her dizzy.

Both Darnell and Marcus reached toward a dazed Tawney Johnson. A pair of large powerful hands grabbed her head near each ear and twisted violently. The snap of Tawney's neck was loud. She died in that instant.

Twelve minutes later another car going from Morrisville to Chester City spotted the disabled vehicle and the driver called the police. Rescue vehicles arrived on the scene within minutes. Obviously injured, Darnell, Marcus, and Bobbie were removed from the battered car were transported to Chester City Hospital for examination. Tawney was pronounced dead at the scene. Her body was taken to the county morgue in Chester City.

Tawney Johnson, once a petite, blonde and physically striking young girl was now dead just five days before her eighteenth birthday.

Shawnee County medical examiner Dr. John Suggs examined the body of Tawney Johnson forty-eight hours after her death. He puzzled over his findings for an additional day before he finally called Chester City senior homicide detective Mike Russo.

Dr. Suggs advised Russo that he had some concerns about the accident.

Detective Russo, in his fifties and with a large gut, prompted Suggs.

"Concerns? Such as?" Dr. Suggs hesitated.

"Well detective, the victim died from a broken neck. I was ready to rule it an accidental death, but my examination indicated that the neck had been twisted, rather than snapped by the sudden forward motion and then a backward motion that you would get in a head-on collision with an embankment."

"So, what are you saying?"

"Uh, I'm sort of twisting in the wind on this one. The break looks like someone twisted her neck. Quite violently. But this was an automobile accident. I've seen all sorts of oddly broken bones in accidents such as this one. So, anything is possible."

Russo shifted the phone away from his ear and scratched the lobe.

"I think I see. You're saying that it could be the result of the accident or could be what? A homicide?"

"Yes, yes. That's it exactly. And remember, this was determined by police investigators to be an automobile accident. If I rule Ms. Johnson's death a homicide or possible homicide that would mean."

"That one of the other three occupants in that car most likely broke her neck. Correct?"

"Yes."

"Well, that's not much to go on. Anything else?"

"There is. She was two months pregnant."

Russo paused for a few seconds then said, "Just how old was she?"

"Seventeen."

"And you see that as a possible motive for murder?" Dr. Suggs sighed deeply.

"I'm a man of science, Detective Russo. If that's a motive for murder, proving it is your department. However, her boyfriend was Darnell Ducette. I can speculate as well as the next man on why a young man with his future earnings potential wouldn't want to be stuck with a seventeen-year-old girlfriend and a child when he is only eighteen years old."

"Oh sure, I can see that too. But that young man is like a god around here and bringing charges against him would require a lot of hard evidence which I don't currently see," Russo said.

"Me either. I'm just passing it on to you. You, of course, may wish to pass it up the chain of command."

"Yeah, I may wish to do just that." The two men rang off. Detective Russo groaned.

CHAPTER 2:
Meet Jack Troop

John Fitzgerald Troop was named after the slain President John Fitzgerald Kennedy, but his parents called him Jack from the day of his birth. He was the second of two children born to Franklin Delano Troop and his wife Clara Mae Troop. Young Jack was born in Fairfield County on August 2nd in 1965. Jack's sister Sarah was eight years older than her infant brother Jack.

Before Jack's fourth birthday, his father Frank moved his family to 12 Willow Lane in the town of Willow Road located eight miles south of Chester City in Shawnee County. Frank Troop sold insurance as a representative of the Great Lakes Life and Casualty Company and had done so well that the company offered to finance an agency for him. Frank had a wife and two young children to support but he was a young man confident of his ability to succeed. Frank took the offer.

Young Jack Troop graduated from Willow Road High School in the late spring of 1983. He loved English composition, competed on the wrestling team for four years and completed high school with a three-point-five GPA. Jack was a physically small man and discovered that he loved competing on the mats because one was matched up with opponents of the same weight. In his senior season on the team, he qualified for the state championships and reached the finals. He lost to his opponent but was pleased with his effort.

When Jack began his college career he reflected often about how hard he tried and how tough he hung in against a more talented opponent in the state wrestling finals. He believed that he could apply that same attitude to achieve success in college.

As Jack began maturing into a grown man, while small in stature, he was handsome with a full head of sandy blonde hair, a strong, and sparkling baby blue eyes. His body was firm with muscle developed while wrestling those four years.

Jack began his freshman year at Chester City State University as a journalism major. That same year, his father opened a satellite agency in the city of Morrisville, eleven miles north of Chester City. His sister had married by that time and moved to southern California with her husband.

In the fall of 1985, Darnell had arrived on the Chester City State campus, which was only six miles from Darnell's home. The regional members of the press had already interviewed Darnell a dozen times concerning his decision to play football for the Chester City State Crusaders. He was a curiosity who had yet to play a down of football at the college level and was in fact, slotted in to play the backup quarterback to junior starting quarterback Chuck Chambers.

When Darnell arrived on campus to begin his freshman year, Jack had already completed his first two years of college and would be entering his junior year. During Jack's freshman year he took the required core courses. Those courses bored him, but his grades were high. His sophomore year involved more core courses but included basic journalism 101 and 102 in addition to courses in expository and creative writing. With the more boring start of his journalism major completed Jack would spend his junior and senior years doing real reporting for the college newspaper which was published monthly and distributed not only on campus but also in Chester City.

Professor John Class, Jack's faculty advisor and administrative advisor to the school newspaper called Crusaders Speak, set Jack up with the school's first interview of Darnell which took place in the press room at Crusader Stadium in early September. Jack had secured permission to tape the interview. When Jack walked into the room Darnell was already standing there dressed in a school logo tank top, cut-off blue jeans and a pair of Nike sneakers. A gold chain dangled from his neck and a bright Stannard High championship ring was on his ring finger. It was a large ring on a large hand. It was easy to see why Darnell could throw a football so far downfield.

Darnell spoke first.

"I guess you're Jack Troop?"

"Yes," he replied simply.

"Okay, good. Then let's sit down here and talk." Darnell said this as he gestured to a table and two chairs. Jack thanked him and sat down. Darnell took the chair opposite Jack.

Darnell then said, "What ya wanna know?"

"Well to start with may I call you Darnell?"

Darnell grinned at this formality. "Sure man. It's my name."

"Thank you. Call me Jack. Now we're here to talk some football. It's my understanding that you will be in a backup role to junior quarterback Chuck Chambers. Is that correct?"

Darnell shrugged, "Yeah."

"Are you okay with that? You are the most well-known freshman quarterback in this region."

"Yeah man, I am. But I'm also new to the team, new to Coach Quinn's system, and new to the university. I got things to learn. But if you're askin' me if I'm excited to be a backup, the answer is hell no."

"The Crusaders won the first game of the season on Saturday with Chuck Chambers starting. How do you see the season moving forward?"

Darnell replied with a blank expression, "We're a good team."

"I see. And how do you like your teammates? Do you all get along?"

Darnell grinned, flashing a bright white set of teeth.

"I'm a happy guy, Jack. I get along with everybody."

"Like Chuck Chambers? How about Coach Quinn?"

"Damn! You are a nosey little sucker man. Why do you gotta know how I get along with everyone? I told you. I'm a friendly guy. Believe me."

Jack chuckled.

"I've been told that before. That's what makes a journalism major. You're a friendly guy but I'm a curious guy Darnell. So, care to answer the question?"

"Coach Quinn is an okay guy. And I'll tell you, he knows his shit. He's a defensive minded coach but he knows how to run an offense too. He's tough but he's fair. He don't take no crap, you know?"

"Good. Does Coach Quinn treat you fairly?"

"Sure. I got no beef with him."

"Have you got a beef with any of the players?"

"Shit man, what a question. Like I said, I'm a happy guy. What, I gotta keep saying it?"

Jack cocked his head to the right. "Darnell, in your estimation, can the team win the conference title this season?" Darnell paused, obviously considering his reply. His brows furrowed, and his eyes seemed to glow a little brighter with intensity.

"Don't know for sure. Maybe. The Lions are really tough and they won the conference last year. They could repeat. They got a lot of starters back. But we will be competitive."

"So, Darnell, I can report that you are fine with your team and teammates, get along with head Coach Quinn, and you expect the Crusaders to compete hard for the conference title. Would that be correct?"

Again, Darnell paused reflectively. Again, his eyes bright and his concentration obvious.

"Not sure I said exactly that man, but you can use it if you want."

"Is that the truth?"

Darnell scowled, "Sure man. Whatever. Call it what you want. But understand, the thing here…"

Darnell points a long forefinger at Jack's chest. "Is that one man's truth is another man's fiction and one man's fiction is truth to another. Truth is how you see things through your own eyes. Understand? Say what you want, Jack. Are we done here now?"

"I do have other questions, Darnell. But I want to switch gears. Get off the subject of football and talk about you personally."

Jack then leans back in his chair and then leans forward into Darnell's space.

"Damn, man. Okay, let's see. Not sure I want to talk about personal stuff." Darnell's eyes narrowed to slits as he stared at Jack.

"How's your life in the Ducette family home?"

"It's good."

"You live at 5550 West Buchcanon Street. Your father George and your mother Estelle live there with you along with your younger brothers Willie and Lamar, and your sister Juliet. Have I got that right?"

Darnell nodded affirmatively, looking bored.

"Do you have good memories of your childhood?"

"Of course. Mom and Dad worked hard to provide for us kids. We always had a roof over our heads, clothes on our backs and enough to eat. We always had birthday parties and presents for Christmas. The tree was always lit up real nice and Mom always cooked us up a big turkey dinner. We had special days like that. I don't forget them. I got no complaints." As he finished he had his big smile on his face.

Jack said, "Sounds like a normal life in middle-class America. Correct?"

Darnell frowned. "What are you saying, Jack?"

"I believe that you have described a normal middle-class life. Am I wrong?"

"You can see me, right, Jack?"

"Of course. Your point?"

"Jack, I'm a black man. You seem to be surprised that a black family can live like a normal white family. We can, you know. And we do. Not all of us grow up without ever knowing who our father was or living in some crappy assed dirty apartment and selling dope on the streets. Lots of us do better. Most of us want to do better. I'm gonna do better. Hell, my parents raised me that way. Look here, some black people are bad people, but so are some white folk. Look at each of us as we are Jack."

Darnell stopped and stared at Jack.

Jack breathed deeply and said, "Sure Darnell, I think I understand. My folks did the same with me. And I meant no disrespect."

Darnell laughed.

"Oh man, you are one clueless dude. Don't you know that white life is way easier than black life?"

Jack narrowed his brow as he looked Darnell in the eyes.

"I didn't mean to imply otherwise. I apologize. So let's move on. You had to deal with a personal tragedy this past winter. Your girlfriend. Tawney Johnson. Care to talk about it?"

"Probably not."

"I see. It's a sensitive subject."

Darnell again pointed a finger at Jack. "You don't see shit! People should stop acting like they understand stuff that they know nothing about. Did your girl ever die in a car that you drove? Know what I'm saying? You can't know, and you can't see shit. Dumb question Jack."

Jack lets a deep sigh escape. He thought again to himself that he was underestimating the intelligence of Darnell. He also understood that life had put a chip on his shoulder. And it was a big chip.

11

"Darnell, I never had a girlfriend die in a car accident while I was driving. How do you cope with such a loss?"

"Careful man. You're seriously pissing me off." Moments passed while the two young men locked eyes.

"Of course, she meant a lot to me. Jack, I'm done here."

"Okay." Darnell stood and looked coldly at Jack and then turned and left. Jack just sat for a moment and then started to review Darnell's recorded responses. When that was done, he began going over the clippings he had copied from the library on the investigation into the death of Tawney Johnson. He was intrigued by this event and more than curious. He thought this guy was one serious piece of work. He's got a large chip on his shoulder and I must never underestimate him. Jack resolved to dig deeper into the life of Darnell Ducette. At that particular moment, Jack didn't understand that this conversation with Darnell would trigger an obsession with following Darnell's life for over the next twenty years.

CHAPTER 3:
The Ducette Family

In the first decade of the twentieth century, the Lockwood family moved north. Henry Lockwood, known as Hank, was tired of life in central Kentucky. There was little work that paid much money to a black man and the rampant harassment and discrimination were too much of a burden. The family left their one-room wooden shack and began migrating northward. They settled and moved and settled and moved, a cycle that would continue for just over two years. Their final stop was Chester City, a growing metropolis with a booming steel industry and a robust manufacturing center.

By the early 1960's Estelle Lockwood's parents were living in the new low-income project that had been built by Mayor Patrick Rooney. Tom Lockwood, Estelle's father, worked in the Carr Steel Works mill just northwest of Chester City on the banks of the Shawnee River. Tom mostly did cleanup work, one of the lower paying jobs in the mill, but better than he had ever done before. Estelle attended Stannard High School where she met a large but affable young black man named George Ducette who was in his junior year.

Able Ducette had uprooted his family in late 1873, not long after the Colfax Massacre in Grant Parrish, Louisiana. Able, too, eventually settled in Chester City. He moved the five hundred miles north and settled in a small town called Bridgeton where he secured a job working as a general hand in a large stable. He cleaned up piles of horse shit. George's grandparents, Amos and Eloise Ducette, had moved further north upon hearing the number of good paying jobs that were available in Chester City. The Carr Steel Works always seemed to be hiring. By the early 1960's George's parents John and Mary Ducette were renting a home in the Roonies. Like the young Estelle Lockwood, George was also attending Stannard High School and had noticed the young and attractive girl many times in the early part of their school years. He eventually approached her in a hallway at the high school and asked her for a date. She accepted. On their first date on a summer Saturday night, they ate pizza slices, drank ice cold sodas and sweated profusely during the course of two westerns at one of Chester City's drive-in movie theaters. By evening's end, they were bloated by too much pizza and too many extra-large sodas. But the magical side of this experience was that they instantly connected with each other. They were completely smitten. From that point on, they continued seeing one another until they both graduated from school. Months after Estelle's graduation, they were married.

George was offered a job at the Carr Steel Works. He was over six feet tall and weighed 235 pounds. He was an impressive physical specimen and a hard worker. He began an apprentice's job working in the oppressive heat on the mill floor where the raw iron ore smelted down. The ore heated to nearly two thousand degrees was poured into various molds. George's job was to maneuver the molds into the correct position. They were heavy and required all of George's strength. Due to the heat of the smoldering ore, his job was highly dangerous. Men had died after hot ore had been spilled on them.

Estelle had a job at Richardson's Market in downtown Chester City. She was involved with helping customers, stocking shelves and ringing up purchases on the cash register. Both worked hard and saved money and when Estelle became pregnant with the couple's first child, they purchased a small two-bedroom house at 5550 West Buchcanon Street in Chester City. Their first child, Darnell Silas Ducette, was born in the mid-spring of 1967. The baby occupied one bedroom, his parents occupied the other.

The late sixties were a time of national chaos in America. There were race riots galore that left city blocks charred and crumbling, a war in Vietnam that no one living in the Roonies gave a damn about, and militant groups of agitators like The Weathermen and the Black Panthers. Presidential candidate Robert Kennedy, along with the beloved civil rights leader Marin Luther King, Jr, were assassinated in 1968. Fortunately for the Ducette family, their West Buchcanon Street home was located almost one mile outside the Roonies and they were spared any potential destruction when rioting broke out in the housing project in the spring of 1968. George and Estelle were able to continue to work, to save, and to survive through it all.

On their 5th wedding anniversary, they indulged themselves by watching TV while drinking a bottle of wine. They went to bed that evening and pretended they were consummating their marriage for the first time.

In the fall of 1970 their second son, Willie was born. It was at that time that four student protestors at Kent State University in Ohio were killed by national guardsmen. The madness of the 60's still plagued America.

With no other bedrooms available in the Ducette home, the infant Willie slept with his three-year-old brother. This turned into a frustrating arrangement for the children and the two parents who were not getting enough rest. The crying of the infant Willie kept his parents awake far too often and of course, would keep three-year-old Darnell from sleeping regularly. Something had to be done.

George resolved to fix up the basement, turning it into a bedroom where Darnell could sleep or play. Willie stayed in the other bedroom. Young Darnell didn't understand why he had been banished to the basement and as he grew he came to resent the fact that his brother had his room. In his toddler's mind, his parents had chosen Willie over him. For weeks he would cry himself to sleep and then wake up mad, pounding his pillow with both fists. In the fall of 1973 the third Ducette sibling, Lamar, was born. Lamar got the second bedroom and Darnell and Willie now stayed downstairs.

Once again young Willie usurped what had to Darnell become his space. Now just six years old, Darnell had come to completely resent the existence of his younger brother. Darnell's resentment would be the foundation of the conflict between the two brothers for the rest of their lives.

The sleeping quarter arrangements came to a head in 1980 when a surprise baby was born. Her parents named her Juliet. It was Juliet who then occupied the upstairs bedroom next to her parents and all three boys now bunked together. George called the basement 'the bunkhouse.' Darnell never thought that there was anything remotely amusing about this situation, although the bulk of his resentment was still directed at Willie. For reasons that were unexplainable to Darnell, he blamed the entire bedroom situation on Willie. Mostly Darnell thought of Willie was a taker. The brother who had taken his space. Darnell complained about the bunkhouse to his parents often and loudly. George had delivered a couple of severe spankings to young Darnell on a couple of these outbursts. But Darnell seemed to view Lamar and his sister Juliet with at least a modicum of affection. This behavior eventually caused Willie to hate Darnell. By the time Darnell and Willie reached their teenage years, the hate between them became more intense. Willie hated Darnell for the way he dismissed him, hated the fact that he was smarter, hated his athletic abilities, and hated the fact that he could date young attractive white girls. In contrast, Darnell had never shown any great animosity toward both Lamar and Juliet. On the other side, he never showed great affection for either one of them. Both Lamar and Juliet were well behaved and studious. That never bothered Darnell. In fact, Darnell ultimately became the defender of the two youngest Ducette's whenever Willie hassled them with his antics, but more because he always wanted to get back at Willie rather than any real affection for either of the younger two Ducette siblings.

In the first couple years of the 1980's, the country went into a recession. The recession hit the Ducette family hard. Business at the steel mill slowed to a crawl and George got fewer and fewer hours. It was also slow at Richardson's Market and Estelle, who had over the years learned every job on the sales floor, kept her job but no longer received the overtime pay she was used to making. The Ducette family budget became tighter and tighter day by day until in early 1982 Ford C. Carr shut the Carr Steel Works down and gave each employee one week's severance pay. The Carr Steel Works was the largest employer in Shawnee County and the ripple effect of 18,000 people being put out of work was felt in every business in Chester City.

The event rocked the Ducette family. The family's economic slide then continued to roll on. It took George almost a year to find other work. Unemployment benefits were not sufficient to sustain the family. George found a new job at the Morrisville Foundry in Morrisville. He made just over half the money he was used to making and had a very modest benefits package. Estelle's pay was cut as business at Richardson's faded. Hard times had hit Chester City.

It was at this point in time that Estelle began drinking a couple of glasses of wine each night. She said it helped her to sleep at night and relieve the distress she felt about the difficulty of simply paying their bills. But the drinking didn't help relieve anything. The wine she drank was unaffordable on a very lean family budget and only exacerbated the situation.

Estelle finally went to the doctor who prescribed sleeping pills. The pills were another extra expense. The pills worked well enough but whenever Estelle ended her shift, she would come home and uncork the wine bottle. Soon her hours were cut and now there were insufficient funds to cover the family bills. George did the bill juggling and calls came in came daily to the Ducette household about payments that were past due. These endless calls put even greater stress on the family. There was now little happiness in the home, only the ceaseless grind of trying to get by day after ugly day. George was worried about Estelle and tried to talk to her about the excess drinking. She just brushed him off time after time, but George would shrug it off thinking that they could talk later. But later never came.

Estelle went into work each day buzzed, bleary-eyed and bone weary. Within two weeks she was fired and given a week's severance pay. She cried daily about the foul package that life had left at the family's doorstep. George kept soldiering on trying to make things work. Estelle just didn't have her husband's strength or spirit. She loved George and all of her children and was disgusted with herself because she was letting her family down. She was the weak link in the family chain and soon loathed herself for her inability to help wherever she could. She kept telling herself that the family was better off if she were dead. The cycle of self-loathing was now complete.

On the evening of the day that Jack Troop interviewed Darnell after the first Crusader football game of the season, Estelle sat on the old couch in the living room dressed in her pajamas and an old, soiled robe. She was sipping red wine straight from the bottle. She usually would fall asleep, drunk on the couch when her children came home from school. George had awakened to clean up and get ready for his third shift job at the foundry. As was the case lately, dinner had not been prepared for him or the four hungry children.

George was a patient man, but he was worn out. He resolved to talk to her again tomorrow morning when he got home. He had tried for a long time to encourage her, to boost her spirits but nothing had worked. George knew deep down he loved his wife and he kept telling her that. Telling her that things would be better. Telling her to find her strength and stop the drinking. He told her that he believed in her. But he knew that he wasn't getting through to her, but he also knew he was becoming disgusted with her. And somehow, he must overcome his own doubts about his wife and his ability to help her.

He put soup on the stove and made cheese sandwiches for the children. He would eat nothing until morning. He couldn't afford to. Estelle awakened late that evening and went directly to the refrigerator for her wine. The bottle was down to the dregs, so she finished it off and grabbed one of George's beers. She finished that beer and downed two more before going up to bed, taking her sleeping medication.

She awakened in a stupor the next morning, thinking she needed to hurry up and get the children off to school. In reality, all four Ducette children had been getting off to school on their own since she had started drinking. As Estelle approached the stairs she stepped on to the green throw rug that was tacked at the top of the steps. But as she stepped, the rug slipped, and Estelle stumbled forward, pitching down the steep flight of stairs, tumbling over and over and over.

Toward the bottom of the stairs, her neck snapped, and she reached the bottom and lay there dead. Her final thought as she fell: Please, God, release me from this life. She would never see her children again. Never get to tell them that she loved them. Never to see the sunshine and never again experience the sweet and peaceful feeling of lying next to George in their old and comfortable bed. It had all ended for Estelle Ducette the morning of September 10, 1985. She was only forty-four years old.

She was buried five days after her death. The funeral was ill-attended and somber. Members of the church had helped pay for a plywood casket. George endured the humiliation of being financially unable to bury his wife properly. The shame would stain his outlook on life until his own death.

By early October life in the household was as normal as it could be, and Darnell was getting ready for the sixth football game of the Crusader's season. He was spending little time at home now that he had a room in the athlete's dorm. George now had the burden of raising his children on his own.

Jack Troop had noticed an article on page two of the Chester City daily newspaper about the death of the mother of Chester City State's star quarterback. He went to his mentor Professor Class and urged him to give him the job of digging deeper into the Ducette family story and publishing the story in Crusader's Speak. When Professor Class approved, Jack called George Ducette and arranged for an interview at 6:30 a.m. at the Ducette home. Jack's initial interview with Darnell had been published in Crusader's Speak, and the Professor thought that a follow up about Darnell's family would be appropriate material for the October edition of the newspaper.

At 6:27 a.m. on a rainy October morning, Jack Troop knocked on the front door. George opened it. He was invited into the kitchen where George got a morning beer from the fridge and asked Jack if he'd like one. Jack declined. George drank a couple of swallows of his beer.

He wiped his lips with a bare hand and asked, "How can I help you, Mr. Troop?"

He then took another deep pull on the beer.

"Well, Mr. Ducette, for starters, please call me Jack. And I've got to say sir that I am very sorry for your loss. I'm sure it's a hardship."

George grunted and nodded.

Jack's eyes were sweeping the living room area from the open kitchen.

"Oh, and by the way, your living room looks great. Is that new furniture and new carpeting?"

George nodded again, drank some more beer.

"Mr. Ducette, are you aware of my interview with Darnell that was published in Crusaders Speak?"

Again, Jack only got a nod while George sipped his beer.

"Well sir, I'd like some more background information. What can you tell me about life with your wife and the four Ducette children?"

"A lot, man, but that covers lots of years. Where should I start?"

Great, Jack thought, he's going to talk.

"How about the day you met your wife? Then go forward from there."

"Okay."

For the next twenty minutes, George proceeded to fill Jack in on the early story of his life with Estelle and the birth of their four children. He did this while getting another beer and draining half of it. He continued talking for another ten minutes and then stopped and shrugged his big shoulders.

"I guess that's mostly it."

Jack said, "Sir, I hate to get into this, but how is your family doing now? Your wife has been gone for a month. How are you and your children coping?"

George grunted, "Not sure I care to talk about that."

"She died from a fall down the stairs from the second-floor landing. Help me out here, please. What exactly happened?"

George sighed and spoke, "Shit man. That's hard to talk about. Cops looked into it. They asked me if she might have tripped on the loose rug at the top of the stairs. I tol' them that I kept that rug tacked down. Didn't know nuthin' about it being loose. But here's the thing. Estelle was getting drunk every night and taking pills when she went to bed. She was messed up every day for months. Couldn't get her to stop. Anyhow, she coulda jus' fell. You know? Jack, I always will love that woman. But she just lost her strength. Really lost her will to live. So she drank. She was drinking herself to death."

"Ah, couldn't you stop her?

"I tried. Honest. I'll tell you something, but I don't want to see it in a newspaper. Can you do that?

"Yes sir, if you want it to be confidential then confidential is what you will get.

George nodded.

"Look, I work nights and sleep days. I'd be upstairs in bed sleeping and Estelle was down here drunk. But she would come up the stairs and lay down beside me. Quietly, so as not to wake me. But I always woke. Knew she was there but I pretended to sleep.

George's voice starts to crack. His eyes moisten.

Jack watches a single tear fall from his left eye, roll down his cheek and then over his lip and hang momentarily from his chin before falling on the kitchen table, not making a sound but signifying his grief.

"She'd lay there and whisper in my ear. Please, George. Please let me go. Let me go. I want to. Please."

Several more tears dropped to the kitchen table. Jack's eyes were also moist. He said in a low voice.

"Anything else you can add sir?"

"Well, for a long time we was doin' okay. Then recession hit in '82 and Mr. Carr shut his damn mill down. I still hate that son of a bitch. Then Estelle lost her job so all we had was my foundry job. And that don't pay enough. Things just went bad."

Jack said, "That's such a shame. But tell me something. How did you pay for all that new furniture and carpeting out in the living room? Looks expensive."

George got up and plucked another beer out of the fridge.

"I gotta get the kids up and moving for school pretty quick now."

"Okay. Do you care to answer my question? About the furniture."

"Oh sure, it was with some of my bonus money. From the foundry."

"I see. Almost done. Can you tell me how Darnell got along with his siblings?"

"Good, I guess. Darnell and Willie been gettin' into it a lot lately but nuthin' real bad. Darnell is protective of Lamar and Juliet, kinda like he was their Daddy."

"So, Darnell and Willie get into it some, but Darnell is cool with Lamar and Juliet?"

"Yeah that's it. Willie been hangin' in the Roonies a lot lately so he ain't around much now and, you know, Darnell is mostly at the university."

"Is Willie a problem child?"

"Maybe some. He hangin' with a bad crowd right now. He's real mad that his Mom is gone, and I don't think he knows what to do with all that anger. I gotta work all the time to make ends meet. I just don't get to talk to him. Look, man, I gotta get moving."

He stood and then Jack stood.

"Well sir, thanks again for making time to see me."

"No problem."

They both walked into the living room.

Jack said, "This is really nice stuff. New paint job too?" George frowned.

"Yeah, man."

"Must have cost a bundle, huh?"

"It was a nice bonus."

"That's great."

George said sternly, "Like I said, got to get the kids moving. Bye."

George opened the front door and Jack started down the sidewalk to his car. He couldn't help wondering, just where in the hell did that money really come from? And Estelle Ducette had died of a broken neck. Just like Tawney Johnson. Very, very strange.

As Jack left, George Ducette's tears were gone.

CHAPTER 4:
Being Darnell

Chester City is not a mega city like Chicago, Philadelphia, or Dallas, but a city about the size of Savanah, Georgia, with a population of just over 182,000 people according to the 1980 census. Chester City State University's main campus is located on the northern outskirts of Chester City, with an enrollment of over 17,000 students. The university is a regional football powerhouse and the team had been coached for the past sixteen years by Head Coach Bill Quinn. Coach Quinn's career winning percentage with the university was 62.4%. Under Coach Quinn, the team had won seven conference titles in the past sixteen years and had taken the Crusaders to four regional bowl games and two national bowl games, both of which they won against nationally ranked opponents.

The university was nationally known for its engineering school, its school for the performing arts and its school of journalism. Because of the prestige attached to the school of journalism and because it was close to home, Jack Troop had decided to attend Chester City State University.

The stadium, Crusader Field, and the athletic dorms were located in the southwest corner of the campus. The Crusader football players were housed in dorm 3. They ate their meals together in the dining hall on the ground floor. Junior quarterback Chuck Chambers' room was on the third floor in dorm number three.

It was the Thursday before Saturday's game, the biggest game of the young season. The conference-leading and bitter in-state rival

Fairmount University Lion's was the opposition. A large bonfire and pep rally was held at 8:00pm in the center of the campus. Chuck Chambers, as the starting quarterback, was a speaker at the pep rally. That Thursday afternoon Chuck filled his backpack with the books that he needed to study before the evening festivities. Ready and anxious to get going, he hoisted the backpack over his shoulders and stepped out of his room, locked the door and headed down the hall toward the stairway. As he reached the stairs he sensed a presence behind him and started to turn and look when he felt the force of a powerful shove to his back. He lost his balance and fell down the stairs, tumbling over and over until he hit the landing below. He lay there unmoving, in a heap and unconscious. He didn't know it at the time, but he had fractured his right arm, had a compound fracture of his left leg, had torn the ACL and MCL of his left knee and had a concussion. He didn't know that he would walk with a pronounced limp for the rest of his life and would never play another down of football for Chester City State or anyone else.

Chuck would never have a firm memory of 'the accident,' as he called it. He told people he thought he had been pushed down the stairs, but never had anything in his memory to support the supposition. He had not seen the person who had pushed him. Chuck was a big man at six feet five inches tall and weighing 230 pounds. The speculation was that it took another big man to shove him hard enough to make him stumble. He eventually recovered from his injuries and moved on to obtain his degree in accounting the following year. He was employed by an accounting firm in downtown Chester City.

For Saturday's big game against the Fairmont Lions, it would be freshman sensation Darnell Ducette quarterbacking for the Crusaders. Darnell was excited about his first starting assignment. Going into the game the Crusaders had a record of four wins and two losses. The Fairmont University Lion's record was one game better and they held the conference lead. Darnell Ducette lived up to his billing. The stadium was packed with over thirty thousand fans. On that cool, brisk afternoon Darnell threw four touchdowns and rushed for 77 yards and another touchdown. He was the team's offense. He was a young man on fire. His legendary college career had now begun.

Jack Troop wanted to talk to Darnell Ducette again. The Ducette family intrigued him. In fact, the whole family dynamic seemed out of the ordinary. He thought of Darnell, a talented athlete, a smart and insightful young man but an obviously flawed young man. A man too reflexively defensive and possessed of an inner anger. George Ducette, an obviously strong personality that in the last year or two was unable to cope with a weak woman he loved so much that he couldn't or wouldn't use his inner strength to help curtail his wife's problem with depression and alcoholism. Or Willie, the bad boy of the family? Maybe. Jack didn't really know him. Or Lamar and Juliet? He knew that they were well behaved and exemplary students but what else? What kept Jack scratching his head in bewilderment was the simple fact that Darnell's girlfriend and Darnell's mother had both died of broken necks. Now just how bizarre was that? Two broken necks. Two broken bones.

He had to know more. He asked Professor Class about contacting Darnell for another full interview. The professor told him to give it a shot. It now occurred to Professor Class that Jack had the tenacity and mindset of an investigative reporter.

When he sat down with Professor Class, he told Jack that he seemed awfully eager to pursue the story of the Ducette family.

"Look, Jack, the Professor started, good journalists come in many colors and many flavors so to speak."

"Yes sir, I understand. Right now, I am focused on looking into the Ducette dynamic. This is an interesting family sir and I'd just like to poke around and see what else is there."

"Um, poke around. Like, investigate?

"Exactly."

"Jack, are you sure that you want to report the news or are you more comfortable in finding the news? Seeking it out?"

"I think I'm an investigator at heart sir. Maybe I should think about becoming a police detective."

"Bad idea. A good investigative journalist makes a good deal more money than a cop. And I believe you've got what it takes to command that kind of money Jack. Go for it. You want to do a piece on the Ducette family, then do it. But keep me in the loop."

When Jack left the Professor's office he walked slowly toward his dorm room thinking about how to approach his new assignment. As he walked something else hit him. Broken bones. Broken necks, but how about a broken arm and a broken leg. Chuck Chambers! Wait a minute! Chuck Chambers the starting quarterback for the Stallions now severely injured and out for the season. The beneficiary of this accident. The new starting quarterback Darnell Ducette. Jack thought that he now had two broken necks, a broken arm, and a broken leg and they all happened to people who were in Darnell's life's path. All of whom Darnell affected in different relationships.

Jack thought about the timeline. Tawney Johnson had died in February of this year, followed by Estelle in September and then the very recent accidental fall of Chuck Chambers. In Jack's mind, there was something here beyond coincidence. He resolved to call Darnell and set up another meeting.

The interview took place in the conference room at Crusader Stadium. Again, Darnell consented to the taping of the interview. Darnell was seated wearing a school logo sweatshirt and jeans. He stood, offering Jack his hand. Jack shook it and they both sat.

"Hey, how you doin' Jack?"

"I'm good Darnell. You?"

Darnell smiled, "Couldn't be better, man." Darnell tipped his chair back on two legs, clasping his hands behind his neck and focusing his bright eyes on Jack.

"So, Jack, what's up today?"

Jack looked straight into Darnell's bright but smoldering eyes. He sensed some hostility in Darnell.

"You're up. I want to know more about you."

"Meaning what man?" Darnell challenged.

"Meaning tell me something about yourself. I've talked to your Dad and talked to Coach Quinn. Both men described you as intense and highly motivated. Is that an accurate assessment?"

Darnell rocked the chair forward. He leaned toward Jack so that they were eye to eye. Jack didn't flinch.

"Damn right I am."

"Got it. That you're an intense personality is obvious. You say you're also motivated, but motivated to do what? What motivates you?"

Darnell considered the question.

"I'm motivated to play football at a high level and I intend to be the best NFL quarterback ever once I graduate. I plan on making big-time money and I believe I will be a Hall of Fame quarterback by the time I finish my NFL career. I will command the respect that I deserve. Respect from white people. I will not be thought of as some dumb assed nigger who can only play football. Hell, I even think about being

President of the United States after my playing days are over with. I'm going to be special."

Darnell paused and stared at the ceiling.

"You know, my parents worked hard all their lives and look what it got them. A small old house a mile from the Roonies. Mom died young. Dad is a broken man. He got no money and he got no respect maybe even no self-respect. That just ain't gonna happen to me. I will be respected. You understand?"

Jack nodded, completely flabbergasted.

"And nothing, and I mean nothing, and no one will stand in my way." His eyes glared like a pair of headlights on high beam.

"I hear you, Darnell. But do you know where that comes from? That drive? That intensity? The desire to succeed?"

Darnell tilted back in his chair again, contemplating an answer.

"Hey Jack, you want to hear a good story?"

"Would it answer the questions?"

"I think it might. Hell, it's a good story."

Jack nodded. Darnell's tone softened somewhat.

"Okay. You know that my family is originally from Louisiana, right?"

"Actually, no."

"Well, anyway, way back my ancestors were slaves in Grant Parish, Louisiana. That's in the middle of the state. This story goes back in history. Think 1873, Jack. It's Easter Sunday on April 13th."

Jack nodded.

"Back in 1873, black folks were free men. But they weren't really free. Whites weren't ready to see black folk as anything more than slaves. They were considered to be a lower form of human being. So, what happened was that black people were kept from voting or having any of the other rights they got after the Civil War. Black people finally got angry. Finally found their backbones. On Easter Sunday about 150 of them got their muskets, knives, and clubs and went over to the Colfax Courthouse. They took it over. Then they dug a trench around the building, so they could defend themselves against any white folk they knew would be coming for them."

Darnell paused, deep in thought.

"The white folk didn't let this stand of course. You see, there was this ex-confederate officer by the name of Christopher Columbus Nash."

"Is that a real name?"

"Yeah, man. That was his name. Captain Nash was a big guy with a long, dark beard. He went and rounded up about 150 men. Most were ex-confederate soldiers. They were better armed because they carried Enfield rifles and they were trained soldiers. They even had a small canon. When these men got to the courthouse the black men were ready in the trench. Under a white flag, Nash sent a rider in who asked the blacks to surrender. They refused. They said they would fight. So Nash ordered his men to start firing. The canon blew out gaps in the trenches and killed a lot of the defenders. Then Nash's men charged, but the defenders managed to drive them back. The canon then continued to kill and wound more black men. Once again, under the white flag, Nash sent a rider in to request a surrender. They were told that if they did and laid down all their arms, they could go home and wouldn't be harmed. Over half of the black defenders were dead. So, the rest surrendered."

The story had captured Jack's attention.

He said eagerly, "Then what happened?"

"They laid down their weapons. That was a big mistake, Jack. Nash rode off and left his men with the unarmed black men. Then the shit happened."

"What? What happened?"

"Those ol' white boys just started shootin'. They just kept it up until every last black defender was shot. Killed in cold blood. But you see after the shooting stopped some of those men were just wounded and lay moaning and bleeding on the ground. Those bastards got off their horses and checked body by body. Any man still alive got stabbed or clubbed to death. When it was over around 70 had been slaughtered. My great-great-great-granddaddy was one of those men. Silas Ducette. He had his head cut off. Silas is my middle name in honor of him. All those men were just left in that field to rot in the hot sun. Jack, it just wasn't necessary to kill those men. Those white boys were cruel and heartless and had too much hate."

"Jesus Christ, Darnell. That is one hell of a story."

"Yeah, man. Nuthin' more to say."

"Where did you hear this story?"

"My Dad told me. It's been passed down from one generation of Ducette's to another. It's also found in the history books. The Colfax Massacre. Check it out. It was real."

"Now hold on. You're telling me that this story is a key motivator in your life?"

"You bet it is. Those men stood up for themselves and paid with their lives. I feel that I gotta stand up just like Silas Ducette. But look, Jack, I ain't planning on gettin' myself killed." Darnell broke out into a hearty laugh. Jack returned the laugh.

"Jack, I got a meeting to get to."

"A football meeting?"

"Yeah, sort of. With Mr. Carr."

"Oh. Ford C. Carr?"

"Yeah."

Jack frowned. "Darnell, you are aware that Ford C. Carr is the university's leading booster?"

Darnell replied, "Sure man, I know. He told me. But listen here Jack, we just talk. That's all. He gives me advice. Like on how to be a better football player or a better teammate. He tells me to keep my grades up. He even talks Republican Party stuff. Says I should start voting. That sort of thing."

"So, you've talked to him before."

Darnell's jaw dropped a bit as he said, "Yeah, sure. Why not?"

"I believe there are NCAA rules regarding the association between players and boosters."

"Hell Jack, that's about takin' shit. Like money mostly. He don't give me nuthin'." Darnell flashed the big smile again. "And I don't take no money."

"I hope not Darnell."

"Well, I wouldn't. And you can take that to the bank." With that Darnell laughed out loud. Jack did too. He couldn't help himself. He looked at Darnell and just shook his head.

Darnell said, "Hey later. Gotta go."

CHAPTER 5:
Ford C. Carr

Ford C. Carr's great-grandfather, Arthur Chester Carr, immigrated to America from England in the 1850's. Arthur was nine years old when he entered America through the port of Philadelphia with his parents and siblings. The family eventually moved westward and settled in Shawnee County. While still a child, Arthur began working as a courier for several area businessmen in the county. As he grew and learned more about the business world, it was obvious to his father and the men he worked for that he had the drive and acumen to become a successful businessman.

Arthur worked in both the fledgling oil industry and the young but growing railroad industry. He rose to management positions by the time he became a young man. Instinctively, he knew the value of owning a business or shares of stock in a business. He soon amassed a considerable stock portfolio and became an active trader in the market while in his early twenties. As the railroad industry generated national excitement after the connection of the east and west links of the transcontinental railroad in Utah in 1869, Arthur quickly foresaw the need for steel to build rails and railroad cars. The Carr Steel Works began operation in 1874. The mill grew and prospered under Arthur Carr's guidance. He was soon banking and investing millions of dollars in annual profits. By the time the 20th century arrived in the thriving American business climate, Arthur had amassed a fortune of 300 million dollars. For those times, this was an incomprehensible amount of money. Arthur Carr retired from his business shortly afterward in

1902. He spent his retirement years traveling the world, spending a considerable amount of time in his native England and playing multiple rounds of golf in Scotland. His travels also took him to the capitals of the Middle East and then on to China and Japan. He even circumnavigated the world by ship late in his life. He died at age 77 in 1918. At the time of Arthur's death, his sons Albert and Jacob were running the Carr business empire.

At the age of 42, Ford C. Carr gained control of Carr Steel Works and all of the other Carr family businesses. His sister, who was uninterested in the family business, had married a college professor and had moved to Oregon with her husband. His brother Charles was a completely dysfunctional adult who was often in trouble with the law and eventually died from the effects of acute alcoholism. While Ford was the youngest of three siblings, he was the smartest and most dynamic of the three. In addition to these traits, Ford wanted to grow the family businesses and was ruthless in his pursuit of power and wealth. His ruthlessness often manifested itself in unethical or illegal transactions.

Ford was a rock. Unlike his siblings, he became interested in the Carr family business even as a youth. By the time Ford reached his teens, he was already working at the mill. He would work all day, and then at night be taught his lessons by the tutor his very wealthy parents could easily afford. He was born a bright child and learned his lessons well, along with learning the ins and outs of the steel mill business. He learned every job in the mill, including the functions of a chief executive. When his father Charles died of a heart attack at the age of 68, Ford inherited control of the mill.

The business continued to stay in the hands of the Carr family when Ford took control of the company in 1971. In 1972 profits dropped for the first time in 98 years of operation. The gas crunch in 1973 spurred a slowdown in auto sales, which in turn triggered a further slowdown in the need for steel. Ford Carr, being a man of some vision, foresaw the day when the dwindling need for American steel would render the Carr Steel Works completely unprofitable. He began moving the company's assets into other lines of business.

The first business opportunity Ford looked into was media. He purchased the Chester City Chronicle, the region's major news publication. He followed that purchase with the purchase of two smaller papers in Shawnee County, the Morrisville News, and the

Scarsdale Daily News. He also purchased the largest radio station in the region and four other stations in cities outside the region.

In the 1900's the Carr family had done a considerable amount of business with Henry Ford and the Ford Motor Company. The steelworks provided Ford Motors with much of the needed steel to build automobiles. Arthur Carr made enough money doing business with Ford Motors that he was able to purchase a considerable amount of stock in the company. Ford C. Carr got his name from the close business relationship between Henry Ford and Arthur Carr. So, in the 1970's Ford further diversified the Carr business by purchasing auto parts companies, tire companies, and eight Ford dealerships.

Ford's next interest was real estate in the early 1980's after the recession. What followed was the purchase of nearly a dozen office buildings in Chester City's downtown business district and later the construction of the massive Ford C. Carr Convention Center. He went on to build the Living Greens luxury community just north of Chester City. The community featured million-dollar homes and Ford built his own 15,000 square foot mansion within the gated, high- security community. This enterprise proved highly successful and with the economic upswing in the 1990's he built six more communities near major cities in the country, including New York City, Los Angeles, and Chicago.

As a grown man and businessman, Ford Carr was an utterly amoral man. In acquiring his many new business interests, he used blustering, bullying and threats to intimidate potential sellers to sell to him at his suggested price. He also used thuggery. When he needed to persuade a reluctant businessman to make a deal with him on his terms, he used a hired thug to mess the man up to whatever degree Ford deemed necessary.

This man was known as Mitch the fixer. Problems that couldn't be solved by less forceful means, Mitch fixed them with the application of violent means.

Ford was also a man who lacked empathy. He had no concern for people unless those people helped him make money. These people included his employees, accountants, lawyers, and financial advisers. His favorite people were Republican Party operatives. Ford was active in the party and was Shawnee County's largest donor to Republican candidates running for both local and national offices.

Ford never married. When his libido overpowered his relentless pursuit of wealth, he paid an attractive call girl. To Ford Carr, anything he wanted could be purchased. That which could not be purchased could be persuaded by violence or the threat of violence. He was a man whose only concerns were himself and his ever- increasing wealth.

By the time Jack Troop was aware of Ford's influence and wealth, Ford was the richest man in the region and on the Forbes list of America's richest men.

While Ford enjoyed amazing wealth, Jack's father had opened three more satellite agencies while continuing to grow his Willow Road Agency. Frank Troop, while no Ford Carr, had accumulated enough wealth to pay qualified managers for all four agencies and employ an executive manager to oversee the entire insurance operation. Frank still kept an eye on his business but as he got ready to turn fifty years old, he was ready to kick back and enjoy life with Clara. Both wanted to travel the world, but Frank had always been too busy. This summer they would travel throughout Europe.

One day Jack asked his father about what he knew of Ford Carr.

Frank paused, then said "Jack, he is a very rich and powerful man as you know. One of the most powerful in the country because he is also well connected politically."

"Yes, Dad. What I'm curious about is his relationship with Darnell Ducette."

"Our favorite local quarterback, huh?"

"Yes. Darnell told me he has meetings with Mr. Carr, but they're not football related. Would you buy that?"

"Jack, I'll put it this way. Depends on who you talk to. Some will tell you Ford is tough but fair in negotiating business deals. They insist he is a generous man, which, by the way, I believe. That's the upside. The downside is that there are a whole bunch of local businessmen that will tell you Ford Carr is the biggest crook in Shawnee County. They also say that if he ever gets anything on you, he'll own you for life."

"Oh shit, Dad." "So to answer your question. Darnell is young and naïve, and Ford is very cunning. He probably sees Darnell as a future superstar and somebody who he'd love to get his hooks into so he could mold Darnell into a profitable or influential resource. It's the talk. I tend to buy it."

SON OF A BITCH!

Jack's interest in Darnell's meetings with Ford Carr magnified over the next few months. He could picture Ford as a giant squid that grabbed you with a long tentacle and then pulled you little by little into his dark and dangerous maw. Was Darnell the next person to succumb to Ford's nefarious influence?

CHAPTER 6:
The Next Broken Bone

Darnell Ducette finished the 1985 football season for the injured Chuck Chambers. He had a spectacular performance against the Fairmont University Lions and then guided the Crusaders to another two wins before being knocked unconscious in the next to last game of the season. Third-string quarterback Cody Packer took over, but the Crusaders lost that game and then lost the final game of the season. The team ended the season with seven wins and four losses, receiving a bid to a minor bowl game which they also lost. It was clear to Coach Bill Quinn and Crusader fans that Darnell was the key to the team's success.

When the spring of 1986 arrived Jack Troop was studying hard for the final exams that marked the end of his junior year. He was also applying for summer internships to various newspapers in Shawnee, Holmes and Carrollton Counties.

Darnell had fully recovered from the late-season concussion and spent the next semester hitting the books and getting ready for his sophomore year. He was able to participate and excel in spring football practice and guided the silver team to a lopsided victory over the blue team in the annual spring scrimmage. Darnell was popular on campus and he had been invited to a semester-ending celebration at one of the fraternity houses where many of the campus athletes were members. Even though Darnell was encouraged to pledge to a fraternity, he did not do it. He was, after all, his own man.

The party took place in an old but sizeable Victorian home on Oak Leaf Street on the night of May 8th. His childhood friend Marcus Wayne was also attending the party. Marcus was on the football team as a second-string defensive end. Like just about any college frat party in America, the alcohol flowed like water over the Hoover Dam. There was the usual young male young female interaction that the alcohol and loud music seemed to inspire. With the testosterone flowing freely among young physically fit males, the recipe for trouble was obvious.

Darnell had managed to hook up with an attractive blonde dressed in shorts and a tank-top, showing off as much skin as she could without getting arrested. Her name was Wendy and she danced, drank and flirted with Darnell through most of the evening. Wendy and Darnell were standing together in the corner of the main room when the captain of the university's wrestling team, Brent Reedy, walked rather unsteadily over to them and asked to dance with Wendy, who he had dated in the past. Wendy said no but Brent persisted obnoxiously. Finally, Darnell intervened and told him to leave them alone. Brent responded by shoving Wendy aside and then with a two-handed shove, pushed Darnell into the wall. Brent was close to Darnell's size but in a boozy fog, he proved to be no match for Darnell. He recovered quickly and confronted the semi-drunk wrestler. Reedy took a swing but Darnell avoided it and hit Brent square in the jaw with a hard right cross. The cracking of young Brent's jawbone was audible. Some of the girls attending the party screamed, some of the boys gasped. Darnell followed with a quick left and right uppercut combination to his opponent's rib cage. Brent Reedy hit the floor like a trash bag of rotten garbage, blood spewing from his mouth. One of his teeth lay on the floor by his open mouth. The body blows had cracked two of his ribs.

Both an ambulance and the campus security guards were called. The incident was printed on the second page of the Chester City Chronicle the next day. Brent Reedy was hospitalized. Darnell was questioned and released. Most of the student witnesses told police that Reedy had shoved Darnell into the wall and Darnell had only hit him three times.

Later, both Brent and Darnell were fined one thousand dollars each. No charges were brought against Darnell by the Chester City DA's office. By early July, a lawsuit was filed by Steven and Dora

Reedy on behalf of their son Brent for malicious and unprovoked assault. They were suing for compensatory and punitive damages of one hundred thousand dollars.

Jack Troop was an avid reader of newspapers. He read the story about Darnell's fight with Brent Reedy and thought to himself, more broken bones. This time a jawbone and some cracked ribs. Wherever Darnell went and whatever he did, broken bones seemed to litter his path in life.

Jack called Darnell after the suit was filed and questioned him for ten minutes. Darnell added nothing that had not already appeared in the Chronicle's initial story or any of the follow-up stories.

Toward the end of the spring of Jack's junior year, he received a summer internship offer beginning the day after Memorial Day. The job would be at the Morrisville News in Morrisville, a town of about ten thousand people located ten miles northeast of Chester City. He accepted and was advised to report to Mr. Clyde Bernhard at 8:00 a.m. Tuesday.

CHAPTER 7:
Jack Troop's Summer of '86

At 8:00 a.m. on the Tuesday following Memorial Day, Jack Troop stood in the offices of the Morrisville News located on 25 South Main Street in the small town. He stood before a middle-aged woman named Joyce who was the secretary for the news' manager Mr. Clyde Bernhard. Joyce ushered Jack into Mr. Bernhard's office.

Clyde Bernhard was standing when Jack entered. He was a man of average height with an unusually prominent Adam's apple. The two sat down to talk and throughout the entire discussion Jack couldn't help but watch the incredible Adam's apple bob up and down as Mr. Bernhard spoke.

By the end of their meeting, Jack learned he would be spending his summer selling ad space to new clients and checking in on existing clients to say hello and see if they had any new advertising needs. Jack finally asked if he would get to do any reporting and was told it might be possible later in his training.

Jack was then returned to Joyce's desk to fill out employment forms and other paperwork. He returned after lunch and was given a list of clients and prospects to contact that afternoon. Mr. Bernhard sent Jack on his way after a few basic sales tips.

Jack grimaced on his way out the door to work on his list. This was not what he had bargained for. He was a serious reporter, not some pushy salesman. He felt betrayed. He had signed on to learn more about reporting the news and now he was to become a salesman. Jack returned home that evening and had supper with his parents. He grumbled frequently during the meal about what a waste of time his summer was going to be. When the meal was eaten, Frank Troop took his son aside.

"Look, Jack," he began. "I've got to explain a couple of things to you. I think it's time that you learn something about how things happen in this competitive world we live in. The Morrisville News is owned by Ford Carr, as you know.

Jack nodded, listening carefully to what his father said.

"I personally don't know Ford. But I do know Clyde Bernhard. I handle his business insurance and some of his personal insurance."

"I didn't know that, Dad."

"Clyde does the hiring and firing. He had four applications that he considered for the internship position. Yours was among them."

Jack interrupted, "How do you know that Dad?"

"I was just coming to that. The name on your application was John Fitzgerald Troop. Clyde recognized the last name but not your full name. He called me and asked if you were any relation to me. I told him."

"And?" quizzed Jack.

"He said okay and told me he'd take care of it. Clyde hired you, Jack because I do business with him. He picked you over the others because he knows me and trusts me. That is how you got your summer job, Jack. You need to appreciate this simple truth about what makes the world go around and do the best you can with the opportunity you have. This is how the business world works. Business relationships matter. Cultivate them. Always remember that."

"I had no idea, Dad."

"Look, Jack, I know how badly you want to be a reporter, but learning the business end of the news business is a good thing. Advertising keeps a newspaper in business. It's a primary revenue source so just embrace the opportunity and do your best."

Jack thanked his father and spent the evening reflecting on what he had learned. He was back at the office early Wednesday morning feeling ready to become a good salesman and learn as much about the newspaper business as possible.

By week's end, Mr. Bernhard told Jack he was very pleased with Jack's sales production for his first week. He also told him he would expect more the following week and then, as a reward, he gave Jack the afternoon off.

Jack knew exactly what he wanted to do with his unexpected free time and headed into Chester City and soon pulled up in front of the house at 5550 West Buchcanon Street with the expectation of speaking to George Ducette again. However, he immediately noticed a realty sign on the front lawn. The house was sold.

The agent pictured on the sign was of a middle-aged woman with snow-white hair named Priscilla Clift. Jack was flabbergasted. He exited his car and knocked on the front door. Of course, there was no answer. He knocked again and then peered into the front window. The house appeared to be empty. What to do?

When Jack's mind clicked into gear again, he drove over to the main office of the Chester City Chronicle and requested to look at the microfilm of the deeds recorded section in the newspaper. He quickly found Mr. George G. Ducette with a newly recorded deed at 2131 Green Apple Lane in the Living Greens community.

Now how in God's name could he afford a home in Living Greens, Jack thought.

SON OF A BITCH!

There was only one way to find out. The Living Greens community was northwest of the main business district in Chester City. It took Jack about 25 minutes to arrive at the guard shack of the gated community. He told the guard that he was there to see Mr. George Ducette and was requesting just ten minutes of his time. The guard called Mr. Ducette and to Jack's surprise, George Ducette assented to the request.

When Jack arrived, George was standing in the open doorway with a beer in hand and wearing a pair of old, stained shorts and a white tee shirt with what looked like ketchup stains on it.

"Well, well, well. Jack Troop." He was scowling at Jack. "What the hell do you want now, Jack?"

"May I come in? I'd like to talk for just a few minutes." George sipped some beer.

"Okay. A few minutes. That's all you get. I got to get to bed pretty quick."

"Thank you, sir."

Jack stepped into the house and couldn't help looking around. It was plush. "Really nice place you've got here, sir."

George was still scowling.

"Yeah, I know. Are you just here to snoop around or is it something important?"

Jack watched the younger children Lamar and Juliet walk across the far end of the large living room and disappear into what he believed to be the kitchen.

Jack pointed in their direction, "Your kids enjoying it here?"

"I believe I asked, what is it that you want?"

"Is Willie here, or Darnell?"

"Darnell comes and goes. He ain't here. Willie lives in the Roonies now. He ain't here either. Is that it?"

"In the Roonies. Wow, this is such a beautiful home."

"Look, Jack, I kicked Willie out. He's runnin' with the gangs now. He's screwing up his life, but I won't let him mess up Lamar's or Juliet's. Hell, Willie ain't been right since his Mama died."

George drank the remainder of his beer.

"Well, I did want to talk to Willie about his relationship with Darnell."

"It ain't good. We done yet?"

"Have you got an address for Willie?"

"Sure." He gave Jack the address, who wrote it down along with a phone number. George was laughing.

"Now remember, white boy. It's the Roonies. You best be careful if you go there. You know what I'm sayin'?"

"I do, sir. Thanks for your time." Jack looked around again.

"Real nice house you got here." George responded harshly,

"Now listen here, Troop! Know what I think? I think you just wanted to see my house. See how a poor nigger like me came up with the money to pay for it."

Jack stepped toward George Ducette.

"Okay, how did you pay for it? Sir."

"Ain't none of your fuckin' business. So just stay out of my life. Hear me! Stay the hell away from here."

Jack paused several moments openly assessing George Ducette.

He lingered long enough so that George understood, man to man, that he was sizing him up.

Then Jack turned and opened the front door.

"Have a nice day sir. But I will find out about your house."

Jack left as George Ducette cursed him. But Jack's inquiries were making George Ducette nervous. As Jack pulled out of the driveway,

George's shaking fingers dialed the private number that he had been given. The one that he was told to call only if he sensed trouble from whatever source. His call was answered by a man with a soft, mellow voice. The man listened patiently to George's concerns. The man then thanked George for calling and told him not to worry.

It was late afternoon and Jack had decided to head home to the Troop residence on Willow Road. As he drove his only thoughts were how George Ducette could acquire a home that had to have cost eight hundred thousand dollars or more. It had to be Ford Carr. Ford wanted to own Darnell Ducette. Ford saw Darnell as a commodity, a future professional athlete with upside earnings potential that his sports management company could make millions from. The key to owning Darnell was simple. George Ducette must be obligated to Ford. Simple enough.

Later that evening Ford Carr was advised by his head of security that a meddlesome young reporter named Jack Troop was pestering George Ducette. Ford told the man that Jack Troop was an intern at the Morrisville News and now worked for him. Ford said he would handle the problem. Monday morning would hold a surprise for Jack Troop.

A stunningly beautiful young woman drove her rented Lincoln up the long driveway to Ford Carr's mansion. She parked the car and walked toward the immense front door. Reggie, Ford's houseman, was already at the door.

"Good evening Miss Marlene," he said smiling.

"Good evening to you Reggie. And how have you been?"

Reggie was still smiling as he replied, "I'm just fine Miss Marlene." Marlene entered the house. Reggie shut the front door.

"Miss Marlene, Mr. Carr is upstairs waiting for you as usual."

"Thank you, Reggie. I know the way."

Reggie had buzzed Ford Carr when Miss Marlene had arrived, and so Ford was eagerly waiting to greet her at the door of his bedroom suite. He opened the bedroom door as he heard the click of her high heels on the stairs. He was dressed in a new silk robe, under which he was buck-naked.

As she arrived at the doorway, Ford stepped aside and with a dramatic sweep of his arm gesturing for her to enter.

"Marlene, Marlene. So good to see you again."

Marlene turned to face him. She was a tall woman with long blonde hair that reached the small of her back and cascaded over bare shoulders. She was blessed with bright blue eyes, full lips, and a flawless complexion. She wore a black, scoop neck cocktail dress that showed the swell of her breasts. A string of pearls decorated her neck. The dress stopped eight inches above her knees and showed plenty of her gorgeous long legs.

Ford took his time admiring the beauty of the woman. Then he stepped forward, putting his hands on her hips and leaning into her to gently kiss the swell over each of her breasts.

Marlene put her hand on the back of Ford's head, stroking his hair and the back of his neck. With her other hand, she reached down between Ford's legs and felt the hardness of his penis. She gave his penis a playful squeeze. Ford groaned.

"Well, Ford," she observed. "I do believe that you are more than ready for me."

"Oh yes, Marlene. Ready, willing and able. You'll see."

Marlene walked to an overstuffed chair, kicking off her heels and unzipping her dress, letting it drop to the floor, then removed her bra and panties. Ford watched her intensely. He was almost unbearably hard. He pulled open his silk robe and let it drop to the floor.

He and Marlene stood looking at each other for several moments.

"I never can get over how beautiful you are," Ford gasped.

Marlene just smiled. Every man that she'd ever been with told her that. Okay, she thought, let him have his fun. After all, she was being paid well.

Ford took her hand and led her to the huge, California king- sized four-poster bed.

After they had sex they washed up together, then sat naked at a circular table where a plate of fresh strawberries and some crisp red grapes sat. A chafing dish with warm dark chocolate sauce sat next to the fruit plate.

"Please, Marlene, enjoy a little appetizer while we wait for dinner."

Marlene took a strawberry, dipping it in the chocolate and then licking it lasciviously with her tongue while looking at Ford. Ford was popping the cork on a bottle of fine champagne. Pop went the cork as Marlene swallowed the strawberry. Ford filled two crystal flutes with the bubbling champagne. Watching Marlene lick the strawberry had made his groin ache.

"Well, Marlene here's to a beautiful evening."

They touched the flutes together and both eagerly drank several sips.

"Oh Ford, this champagne is so good."

"Six hundred dollars a bottle, my dear." He winked at her. Marlene took another strawberry, dipped it, and then held it out to Ford. He opened his mouth and she dropped the fruit in. As he began to chew, Marlene leaned over and kissed him hard on the lips, causing some chocolate sauce to escape through the corners and run down his cheeks. He was startled but finished chewing and swallowed. Marlene licked the chocolate off his chin.

"Jesus Marlene, you never cease to please and amaze me."

Marlene smiled while tonguing another strawberry.

"And I always will, Ford darling. Just watch." She dipped a finger into the chocolate and smeared it on each of her nipples. She thrust her breasts toward Ford. "Want some chocolate, big boy?"

Ford's eyes widened.

"Oh yes. Oh yes, I do."

He proceeded to lick each nipple clean.

The two continued to talk and drink over the next hour while Ford frequently touched her naked body. Marlene would give his penis a playful squeeze every so often.

Finally, Ford buzzed Reggie to bring up the evening's supper. He then put his robe back on, went to the large walk-in closet and fetched an identical robe for Marlene.

They ate a meal of braised beef in wine sauce with garlic mashed potatoes and a salad of mixed greens, cherry tomatoes, diced apples, and crushed walnuts. When their meal was finished they both drank another bottle of champagne.

Ford sighed.

"Marlene honey, I believe I'm tired, but come with me to the bed." He stripped off his robe and undid Marlene's, letting it drop to the floor. They both crawled up on the large bed and Ford sought her body. Tired and with a full stomach and a warm, peaceful glow, Ford gently began to make love to Marlene again. She accepted him with a smile.

A half hour later they lay quietly in the bed saying nothing until Ford spoke.

"Marlene, you must stay with me tonight."

"But Ford, you know that I'm catching the redeye back home."

"Please, surely it can wait."

"Ford, you know I have to work tomorrow. I mean I have other clients."

"Yes, yes of course. But my chauffer Clark will drive you to the airport as early as you wish in the morning. He will take you to my private jet. You will be back home in plenty of time. And don't worry about returning the Lincoln. I'll take care of that."

"Oh," she said. "Then I guess I'll stay."

"And Marlene, over on my dresser I've made out a check to you for twenty-five thousand dollars. That should reward you handsomely for the extra time."

She beamed. "Why yes, it will Ford."

They curled up together, Ford dimmed the lights and they both slept like the dead.

Ford gave her a nice pat on her butt as she left early the next morning.

"Marlene dear, I must tell you. Last night was the best twenty-five thousand dollars that I've ever spent."

"Why thank you, Ford." As Ford closed the bedroom door Marlene walked down the hallway thinking, that was one of the tougher twenty-five thousand I've ever earned Ford, you sleazy old dirtbag.

On Monday morning, Jack's second week at the News, he arrived early and ready to attack the job with more enthusiasm. Joyce was waiting for him and immediately escorted him into Mr. Bernhard's office. As Jack entered he noticed a man of average height and a slim build sitting at Clyde Bernhard's desk. The man sported a full dark mustache. Clyde was standing beside him.

Clyde looked at Jack and said, "Jack, it is my pleasure to introduce you to your employer, Mr. Ford C. Carr."

Jack wondered what this was going to be about.

"Pleased to meet you, sir."

"Sit down young man." Jack sat in the chair Ford pointed to.

"Well John," Ford began. "Clyde tells me that you did some good work last week. I've looked at your contact list and I agree. Of course, you know that you need to improve. Yes?"

"Yes, sir. I can make that happen. And sir, please call me Jack. Nobody calls me John."

"Well, John, keep up the good work. Just stopped by to meet you. Now go on out there and double those sales numbers. That will make me smile." Ford narrowed his eyes looking directly at Jack.

"Oh, and John, by the way, I heard that you were out at Living Greens on Saturday."

Jack was startled but said nothing.

"You don't really need to be there. So, stay the hell away. Don't forget that. Just don't worry about what does not concern you. And yes, that's your first and only warning. Now you have a nice and productive day. Here me!"

Jack nodded stupidly.

Ford Carr then stood and walked out of the office without another word to either one of them.

Later that day it finally hit Jack that Ford just confirmed what Jack had thought all along. Ford had been giving money to George Ducette. Lots of money. George was in Ford's pocket and so was Darnell.

SON OF A BITCH!

Jack spent his second week at the news concentrating on becoming a better salesman. By Friday afternoon he had nearly doubled his prior week's sales and received praise from Clyde Bernhard. He drove home to Willow Road late that afternoon to say goodbye to his parents. Frank and Clara were ready to embark on their first trip to see the rest of the world. They had rented a limo to take them and all their baggage to Philadelphia where they would catch an Air France flight to Paris. They wanted to spend ten days touring Paris and then move on to tour continental Europe. They would not return to Chester City until mid-August. They would miss Jack's 21st birthday but promised him gifts from Europe and a late birthday party when they returned. Jack was given their itinerary plus a list of things to remember while he watched the house.

The Sunday after the Troop's departure, Jack drove into Chester City to the Roonies to Willie Ducette's address. Willie wasn't home, and Jack took note of several nefarious looking black males keeping an eye on him. George Ducette was right: the Roonies was no place for an undersized white boy. Jack spent the next two weeks dialing Willie's number twice a day and not getting any response. Finally, Willie called. Jack explained he wanted to speak with him about Darnell and offered to buy him lunch. He agreed but told Jack he wanted dinner and they should meet at a McDonald's two blocks down the street from his home. He also told Jack that he wanted fifty dollars in cash. He was short on money.

Jack told Willie what kind of car he drove and they agreed to meet on the following Sunday at 5:00 p.m. As Jack arrived that Sunday Willie was standing outside waiting for him. He was a tall thin young man wearing the obligatory baggy pants down his butt and a dirty white t-shirt. As Jack exited his car Willie walked up to him and stuck out his hand. Jack assumed he wanted to shake hands and offered his hand.

Instead, Willie said, "Give me the fifty bucks." Jack complied without saying a word. "Good," Willie continued, "now let's get some burgers."

They both entered the restaurant and ordered. Willie ordered two Big Mac's, two large fries, a large coke, and an apple pie. Jack settled for a small black coffee.

Willie led Jack to a corner table in the rear of the building. They sat, and Willie pointed to Jack's coffee.

"You ain't hungry man?"

"No, not really. I can eat later."

Willie just shrugged.

"Suit yourself, man. I can never get enough." Jack believed him. He was that thin.

Jack started, "So Willie, have you seen Darnell lately?"

"Nah. He's a big shot collitch boy now. Got no use for a nigger like me. Even if I is his brother."

"Wouldn't you like to see him?"

"Nah, we never did get along much. Darnell think he too good for us. Like I said, collitch boy. Big shot football player. Hangs out with white girls like he always did. Hell, he ain't even got much time for Dad now that Mom's dead."

"Why don't you live at home? Your Dad's got a really nice place."

"Yeah, yeah. But it's a white man's house. He lives around white folk. I don't need that. My friends all black and Dad don't like them. So I left."

"Your Dad said he kicked you out."

"Don't matter, either way, I'm out. Gonna make my own way now."

"Then you got a job?"

"Sure man. I do some of this and some of that. Odd jobs. Know what I'm sayin'?"

Jack's thinking that George had been right. Willie was running with the gangs and dealing drugs.

Jack replied, "Sure Willie, sure I do."

Willie flashed a half smile.

"Glad to hear it."

Willie began eating his second Big Mac. Jack noticed that Willie usually took two large bites at a time so that each of his sunken cheeks puffed out like a chip monk with its pouches stuffed with nuts.

Jack said, "Your Dad said that you and Darnell used to fight a lot after you all moved downstairs to the bunkhouse."

"Yeah man. Like I keep sayin', Darnell think he's some rich white boy. Always better than me. When he was dating white girls he and Mom was fighting over it. My Mom was a sweet woman man. Treated us good. He shoulda not done that."

"They fought about his dating white girls? Like Tawney Johnson?"

"Yeah. That was the white girl he was fuckin'. Mom told Darnell she was jus' white trash. But Darnell wouldn't listen. He got to always prove that he can get white pussy. He thinks he ain't black. Shit man!"

"Willie, your Dad told me that things went bad for you after your Mom died. That right?"

Then he said, "Mom was a good person. Know what they say about accidents?

Willie looked at Jack but said nothing. He was busy wolfing down french-fries. Jack was shaking his head.

Willie swallowed and said, "They happen. Guess she just tripped over that rug. It being loose and all." Jack stared at Willie.

SON OF A BITCH!

An itch had just been scratched.

"Ah, Willie, your Dad said that he had no clue that the rug was loose. Did you?" He paused, swallowing a French fry then washing it down with some Coke. All this time that they had been talking he'd been eating steadily with his head down. But now he stopped eating and looked Jack in the eye.

"Man, don't know nuthin' about no rug. Hear me?" Jack looked right back at Willie, each man now trying to read the other.

"Why sure Willie, I hear you. But, to be clear, you did mention the rug." Willie scowled and went back to gobbling down his food.

Jack felt that Willie, by looking him in the eye, was trying to convince Jack that he was telling the truth. Jack thought just the opposite. Bullshit. Willie knew something, but Jack wasn't sure how that piece of knowledge fit the puzzle that was Estelle's strange death. When Willie finished eating he stood up.

"I'm outta here man." Jack also stood but Willie turned and left without saying another word. Jack drove out of the Roonies as fast as possible.

On a Sunday in mid-July Jack was sitting outside at the backyard pool going through about six days of mail he had not yet attended to as his parents had requested. One letter was addressed to him. He opened the envelope and unfolded the letter.

In the upper left corner it said:

From the desk of Richard A. Jolly, President Ford C. Carr Media Company

Dear Mr. Troop:

Based on your excellent work to date with the Morrisville News, Mr. Carr and I invite you to apply for a full-time position with the Ford C. Carr media company after the first semester of your senior
year at Chester City State. Your supervisor, Mr. Clyde Bernhard, has highly recommended you.

We have most of your relevant information from this summer's internship. In January please forward any updates from the first semester of your senior year including grades and any awards or unusual assignments.

We are confident that you will fit in with our organization.
Sincerely,

Richard A. Jolly

Well, son of a bitch.

Jack's first thought was great, I have a job—but then his father's words came back to him about Ford Carr getting his hooks into you. Oh shit. But then he thought, What the hell, I will need a job.

The week before Jack's parents were due to return home from Europe, Brent Reedy was preparing for his senior season with the Chester City State wrestling team. It was a warm evening in August as the sun was setting. It was nearly dark. Brent had just left the school gym after a vigorous workout. He wore blue shorts and a silver t-shirt with the Crusaders logo on it. He walked casually, his head down, toward his car parked on the far side of the parking lot. He was thinking about the upcoming season and his chances for making it to the NCAA tournament this winter. He also had the lawsuit on his mind. He would have to testify against Darnell Ducette in the upcoming trial. The idea of testifying under oath unnerved him.

As Brent walked toward his car he had no idea a tall man dressed in black was hunkered down behind his car. The man carried an eighteen-inch section of lead pipe in his right hand. The man was a hunter by nature and didn't see Brent but listened to the sound of his footsteps on the warm pavement. Closer and closer. He wasn't nervous but was tense and ready to strike. He had done this kind of thing before.

Brent reached the car and moved to the driver's side door, setting down the gym bag and fishing his keys out of the right-side pocket of his shorts. He was facing the hood of his car while the man in black moved in quietly behind him. He was standing now, stepping silently with Brent unaware of his presence. He closed in. Eight feet, then seven, now five feet. He raised the section of pipe. Four feet, three, two and then he struck, tapping Brent on the head just hard enough to knock him cold. The man then flipped Brent over onto his back. He raised the section of pipe and cracked Brent's right knee with a forceful blow. The man then delivered another blow and then another. The knee was pulverized. Blood flowed from the wound and stained the pavement.

Brent's assailant plucked a note from his own pocket and stuffed it into the pocket of Brent's shorts. It read: BACK OFF. FIRST AND FINAL WARNING BRENT!

Then the man walked quietly away, confident that he had fixed the problem.

The lawsuit against Darnell Ducette filed by Brent's parents was dropped within the week.

August 2nd, Jack Troop celebrated his 21st birthday by himself. Two miles north of Willow Road, the Willow Road Bar and Grill sat just off the main route north toward Chester City. Jack had occupied a barstool there since late afternoon. He had ordered a T-bone steak with baked potato and salad bar, washing it down over the course of the evening with multiple tumblers of ice-cold vodka. He then returned home and slept. The next day would be just another day on the road selling newspaper ads.

Soon after the assault on Brent Reedy, Jack read the newspaper article. He shook his head. Someone had now shattered Brent Reedy's knee. Another broken bone!

His parents returned home on August 15th. Frank and Clara took Jack to the Willow Road Bar and Grill for a steak dinner again, not knowing that Jack had celebrated his birthday there thirteen days earlier. Jack said nothing about it. Several days later packages arrived from overseas. Gifts for Jack included a custom-made suit from Italy along with hand-crafted loafers of fine Spanish leather and a selection of smooth Polish vodka.

Jack finished his internship at the News on a Friday near the end of August. The following Monday Jack returned to Chester City State to finish his final year. He knew one of his first tasks was to interview sophomore quarterback Darnell Ducette about expectations for the coming football season.

CHAPTER 8:
Jack Confronts Darnell

Jack got in touch with Darnell on his first day back on campus. Darnell had arrived earlier in August to prepare with the team for the new football season. Darnell had expected Jack's call and they agreed to meet in the pressroom under Crusader Stadium two days later. The meeting took place in the late afternoon once Darnell had finished practice for the day.

Jack was there before Darnell and looked up at him as he entered.

"Hey Darnell, good to see you again." Darnell nodded in acknowledgment.

"Listen, before we get into football talk, I need to ask you something about a different topic." Jack paused and made eye contact with Darnell.

"Now, Brent Reedy. You remember him? The wrestler that you got in a fight with at the frat party last May." Darnell had taken his seat.

"Yeah man, I remember."

"Well, the Chester City Chronicle reported that Brent Reedy was assaulted in the parking lot at the gym a couple of weeks back. Do you have any comments or input?"

"I don't think so, Jack. I mean hell, why would I care?"

"Allow me to follow up. In the fight that you two engaged in, Brent received a broken jaw and two cracked ribs. Correct?"

"Sure, but as far as the law is concerned it was self-defense.

But Brent's parents filed a lawsuit against you—" Darnell interrupted.

"Which my attorney said would go nowhere based on eyewitness testimony and the fact that I wasn't charged. I was supposed to see their lawyer to give a deposition but then that got cancelled."

"Exactly Darnell. But that happened after Brent was attacked in that parking lot by an unknown assailant. He was knocked unconscious and his right knee was shattered with a blunt object. His knee joint had to be replaced and he won't ever wrestle or walk normally again."

Darnell just shrugged.

"I don't know about that Jack and I don't give a shit. His problem, not mine."

"So you had nothing to do with it?"

"Ah, fuck man."

"You have no knowledge of the incident?"

"Same answer," Darnell said.

"Alright fine. On to football. What expectations do you have for this season?"

"Team's going to have a good year Jack. So am I. You see, Jack, I don't see any reason why I can't set the school record for touchdowns and passing yardage for a single season. And this will only be my first season as starting quarterback. Stuff like that will get me some national attention. Full media coverage game after game. By the end of the season, those NFL scouts will know who I am. I guarantee it." The big smile of his was plastered across his face.

"Actually, I believe the NFL boys know all about you. Sounds like you got it all figured out, Darnell."

He was still smiling. "Sure, I do, man."

"Yeah, but you were talking about your accomplishments. How about the team?"

"Shit, Jack, as I go so goes the team. It's that simple."

"Have you discussed your goals with Ford Carr?"

Jack felt that he had asked a hard question to Darnell. He wanted to probe the depth of the relationship between the two men. "That ain't your business, man."

"I see. So, you did talk to him."

"Not what I said, man."

"I know. But you sort of did."

Darnell paused and looked coldly at Jack. "Jack are you here just to piss me off?" Jack said nothing.

"Not a good idea man."

Jack replied, "Okay, okay. It wasn't Ford Carr."

Jack sucked in a deep breath and took the plunge.

"But it was Richard Jolly. Right? Don't tell me I'm wrong."

Darnell stared at Jack. He blinked three times.

"Who?"

"Richard A. Jolly. He's the president of Carr Sports Management."

"You're bothering me, man. Like a little piss ant. And guess what. Piss ants get stepped on. Know what I'm sayin'?" Jack leaned in toward Darnell.

"By you?" Darnell smiled again.

"Nah, not by me. It would prob'ly be by someone who likes me."

"I see."

"Oh, hell no you don't. And because you don't, you won't see it coming."

"Like Brent Reedy, Darnell?"

Darnell busted out laughing.

"Ah man smile a little. I'm just funnin' with yah. But now I'm out of here. Not sure if we gonna talk again any time soon. You need to learn how to be nice."

CHAPTER 9:
Jack Meets with Marcus Wayne

On the Friday before the first game of the season, Jack had a joint interview with Coach Bill Quinn and Darnell. In the interview, the only topic discussed was the first game of the Crusaders' football season and the prospects for the upcoming season. Darnell was reserved, never smiled, and only echoed anything that Coach Quinn said.

The Crusaders went on to win the first game and the two games following. Early in the second quarter of the fourth game of the season Darnell was blitzed by an outside linebacker and caught a helmet in the face. He was taken off the field and later diagnosed with a concussion. He would not return to active play for ten days. His backup, Cody Parks, took his place at quarterback to finish game four. He also started in game five. The Crusaders lost both games.

While Darnell was recovering, Jack was able to secure an interview with Darnell's longtime friend and fellow teammate, defensive end Marcus Wayne.

The meeting took place at a Burger King two blocks from the main campus on a crisp October afternoon. After Jack asked Marcus about his football career to date, he moved on to explore his relationship to Darnell, which was the information that interested him the most.

"Tell me, Marcus, how long have you known Darnell?"

"Ah, well, ah we been friends since we was kids."

"Do you also know his Dad? His brothers and his sister?"

"Yeah sure. A little I guess. But his Dad don't like me much, so I don't go to Darnell's house much."

"Was that the one on West Buchcanon Street?"

"Yeah, that one."

"How about the new house in Living Greens?"

"Never been there."

"Okay. How did you two get to know each other?" Marcus paused, obviously thinking.

"When Darnell was a kid he'd come down to the Roonies from time to time. Later we both played football at Stannard High." Jack paused. Marcus had purchased a whopper, large fries and a large coke, which Marcus ate in between questions. Jack only sipped on a small coke.

"So, Marcus, what happened when the family moved to Living Greens? There's something like six to eight miles between the new home and the West Buchcanon Street home." Marcus just sat and chewed on his burger. He was thinking again.

"Me and Darnell still played football together, you know. Darnell also got a brother named Willie. Willie hang in the Roonies a lot. I know Willie pretty good too. We talk a lot."

"Oh, about what?"

"About stuff. Talk about Darnell some too."

"Really. What does Willie say about his brother?" Marcus sucked in a deep breath then took another bite of the burger. He looked at Jack.

"Darnell and Willie. They don't get along much."

"Didn't get along much? How much Marcus?"

"Aw, shit man. Willie see Darnell like he a white boy. You know, goin' to collitch, datin' white chicks. You know. Stuff like that."

"Yeah, I guess I heard that they don't get along."

Marcus said, "Hell, Willie say there's times he wish Darnell was dead." Then he laughed. Jack furrowed his brows and looked at Marcus.

"He said that about his own brother?" Marcus was chewing on fries and grunted a yes.

"Say, Marcus, you knew Tawney Johnson. His high school girlfriend." When Jack said this Marcus stopped chewing and gave Jack a hard look.

"Yeah, sure. Why you askin', man?"

"You were in a car accident with Darnell, Tawney and your girlfriend Bobbie. Tawney was killed in that accident but the rest of you survived with only minor injuries."

"Yeah. So?"

"So how did that happen?"

Marcus shrugged.

"Car slid off the road. Inna ditch. She busted her neck. Shit happens. You know?"

"Sure. But it is odd that one person died and the others all survived."

"Like I said, man. Shit happens." Jack realized he was going nowhere with the Tawney Johnson questions, so he switched gears.

"Marcus, would you have any knowledge of how George Ducette got the money to buy a new home in Living Greens?"

"Don't really know, but I heard he come into a whole bunch of money."

"Any idea from where?"

"From some church, I think. That was the rumor goin' around the Roonies."

"Do you know anyone who could tell me more?"

"Maybe Chimp. If somethin' goin' on in the Roonies, Chimp know it."

"Good. How do I contact this Chimp?"

"You don't." Another pause as Marcus finished his meal. "But, I maybe could get a hold of him."

"That would be great."

"But for a price."

"What kind of price?"

"Don't know until I talk to Chimp. Call me again in a week. Then we'll see." Marcus stood, nodded at Jack, and left the Burger King. Jack sat and thought for a few minutes before leaving.

Jack settled into his usual routine with classes. At the end of the week, he called Marcus but got no response. He called again several times for each of the next three days. Still nothing. Jack decided to seek him out after football practice but dismissed the idea and called again. This time Marcus answered.

"Hey Jack, I might have somethin' for you."

"You talked to this Chimp guy?"

"Yeah, man but I ain't sayin' nuthin' until you pay me."

"Okay. Sure. But tell me something, Marcus. Why is this guy called Chimp?"

Marcus started laughing.

"Cause, man, he got big ears like those monkeys that you see on TV. You know, the ones always wearin' diapers so monkey shit don't get all over. Know what I mean?"

Jack also laughed and finally said, "I sure do, Marcus. Where do we meet and what's your price?"

"At the Burger King again. Bring two hundred fifty dollars."

"Two hundred and fifty dollars! Damn it, Marcus. I'm a college student, too. I'm not rich."

"Cut the crap white boy. Your Dad makes plenty. He got a nice house with a pool where ya'll live in Willow Road. I seen it. I know where you're at." A chill shot through Jack's body.

He shook it off and said, "How about two hundred?"

"Fuck that! I ain't haggling man."

"Okay, Marcus. I'll have the money."

"Good. See you at the King. Got it?"

"Yeah."

The weather had turned cold and crisp the next afternoon when Jack again met with Marcus at the Burger King. Jack walked in and saw Marcus already seated at a rear corner table. Jack approached the table with his right hand in his pocket. He was clutching five fifty-dollar bills. He sat opposite Marcus and withdrew his hand from his coat pocket, slapping the fifties on the table and keeping his hand over the bills. Marcus had been right; Jack's wealthy father had given Jack the money with no strings attached.

Marcus looked at Jack's hand covering the money and said, "See you got the money."

"Yes. But I want the information first."

Jack was staring Marcus down. Such bravado from a man half the size of Marcus. Marcus nodded.

"Okay, man. I talked to Chimp. Seems he got an aunt who lives in his building one floor below him. Now see, this aunt got a daughter. She nineteen. Gets paid to clean up at the First Presbyterian Church on the corner of Market and Harlow Street. You know it?" Jack nodded.

Marcus continued, "It's a big old building about a hunnert years old. You see, Teeka, that's Chimp's aunt's daughter that cleans it..."

Jack interrupted, "Fine, so what's the deal?"

Marcus resumed, "She hears talk, see? From the church folk. She say them folk is mostly white. Folk got money too. Anyhow, she hear talk that they are givin' money to George Ducette. She say they said his name. It's to help him out, see. But she say she can't figure why them rich white folk would want to help out a black family. So, George got the money from the white folk at that church. You see?"

Jack said nothing for a moment, choosing to silently digest this information.

"Marcus, are you sure about this? Can I trust Chimp's information?"

"Aw, shit, yeah man. Everybody in the Roonies know Chimp trade information for money. It's how he get by. If what he say is bullshit, then he gonna get hurt, hurt bad. By someone. Unnerstand?"

"Got it," said Jack firmly. Jack slid the money over to Marcus and both men nodded and left the restaurant.

CHAPTER 10:
The Church Lady

For the remainder of the semester, Jack concentrated on his studies, final exams, and the small assignments that Professor Class had handed to him. During that time the Crusaders' finished their season with a 9 and 2 record. That tied them for the conference championship, which they won in a playoff game. They also qualified for a minor bowl game against Stone Mountain State University from Stone Mountain, Georgia. The Crusaders won that game to complete a very successful season under sophomore quarterback Darnell Ducette. Regional sportscasters gave him rave reviews for his dynamic plays and leadership of the team. Darnell basked in the light of the countless news releases regarding his superlative play during the season. His abilities were analyzed multiple times by pundits on the national sports networks.

With finals completed, Jack moved into his final semester at Chester City State. His course load for the coming semester was a light one and Jack's thoughts were firmly fixed on the money that the First Presbyterian Church had passed on to George Ducette. But before he tackled this problem, he got his resume out to Mr. Richard Jolly. After all, he would graduate soon and would need a job. Hopefully, it would be a job as a print news journalist. With time between semesters, Jack returned to his pet project: learning all about Darnell Ducette.

With January snow lying on the ground, Jack arrived at the First Presbyterian Church on a Wednesday morning. He was dressed in a fine camel colored topcoat and a matching fedora. Underneath he wore a dark gray suit with a pale blue shirt and a flashy purple tie. Shiny black wing tips completed his attire for the occasion. He had also dyed his light sandy hair a dark brown and put some flecks of gray at his temples. Green tinted sunglasses completed the look. For the role that he was about to play, he needed to look older. He felt like James Bond and loved it. But better yet, he felt like an investigative reporter.

He entered the church and strolled casually down the wide center aisle. The nave was huge, the ceiling high, and the decorations sparkled in the spectacular lighting. Before he reached the end of the aisle he was intercepted by a well-dressed young woman who politely inquired if he had business there or was just stopping in to pray or to rest.

Jack introduced himself as Mr. Herbert Hoover and explained that he was interested in making a substantial contribution to the church fund for purposes of aiding the needy. She said he could talk to her and introduced herself as Ms. Cheryl Pederson.

She smiled and said, "Please follow me back to my office."

"Certainly," Jack replied, realizing that she didn't understand that he was using the name of a deceased president of the United States. Jack enjoyed small pranks.

They were soon seated in Ms. Pederson's office.

Jack began, "I represent a conglomerate of regional businessmen who are interested in helping people in need. We are particularly interested in helping people in minority communities. I have been advised that you do that sort of work here."

Cheryl Pederson was listening to Jack attentively.

"Now Ms. Pederson, what I have in mind is exploring the possibility of donating a sum of one million dollars to be used to benefit these disenfranchised minority families. Would that interest you?"

Cheryl almost choked. She coughed several small coughs.

"Why...why, yes. Yes, Mr. Hoover. We would be very interested in such a donation."

"Good, good. Now, Ms. Pederson, I have information that the church has donated a significant gift to a Mr. George Ducette who now resides in the Living Greens community. Would that be correct?"

"Well Mr. Hoover, ah—well, we really can't disclose the names of our beneficiaries. Surely you understand that?" Jack just shrugged.

"Yes, I suppose I see. What a pity. We wish to specifically help people of color who have not shared in life's bounties to the extent we have. My sources tell me that Mr. Ducette received such a donation, so I had hoped that you would be more forthcoming. I am merely seeking a confirmation that this church was the source of aid to Mr. Ducette."

Cheryl replied, "Then it is specifically people of the Negro race that you wish to be the beneficiaries of your donation?"

Negro race, Jack thought. Did anyone use that word anymore?

"Exactly. May I ask, Ms. Pederson, who your management firm is for these kinds of accounts?"

"I can tell you that, Mr. Hoover." She smiled. "It's Ford C. Carr Accounting, Inc."

Well, son of a bitch.

"Ah, that's a reliable firm. Now come on, Ms. Pederson, come clean. Was George Ducette a beneficiary?"

Cheryl Pederson sighed and then clasped her hands in front of her. Girlishly, she said, "Can you keep a secret Mr. Hoover?" He smiled.

"Of course," Jack replied with all the sincerity he could muster.

"Then I can tell you this much. George Ducette was at one time on our list of eligible beneficiaries. I can't say any more than that."

Jack flashed an even bigger smile.

"Very good. Thank you, Ms. Pederson. Would you perhaps have a card so that I may get back to you?" She plucked a card out of a holder on the desk and handed it to Jack.

"Thank you. You will hear from me in two to three weeks after I consult with my partners."

The usual pleasantries were exchanged, and Jack stood and started to leave.

"Oh Mr. Hoover, may I have one of your cards?"

Shit, Jack thought. I didn't think of that. Dammit.

He began fishing through a couple of his pockets then said,

"Well that's strange. Ms. Pederson, I'm afraid that I must have misplaced them. But don't worry. You will hear from me. Thank you so much."

Cheryl Pederson watched Jack leave. Strange, she thought. A businessman without a business card.

As Jack left the church, his head was spinning. While Cheryl Pederson didn't confirm the gift to George Ducette he felt that without a doubt that Ford Carr had purchased an eight hundred-thousand-dollar house in Living Greens for Darnell's father. This was a clear violation of NCAA regulations involving boosters and their relationship with athletes. This gift must have been made with Darnell's knowledge and with some form of quid pro quo.

CHAPTER 11:
Jack Alone with his Thoughts

After leaving the First Presbyterian Church, Jack Troop's brain was awash in a sea of bizarre and crazy thoughts. Tiny's Bar and Grill was located within a half mile of the church and Jack decided to stop there, drink some vodka, and try to assemble his thoughts into something that resembled a rational picture, even if that picture would be somewhat blurred.

He entered the bar and took a stool at the far end of the counter. Jack's father Frank had introduced him to adult beverages in his late teens. Frank was a vodka man himself. Frank's wife Clara preferred white wine. Jack had acquired his father's taste for vodka. The Troop household had a second refrigerator that was especially used to keep several brands of white wine chilled and multiple brands of Russian and Polish vodka cold. This fridge also held bottled beer for those guests who were beer drinkers. In the cabinet above the fridge, several bottles of scotch were stored. Alcohol had always been a staple in the Troop household.

Jack preferred to drink his vodka in a four-ounce tumbler half filled with ice. Vodka filled the rest of the glass to one-half inch from the top. On occasion, Jack liked a wedge of lemon or lime. On this particular day, Jack told the bartender that he wanted his drink fixed with a wedge of lemon.

Jack had much to consider. It was most likely true that George Ducette had purchased his new luxury house through funds provided by Ford C. Carr. Jack further believed that the funds used to fix up the Ducette's old West Buchcanon Street home could logically have

come from Ford also. Jack's father had told him Ford liked when people owed him. He wanted people of influence to be under his control. Ford obviously believed that Darnell was destined for a rewarding career as an NFL quarterback. It followed that if Darnell was obligated to Ford, then Ford would have another asset that could make him millions of dollars. That Darnell would receive a couple of lucrative contracts during his career in the NFL seemed to be a given. By giving George Ducette the money for a new luxury condo, Ford believed that Darnell would be obligated for a quid pro quo.

Management would then get a share of Darnell's contracts as a management fee. While Jack was no expert, he was confident that Ford Carr's large gift to Darnell's father was a major violation of NCAA rules and could probably kill Darnell's college football career if discovered. Granted, Ford had covered his tracks by using the church as a charitable conduit for the gift to George. But Jack believed if he could figure this out, so could a smart NCAA investigator.

Jack ordered a second vodka.

Now that he thought he understood the money trail, there was Darnell the man to figure out. Darnell had told him without equivocation he intended to get somewhere in life. Somewhere big and somewhere where there was serious money to be made. He had even told Jack no one would be allowed to stand in his way. Jack thought, why hell, he had even threatened me and laughed out loud about it. So, who else had Darnell threatened? Had he already acted to make sure no one would obstruct him on his path to fame and fortune? Had his own mother gotten in his way? Had Darnell arranged an accident when Estelle Ducette stumbled on a loose throw rug and tumbled down the stairs to her death? Possibly, but Willie's knowledge of the loose rug seemed to indicate otherwise.

And what about Tawney Johnson, the pregnant seventeen-year-old girlfriend? Wouldn't she be an obstacle? She had died of a broken neck, just like Estelle. Coincidence? Seemed unlikely. And Chuck Chambers? The starting quarterback had a serious fall down a flight of stairs that had injured him for life and opened the quarterback job up for Darnell to step into. Another obstacle eliminated. Finally, there was the lawsuit filed against Darnell by the family of wrestler Brent Reedy.

An unknown assailant had shattered his knee. Another problem for Darnell had been eliminated. Jack was thinking just too

many broken bones. How could this possibly be mere coincidence? Something strange was happening here, Jack thought. Something rotten and nefarious. If he could connect all the dots, Jack knew he would have one hell of a news story.

Jack was nursing his third vodka now, mentally chewing on the wealth of information that he had gathered. The thought occurred to him that if Darnell was behind this trail of broken bones, then he may well be a sociopath. He thought of Darnell's constant smiling. His attempt to appear affable. But the smiles always disappeared and were replaced by cold glaring eyes and words of intimidation. He found these thoughts chilling.

With his head still spinning partly from trying to piece together Darnell's actions and partly from three vodkas, Jack carefully drove back to his home on Willow Road.

For another couple of months, Jack returned to his studies. In mid-March, he received a letter from Ford Carr Media Inc. offering him a job with the Scarsdale Daily News as an intern in training to become a crime reporter. He would be expected to start on the third Monday in May and was offered a full salary, benefits, and an expense account. While Jack had hoped to land a job with the Chester City Chronicle he was happy with what he had in hand. It was a start. He wrote a letter of acceptance and then proceeded to cruise through the remainder of his senior year.

He was excited by this opportunity. He was being offered a job as a crime reporter, his fondest wish.

As Darnell was busy finishing his sophomore year at Chester City State, he was now dating the hottest honey on campus, head cheerleader Candy Champion, a spectacular, tall, blue-eyed blonde peach of a young woman. This relationship was about to blossom.

CHAPTER 12:
Buzz Cutter

The Scarsdale Daily News office building was located in downtown Scarsdale at 315 Vanover Street. The building was one of the larger buildings in Scarsdale. It was three stories high and occupied most of the 300 block of Vanover Street. It was an old building built with brick that was scared and weather-worn and stone that was rain and grit stained. The expanse of sidewalk that fronted the building was cracked and chipped with an assortment of weeds growing up through the breaks in the aging slabs of concrete. Jack was in the office at 7:45 a.m. Monday morning after having spent the night in a roach motel only three miles away. Staying in this crappy motel saved him the one-hour commute from Chester City. He had entered the building and approached the receptionist. The nameplate on the desk read Diana DeLeo.

When she asked Jack his name, he stood there staring stupidly at her. She was drop dead gorgeous with long raven black hair, large expressive brown eyes, full lips, and a big killer smile. Jack shook off the fog he was in and introduced himself. Diana smiled again and buzzed the office of the editor-in-chief Buzz Cutter. Diana ushered Jack into Buzz Cutter's office. During the brief journey from the front desk to the office, Jack could not help staring at Diana.

Buzz Cutter looked just like you would expect a guy named Buzz Cutter would look. Something like Gomer Pyle's drill sergeant on *The Jim Nabors Show*. About average height, wide across the shoulders with thick arms and forearms and fingers the size of carrots. He wore his steel gray hair in a buzz cut. Bright blue eyes completed the look. He stood and shook hands with Jack. He felt like he'd just shaken hands with a vice grip.

Surprisingly to Jack, Buzz spoke with a soft voice.

"Good morning. So, you would be my new intern, Mr. John Fitzgerald Troop?"

"Yes sir, but—"

"Should I call you John or Jack?"

"Jack, please, sir."

Buzz grinned. "Jack it is then." Jack returned the grin.

"Let's get down to business. Okay? I've got a lot to cover with you. Please sit down." Jack sat.

"Now I need you to understand your assignment here at the Daily News. Working the crime beat is long, hard work. Criminals don't take days off. So, the job is very unpredictable. But it is often exciting, sometimes depressing, and sometimes a bit dangerous. But it can also be a lot of fun and very satisfying once you get the hang of the job."

Jack nodded.

"Good. You will be working in the beginning with a partner. He'll help break you in. His name is Max Hurley. He wants to retire in January when he turns seventy. That's why you're here. Listen to Max. He knows this beat and knows all there is to know about crime reporting. I can't emphasize this enough: listen to Max. Understand?"

"You've made that very clear, sir."

Buzz reached out and handed Jack a list that contained a column of names, addresses, phone numbers, and alternate phone numbers.

Jack glanced at the list. He then looked up at Buzz with a puzzled expression.

"Jack, you're holding your first task in your hand. You are to contact all those people and meet with them. And I stress that I do mean all. The meetings will be a formality. You say hello, how are you today. I'm the Daily News' new crime reporter, then blah, blah, blah. Understand? Buy them coffee, lunch, or a drink or two at Gino's. The paper has an account there."

Jack's eyebrows arched.

"You're on the expense account now so don't sweat it. Save the receipts and give them to me. Got it?"

Jack replied, "I believe so, sir."

"Believe so or have you got it?"

"Got it," Jack replied firmly.

"Jack, have you got any idea who all these people are?"

"No."

"Well, when you work the crime beat, you need to know people: cops, judges, politicians, community leaders. They'll eventually become sources for you. Throw in some gang leaders too. And any residents in crime-heavy areas of the city. Any of these kinds of people can be useful in developing a story.

"This is another point of emphasis. You need to develop sources. They are literally your meal ticket if you want to be successful on the crime beat. I can't stress to you enough the importance of developing sources. Your job will depend upon it. Have I made my point?"

"Yes, sir."

"Again, Max will help you. Work on the contact list over the next week to ten days, and then we'll sit down and chat. Max knows all of these people well. Use him. And Jack, when I said meet with them, that's what I meant. Face to face. No quick 'hi' and 'goodbye' phone calls. I'll want a detailed report. Any questions?"

"No, sir. At least not at this moment."

"Okay then. I'm going to send you back to Diana. She'll give you a tour of the building and have you meet some of our key personnel and get you upstairs to sit down with the HR people. They'll give you a pile of paperwork to fill out and go over your salary and benefits package. They'll also highlight the employee handbook with you. Later this afternoon I'll have Max get together with you."

Jack was excited. A building tour with the luscious Diana DeLeo.

When Jack's first day had finally ended, he took a shot and asked Diana out for a couple of drinks. He got the standard 'I have other plans' brush off. Ouch!

Jack drove around the town looking at the local neighborhoods and finally found a local tavern that looked good from the exterior. At least it looked better than many of the other buildings in downtown Scarsdale. Jack walked casually in the front entrance, glanced around the combination bar and dining room and took a small table in the rear. Once seated, he used his phone to call the motel he was staying in and booked his room for another two weeks. Hopefully, he thought, maybe he could get a decent apartment rented within that time span. Next, he called home to his mother and explained his situation. She was disappointed that he wouldn't be coming home for a while, but she understood.

His calls completed, he ordered a cheeseburger and washed it down with several ice-cold vodkas. While eating his dinner, Jack became immersed with thoughts of how wonderful it would be to date Diana DeLeo. He thought about touching her, about kissing her and holding her beautiful body against him. He fantasized seeing her naked before him and started to become aroused even as he ate. Good God, stop it, Jack, he thought. You're going to drive yourself crazy over that woman. Hell, she flat out turned you down for dinner. She's probably dating someone. Some stud I'd bet. Then he remembered that she didn't wear a ring and that much was encouraging.

He left the tavern and could think of nothing else to do but return to the Blue Lagoon Motel. It was nearly eight o'clock in the evening, so he decided to walk around outside in the dying daylight. About one hundred yards behind the motel was swampland that was known locally as the Blue Lagoon. Hence the name of the motel. The swamp was full of dark, muddy sludge and dirty looking water. There was nothing blue about it. Scrub pine, scruffy shrubs, and weeds protruded from the dark water and swamp goo. The stink from the swamp stung Jack's nostrils. As Jack surveyed the swamp he speculated that one could probably find human remains in all that muck. He would later learn that he was correct.

As night descended, Jack returned to his room and stripped down to his underwear. He turned on the TV and fluffed a couple of skinny pillows with brownish gray pillowcases. The sheets showed splotches of stains from unknown substances. Jack decided not to think about it.

SON OF A BITCH!

Here he was, now out of college and starting a new job. He was excited but felt depressed. He picked up the TV clicker and stretched out on the stained sheets. Hopefully, there would be enough boring crap on TV that it would help put him to sleep. As it turned out, there was plenty.

CHAPTER 13:
Scarsdale

After Jack spent that first sad and lonely night at the Blue Lagoon Motel, he went to work early the next morning. Buzz Cutter gave Jack a reference to a widow who lived on the south side of Scarsdale named Myrtle Merriweather who rented some of her upstairs rooms. She lived in a large old Victorian home with a porch wrapped around three sides of the house. The house had four bedrooms and three baths. Mrs. Merriweather liked to keep two of the upstairs bedrooms rented out to supplement her social security income. Jack called her and made an appointment to meet with her late that afternoon.

She was a large woman, 81 years old with bright blue eyes and one of those kinky perms that older women seemed to prefer that left her silver hair looking silver blue.

As it turned out, both of the bedrooms were empty, and Jack was able to rent the larger of the two. He wrote a check for the first month's rent and a security deposit. During the time Jack spent in Scarsdale, he and Mrs. Merriweather became good friends.

Scarsdale was the second largest city in Shawnee County with a population of just under forty thousand people. It is also the oldest city, having been founded by a group of three hundred settlers on the land that is now inner-city Scarsdale in 1806. Scarsdale was located in the far southwestern corner of Shawnee County with Holmes County just a mile and a half from the city's western limits and Carrollton County just three miles from the city's southern limits.

If drab was a color that would be the color of the entire city. Drab old homes, a drab and graffiti-ridden business district, a drab population of older residents all moving about on rutted and pot-holed roads and drab, rusty bridges. It was a city aching for an infusion of cash and starving despite its best efforts to stay alive. It had a too small police force, a too small fire department and a too small and chronically understaffed local hospital with an emergency room crowded each Friday and Saturday night with people beaten in bar fights, stabbed in domestic violence disputes and shot in gang fights. The public service employees who worked in these places were constantly stressed and grossly underpaid. Old neighborhoods were replete with the poor, the black, the Hispanic and the homeless. If you were to page through a thesaurus looking for another descriptive word for depressing, then Scarsdale would surely be listed.

Jack's crime beat proved to be endless work. Scarsdale was cancerous with every form of lawlessness that is prosecutable. As Buzz Cutter had forecasted, the job proved to be hard work, often exciting and almost endlessly depressing. To Jack, it was certainly interesting but as yet, fun was not how he would describe his days this early in his career.

On his second day, Jack began working on the list of people to get to know. He first contacted Mayor Leroy Taylor. Both men hit it off from their first meeting and Jack was later invited to dinner with the Mayor and his wife Sue several times while working in Scarsdale. Scarsdale's chief of police was a man in his sixties who had fought in Vietnam as a Marine Corps officer. Dick Franklin was a stern but likable man who Jack developed a solid relationship with over the next several years. King Faraday, known as King-for-a-day to Scarsdale police officers, and Dino Giamati were the two senior sergeants on the force. Jack would get along well with King but not as well with Sergeant Giamati. Jack also met with Scarsdale District Attorney Abe Frankel, a small and spritely Jew of quick wit and intelligence. He met the others including both ADA's, criminal court justices Maria De La Rosa and Martin Tomlin, black community activist Rev Samuel Pickler and the Hispanic community spokesman Juan 'Taco' Ramos.

Jack's mentor Max Hurley assisted him in meeting with everyone and providing him with tips on how to best get along with them. Max advised Jack to invite Captain Franklin to Gino's Tavern and buy him a couple of Dewar's on the rocks. The Captain loved his scotch. He told Jack to take Sergeant Faraday fishing and bring plenty of beer. Rev Pickler liked a good cheeseburger with a side of coleslaw for lunch. There was a restaurant on the south side of town that specialized in Jewish cuisine that Abe Frankel was found of. Jack got the message. It was also Max who was able to set up meetings for Jack with the black and Hispanic gang leaders.

On a hot summer afternoon, Jack and Max met El Diablo, the Hispanic gang leader of Los Lobos. The wolves. El Diablo sported a braided ponytail of black and greasy looking hair and multiple tattoos. He was clean shaven and had dark, cold slits for eyes. On the back of his hand was a tattoo of a black and red devil. El Diablo. The three men stood on the cracked pavement outside the building that El Diablo had said he lived in, although Max would tell Jack after the meeting that El Diablo had no known address.

Max introduced Jack as the new crime beat reporter and continued to chat with the gang leader.

"So, hey man, you gonna be the new crime boy in town. You know anything about gangs? Gangs in Scarsdale?"

Jack replied evenly, "Not much. But I am a fast learner." He smiled at El Diablo.

"That's good. You learn. Me and Max get along. He unnerstands. You . . . you I don't know about." El Diablo extended his right pointer finger, tapping Jack on the sternum several times.

Jack didn't flinch and stared back at the gang leader, standing his ground but shaking on the inside. But he stood in place unwilling to retreat and show any fear.

El Diablo said, "Be good and maybe I be good to you. But . . ."

He extended the finger again. "Don't ever fuck with me and never lie to me. Unnerstand?" Jack just smiled.

"El Diablo," Jack replied, "I think I can work with you. Do you understand?"

The gangbanger grinned and then nodded. "Maybe. We see."

"Hey, look, man. I'm new. I get that. But I'm here to do what Max does. Like maybe something happens that doesn't look so good for Los Lobos. Maybe you need to tell the media your side of the story. Right? Then I'm your guy. Maybe something bad is going to go down that you want stopped. Tell me. I—"

"Hey. Hey! I don't snitch man!"

Jack paused, letting the gangbanger calm down. "Sure. I get it. But I'm here to report your side of things if you want me to. Okay?"

El Diablo grunted a yes. Without another word to either man, he walked away. Max had next arranged a meeting with the new leader of the black gang called RED. The former leader known as 'Crazy' Brown had disappeared nearly a month ago. A new leader named Willie had taken Crazy's place. They met at the Scarsdale Municipal Park on the north side of town. Willie Ducette walked up to both men. Jack's mouth was agape as he gazed at Willie.

"Jesus, Willie, what a surprise to see you in Scarsdale." Willie let out a small laugh.

"You know man, I been movin' up in the world. Pretty cool, you know." Max is surprised that the two men know each other. Max asked, "Ah you two know each other?" Both Jack and Willie nodded a yes at the same time.

Max threw his hands up, "Well hell then."

Jack chimed in, "So Willie. Being the new leader of RED. Is that a step up?"

Willie scowled.

"Damn right, man. Let me know when you move up."

"Max called you to meet with the new crime beat reporter. That's me. I'm not a college boy anymore."

Willie chuckled. "Good for you. 'Bout time you got a real job. No more collitch shit."

"Fair enough. But hey. We've worked together before when I was at school. We can do that again."

"Yeah man. I remember. But what I gave you cost some money."

"Sure," Jack said. "Twenty bucks. No big deal."

"Oh man! Cost you a whole lot more now. I'm an executive now. Don't work for no chump change."

"Sure, Willie. We'll work it out. You or one of your guys get jammed up by the cops, call me. I'll get your side of the story out in the Daily. The Daily can pay." Jack extended his hand. Willie stared at it for several seconds and then took it.

"We good man. Just don't fuck with me. I got responsibilities now."

Jack nodded. He heard the same sentiment uttered by El Diablo. And both gang leaders were right. This wasn't college anymore. School was out for Jack Troop and reality was in. Danger certainly lurked in more places than Jack knew about.

CHAPTER 14:
Darnell and Candy

When Jack began his new job in Scarsdale he began losing touch with the life of Darnell. He would, of course, follow that articles written about Darnell or his family in the Chronicle but never had the time to communicate further with him. Jack was occupied with learning his job and learning about Scarsdale and its people. But he also became preoccupied with the daily presence of Diana DeLeo, whose attention he wished to attract.

Darnell was busy completing his education at Chester City State and playing football for the Crusaders each fall. During his junior and senior seasons, Darnell sustained three concussions, two broken ribs, a broken thumb on his non-passing hand, three sprained ankles, a chipped tooth, and a pulled groin muscle. These injuries caused him to miss seven of the 24 games that the Crusaders competed in during that time period. Pro scouts had started taking a hard look at him starting in his junior year. Not a game passed during this time that there weren't at least a dozen or more pro scouts attending the games. Many of them expressed concern over Darnell's injuries to the general managers of the teams they represented.

During his junior season, the Crusaders finished with an eleven and one record and the conference title. They were invited to a minor bowl game that matched them against an opponent from eastern Montana. The Crusaders lost the game by four points despite a heroic performance by Darnell, who played the final two-quarters of the game with an injury. Darnell was also being scrutinized by members of the national sports media. He was frequently interviewed by sports journalists and Darnell enjoyed every minute of it. He craved the attention and was always flashing the big smile of his to the cameras.

During his senior season, Darnell continued to excel. This only attracted more NFL scouts and more members of the media. Halfway through the season, Darnell was being touted as the number one quarterback prospect in the nation. This engendered even more interviews and Darnell's face started appearing on the television sets of football fans across the country. The Crusaders finished the season with a ten and two record, which was still sufficient to capture the conference title for the second straight year. Three days before Christmas the Crusaders met the nation's twenty-third ranked team, the Rebels from Sloane University in Cross Rivers, Alabama. In this game, the final game of Darnell's college football career, Darnell threw four touchdown passes and ran for one, as the Crusaders defeated the Rebels thirty-eight to thirty-five. It was a fine ending to Darnell's outstanding college career.

Darnell finished college as the career leader at Chester City State in passing yards, touchdowns and completion percentage. His statistics were second best all-time in NCAA history. That he would be a first-round NFL draft pick was now a certainty; the only questions were how high in the draft would he be picked, and which team would take him. The lucrative future that Darnell had told Jack he wanted so badly was now firmly within his grasp.

During those years Darnell and Candy Champion had continued to date regularly and were easily the power couple on campus. Before the first game of Darnell's senior season, he gave Candy a diamond ring. Darnell bragged to his buddies that the ring cost him over four thousand dollars. That prompted some speculation from his detractors about how he could possibly come up with that kind of money. No one ever reported this potential violation to the NCAA.

After the football season, a celebration occurred at a frat house on Lemont Street. It was attended by the soon-to-be-graduated senior football players and their girlfriends, along with a list of selected classmates who were specifically invited. The large Victorian fraternity house had as many as sixty young college students in it into the wee hours of the next morning. Beer and liquor flowed freely among the guests. As the evening wore on Darnell was continually asked by male attendees if they could have a dance with Candy. Darnell mostly smiled at the young men and granted permission. After a couple hours of these requests, his finance got tired of dancing with strangers and Darnell, sensing her anger, decided to cut it off. The next person who requested permission was turned down.

The young man making the request was a backup linebacker on the team and roughly the same size as Darnell. He was well buzzed and hostile when Darnell had told him no. A shouting contest broke out between the two young men. Darnell turned away to talk to Candy when he was tackled and shoved into a wall. Darnell's attacker, Douglas Ward stood over the fallen Darnell, challenging him to get up and fight. Darnell accepted. He caught his opponent with a left uppercut in the rib cage then a hammer of a right cross that caught the young man in the nose and upper cheekbone. The nose broke and the cheekbone shattered from the force of the blow. The young man dropped to the floor like a sack of flour.

An ambulance was soon called, and the police were summoned. Darnell and nearly a dozen witnesses gave their statements. The victim, Douglas G. Ward, was interviewed the following day after receiving the needed medical attention. Two weeks later it was announced that no charges would be filed against either of the two combatants. In March, a civil suit was filed by the parents of Douglas G. Ward for financial and punitive damages. They were asking for compensatory damages in the amount of one hundred thousand dollars and punitive damages of two hundred and fifty thousand dollars.

Darnell had remembered this same thing happen earlier in his college days when he was attacked by Brent Reedy. The Reedys had also sued him and now it was happening again with Douglas Ward. Darnell just wanted to make it all go away.

In early April, a small but lavish wedding took place at one of the ballrooms in the Ford C. Carr Convention Center. There were fifty-three invited guests and the master of ceremonies was Ford Carr. It was a plush and peaceful wedding for the new bride and groom. Candy was dazzling in her wedding dress and Darnell was handsome and stylish in his bright blue tux. The couple ate, drank, and danced throughout the glorious evening. A dozen local reporters and several reporters from the national press had been invited to cover the event. Interviews with the young newlyweds were frequent and a gallery of photos were taken. In a town like Chester City, the event was nothing short of a happening. Neither the bride nor the groom had any idea that their wedding day would be the happiest day of what would be a short marriage.

When the newlyweds graduated two weeks later, they went on a two-week honeymoon touring Europe. The speculation was that Ford Carr paid for the trip. Darnell signed a contract with the Ford Carr Sports Management Company the day after graduation. Richard A. Jolly had signed the contract as the president of the sports management company. The NFL draft would be held in Madison Square Garden in New York City four days after Darnell and Candy returned from their honeymoon.

There are a number of people who earn their living analyzing the NFL draft. Despite his stellar college football career, the speculation was rampant among these pundits that because of Darnell's injury history and the pending lawsuit initiated by Douglas Ward's parents, Darnell might not be a high first-round pick. He had some baggage. While he may not go at number one or two, the pundits believed he would be picked between the tenth and fifteen slots. As it turned out, Darnell was picked number five by the Washington, D.C. Red Knights. Darnell would start his NFL career in the nation's capital.

The Red Knights' had been searching more than a decade for a franchise quarterback and management believed Darnell could be that man. He received a huge signing bonus rumored to be in the neighborhood of twenty million dollars. Whatever the number, Darnell, and Candy used some of that money to purchase a luxury two-bedroom condo in Georgetown.

Soon after Darnell reported to the Red Knights' practice facility to participate in spring training. Candy decided she would return to Chester City for a week to visit her parents and friends. Unknown to Darnell, she also did a photo shoot for a calendar that featured the nation's hottest cheerleaders, despite her being a recent graduate. Candy was handsomely compensated for her work, which did not require her to wear too many garments.

Upon completion of her work, a check was made out to Candy Champion and Candy quickly deposited it in her newly opened account. Candy had signed a contract to do other photo shoots for TV ads and magazines. Darnell knew nothing about either of these happenings. Candy had ambitions of her own. She knew that she had married a man who would make millions, but she also knew that she could make millions herself. She would always retain the name of

Candy Champion and would never be Candy Ducette. Darnell had also not foreseen this.

CHAPTER 15:
Pretty Woman

In the pre-dawn hours of Monday morning, six weeks after he had started working at the Scarsdale Daily News, Jack Troop was dreaming. He dreamt he had been shot in the heart. But he was still alive because he hadn't been hit by a bullet. Instead, it had been an arrow. An arrow would have killed him, but this was not an ordinary arrow. Its archer was the legendary Cupid. Jack reached for the arrow and clutched it in both hands, holding it firmly so it would never dislodge from his heart. When he held it the picture of the most beautiful woman in the world passed before his eyes, smiling at him. The woman was Diana DeLeo. In the dream, Jack smiled at her. She smiled back at him.

"Come with me," she said, motioning toward him with her hand. "Be with me. Be with me forever."

It was such a beautiful dream, but then her image faded from his hungry eyes and he yelled out, "Come back! Come back please!"

But she didn't and then he awakened, startled at first and then disappointed.

Jack rubbed the sleep out of his eyes and put his legs over the edge of the bed. Time to get cleaned up and ready for work. Jack knew that he was obsessed with Diana's beauty and at least in love with the idea of being with her forever. He had asked her for a date four times over the last six weeks and had been turned down all four times. He had been ready to give up, but the dream changed his mind for him. She had said, "Be with me" in the dream. The reality was that she never would be with him until she said yes to a date with him. He resolved to ask her again that day. That day, for the fifth time. The dream was telling him that this time she would say yes. He just knew it.

As Jack's workday progressed he struggled to focus on the story he had to complete for the afternoon's deadline. His focus constantly drifted toward the moment when he would approach Diana and ask her out. He finished the story and as the clock ticked toward 5:00 p.m. he decided he was ready.

Diana was straightening out her desk as she prepared to leave for the day.

"Hi Diana," he chirped. "How was your day?"

"Just fine," she replied. "You know, same ol' same ol'."

"Well, I stopped by to make your day a little bit brighter."

She chuckled, "And how would you do that Jack?"

"It's simple. By asking you out to dinner with me. So, would you like to have dinner with me?"

Diana chuckled again. "Jack, tell me something. How many times have you asked me out since you've been working here? Jack smiled and said, "This is number five."

"Five, huh. And I've turned you down the previous four times?"

"Unfortunately, yes." He kept on smiling but sensed that this once again was not going his way.

"Well then, I suppose I have played the game of hard to get long enough. So, yes, Jack I'd love to have dinner with you." Jack couldn't believe his ears.

"You said yes."

"I did. When and where?"

"That's great. Thank you. How about Gino's Italian Restaurant this coming Thursday at seven? I'll pick you up around 6:30 or a little after."

"No."

"No!"

"Jack, I mean no don't pick me up. I'll meet you at Gino's at seven. It will be easier for me that way. I'll explain over dinner."

"Okay, sure then. I'll be looking forward to it."

"Me too. Jack. And Jack, you are a handsome devil you know."

"Thank you," Jack replied stunned.

"See you then. Jack."

"Yes, you will." When Jack went to bed that night, he lay there looking up at the ceiling and the heavens above. He was not a great believer in a deity or a spirit world but for whatever unfathomable reason he was sure that the dream that morning was the motivator that prompted him to ask Diana one more time for a date. And that dream had forecasted his success.

Gino's Italian Restaurant was only about a mile from Jack's apartment in Mrs. Merriweather's large Victorian home. He arrived at the restaurant a half hour early, sitting at the bar and ordering a chilled vodka on the rocks. He wished to calm down as much as possible. He sipped the vodka, waiting patiently until Diana came through the front door.

When they had been seated at a quiet table near the rear of the restaurant Jack asked Diana if she wished to order a drink.

"I'd love to Jack, but you see, I'm not twenty-one yet, so I'll settle for an iced tea."

"Oh, I didn't know. I'm sorry."

"Don't be. It's alright. I turn twenty-one next Thursday. Perhaps you can buy me a drink then, but for now, I can wait. If you want one go ahead and order one. It's fine by me."

"Thank you. So, your birthday is on the 29th. My twenty-third is just four days later—on the second."

A quick laugh escaped Diana's lips. "Jack, it sounds like multiple celebrations are in order."

"Yes, it does. Should we make plans?"

She tilted her head, looking at Jack and appraising him.

"Perhaps. Let's see how this evening goes first."

Jack was slightly deflated but replied, "Yes, yes let's do that." There was a brief silence as the two young adults just looked at each other.

"So, tell me, Diana, I'm interested in hearing this. Why did you choose to meet me here? I would have been happy to come to your home and pick you up."

"I did promise you an explanation, Jack. You may have noticed that I am Italian."

Jack nodded.

"My family is very old school. Particularly my father and my mother. Dad sees me still as his baby girl. His little princess. I am the youngest of four children. I have three older brothers. Are you getting the picture?"

"Not exactly. I assume that you and your family members are Catholics?"

"Yes, but that's only some of the problem. You see Jack, Dad and Mom are very, and I mean very, protective of me. So are my older brothers. So, I told my parents that I was going out with Margie and Sue. Those are two of my friends and they know what I told my parents. They'll cover for me if I need to be covered."

"Diana, covered how? From me?"

"Precisely, Jack. From you." Jack gave her a palms-up gesture and shook his head.

"Look, Jack, Dad would never let me go on a date with a man that he has not yet met and approved. That's the old-fashioned Italian male in him."

"I see that you're not kidding."

"No, I'm not. So technically I'm out tonight with Margie and Sue. But I'm much happier being here with you. How's that?"

Jack just smiled. "That's great. I'm happy too."

"Now that we have that out of the way, tell me, Jack, why did you become a reporter? I'm curious."

"Well, I liked writing stories even as a child . . ."

Jack and Diana ordered fresh drinks and ordered dinner as Jack told a shortened version of his childhood and his college years as a student of journalism.

They ordered dessert as Jack asked Diana about her childhood. Diana explained that her upbringing was strict, and the Catholic Church played a significant role in her daily life. In high school, she had taken courses in typing, shorthand and a course in basic bookkeeping. This had prepared her for the job she currently held at the Scarsdale Daily News.

When they had finished their desserts, Diana asked Jack for the time.

Jack said, "Oh no, have I been boring you?" Diana grinned.

"No way, Jack, this has been a delightful evening. But, don't forget that I'm really out with my girlfriends Margie and Sue. My parents won't be expecting me to be home very late."

"Oh, I suppose not. You must understand that your situation is rather, well . . . rather odd to me. Can I say that?"

"Oh, hell yes. To me, it's screwy as all hell!"

Jack laughed. "In that case, it's almost ten o'clock. Damn, this evening went awfully fast."

"It did, Jack. So let's do it again. Next Wednesday. My parents will be holding a birthday dinner for me with family and close friends on Thursday."

"Good. Do you like beef? Steaks and all?"

"Sure."

"Then I know just the place. I suppose I still can't pick you up?"

"Not just yet, but soon. How about I meet you right here in the parking lot."

"Sold. How about at 6:30. It's about a half hour drive to the restaurant I have in mind."

"Sounds good," she said. "Let's go please."

The young couple left and walked out to the parking lot. Diana guided him to her car. As they stood there facing each other, Jack slowly put a hand on each of her shoulders. She didn't flinch. He slowly leaned in to kiss her and was delighted when she leaned into him. They kissed. Gently at first, then with more firmness and passion until the gentle kiss morphed into a long, firm, wet kiss that lasted over a minute. They slowly pulled apart.

"God, Jack," Diana said breathlessly, "Where did you learn to kiss like that?"

Jack shrugged and replied sheepishly, "Not trying to brag Diana, but I've been told that before. I honestly don't know where it comes from. Just natural I guess. Did I offend you?"

"Good God no, don't you ever stop kissing me like that. So, I'll see you next Wednesday."

"Yes," Jack said. "Does this mean that we are officially dating now?"

"It sure feels that way, Jack." They both said goodnight.

CHAPTER 16:
Jack at the Blue Lagoon

Max Hurley proved to be a good mentor and a better friend to young Jack Troop. Max had worked with Jack on multiple stories involving domestic abuse cases. Max then encouraged Jack to do an extended story on the subject for later publication in the Sunday edition of the Daily. He had also done two murder stories, a robbery, and several car theft stories and was currently working on a major story on the state of the Scarsdale police force.

In addition to crime reporting, both men enjoyed golf and had already played together several times at the Scarsdale Country Club where Max was a member. Both discovered they enjoyed a few drinks at some of the local taverns. Max boasted he knew every bar, tavern, and dive in the city. Jack quickly discovered that indeed Max did.

A warm summer in Scarsdale had morphed into a cool early fall. On Wednesday, October 1st, both Max and Jack had been in the Vanover Street office of the Scarsdale Daily for about an hour working on a couple of stories. Jack had put time and energy into his job over the past months and discovered that his job could be a good deal of fun. The in-depth stories that he had been working on under the guidance of Max were both exciting and challenging. As Jack was refining these stories a call came in from Sergeant Faraday.

"Faraday here, Jack. You doing anything real important right now?"

"Not overly. What's on your mind, King?"

"I'm over at the Blue Lagoon with my partner. We got a floater in the lagoon. Could be a homicide. Thought you might want to take a look. I think this will be your first time seeing a body fished out of the lagoon. It may not be your last."

Jack said, "Ah, yeah sure. Should I bring Max?"

"Max has seen his share. Just thought I'd give you a shot at this. Could be a good story."

"Sure, King. I'll owe you."

"Yes, you will. Lunch at Gino's Tavern?"

"Deal. I'm on my way." Jack told Max what was happening, and Max told him to get his young ass over there. This could be big. Excited, Jack hustled out of the office, hopped into his car and sped over to the Blue Lagoon.

When Jack arrived at the scene, a police van had already arrived with the equipment needed to recover the body from the swamp. Four newly arrived officers were sliding a small boat into the murky swamp water. Jack parked his car and walked over to Sergeant Faraday and the other officers with his pocket recorder and camera in hand.

Hey, King." Jack said. "What do you have at this point?" Faraday looked at Jack and pointed toward the lake.

"The guys put the boat in and have just snagged the body. It's probably bloated with decomposition gasses, which caused it to float to the surface. We'll see what we got soon."

"Good," Jack replied somewhat lamely.

Jack aimed the camera toward the boat and took snapshots as it moved slowly toward the shoreline as he watched the officers poling the boat forward toward the shore. When it reached the shore, the officers at the shoreline grabbed the rope securing the body and pulled the corpse into the swamp grasses lining the shore. Faraday moved closer to the body and Jack followed.

As Jack moved closer, the officers were wiping some of the swamp goo off the head and face of the body. The back of the victim's head came into full view and revealed a large hole in the back of the skull. Jack watched as several small swamp insects emerged. For reasons Jack couldn't explain, his stomach cramped violently, and he had to turn away as bile and leftover stomach contents spewed out through his mouth and nostrils. His stomach recoiled again, and the bile shot from his mouth. Jack was down on his knees, hands on the ground, trying to gain control of his stomach spasms. He coughed multiple times as his body shook.

King Faraday and the other police officers just stared briefly at Jack and then started to chuckle.

Faraday teased, "Hey Jack. I was right. This is your first time."

Jack just continued to cough and spit the remainder of the fowl crap out his mouth. Slowly he stood and looked over at the assembled group of officers.

Jack grumbled, "Shit! Sorry guys. Didn't see that coming."

Faraday replied, "First time for everything. Even dead bodies. You okay?"

"Yeah. Embarrassed but okay." He moved closer to the body and his stomach now stayed steady.

Faraday then said, "Jack look here. The size of the hole in this guy's head. Gotta be a .45 caliber. Gang execution I'd say." Faraday waved the other cops over, who all nodded in agreement. Jack also risked a look. Luckily his stomach held.

"Flip him over, guys. Let's get a look at his face." Once the body was turned on his back an officer wiped the face free of most of the remaining swamp goo.

Faraday spoke loudly, "Well, well, well. Looks like Tyrone Brown. Now, officially, the former leader of RED." Jack moved in closer.

"That's Crazy Brown?"

"Yeah. It's him," Faraday said.

Jack offered, "And Willie Ducette is his replacement. How long you figure Crazy's been in that swamp. King?"

"Hard to say, but probably as much as a month or two. No more."

"So, what's the next step?"

King considered. "I call Chief Franklin and then get a coroner's bus to transport the body to the county coroner's office in Chester City. Go ahead and write the story, Jack. We've found Crazy Brown."

The story appeared in the Thursday edition of the Daily News. After the story was in the newspaper, Jack felt he needed to talk to Willie and El Diablo. He spent several weeks trying to meet with either man but without success. Jack combed the neighborhoods where the members of both gangs hung out, asked questions of some members who were out in the streets or sitting on concrete front porch steps of the many neighborhood homes. But his efforts got him absolutely nowhere. For the matter, neither had the Scarsdale police. Both El Diablo and Willie had vanished. Dead end.

CHAPTER 17:
Jack and Diana

The following Wednesday, Jack and Diana were seated at the Hillsdale House of Beef located in the town of Hillsdale just over the Shawnee county line in Carrollton County. They were approximately fifteen miles south of Scarsdale.

They were chatting when the waitress came to their table and asked if they would like something to drink.

Diana looked up and said, "I'd like a glass of red wine." "What kind of red would you prefer?"

"Any dry red would be fine."

"Very well. And you, sir?"

"Grey Goose on the rocks, please?"

"Very good. I need to see your ID's, please." Jack handed the waitress his. She took it, glanced at it, and nodded.

"And you, miss." Diana handed the waitress hers thinking, oops. She glanced at it, then looked at Diana and smiled.

"Well, miss, I guess you turn twenty-one in a little less than five hours. Very good."

When the drinks arrived the two started looking through the menus. Jack decided on a sirloin steak with baked potato and salad bar. Diana opted for the braised beef with sautéed asparagus tips and mushrooms.

"Well, Diana, I guess tomorrow will be a big day in your life. You'll be officially legal. An adult."

"Actually, what I will really be tomorrow is my own woman. I will be making my own decisions about the remainder of my life. Jack, I love my parents and I love my brothers, but their ways are not my way. I'm a modern woman, not a dinosaur."

She paused and sipped some of her wine.

"You know, Jack, women in my family have, for generations, been expected to grow up, get married and have a bunch of kids. Big families. Italian men of the old school are providers and the women stay home, to cook and clean and raise kids. Not what I'm after, Jack."

"Really?"

"Well, sort of really. I mean I've got no problem marrying. None at all. I—"

"You would marry me, wouldn't you?"

"Perhaps. We'll see, won't we?"

"Fair enough."

"Anyway, the man I marry would need to accept me on my terms. I mean his terms would also count but I can't play house. I can't play the compliant little woman who spends her time in the kitchen barefoot and pregnant all the time. So, to speak I mean."

Jack cocked his head and looked at Diana appraisingly.

"How do you see me, Diana? What kind of husband do you see?"

"Oh my, Jack. What a question. I—I mean . . . I don't really know. I think I would know in time."

"How much time?"

Diana laughed. "Are you in a rush Jack?"

Now Jack laughed. "Oh, I don't know. Maybe, maybe not. I do know one thing. I'd marry you in a heartbeat."

"Come on, Jack. We don't know each other that well yet. I do really like you. Does that help?"

"Of course it does. But seriously. My heart knows you and I would marry you. When you're ready."

"What if I'm never ready?"

"I can't let myself think like that." The two fell silent and drank some more. Their food arrived so they began to eat.

Diana was a petite young woman at five feet two inches and about one hundred and fifteen pounds. But she was not a dainty eater. She attacked her food with gusto and ate eagerly. Jack was surprised by this when they had eaten together last Thursday. But he decided that he liked a woman with a robust appetite. Perhaps her other appetites were equally robust. He knew that he would love to find out. When they had finished they ordered desserts, and each ordered another drink.

"Tell me, Jack, do you know if there is a playhouse near here. I'm thinking that there is."

"Yes," replied Jack. "It's called the Players Playhouse. It's about five miles north of here, near the resort area around Bluebird Lake."

"That's right. Our family went there once when I was a child. I love live theater. Do you know that I can sing well? I was in my high school chorus. I was the soloist. I also appeared in the senior play, My Fair Lady. I played Eliza Doolittle. Surprised?"

"Wow. Yes, I am. There's obviously a lot more to you than a pretty face."

"Why, of course, there is. You'll see eventually. I am a catch, Jack."

"Damn. You are that, Diana."

They left the restaurant soon after dessert and headed back to the parking lot at Gino's Restaurant. Another long, deep kiss was exchanged between them before they parted company. The following Sunday afternoon they went to the Players Playhouse for an afternoon matinee, followed by beer and burgers at the Old Piney Tavern in the Bluebird Lake Resort area.

They continued to date regularly over the next month and discovered they were both joggers. Occasional weekend morning jogging dates were followed by a picnic. Jack played golf and Diana wanted to learn how to play, so he began teaching her the game. The couple was bonding quickly and with each date, the sexual tension growing between them was becoming too intense to ignore.

They were having dinner one evening at a small Mexican restaurant north of Scarsdale in Culver City, a town of just over five thousand people. At the end of the meal Diana spoke.

"Jack," she said seriously. "I think it's time."

Jack looked curiously at her. "Time? Time for what?"

"Time for you to be introduced to my family."

"Oh. For a moment I thought you meant something else." She smiled. "Ah yeah, that, too. All the more reason to get this over with."

"Diana, I have told my parents about you. They would love to meet you so maybe we ought to get the social niceties taken care of."

"Yes, we should. I have already taken the liberty to explain to my parents that I have been seeing you. You are invited to Sunday dinner. That's next Sunday at one o'clock after our family is finished with our church services. Wear your Sunday finest. You know the address. I'll be waiting for you. You make the arrangements with your parents."

"Good. I guess we have a plan. Oh, by the way, how about the other situation."

Diana laughed out loud. "Just hold your horses, ace. I'm worth the wait, you know."

"I know, Diana. I know."

CHAPTER 18:
Dinner at the DeLeo's

Jack Troop took a deep breath and knocked on the large front door of the old mansion that was the DeLeo family home. Diana answered the door. She was dressed in a pale yellow dress accented with a flower print sash. She wore a string of pearls around her neck. Her dangling earrings sparkled. Her long black hair had big curls that hung over her bare shoulders.

Jack thought he looked appropriately dressed in a tan suit with a light green shirt and a pale yellow tie. He had polished his wing- tipped shoes and sported a fresh haircut. He took another deep breath and entered.

Diana's parents were standing at the end of the hallway. Dom was a slim man, around six feet tall and about one hundred and sixty pounds. He wore a custom-made, dark gray Italian suit. He wore a pale blue shirt with French cuffs and a dark blue tie. He also had brightly polished wing-tipped shoes. Dom's DeLeo's hair was snow white and he wore it long in the back, down to his shirt collar. He sported a thin silver mustache over his upper lip.

Sophia DeLeo was Diana's height and somewhat heavier. She wore a print dress and several pieces of what Jack expected were very expensive jewelry.

Jack plastered a big smile on his face as Diana led him before her parents.

"Daddy," she said, "This is my boyfriend, Jack Troop."

The two men shook hands as Jack said, "I am delighted to meet you, Mr. DeLeo."

Dom nodded and replied, "Pleased to meet you, Jack." Jack turned to Sophia. She extended her hand and Jack shook it. He said, "I'm very glad to meet you, Mrs. DeLeo."

She replied, "I am happy to meet you, young man."

With pleasantries exchanged Diana moved the group into the living room. There, Jack met Diana's older brother, Nick, and his wife, Sherry, and the couple's three children. Nick was taller than his father with dark hair and dark eyes nested in narrow slits. Then her brother, Lou, and his wife, Kate, and their three children, and finally the youngest brother Gino, a bachelor. Lou was the shortest of the three brothers, fifty pounds overweight and a face scarred by acne. Gino was as tall as Nick but with a distinctly more muscular build.

Dom signaled the assembled family members and Jack to enter the dining room, where it was obvious to Jack that everyone knew where to sit. Diana guided Jack over to a chair beside hers. Sophia left the dining room and disappeared. Jack had watched her leave. Diana noticed this and whispered to Jack that she was going to the kitchen to make sure the food was ready. Sophia soon returned, and Dom pulled her chair out for her. Jack smiled. She had told Jack that her father was an old school gentleman.

Two maids then entered the dining room with carts of food that they began distributing on each end of the table.

Jack had a moment to take in the dining room. It was massive, probably over a thousand square feet with a high ceiling holding a magnificent chandelier over the center of the table. There was a large window to the rear of the room that exposed a view to the yard outside. Several potted plants decorated the sill. Two narrower windows faced Jack. A variety of knick-knacks sat on each sill. The dining table was as large as a bus and made from a type of highly polished wood. Jack had no idea where a tablecloth big enough to cover it could have been purchased. He decided it had to be custom made.

When the platters of ravioli, lasagna and garlic bread had been placed on the table along with bowls of fresh salad, everyone became silent and bowed their heads. Dom said grace. He was kind enough to mention that the family was thankful for the company of their newfound friend, Jack Troop.

As the head of the family, Dom said the grace. Heads were bowed, and Dom began solemnly,

"Heavenly Father we thank you for the health and well-being of all members of the DeLeo family and our special guest Jack Troop. We thank you for the food that we are about to receive from thy bounty through our savior Jesus Christ. Amen."

The grace completed, carts with bottles of wine were wheeled into the room. The two maids uncorked them and set a cart at each end of the table. Jack counted ten bottles on each cart. The wine was then passed around and plates were filled. Once that ritual was completed everyone began eating. To Jack, the smell of the food was heavenly. To a man who was used to subsisting on microwaved Hungry Man dinners and fast food, Jack believed he had entered the home of culinary paradise.

As everyone ate hungrily, Dom put down his fork and said,

"So, Jack. Diana has informed us that you are the new crime reporter at the Scarsdale Daily. I have seen your byline. You write well. Now let me see, you have been there for how long now?"

Jack put down his fork. "Well, sir, I've been working the crime beat since the end of May. I work with a mentor. His name is Max and he is teaching me the ins and outs of the job. I like the work, but the hours are long."

Dom looked down the table toward Jack.

"Well, good Jack. Tell me about these ins and outs. What are they?"

"Oh, you know sir, like—"

"Excuse me, but I don't know. It is why I ask. Enlighten me please."

Oops. Jack realized he didn't say the right thing.

"Sir, I guess I'm talking about doing the job properly. Like doing good reporting. Working with the police and the DA's office to develop information to give the public a fair and accurate story."

Dom replied, "Now that I understand, Jack. Thank you. But tell me something. Why do you news people call them stories? A story is like Jack and the Beanstalk. It isn't real. Why not call them reports or something?"

"I guess I don't really know, sir. A news story has been called a story since well before I was even born."

"Like something old and settled? Tried and true? That stuff I get."

"Yes, sir. Well said."

Dom just smiled. Jack was starting to sweat a little. It was like he was being grilled by a congressional committee. Come on Jack. Relax. Diana told you this was coming.

Dom started eating again. Sophia put down her fork and grabbed the opportunity to jump in. Jack also was told this switch would take place. Diana knew her parents.

Sophia began, "Jack, please tell us. Which of the Catholic churches do you attend? It's clearly not our church because I've never seen you there."

Jack's heart starts to race. He took a deep breath before speaking. "Jack?"

"Well, you see, Mrs. DeLeo, that's sort of because I don't . . . I don't . . . attend a Catholic church." He cringed at his response.

"Then where do you attend church? Diana's father and I would like to know."

Jack muttered he often worked Sunday's and didn't get much opportunity to attend church.

Sophia retorted, "Oh, I see. But I'm not sure I understand." She had a puzzled look on her face.

Clearly, she didn't see at all. Jack knew he was in a jam.

"Please, tell us, Jack, of what faith are you?"

Slam, bam. Jack Troop went down for the count. He clearly had no decent answer to this question despite Diana warning him this would be the blockbuster bomb that he must defuse.

Jack looked at her with a wry smile on his face followed by a big shrug of his shoulders and took the plunge. He flashed Sophia his best smile.

"Mrs. DeLeo, actually, I'm a Democrat."

He kept smiling sheepishly. Both Dom and Sophia dropped their forks and picked up their wine glasses. Jack could see Diana out of the corner of his eye with a silly I-told-you-this-would happen grin on her pretty face.

Sophia regained her composure first.

"Jack, both Dom and I are Republicans. We serve on and give to the Scarsdale Republican Committee. So, I expect that we will be having many entertaining dinner conversations in the future. Don't you think?"

SON OF A BITCH.

She had made it easy for him. Jack passed inspection.

With great relief, Jack said, "Mrs. DeLeo, I will look forward to it."

During the next year, Jack was a guest at the DeLeo home at least once a month. Over time the DeLeo's became comfortable with him and he was comfortable with them. It was obvious to Sophia that Diana had fallen in love with Jack.

One late summer evening Jack and Diana were sitting on the front porch of the DeLeo's old Victorian home drinking lemonade. Jack was interested in a cold vodka but stuck with the lemonade. They were holding hands, gazing at the stars on a warm evening. Diana leaned into her man and looked up into his eyes. Jack thought she was about to say something romantic or perhaps profound. The warmth and softness of her body created an ache in his groin that they both knew had yet to be satisfied.

"Jack, screw this lemonade shit. Can we go somewhere and get a real drink?"

Jack smiled and hugged her. "That's my girl."

CHAPTER 19:
Back to the Crime Beat

After the discovery of the body of Tyrone 'Crazy' Brown, Sergeant Faraday was again called out to the Blue Lagoon. He decided to call Jack Troop again.

"Jack Troop here."

"Jack, it's Faraday. You busy?"

"Sort of, but what's up?"

"The lagoon. We're gonna pull out another floater pretty soon. Looks like another homicide, Jack. You want to give it another try?" Jack responded with excitement in his voice. "Oh, hell yes. And don't worry. I'll be fine this time around."

"Okay, get your butt out here ASAP."

Jack shoved aside the work he was doing at his desk, got in his car and arrived at the lagoon fifteen minutes later. Jack hustled over to the edge of the lagoon where Sergeant Faraday stood along with two officers. Two more officers were in the boat bringing the newly discovered corpse to the shore. The two in the boat were obviously straining as they poled the boat to the shoreline. Jack watched as the boat arrived. The officers jumped out while sucking wind dragging the body onto the grass. Jack observed the body was that of a large man, well over six feet and over two hundred pounds.

Jack again felt the bile in his stomach start to churn. Oh shit. He began taking slow deep breaths to settle himself. The urge to vomit quickly passed. Good, he thought, not this time.

"What do you think, Sergeant?" Jack asked. Faraday was bent over the body staring intensely at it.

"I don't see a large amount of deterioration. The body hasn't been there more than a few days." Faraday pointed to the skull.

"Damn. Look at that hole in the back of this guy's head. Its fucking huge. Gotta be a .45 caliber again. God damn gangbangers!" The other officers nodded in agreement.

"Any idea who he is," Jack inquired.

"I think so. Let's turn him over, guys."

The other officers rolled the dead man onto his back.

Faraday said, "Oh yeah, that's him. Pedro Ruiz. They called him 'Two Gun' because he carries a forty-five in his waist, and a thirty-eight-revolver strapped to his leg. He's believed to be a hit man for Los Lobos. Looks like the RED bunch finally got him. Payback for killing Crazy Brown. At least that would be my guess."

One officer echoed Faraday, "Yeah that's 'Two Gun' alright." Another said, "Someone from RED got him, for sure." Another said, "Hey Sergeant, the thirty-eight is still strapped to his leg."

Faraday walked over to the corpse and said, "Let me see." The officer pulled the pants leg up again. Jack now looked at the body.

"Have we got a gang war going on here, King?"

"Could be. Or it could stop right here. Hard to say for sure. You know you got our guy and now I got yours. It's even. Right?" Jack shrugged.

"Even Steven, as we said as kids," Jack replied.

"But we could soon have a shooting war between the gangs. Time will tell."

"Maybe it can be stopped."

Faraday held his hands out palms up.

"Maybe, maybe not. If they really want a war it will happen."

"I see."

But Jack didn't see. Maybe Willie and El Diablo could get together. Maybe talk things out.

The body was soon bagged and put into the van and Jack thanked Faraday for the tip. Jack left the scene feeling that maybe he could do something. He needed to visit the neighborhoods where the gangbangers hung out. He had done this before with no tangible results. Perhaps he would give it another shot. But first, he needed to write this story.

The next morning Jack was in the heart of Los Lobos territory. He had been walking the streets since before 9:00 a.m. asking anyone he ran into if they knew where he could find El Diablo. An hour later, he was on Blackberry Street knocking on doors and still asking about El Diablo. Everyone he talked to, man or woman, said that they knew nothing. He was not making progress. He reached the end of Blackberry Street and turned uptown on Green Street, where a group of four young men were moving down Green Street walking with a purpose toward him.

"Hey man," one yelled to him.

Jack stopped, watching them with apprehension as they approached at a steady pace.

The largest of the four men pointed his finger at him.

"Hombre. You! Get the fuck out of this neighborhood before something bad happens to you. You got no business here, man."

Jack stared at the man while taking some steps backward as the group approached to within several feet of him. Jack turned to run as all four men sprang at him. The big man grabbed him by the back of his jacket. Jack swung a couple of fists at the man and connected with an inconsequential blow to his sternum. By then the other three men grabbed him and knocked him to the ground. On the ground, he was assaulted by a succession of kicks. Jack attempted to curl himself into a ball, but more hostile boots assaulted his kidneys, a couple to his head, and then to his ribs. His hands, arms, and legs were also stomped on by the four booted men. It was over in half a minute. The men scattered as Jack lay on the ground stunned, bleeding, and barely conscious.

Apparently, a Good Samaritan had called 911. An ambulance and a police cruiser arrived and eventually Jack was taken to the Scarsdale General Hospital's ER where he received emergency care and was admitted to the hospital. Jack was pissing blood, had two broken ribs, a broken left thumb, a concussion and multiple bruises and abrasions over a significant portion of his body. He spent a week in the Scarsdale hospital recovering before being released. He returned for a long rest in his room at Mrs. Merriweather's house, attended to by Mrs. Merriweather and Diana. Both Sophia DeLeo and Jack's parents also spent time with him.

While in the hospital, Jack gave his report to Sergeant Faraday with as much information as he could remember, which wasn't that much. The only assailant that he remembered was the tall slim Hispanic who had first challenged him. Faraday was sure he knew who that was and would bring him in for questioning.

After several weeks of recuperation, Jack felt that he was ready to return to work. When he returned, he was summoned to Buzz Cutter's office.

CHAPTER 20:
Another Talk with Buzz Cutter

Jack returned to work after the assault by four members of Los Lobos. But he had taken a severe beating and he did not feel fully recovered from the injuries he had sustained. He worked as long as he could each day until he tired.

He was unexpectedly summoned early one morning to the office of Buzz Cutter. Tired and still sore all over, he walked slowly into the office. Buzz saw Jack obviously moving with some pain and motioned for him to take a chair in front of the desk. Jack did just that, sat and released a deep sigh.

"Good morning sir. Sorry. I'm pretty gassed this morning.

"Understandable Jack. And I'm not going to keep you very long. I have been extremely happy with the job you've done since you first started. I've been talking to Mr. Jolly about how quickly you've adapted to the crime beat. We have both come to a conclusion about your future."

Jack's heart skipped a beat.

"Yes, sir. Ah, you know that I'm not yet up to full speed. But it won't take much longer."

"Relax Jack. Everybody understands your situation. Take the time you need and then be ready to roll. Okay? As I was saying, we believe that we should upgrade your assignment. It comes with a pay raise of $400 a month. How does that sound?"

"Well sir, it sounds fine. But . . . but what would that assignment be? I like what I'm doing."

"It shows. You're good at it, Jack. But I want you in the van a couple of times a week and then more often as you gain confidence in front of the camera."

The van was the Scarsdale mobile news van, filled with electronic equipment to broadcast news live from the scene.

Jack stammered, "B—But . . . but sir, I—I . . . I have no experience in . . . in front of a camera."

"Oh, stop it, Jack." Buzz was holding out his right hand like a traffic cop.

"Six months ago, you had no experience as a crime reporter. Now you're damn good. Max told me you are the best young reporter he has ever seen. And that's saying a lot. Look, you are very well spoken. You've got the big blue eyes and the strong jawline, and you'll look great when you are on camera. I have no doubts." He winked. "Diana sure thinks so."

That brought out a smile from Jack.

"Don't worry, you'll catch on fast. Besides, Joanie Blake will ride with you until you get the hang of it. You'll be fine."

Great, Jack thought. Joanie was a dozen years older, but like Diana, also a knockout. Behave yourself, he thought.

"Well sir, if you're sure."

"I'm positive."

Two weeks later, after Jack had more fully recovered, the van's driver Emilio Torres pulled the van up to the scene of a shooting and Jack took the mic.

"This is Jack Troop reporting live from . . ."

CHAPTER 21:
The Crime Beat

Jack was healthy now and working from the van on Friday and Saturday nights. Criminals in Scarsdale were always busy on those nights, as were the cops and crime reporters. He had returned to work the week before Thanksgiving. During his recovery, his parents Frank and Clara had visited him on several occasions. He took one such opportunity to introduce his girlfriend Diana to them. His parents were impressed with Diana and approved of his choice. He and Diana spent Thanksgiving Day visiting Jack's parents in their Willow Road home for a Thanksgiving dinner and then drove back to Scarsdale to rest and relax together free from family and happy to enjoy some time alone with each other. They ate delivery pizza and drank wine late into the evening. Once both sets of parents were comfortable with the two as a couple, Jack and Diana felt completely free to spend as much time together as their work schedules would permit.

The Friday evening after Thanksgiving Jack had to work. But he decided to take Diana to an early dinner at Gino's Italian Restaurant. Scarsdale, having a large population of people with Italian ancestry, had several businesses owned by men named Gino. In addition to Gino's Italian Restaurant, there was Gino's Tavern, Gino's Dry Cleaning, Gino's Auto Repair, Gino's Real Italian Pizza, Gino Rizzo's Tire Outlet and Gino's Tool and Die Inc. They ate a large Italian dinner followed by Italian pastries for dessert. After taking Diana home, Jack headed into work and got there as Joanie and Emilio finished readying the van for the evening's prowling around the city of Scarsdale.

Toward ten o'clock that evening Emilio was guiding the van through one of the more crime infested areas of the city. While the van frequently patrolled Scarsdale's more depressed neighborhoods where crime was most likely to occur, they also scheduled themselves to patrol more affluent neighborhoods looking for stories. They stumbled across such stories often enough, particularly those involving domestic violence, which proved to be the kind of crime that knew no economic limitations.

They all heard a long burst of gunfire coming from a couple of blocks of their location. The shots were very loud and came from a powerful gun. Probably an AR-15, Jack, and Emilio thought. Emilio quickly headed the van toward the sounds of the gunfire while the van's police scanner picked up the calls summoning police. The shooting took place on the corner of Lombardo and Maple Street. As they approached the location, a police car was arriving. The sirens of other police vehicles could be heard nearby. Curious people began emerging onto the sidewalks.

The corner of Lombardo and Maple was occupied by an old brick apartment building. The bricks were full of cracks and some of the mortar that held them in place was worn and crumbling. Gang insignia was spray-painted over the brick. The blacktop was cracked and littered with an assortment of crushed beer cans, various crumpled food wrappers, and cigarette butts. As the van pulled into the parking lot, its headlights glared on what appeared to be three male victims of the shooting laying on the cold black asphalt. One of them was wiggling around in distress. The other two lay still. Emilio inched the van closer. Two officers exited the cruiser with guns drawn and moved cautiously toward the fallen men, the headlights from the cruiser illuminating the bodies. One officer waved Jack and his crew back. Emilio put the van in reverse and inched the vehicle backward. Joanie and Emilio got the camera running and Jack grabbed the mic.

"This is Jack Troop coming to you live from the corner of Lombardo and Maple Streets. We are on the scene of an apparent shooting. I can see three males lying on the parking lot. One of the men is moving, writhing around, perhaps in some pain. Two officers are now attending to the victims. I see another police cruiser is now entering the lot. I'm going to try to get closer."

One of the cops was on the radio and the other was motioning Jack to stop where he was. Jack then re-keyed the mic and passed on some additional observations. Emilio and Joanie kept the camera running pointed at the scene. Jack recognized Officer Bill Pullman, who he had talked to several times since he started on the crime beat.

"Officer Pullman. What information can you give us?" Jack began slowly moving forward toward the three men on the blacktop.

An ambulance from the Scarsdale Community Hospital had now arrived. Pullman had waved Jack off, so he killed some time explaining the crime situation in general in this section of the city. The crew then cut the broadcast as Jack signed off.

Jack again moved closer. He could clearly see that both of the dead men had been killed by multiple gunshot wounds. Two of the men were black and the other white. Paramedics were working on the struggling victim's right foot and as he rolled his head back and forth groaning in agony, Jack got a good look at his face.

SON OF A BITCH!

It was Willie Ducette. The crew then headed back to Vanover Street where the story would be put together for the late evening news and the Saturday morning news broadcast.

Saturday morning Jack went to police headquarters located in the center of Sumner Square. He learned that Sergeant Dino Giamati was lead on the case and Jack silently cursed. For reasons he couldn't explain, Giamati obviously disliked him and always gave him as little as possible.

"Sergeant Giamati, what can you tell me about the shooting last night at Lombardo and Maple?"

"Well Troop, not a whole hell of a lot. Here's what we know. Two of the victims were killed and one is wounded and currently hospitalized. He will recover. This was a drive-by gang hit. The shooter used an AR-15."

"Do you have any names?"

"Yes, but I'm not releasing them for now." Jack grimaced at Giamati's lack of cooperation.

"Any obvious motive?"

Giamati frowned.

"The obvious. Drugs. Fighting over territory. That kind of thing. Use your head, Troop."

Jack ignored the taunt.

"I recognized Willie Ducette, who is the new leader of RED. Who are the other two?" Giamati shrugged.

"They both have a past association with Los Lobos."

"Is there anything else you can give us?"

"No. See you." And he began walking down the main hallway. In the late afternoon of that same day, the names of the shooting victims were released. The deceased black male was Tyrod Grayson and the white male was Bucky Kent. Both men had criminal records filled with minor offenses. The early speculation was that Willie had been trying to recruit both Grayson and Kent, but El Diablo found out and put a hit out on all three of them.

Jack badly wanted to talk to Willie. His brother Darnell was now a well-known quarterback in the region and the potential of the story about a famous athlete with a brother involved in illegal drug sales would make the headlines in every newspaper and TV news show in the area. Jack arrived at the Scarsdale Hospital during visiting hours, but Willie had requested not to see anyone. A police officer was on guard at the door of Willie's room.

Jack went to the waiting area and sat down alone with his thoughts. He was there for over three hours when a surprise visitor made his large presence known to Jack. All six feet five inches and 280 pounds of him. Marcus Wayne was dressed in jeans, a purple shirt, and a waist-length gray jacket. The two men locked eyes.

"Hey, Jack. Watcha doin' here, man?"

"Hey, Marcus. How are you?"

"Doin' real good man. Like I said, what's up?"

"Well, I'm here waiting to talk to Willie."

Marcus scowled. "He got shot you know. I don't think it be possible to see him."

"Yeah, he's got a cop outside his door but surely he'll be able to talk to me sooner or later."

"Cop here by family request."

"Ah . . ."

"Oh yeah, man. Come from Darnell. Willie ain't available."

"Why not Marcus?"

"Cause Darnell says so. I'm helping with security. Darnell wants Willie safe and secure. I secure him. You know?" Jack rose from his chair. Marcus, with his hulking size, stood less than three feet from him.

"He told you to keep Willie safe?"

"Sure. Paid me some money to help him out." He cracked a big shit eating grin at Jack.

"He paid you?"

"I already said he did. So, listen here, Jack. You don't get to see Willie."

"Look, dammit. All I want to do is to find out what happened to him." Marcus slowly extended a long thick finger and touched Jack on the forehead.

"You don't need to know that little man. You—"

"Keep your hands off me, you son of a bitch!" Jack interrupted, slapping away the finger that was touching him. Marcus smiled.

"Hey! You wanna fight me, little man? Should we get it on?"

"Eat shit," Jack yelled at him.

Marcus just laughed. In no position to go one-on-one in a fight with Marcus, Jack slowly walked away and left the hospital. Within ten minutes he arrived at Gino's Tavern and settled himself onto a bar stool and ordered a double vodka on the rocks. He sat there drinking for several hours and then went home to his room at Mrs. Merriweather's.

Willie Ducette was released from the hospital on Monday morning. At the time of the shooting, there were no drugs in his possession and no firearms. He was free to go. Jack called Sergeant Giamati, but he was busy, so on impulse, Jack called his friend Sergeant Faraday.

"Look, Jack, you know this is Giamati's case, right?"

"Yeah King, but he's busy again. I'm in the news business and I need to be able to get the news from someone."

Faraday was momentarily mute. "Well, the Sergeant ain't too high on reporters."

"Oh, I know."

"Okay look," Faraday began. "A witness came forward telling us the vehicle involved was a black or dark colored SUV. There was a driver with a shooter in the back seat of the vehicle. The shooter had the rear window down, sticking the gun out and emptying the clip. He killed the two Los Lobos guys, but we believe that Willie Ducette was the real target."

"Sure, I've thought about this and that's the way I see it. They missed the guy that they really wanted. You got an address on Willie?"

"815 Locust Street."

"Is Willie still the target in your opinion?"

"Shit yeah, Jack. And now the punk can hardly walk. The bullet busted up a bunch of the small bones in his foot."

"Makes him an easy target, huh?"

"Like shootin' ducks on a pond," said Faraday with conviction.

"You figure he's home?"

"Only if he's stupid."

"Yeah . . . oh hey, I need to ask you for a favor."

"Sure, if I can."

"I've gotten into a couple of close scrapes lately. I want a gun. And a concealed carry permit. Can you help me out?"

"I think what you do has some danger associated with it. After all, you did get the crap beat out of you several months ago. You could easily get a permit. What do you know about handguns? Ever shoot one?"

"Nothing, and no, I haven't."

"Well sure, I'll help get you started. Dinner at Gino's?"

"Oh, hell yeah, I'm still on the Daily's credit account." Later that same week, King Faraday took Jack to a Scarsdale gun shop called Gun Guys. Jack filled out paperwork for a conceal carry permit and with King's assistance picked out a .380 caliber six-shot automatic. It was a small weapon that would be easy to conceal but still packed sufficient stopping power. In addition, Jack purchased an extra clip and four boxes of ammunition. At King's suggestion, Jack bought a razor-sharp knife with a three-inch blade that could be clipped inside his front pants pocket. Gun Guys had a range in the basement of the building and King took Jack downstairs for his first shooting lesson. An hour later Jack had shot two boxes of ammunition and was getting the hang of shooting accurately at short range. King also suggested that Jack visit Lee Quan's Studio of Martial Arts and learn a few moves for hand-to-hand combat. He advised Jack to talk to Lee about how to effectively use the knife in close combat encounters.

Over the next several months Jack spent a lot of his free time practicing his shooting, martial arts and using the knife. He received the conceal carry permit five days after making his application. He felt relieved that he was in a much better position to protect himself, and perhaps his future wife.

Jack felt that things were now coming together in his life. He believed that his job was secure and his potential to grow in this kind of work was boundless. Now, he also felt that he had acquired the ability to handle himself in the event of trouble. The strong relationship that had developed between him and Diana was definitely leading someplace, and Jack was about ninety percent sure he would ask her to marry him. He was certain that he was ready for this leap, one of life's most awesome leaps.

CHAPTER 22:
The First Night

It has often been said among men and women that the best sex is spontaneous. In Jack and Diana's case, this supposition turned out to be false. The week after Thanksgiving the Christmas party season was already shifting into high gear. Jack's mentor Max Hurley held a party for a select group of co-workers at his home in Scarsdale. Max was a drinker and always had a generous selection of liquors, wines, and beers on hand. Not only was the selection generous, but so were the quantities. The food was a catered selection of pasta from Gino's Italian Restaurant.

Jack and Diana thanked Max and left the party around midnight in search of some alone time. As he started the car, Jack asked Diana, "Gino's Tavern?"

Diana said no and suggested a small bar called Mickey Rourke's. Rourke's was a small Irish bar located just on the outskirts of Scarsdale. It was known for catering to couples who simply wanted to talk quietly and share some moments of their time together. Jack realized this was the perfect place to end their evening and wished he had thought of it.

Rourke's was a rectangle, with a long bar along the rear wall of the interior. The other three walls were lined with tables for two and tables for four. There was no room for video games, pool tables, or a dance floor. There was a jukebox and one TV hung over the middle of the bar. Rourke's was a place for drinks and conversation. It was not an eatery; the only food items available were bar-sized bags of chips, pretzels, nuts, and candies. Single packs of cigarettes were offered as well, but pipe and cigar smoking was prohibited. Jack and Diana found a table for two. When the waitress arrived, Jack ordered the usual chilled vodka and Diana ordered red wine. When she returned with their drinks, Diana looked at Jack. A late-night comic could be heard on the TV. The jukebox was silent. Diana had picked the perfect place.

"Jack," she said seriously. "We need to talk."

"Sure Di, but you sound serious."

She smiled, "I suppose I am, but it's not like seriously serious. Just sort of serious."

Jack chuckled. "Well then, you have my attention."

"Hm.... I'm not sure how to start. I guess what I want to say is that I went to the doctor's several weeks ago."

Jack jumped in, "Diana, is something wrong?"

"Oh no, no. Nothing like that. Actually, it couldn't be more right. Look, Jack, what have we been talking about since before you got hurt? What do we both want so badly to do?"

Jack let the question hang and just sat silent for half a minute.

"Okay, sex, right?"

"Jack, I've been on birth control pills since I saw my doctor. We both know it's past time for this."

"No arguments from me. I suppose I need to make arrangements?"

"No. No, you don't. I already did."

"Really? Here I thought I knew you, but you've gone and surprised the hell out of me."

"What have I always told you, Jack?" She didn't wait for an answer. "I am a modern woman. I am not a dinosaur from the ancient past. I know what I want and when I want something I intend to get it. And what I want now," she lowered her voice to a whisper, "Is you. Alone with me, in a king size bed. Naked and excited. That's what I want." Jack laughed softly.

"Then Diana, I want you to have it."

"Look, next Wednesday, we have reservations at the Players Playhouse for dinner and the play. It's called The Pretenders, about people in relationships. When the play ends I rented a cabin in the woods at the resort for us to spend the night. It is your job to bring a bottle of quality champagne. I think we should drink it afterward. Am I being too forward? I'm not acting like a proper Italian Catholic girl, I know."

"I suppose it's a man's job to make these kinds of arrangements, but I'd say you did well Di. And I think I am going to like you better when you're not a proper Italian Catholic girl."

"Thank you."

"Can I ask you a question?"

"Yes."

"Have well, have you ever done this before?" This time Diana laughed out loud.

"Twice. Once after prom night with Gary Sampson. In the back seat of a car no less. I think we both had too much alcohol."

"That doesn't sound that great Di."

"No. It sucked and it hurt. Then there was this guy I dated for a couple of months a little over a year ago. He was kind of rough. Well, maybe not, but he didn't make love to me really. When he was finished, I just felt used. Felt like I needed a shower. Does that make sense?"

Jack nodded.

"How about you, hot stuff? Got to be more than two for you."

"That's funny Di. No. Only two for me also. Both with semi-inebriated females after a frat party. Neither experience was that great."

"Well then, lover boy, surely we can do better."

"No, Diana, we will be better." Diana's eyes flashed, and her smile was wide.

On Thursday morning of the following week, the morning sun shone brightly against the drapes of Jack and Diana's bedroom in their rented cabin. Though it was only twenty degrees outdoors, it was a perfect seventy-two degrees in the comfort of the king-sized bed where they lay sleeping, naked and in each other's arms.

During dinner the night before, Diana informed Jack that she had also talked to Buzz Cutter, their boss, about both of them taking the day off to be together. Buzz had smiled and said yes. Diana did not even hint at what the couple would be doing the night before.

After dinner, they both sat impatiently watching The Pretenders. Both of them were beyond distracted and when they got to their cabin after the performance, they confessed that they hadn't a clue what the play was about, but both agreed that they were glad it was over.

Jack took the bottle of pink champagne he had purchased for nearly a hundred dollars along with two champagne flutes that he had bought and put them in the refrigerator. With that task completed, the two of them stared briefly at each other.

"Come on, Jack, let's do this."

She stepped over to him, grabbed his right hand and the two entered the bedroom.

"Time to get naked darling," she giggled.

They both peeled their clothing off eagerly, lustfully. Neither had ever seen the other naked before. They gasped at the sight of the other, looked at the large, soft bed and jumped in. They spent time touching, stroking each other with joy and abandonment. They both were responding rapidly into a passion neither could resist. When he entered her the built-up sexual tension morphed into uncontrolled passion. The floodgates opened, and the wave washed over them.

They laid in the bed panting, sweating, hearts thumping revealing in the feelings.

"Jack. God, that was incredible. I had a dumb thought in the back of my head for a long time that sex really wasn't that great. Like, you know, it was all hype. Like it was great in the movies and sucked in real life. Damn, I'm glad I was wrong."

Jack was laughing.

"Me too honey, me too."

"Hey Jack, I need a shower. Want to join me?" Quickly they were both in the shower stall feeling the warm needle-like spray of water massaging their bodies. They agreed to wash each other and then spent nearly half an hour discovering what they could do to each other's bodies with soapy hands.

When they had dried off, they returned to the bed and chatted while each drank two flutes of the pink champagne. By then their libidos kicked into gear and this time they made love to each other tenderly, but not without passion. When it was finished they again washed and then finished off the remainder of the champagne. Still naked, they dimmed the lights, pulled the covers over themselves and soon fell sound asleep. Exhausted, they both slept like the dead.

When they had both awakened, they spent some time holding each other and one staring into the eyes of the other. Neither said a word.

Finally, reading each other's eyes, Jack said, "Me too."

They began touching and feeling one another at first slowly and then with more urgency until they reached a level of pent-up desire almost like the first time the night before. Their two bodies merged into one. When it was finished Diana said, "Jack, we are so, so good together."

"Yes, we are. I knew we would be when I first laid eyes on you."

"Really? Me too."

"What do you mean, you too? Di, I had to ask you five times before you would even go out with me."

"Come on, Jack. What kind of a girl worth having is easy?"

Jack threw up his hands. "You're right. You're right."

"Jack, oh my God. Look at the time. We gotta go."

"What are you talking about? Who cares about time?"

"It's after ten, dummy. Check out is no later than eleven."

"Oh shit."

After they had checked out, having satisfied one kind of hunger, they knew there was the other hunger that needed to be satisfied. They stopped at the Carrollton Diner for a late breakfast and then headed back to Scarsdale.

Diana returned to her parent's house to clean up and get ready for the remainder of the day and Jack returned to his apartment and did the same. They got back together again in the late afternoon at Rourke's for some more quiet talk. After a couple of hours together they both kissed goodbye and headed home and went to bed early that evening.

CHAPTER 23:
Finding Willie

Back to work early the next morning, Jack Troop was determined to locate Willie Ducette to get an extensive in-depth interview with him. Unable to speak with Willie when he was recuperating from the gunshot wound to his foot, Jack had filed a story on the shooting of Willie Ducette without an interview. He had included the fact that Willie was the younger brother of Darnell Ducette, the star quarterback for the Chester City State Crusaders. The story was picked up nationwide with Jack's byline. He hit the jackpot. Jack achieved national recognition as a news journalist.

But Jack wanted more. He wanted a follow-up story replete with information from an interview with Willie. He began his search for him by combing the gang neighborhood where Willie lived at 815 Locust Street. Jack was more confident about canvassing this neighborhood because he now carried a gun and was certain that he could use it effectively if he needed to. He knocked on Willie's front door many times, but Willie was never home. He stopped at many doors and talked to many people in the neighborhood, but nobody ever admitted to knowing where Willie was. He tried combing the Latino neighborhood, going to door after door and getting nothing. He had managed to locate and talk to El Diablo who told him he had no idea where Willie was hiding out. El Diablo concluded the discussion with Jack by saying, "I hope he dead, man."

Jack had forced himself to call the always-uncooperative Sergeant Giamati several times. The Sergeant always had the same answer: the police also wanted to talk to Willie, but they couldn't find him and had no promising leads as to his whereabouts. It occurred to Jack that maybe Willie was hiding out in Chester City. In early January he began combing Willie's old neighborhood in the Roonies. He got no useful information. He visited police headquarters and talked to the detective in charge of the gang unit, Barney Jefferson. Detective Jefferson told Jack that, in cooperation with the Scarsdale police, the Chester City police were also looking for Willie Ducette. They had been looking for several weeks and had come up dry to this point. Jack thanked the detective for his time.

Jack's next step was to go to the Chester City Chronicle building and speak with crime reporter Ken Stanley. Jack quizzed him about what his sources might be saying about where Willie may be hiding. Ken told Jack he had been actively talking to all his sources but had nothing at all. Frustrated, Jack took the opportunity to stop in at Barney's Tavern for a couple of vodkas. As Jack sipped his drink he allowed his mind to go over what he had learned. He finally concluded that he had learned nothing other than what he now believed was fact. Willie had simply disappeared.

Jack ordered a second drink and continued to think. He hadn't talked to George or Darnell Ducette yet about Willie's disappearance. He walked to a quiet corner of the tavern and first called George, then Darnell. Both men were home but neither admitted to having seen or talked to Willie for a couple of months. Jack returned to the bar and sipped his drink. That's right, he thought. Willie had disappeared for what was now just over two months. For a reason he couldn't explain, thoughts of Willie's predecessor entered his head. Tyrone 'Crazy' Brown had also disappeared. Nobody knew where Crazy was for over six weeks. As it turned out, Crazy was dead. His body was eventually fished out of the swampy Blue Lagoon. As Jack contemplated the death of Crazy, reality hit him like a punch in the face. He knew where Willie was. Well, he thought, I don't really know for sure, but I'm certain I know his fate.

Jack finished the remainder of his vodka and left. He got into his car and drove back to Scarsdale. It was early evening by then, so he drove to his apartment, watched some TV and decided to see Sergeant Giamati as soon as possible the next day.

He was able to meet with the Sergeant first thing that next morning. Giamati gestured for Jack to take a seat by his desk.

"So, what's on your mind Troop. I'm a busy man."

"Of course you are, Sergeant. So, I'll keep this short."

"Please."

"I've been searching everywhere for Willie Ducette since mid-December. I've looked over all the possible neighborhoods in both Scarsdale and Chester City. I checked with multiple sources, I've talked to family members. Nobody has seen or heard from him in about two months. There is only one rational explanation to his disappearance."

"Which is?"

"He's dead, Sergeant. Nothing else makes sense."

"And you have evidence of his death Troop?"

"Well, no. But there is no other explanation. Willie lived his entire life in Chester City. He then came to Scarsdale last May as the new gang leader of RED. He knows no other place. If he's not in Chester City and not in Scarsdale, then he's dead, Sergeant, it has to be."

"Okay, Troop. I'll consider it, but you're offering me no proof. You're giving me speculation."

"Fine. But I'm right. I know it. And you know what else?"

The Sergeant shook his head no. "Think of Crazy Brown. He couldn't be found either. That's because he was dead. And where did you find him?"

"In the Blue Lagoon."

"Exactly. And that's where you'll find Willie." Giamati snickered.

"Yeah sure, Troop. Thanks for nothing. I got work to do." Jack stood.

"See you, Sergeant. But I'd check the swamp if I were you."

On a sunny, breezy and cold weekday, Jack received a call from Sergeant Giamati. The Sergeant advised Jack there was a body in the swamp and that he should get his butt over there ASAP.

Jack got Joanie and Emilio and the three headed over to the Blue Lagoon. Emilio parked the crime van near the swamp's shoreline. A police van and a cruiser were also parked. The lagoon appeared to be frozen solid. Several crime scene technicians were dressed in wetsuits and carrying ropes, metal hooks, and axes. Slowly and cautiously they walked to the shoreline and then proceeded to walk out onto the frozen ice. Giamati motioned for Jack, Joanie and Emilio to come over. Jack and his crew watched expectantly as the crime scene techs moved out further and further from the shoreline. As Jack observed the direction they were heading, he saw what looked like two human legs sticking up above the ice. As the men reached the body Jack was convinced he saw an orthopedic boot on the right foot.

Bingo, Jack thought, knowing that it was Willie who had worn an orthopedic booth after being shot in the foot.

After nearly forty minutes of careful chipping away with axes, the techs set some metal hooks and ropes to secure the body and began to pull, then pull again. The body appeared not to move, so they stopped and used the axes again. It was then back to the ropes and with a little more force applied, the body popped free. They stopped and knocked off some ice clumps that had adhered to the body, then started the laborious tugging of the frozen corpse to the shoreline.

Giamati waved Jack closer as the men tugged the body onto the ever-present swamp grass. The men flipped the body onto its back, face up. Jack observed it was indeed an orthopedic boot on the right foot. The face was covered with ice and dirty water, so one of the techs took out a spray can of chemical de-icer and sprayed. A minute later he used a rag to wipe down the frozen face. Jack leaned over and looked closely. It was Willie Ducette.

"Sergeant, that's Willie. Not a doubt in my mind." Giamati grimaced.

"Yeah, it is. Troop, I'll give you the credit. I finally thought about it and decided to come out here and take a look. I spotted the body, so I called you and the tech team."

"Thank you, Sergeant. See any obvious signs of what killed him?"

"No. We'll let the M.E. figure that one out. Hell, he could have just been knocked over the head and tossed in the lagoon to freeze to death. No telling."

Jack nodded.

The news crew left the scene after taking a couple of pictures.

Jack knew he had to file this story before tonight's deadline, but it was still early in the afternoon and he wanted to see Diana.

"Hey, Di. Are you up for an early dinner? We could go over to Gino's for burgers and drinks."

"Well, Mom's cooking spaghetti tonight. There will be more than enough to set another place."

"Well sure, but I was hoping for some you and me time. I got to work tonight, but I really wanted to see you for a couple hours. How

about Gino's Italian Restaurant instead and we'll have spaghetti there?
What do you say?"

Diana laughed.

"Jack, I'll follow you anywhere. But let me talk to Mom first." And
that's what the young couple did: spaghetti with an Italian salad and
freshly baked Italian bread followed with fine wine. They spent a
delightful couple of hours together and then Jack headed back to
Vanover Street and Diana went home.

In the days that followed, events started popping. George Ducette
had officially identified his son's body. Despite father and son being
alienated for some time, George was inconsolable. He had to be
sedated to get any sleep that evening. Darnell had been notified of his
brother's death.

Jack would file a couple of stories on Willie's death. These stories
were widely circulated and did nothing but enhance Jack's growing
reputation as an outstanding young journalist. Members of the national
press started to show up in Scarsdale and Chester City to get more
information about the gang leader who was the younger brother of
quarterback sensation Darnell Ducette. But the bomb that blew Jack
away was when the medical examiner, Dr. John Suggs, announced the
cause of death. Willie Ducette had indeed been murdered. He had died
from a broken neck, the vertebrae snapped by the hands of a large and
powerful man. No water had been found in his lungs. He had been
murdered somewhere else and then his body dumped into the lagoon.

SON OF A BITCH!

I was right, Jack thought. I nailed it. I was damn well right.

CHAPTER 24:
Willie's Funeral

Within a week's time, Willie Ducette's funeral was held. He was buried in the Peaceful Meadows Cemetery located just north of his father's home in Living Greens. The funeral service was attended by family members and several unidentified black males. The Reverend Emanuel Pickler conducted a brief twenty-minute service. The Reverend didn't know Willie but performed a credible service. After all, there is a lot that can be said when a young life is cut so short, regardless of how well or poorly that life had been lived. When the Reverend had finished George wanted to say a few words, but he became too choked up to speak. Instead, he just stood and looked at his son's casket, tears running down his cheeks as he shook his head. Darnell and his brother Lamar and his sister Juliet also approached the casket and looked at it for several minutes. Then the small gathering turned and headed toward the exit of the cemetery.

As the family members and guests approached the exit from the grounds, Jack walked slowly toward them. He could see tears running down George Ducette's face. His grief was evidence of the awful truth that losing a child, regardless of the circumstances, was a parent's worst nightmare.

Jack moved toward the family, but Marcus Wayne stepped directly in front of him. Darnell quickly motioned to Marcus that there was no problem, so he moved aside and let Jack stand there facing Darnell. Jack said solemnly, head tilted downward.

"I am sincerely sorry for your loss, Darnell. Sorry for your family."
Darnell stopped while the remainder of the family kept moving.

"Jack, you want something?" He stood just staring at Jack.

"No, not really. I just wanted to offer you and your family my
condolences. That's all."

"Okay. Thank you. I gotta go."

"You want to talk a minute or two?"

"About what?"

"About Willie. About how things turned out this way for him."
Darnell shook his head. "I don't know. I ain't that smart. I just play
football."

"And you just lost a brother. That's got to be tough."

"Jack, I don't know what it is. But I'm tired. Gonna go."

"Sure, Darnell." Darnell took several steps forward then stopped
and turned toward Jack.

"Shit. You know, and I know that we didn't get along real good."
He paused and shrugged his big shoulders. He turned and moved
rapidly off the grounds to catch up with the other family members.

Jack just stood there shaking his head. Family dynamics, he
thought. Always so hard to figure out.

Jack soon learned of another pending event that would prove
consequential to his life: he was summoned to Buzz Cutter's office one
morning.

"Morning, Jack. How are you doing today?"

He rose and shook Jack's hand. Once again, Jack winced at the
power of his handshake.

"I'm good, sir. What's up?" Buzz sat and leaned back in his chair.

"A good thing, I believe. You know, Jack, since you've been on
TV news from the van, the Daily has seen a significant increase in sales
and, more importantly, profits."

"Why, that's great! Are you telling me that I get some credit for
this new growth?"

"No. No. All the credit! Every bit of it."

"Thank you. But Joanie and Emilio. They play a role. I couldn't
do what I do without their help."

"Nice of you to say so. And I agree. But Ford Carr says you get
the credit." Buzz paused. "Who am I to argue?" He tilted his head and
looked at Jack.

"I understand. I guess I won't either."

"Yes. So anyway, here's the deal. Mr. Carr has authorized me to increase your salary to $1,000 per week."

Jack's eyes popped wide open.

"Mr. Carr is out of the country right now. A combined business and pleasure trip. He won't be back until late April. When he returns he wants to meet with you. He said to tell you to keep it up. Push harder, Jack. You've got a future in this business."

He paused again.

"Something's in the works, Jack, and I believe it's headed your way. Could be something big."

"Any idea what?"

"Mr. Carr called it an opportunity. Said he feels you'll like it."

"Damn. That's it?"

Buzz smiled. "For now, yes."

"I guess I'll have to remain patient."

"Yes, you will, and keep doing what you do."

Jack hesitated then said, "Ah, that raise sir. When would that go into effect?"

"Now." Buzz winked. "You might want to go out to the front desk and tell that young lady of yours that you can now afford to marry her."

Jack just nodded, thinking he would do just that.

Mid-March arrived, and Jack purchased a diamond for Diana. He asked Buzz Cutter if he could borrow Diana for fifteen minutes and use the conference room. When Buzz asked why Jack showed him the ring he had in his pocket and told Buzz he wanted to give it to her. Buzz nodded and smiled. The ring had as big a diamond as he could afford, and Diana accepted it joyfully. They both went back to Buzz's' office and Diana showed him the ring. Buzz congratulated them both.

Both Jack and Diana understood a simple truth. They wanted to spend their lives together. However, they were in no rush to set a wedding date. Jack, in particular, knew he was now moving up the ladder in the news business and wanted to be able to support a wife and eventually a family in style.

Their next move was to inform each of their parents. On each of the next two Sunday afternoons, the couple first had dinner with Dom and Sophia and then the following Sunday with Frank and Clara. Diana had presented Jack to her family members as her future husband and proudly showed off her new ring. Jack presented Diana to Frank and

Clara as his future wife and Diana showed her new ring to her future in-laws. Both sets of parents were very happy the two would eventually become man and wife.

CHAPTER 25:
Darnell and Candy Continued

Genetically, Candy Champion was born to be a glamour model. During the winter before she and Darnell were to be married, she had been contacted by a modeling agency in New York City called Hot Stuff, Inc. The calendar that Candy had posed for was published while Darnell was attending Organized Team Activities for the Red Knights at their training camp in Virginia. The calendar was titled America's Hottest Cheerleaders. Candy was Miss May. She was photographed on an open field of grass and wildflowers dressed in a light blue bikini bottom and nothing else. She held a bouquet of wildflowers over her obviously bare breasts. A large fan was used to give the effect of a spring breeze blowing her long blonde hair off her bare shoulders. Any human male with a pulse would find her photo breathtaking.

The calendar was in circulation nationally and eventually became such an outstanding seller that it went through several more printings. It was an unqualified success.

Darnell was the kind of young man who enjoyed the spotlight. He enjoyed his celebrity status as a college football star and eagerly anticipated a career in front of the cameras like the Red Knights' franchise quarterback for a dozen or more years. His glamorous wife, Candy was a decoration that would only enhance his star power. She made him a more magnetic and compelling personality. In Darnell's mind, the combination of Candy and him would help bolster his career and increase his earnings potential. In the game of life, Darnell wanted both fame and fortune. His new wife was to be his helper— or perhaps, as the expression goes, a trophy wife.

With Darnell playing professional football with over fifty other young men, all of whom were strong, fit and overloaded with testosterone, the America's Hottest Cheerleaders calendar was bound to be circulated among them. It was eventually seen by Darnell. In the calendar, his mostly naked young wife was now known as Miss May. He was instantly furious. He had thought Candy would support his career, but now saw she had a career path of her own. In Darnell's mind, she instantly became his competition for the spotlight and an obstacle in his path to fame and fortune. He was mad enough to explode and he did just that on a late July evening before training camp opened the following Monday. The excitement occurred in their Georgetown condo. Neighbors heard screaming, shouting and breaking objects. The police were summoned. When the two combatants heard the police pounding on the door yelling, "Police. Police! Open up!" the quarrel stopped, and Darnell opened the front door.

Two uniformed officers stood before them. Darnell affected his big smile.

"Evening officers. Can I help you?" The taller of the two men explained that they had gotten a call concerning a domestic violence disturbance at this address and they needed to come in.

Darnell asked why.

Again, the tall officer explained. It was standard police procedure under these circumstances.

"Well, if you must. But there's no problem here, officers. Just a small disagreement."

The officers moved into the living area. They didn't observe any injuries to either Darnell or Candy, but they did observe two broken lamps and a broken end table.

The tall officer again spoke. "Sir, there is some obvious damage here. Care to explain?" Candy jumped in.

"Officer, this was just a disagreement. We were discussing our career goals. There's a difference of opinion. That's all it is."

The officer replied, "The damage, miss?" He was pointing to the breakage.

"I guess I have a temper. I just threw a couple of lamps on the floor."

"And the table?"

Darnell commented, "I kicked it. That's all. I got annoyed."

"Either of you hurt?"

They both shook their heads. The officers then took their names and some additional information.

"Okay. Please try to control yourselves. After all, your neighbors did complain. If we get another call, we'll have to arrest you both for creating a public disturbance. Understand?"

They both nodded yes. The officers wished them a good evening and then left.

Several weeks later, the Ducette's neighbors heard more shouting. This time one of them walked over to the Ducette's front door and rang the bell. On this occasion, Candy opened the door. The man asked that they please quiet down or he would have to summon the authorities. Candy assured him that they would and the latest argument between her and Darnell ceased. The following weekend Darnell was away playing in the Red Knights' last pre- season game against Denver. Candy took the Amtrak to New York City.

Hot Stuff Inc. was a subsidiary of Lola Getz Enterprises Inc., which had started as a modeling agency and branched out into publishing. She met with Lola Getz and soon after signed a modeling contract to do additional calendar shoots, as well as magazine layouts for several national publications, most of which were men's magazines. Darnell had never realized Candy had ambitions of her own and that she never had any intention of playing second fiddle to Darnell and his football career. To Candy, it was just exciting to marry a football star and be around the ambiance of the game. She had already realized she didn't love him, just the idea of him. The truth to Darnell was that he was just in love with the idea of a hot, young, blonde-haired white woman.

As Darnell became occupied with the rigors of the sixteen-game professional football season, Candy became occupied with successive photo shoots for magazine layouts. She was quick to make the decision to rent a one-bedroom apartment in New York City since she didn't have the time to continue commuting back and forth from Washington every day. Journalists making their living reporting on the lives of celebrities soon were writing about a rift in the marriage of supermodel Candy Champion and Red Knights' quarterback Darnell

Ducette. These stories were being reported well before the couple reached their first anniversary.

As January of the new decade began, both Candy and Darnell knew the marriage had been a mistake and was now a complete failure. Darnell was not a man used to failure. He had no tolerance for it. The thought of a publicized divorce drove him into a rage that kept him up on a Saturday night before the last game of the season. He sustained a broken finger on his throwing hand early in the game. This threw him into another rage in the team's locker room, where he threw his helmet repeatedly all over the locker room.

Candy was not at home. She had been staying in the city with increased frequency.

While Darnell and Candy's marriage was on a rocky road, the relationship between Jack and Diana thrived. After that first magical night of sex at the cabin in the woods in December, they both wanted to make regular sex a part of their lives. However, this desire was somewhat complicated. They certainly couldn't enjoy sex in Diana's bedroom in her parent's home. Mrs. Merriweather didn't permit female companions for her male renters in her home. The alternative was to return to the cabin in the woods at the resort in Carrollton County. But Diana always had to invent a credible excuse to give to her parents for not returning home after an evening out with Jack. So, they used the cabin a couple of days a week, but only for a few hours. It was winter, and the cabins were easily available but renting them at a cost of $39.95 a day was hard on Jack's budget. It also seemed dumb to pay that rate and only get a few hours use of the cabin. Jack told Diana it was worth the price, but Diana had a practical side to her nature. She wanted sex more often and didn't want to have to pay so much or have to make the twenty-mile drive to the cabin and the twenty-mile return trip. She soon solved the problem.

The road to Culver City ran north of Scarsdale. On the outskirts of Culver City, there was a discount motel that charged a flat twenty dollars per day for a room. The drive would take no more than twenty minutes. It was a win-win situation to Diana. The first night they used the room both she and Jack decided that it would do. It was far enough away from Scarsdale so that anyone who knew her parents would probably not run into her and Jack renting a room. The room had a bed and a bathroom, which was all they really needed. It was certainly not a nice as one of the cabins, but they were there for the sex, not the amenities.

While their first sexual experience together had been magical, the next several experiences had proved to be pleasant and close enough to magical. After several more experiences, they found they had become more relaxed with each other, and learned more about what pleased each of them. Jack loved it when Diana would reach for his groin and gently fondle his testicles. Diana liked Jack to lick her nipples. She also liked when he placed his fingers on her clitoris and rubbed and pressed the flesh gently and then released the pressure—rub and press and release, rub and press and release, until the action became a vaginal massage.

As their comfort level deepened Diana found herself enjoying increased pleasure. Orgasms came more frequently and with greater intensity. When they hit her, they shook her to her core and left her breathless, gasping for air and consumed with the raw pleasure of it all. Jack found that Diana's excitement and obvious pleasure only stimulated his desire to make each sex act last longer and longer before he too released.

By early spring the sexual chemistry was almost beyond powerful. They rented the motel room with greater and greater frequency. Jack found his mind constantly wandering to thoughts of Diana and how wonderful it felt to please her sexually. Diana's mind was constantly occupied with the thoughts of how great it felt when Jack's erect penis was inside her. It occurred to both of them that having sex would never be an issue in their marriage. They also thought it was time to set a wedding date.

CHAPTER 26:
Jack and Darnell's Long Talk

It was a sunny, cold Friday in early March and Jack was busy at his desk putting the finishing touches on the latest story he was writing. He was working with only a few hours' sleep and was drinking his third cup of hot black coffee. Diana buzzed him and advised him that there was a man on the phone for him who wouldn't divulge his name. Jack said he was busy, but Diana told him the man insisted on talking to him. So, Jack told his finance to put the caller through.

It was Darnell.

"Hey, Jack. How you been?"

"I'm good, Darnell. Getting up in this world. Just like you."

Darnell laughed. "Yeah man. We each have some new-found success."

"Exactly. But you called me. What's up?"

"Well the season is over. I got a place back at Living Greens. I'm thinkin' that I got some time to kill. Thought we could get together and chat some."

"Oh. You do know that I'm a crime reporter now, right? So, are we chatting about a crime? On the record? Or are we just going to have a nice, sociable conversation?"

"Let's keep it strictly social. Nothin' on the record. Okay?"

"Fine by me. Where and when?"

"Are you free this afternoon? Around three o'clock? I'm a member of the Living Greens Club. It's plush, man. The place doesn't get busy 'till around five o'clock, so we could get a quiet seat at the back of the room. Have some drinks. Get some eats. Food is first class. It's all on me. How's that sound?"

"You're buying? Then hell yeah, Darnell. Count me in."

"Good. I'll leave word at the front gate. See you soon." Later that day Jack made the long drive to the north side of Chester City and arrived at the Living Greens Club minutes before three o'clock. Darnell was waiting for him. They shook hands and then took a couple of seats at a high top in the rear corner of the bar. Each ordered a drink and Darnell instructed the waitress to put everything on his tab. When the drinks arrived, each man took a sip.

Jack was looking at the decor of the bar and dining room.

"Nice place, Darnell. So, let's get into that social chat we're going to have."

"Well it's sorta social. I need to ask you a couple of questions."

Jack leaned back in his chair and looked at him with an I-knew-it look on his face.

"You need to ask me questions. That's a switch." Jack then paused as he thought. "Fair enough. What's on your mind?"

"Let's start with Willie. I call the police a lot. Every time I talk to them they say we ain't found his killer yet. Then they say they ain't got no leads either. Jack . . . you're on the crime beat. What do you hear? Are the cop's bullshitting me? Maybe they don't care cause he's just a dead, black dope dealer."

"Look, Darnell. Willie was fished out of that stinking swamp after he was killed. Someone broke his neck and just dumped his body in the lagoon. The county M.E. said the killer was a big, powerful man. Police haven't come up with much else. I have sources, including some on the police force, but I've also heard nothing else." Jack stopped and looked at him.

"And I will add that I check my sources regularly."

Darnell considered this.

"I asked the cops if they were looking at the gangs for suspects and they said yes. Then I asked if they were looking into alternative suspects and they said yes. Is that bullshit?"

"No. Sounds right to me. They say that's what they're doing. I know of nothing to contradict that."

Darnell tapped his glass loudly on the table. He put his hand in the air, holding out two fingers. Within minutes the waitress returned to the table with fresh drinks.

"Is Willie turning into one of them cold cases, like you see on TV?"

He paused, appearing to be lost in thought. Then he surprised Jack and changed the subject.

"My Dad, George. Couple of years ago you were looking into where he got money to buy his new house. Right?"

"Okay."

Now Jack knew why he was here. Darnell was grilling him. He wanted to know what he knew about his family. So he paused, putting on his poker face.

"Ah, are you still looking?"

Jack held his poker face for another half minute.

"Not anymore. I know where it came from."

"Oh. Do you really?"

"Sure. It came from the First Presbyterian Church in Chester City. Ford Carr, who I know you know, is a big shot in the congregation."

"You sure?"

"I believe my source is credible."

Darnell chuckled. "Sure you do. Marcus told you, right? At least he told me that he told you. Right?"

"Yes."

"Jack, let me ask you somethin'. How would Marcus know anything about a church full of rich white people? He hangs in the Roonies, man. He don't know shit."

"Um-----. Back at you, Darnell. Marcus tells me that he works for you. He said you paid him money to guard Willie after he'd been shot in the foot. Is that accurate?"

"Yeah man. Your point?"

"Hell Darnell, you just said a minute ago that Marcus don't know shit. Why is he on your payroll?"

"He don't know shit about that church. But Marcus is my friend, and he's big and real strong. I'm fine with him. He always has my back."

Jack leaned in toward Darnell.

"Fine. But Marcus said he had a source. I paid him for the information. The information rang true to me."

Darnell broke out in a burst of loud laughter. The bartender looked toward them curiously. Darnell noticed and calmed down.

"A source, huh? Marcus got a source? Let me ask you, would that be a little monkey-faced guy called Chimp?"

Jack tried to maintain his poker face, but this time failed.

"Damn. Sure it was. Jack, I'll help you out here. You need to know that Chimp would say anything for money. It's just what he's about."

"Are you saying he just makes it up?" Jack shot back. He nodded a yes.

"But Darnell, when I talked to Marcus he said that if Chimp just made stuff up, it would get him seriously hurt or even worse." "Yeah, maybe. But the thing is that everyone in the Roonies knows that Marcus got Chimp's back. And I can tell you for sure that nobody wants to fuck with Marcus. It's why I hired him." Jack took a long pull on his drink while considering things. "Darnell, your Dad got that money from somewhere."

"Why, sure. From me."

"You?"

"Yeah, I'm a millionaire now. I got a big signing bonus. Hell Jack, it was in the papers." He had that big killer smile on his face again.

"You are a millionaire now. But you see Darnell, you weren't a millionaire when your Dad bought the house."

Darnell was still smiling.

"Jack, every banker in the state knew that I was going to be a first-round draft pick. And that, my man, gave me credit. Lots of it."

Damnit, Jack thought. That had never occurred to him. Shit. What else had he been wrong about pertaining to Darnell's life? His mind was racing as he finished the second vodka.

Darnell signaled again for another round.

At this point, the conversation turned toward the trivial. He told Jack his father had an accident at the foundry and was now on permanent disability. He was receiving checks from a worker's compensation settlement. Darnell also advised Jack that he sent George money when he needed it.

Jack then filled Darnell in on his career path and his engagement to Diana. The conversation finally got around to where Jack decided to ask him about Candy.

"So, how's married life treating you? Is Candy back at the house?"

This inquiry brought a frown to his face.

"Nah, she's in Europe, man. Doing a photo shoot in the Alps. You know, the Swiss Alps, the French Alps and Italian Alps. I think

Austria, too. It's about fancy ski resorts for some magazine. Called American Skier. Ever heard of it?"

"Yeah. Who hasn't?"

"Me, for one. See, I'm a black man. Black men play ball. Black men don't ski. Can you name me one black skier?"

Jack shook his head.

"So, you see what I'm sayin'?"

"Sure. So, is Candy coming home after the shoot?"

"Oh hell no. When she's done in the Alps she's flyin' to the Keys. She's doin' a swimsuit shoot for Barney's Department Stores. For a catalog. You heard of Barney's?"

"I have. They've got one on the east side of Chester City."

"Yeah that's right. I forgot. Anyway, I'm flyin' down to the Keys to meet up with her. We'll have some fun together when she's done with that shoot. Then it's back to Washington for me. Spring practice, you know."

"Then enjoy the Keys."

"I will. Get some quality time together, as they say. I can work on my tan." He busted out laughing.

"Good one, Darnell."

"Hey man, you gettin' hungry?"

"I could eat something. Soak up the alcohol, you know."

Darnell walked over to the bar and spoke to the bartender.

"Hey, sorry man, but it's pushing five o'clock. I gotta be somewhere else soon. Get yourself anything else you want. Food, drinks, whatever. The steaks are great here. I told Lou to keep it all on my tab. It was good talking to you again. Take it easy."

"Sure, Darnell. You too."

It was now after five o'clock and people started coming in to dine. Two new waitresses arrived for the evening shift. Jack signaled for another drink and put in an order for a T-bone steak cooked medium, baked potato with butter and sour cream, and a small tossed salad. He then just sat and reflected.

While in college he became interested in Darnell's high school career. However, he became even further curious about the fact that by the time Darnell was eighteen years old he was already associated with accidents to his mother and his girlfriend in which both women died from broken necks. His college football career began with him winning the starting quarterback job when quarterback Chuck

Chambers took an accidental fall down a flight of stairs fracturing his leg and arm. Then there was the attack on Brent Reedy and the dismissal of a wrongful injury lawsuit after Reedy was left with a shattered leg.

Too many broken bones, Jack thought.

Then there was the money trail emanating from Darnell and Ford Carr to Darnell's father George. Darnell had tried to deflect the obvious by taking credit for financing his father's new home in Living Greens. At the time, Jack had stayed relentlessly on the trail of Ford Carr's dealings with both Darnell and his father. Darnell had provided him with an obvious and very plausible alternative explanation for the source of money to purchase his father's house in the Living Greens. This simple fact caused Jack to reflect. Reflect on the singular pursuit of Ford Carr as the source. Was he too narrow- minded in his quest for the truth? Perhaps too full of himself? Too full of his gut feelings and his rightness? He felt that he perhaps needed to expand his thinking for every investigation from now on. But at this point Darnell was now out of school and playing professional football. The issue of taking money from a university booster was a moot point at best. Time to forget the whole thing.

For Jack, the most serious and consequential part of his conversation with Darnell was his probe into Jack's knowledge of the investigation into Willie's death. Jack knew that the cause of death was another broken neck. Broken neck number three. Way too many for coincidence. And Darnell could easily be considered a suspect in each case. So, Jack thought, am I wrong in pursuing Darnell as the man who was involved in each broken neck?

His fresh drink and the steak arrived, so Jack just thought and ate.

Darnell had left and indeed had another place to be. He was meeting a stranger in Chester City at 5:30 p.m. Darkness was descending on what had been a cloudy day. Darnell was to meet this man in the lobby of the convention center. The man told him he knew what the famous quarterback looked like and would contact him when he felt safe. The man made contact at 5:45 p.m. by bumping him slightly, then waving him to follow with a quick flick of his hand.

Darnell followed him into the men's room. The man was dressed in dark clothing, wore sunglasses despite the approaching darkness, and had a silver beard. He was nearly Darnell's height. The man nodded at Darnell and put his hand out.

Darnell reached inside his coat pocket and pulled out a manila envelope. The man took it, opened it, and flicked through the bundle of cash. He stuffed the envelope into his coat pocket and looked at Darnell.

The man said, "It will be taken care of. Leave through the front doors. Now."

Darnell looked at the man, finally said okay and left the building.

The man waited several minutes before he exited the bathroom and then turned in the opposite direction and left the convention center through the rear door.

After Jack finished his meal, he left Living Greens and drove home to his parents' house on Willow Road. He spent some quality time catching up with his parents on each other's lives and they eventually all turned in for the night. Jack would have breakfast with them in the morning and return to Scarsdale. He met Diana in the early afternoon for dinner and a few drinks. Jack had to be back in the news van for the Saturday night shift on the city crime beat.

Doug Ward had parked his car in the lot of the Chester City State administration building that Friday evening. He was attending a seminar about financing a graduate degree. He had earned his degree in sports management but had been unable to find a job in that field. He decided to look into pursuing a Masters or an MBA.

After the meeting ended he left the building and walked out toward his vehicle. It was very dark by now. He was walking head down, focused on what he had learned and didn't notice the man moving quickly but quietly behind him. The man was nearly as tall as Doug but of a slimmer build and moved with practiced stealth.

Before Doug felt his presence, the man cracked him across the shoulders with a two-foot section of lead pipe. Doug fell face first on the asphalt, breaking his nose. Doug was stunned, and he groaned. His assailant rolled him over and gave him three vicious whacks with the pipe on his right knee. The sharp pain caused him to yelp. The knee was completely shattered, and Doug was only semi-conscious. The man lightly tapped his cheeks to keep him conscious.

The man said, "Now listen to me Douglas. I have a message for your parents. Back the fuck off. No more lawsuit. Understand?"

Doug didn't respond.

The man, louder this time: "Understand?"

Nothing. The man then tapped the shattered knee again.

Doug yelped again.

"Do you understand me?"

Doug finally nodded, shedding tears.

The man continued. "Okay. Dump the lawsuit. Immediately. If I have to visit with you again. . . well, let's just say that it gets worse."

The man stood and tapped the pipe against his left palm. Good night Douglas.

He then walked slowly out of the parking lot and vanished into the night. No one had seen him. The envelope full of cash was still in his coat pocket.

CHAPTER 27:
Chimp

On Monday morning Jack was back at his desk at the Daily. He and Diana had discussed a wedding date that weekend and Jack was in a great mood. They would shoot for a mid-October date. As Jack began working, Diana buzzed him and told him he had a call. She told him the man talked in a whisper and would not give her his name. Jack was intrigued and told Diana that he would take the call.

"Hello, Jack Troop speaking."

The whisperer answered, "You got time to talk?" Jack pulled the phone away from his ear and looked at it as if the inanimate device itself had something to say to him. "Maybe. Who are you, sir?" The whisperer replied, "I got sumpthin' for you."

"Okay fine. But who are you? You got a name?" Jack was now getting a little peeved.

"You don't know?"

"You're talking in a whisper, sir. I can hardly hear you and I don't know your name. You are beginning to test my patience."

"I be Chimp."

"Who?"

"Chimp, man. You remember. From Marcus."

"Marcus Wayne?"

"Yeah. I gave Marcus some information you wanted. On George Ducette. You remember?"

"Yeah. I do now. But can you speak up? Quit whispering." Chimp began talking in a normal voice.

"I got some more stuff that you gonna wanna know."

"How nice," Jack replied with some anger in his voice. "But I just talked to someone recently who told me that your information is no good. That you just make it up."

"Thaz bullshit man! Axt anybody in the Roonies. They tell you. Chimp give it to you straight. I don't, and I get myself kilt."

"That's what Marcus said."

"He say it straight, man." Jack Troop was suddenly unsure of who to believe. This Chimp character, or Darnell. Damn!

"Let's say I believe you. What have you got?" Chimp laughed.

"It don't work that way, man. We need to meet. Stuff I got gonna cost you."

"Sure it will, but give me a clue. What would I be buying?"

"It's about the Ducette's. Their Mom died in an accident. I know something."

"Really. Well, you've got my attention. Now what?"

"Like I said, we need to meet. Say ten o'clock tomorrow night."

"No, no, no, no man. I'm not going into the Roonies at ten at night."

"Not in the Roonies man. I meet you. Ya know the second light comin' east on Rt. 40 out of Scarsdale? There's an all-night dinner there, Spankey's. Know it?"

"I know it. I've passed by it dozens of times."

"Then meet me there. When you turn into the parking lot cut your lights. Take it slow. Pull round back near where the woods be. I be in the woods. I'm lookin' for you. Got it?"

"Got it. I'll—"

"You bring the money. Five hunnert, maybe six. Maybe even seven."

"Holy shit man! Whoa now. That's a lot of money."

"Information is good. Cost you five hunnert to hear it. You like it, cost you more. I be the judge of that. Got it?"

"Yeah. But that sucks."

"I'm thinkin' you gonna like it."

"Well then, tomorrow at ten o'clock. Spankey's. Back in the woods. I'll have the money."

"We good to go, man."

Before Jack headed out on that cold Tuesday evening, he loaded his gun and the extra clip. He slipped the knife into his right pocket. He had no idea what to expect.

At 9:58 p.m. Jack cut his lights as he pulled into the parking lot at Spankey's. He looped around to the rear of the diner and angled the car out toward the woods at the edge of the lot. He stopped but prudently kept the engine running. He started to sweat and cranked down the driver's side window a few inches. His heart was racing, and his feet were cold. At 10:02 a small man emerged from the trees and slowly moved toward his car. He reached the car and grabbed the handle of the passenger side door. Jack had his gun in his hand. He had not yet unlocked it. Jack noted that he was a small black man, so he cautiously opened the door. Chimp entered the car. He wore a knit cap and a sweatshirt. The cap accented the larger than normal ears.

Chimp turned toward Jack. He noticed the gun in Jack's hand.

"Hey, you don't need that gun. You Jack Troop?"

Jack nodded, still holding the gun.

"I guess you're Chimp. You fit the description." Chimp smiled and fingered his large ears.

"Monkey ears. I be Chimp. Now I want you to go into that diner and get me a cup of coffee and some sweet stuff to eat. Got it?"

Jack took a deep breath and slowly exhaled. He put the safety back on the gun and tucked it into the holster on his belt.

"What the hell for?"

"I'm hungry. Ain't gonna do no talkin' 'til I eat."

"Shit Chimp. I'm no waitress. But I'll go. But before I do, you get out of the car and get your ass back into the woods."

"Oh, hell no! It's cold."

"I'm not going to get you anything while you sit in my car. No way."

"Sucks, man."

"Take it or leave it." Chimp grimaced. He opened the car door and headed over to the woods. Jack re-locked the car. Ten minutes later he returned with two coffees and a brown sack filled with sweets. Chimp saw him and headed back to the car.

"Now keep your lights off and pull around the diner and get back on Route 40 toward Scarsdale. Go past the first light and take a right." Jack complied with the instructions.

Chimp said, "Slow down. See that gravel spot there on the right? Pull into it." Jack did.

"Go real slow into the trees and cut the engine." Jack again did as instructed.

"Do you got the money?"

"Yes." Jack patted his pocket. "I got the money. And the gun. So be careful."

Chimp frowned.

"Let me see the money." Jack pulled out a wad of cash.

"Okay. Now we talk."

"Finally. What have you got for me?"

"I'm gonna tell you a story . . . You see there was these four brothers. Me—"

"Not real brothers, right? Like brothers in the hood?"

"Hell yeah. It was me, Willie, and two other brothers. We was at a pad in the Roonies. Around last Christmas time. We was all drinking gin and smokin' some weed. Got it?"

"Yes, so far."

"We was all just sort of bull shittin' and gettin' high. Willie starts gettin' sad. Real sad. Says he don't even know how he got here. He say his brother Darnell is this big star quarterback and his brother Lamar and sister Juliet are both real smart and don't get in no trouble. He say what the fuck he doin' here smokin' weed and dealing crack on the streets. He say a lot of shit like that. See?"

Jack gestured for him to proceed.

"He keep gettin' more sad. I'm sittin' by him and see tears go down his face. I say, 'Hey bro, lighten the fuck up. You gonna be okay, you know. But he's shakin' his head and sayin' he fucked up his whole life. He say he ain't been worth a damn since his Mama died. I say shit man that was an accident. But he just sittin' there crying. Then he starts moanin' and groanin'... Cryin' real hard. I slap him side his head. I say get a hold of yourself man. Shit, took him fifteen more minutes to calm down."

Chimp paused and finished his coffee. He pulled a candy bar out of the bag and took a bite.

"What was he so upset about?"

"Now you axt the big money question, man. Well, Willie pours herself some gin. Drinks it. He say, 'You know, it's my fault my Mama died. Mama was my best friend. She loved me, and I didn't think no one else did. And I fucked up. I kilt her.'" Chimp paused.

"Is there more?"

"Sure. The best part. Willie say that the night before his Mama fell, he got up while everyone was sleepin'. Had him one of his Daddy's screwdrivers. He go upstairs and pry up the rug at the top of the stairs and smooth it out. He say it was Darnell always wake up first, go upstairs and use the bathroom first and then come back down. Willie say he tryin' to fuck up Darnell. You know, fall and break a leg or arm. He say he sick of Darnell actin' like a big shot white boy with a white girlfriend. Teach him a lesson, see?"

SON OF A BITCH!

"I believe I get the picture."

"So, I get my money?"

"Sure." Jack reached into his pocket and counted out five hundred dollars.

"Only five hunnert? You liked what I said. Worth at least 'nother hunnert. Maybe two."

"Maybe you're right, Chimp. But first, who were the other two dudes with you?"

"Not in the deal, man."

Jack's voice hardened. "It is now."

"I don't know, man."

"I can get the gun out again, bud."

"Yeah, but you know what I give you worth 'nother fifty."

Jack sighed and relented. He handed him another fifty. "The names. Now."

"Oh, shit man. Okay. One brother is called Brick. Don't know no last name. The other was Marcus."

"Marcus Wayne?"

Chimp nodded.

DOUBLE SON OF A BITCH!

Jack gave him another fifty. "Why is the other guy called Brick?"

"Cause he's stoned all the time. He never know shit, man."

"Okay." He handed Chimp the final hundred. "Alright my man, you're holding seven hundred dollars of my money and a bag of candy bars. We're done here." Chimp nodded and left Jack's car, heading back into the woods.

Jack watched him cut toward Scarsdale and he instantly felt he knew where the mysterious Chimp was headed. He entered the town limits and made several turns before pulling into the parking lot of the Greyhound bus station. A bus was waiting, ready for boarding.

Jack stayed out of sight as he watched Chimp leave the woods and sprint over to the entrance of the bus station. Several minutes later he exited the station and climbed on board the bus. Jack watched until the bus left the station.

Jack entered the station and walked up to the ticket counter and spoke to the man on duty. He was an older, wrinkled man who looked perpetually bored. Jack inquired about the final destination of the bus that had just left. The man said Cleveland, Ohio.

So, Jack thought, Chimp would soon lose himself in the dirty, dingy projects of downtown Cleveland. Well, good luck.

Jack returned to his Scarsdale room after midnight. He poured himself some vodka and stretched out on his bed. He had several vodkas before he fell asleep.

CHAPTER 28:
Jack Meets with Ford Carr

The following morning Jack Troop sat at his desk with a story to work on but found his mind wandering in the weeds that seemed to represent the story of Darnell life over the last half dozen years. Jack was about eighty percent confident that the information he had obtained last night from the mysterious Chimp was credible. If he accepted that premise, then Darnell had nothing to do with the death of his mother Estelle. Tripping over that loose throw rug was a trap set for Darnell by Willie. But as it often happens in life, the victim of the trap was an unintended victim. In reality, Estelle was the only person that loved Willie regardless of his faults. A mother's love for her child has no boundaries and Willie would never have harmed her intentionally.

But Marcus was also present for Willie's boozed-up confession. Marcus and Darnell were close friends. To Jack, it seemed more than possible that Marcus would have passed that information on to Darnell. Given that assumption, would Darnell want to eliminate his own brother? Was a drug-dealing gang banger brother such an embarrassment to Darnell that he had to be removed from Darnell's path to fame and fortune? Darnell himself had told Jack that no one was going to stand in his way to what he wanted in life. And it really was beyond coincidence that Chuck Chambers, Brent Reedy, and recently Doug Ward, all clearly in Darnell's path to success, would have had their right legs shattered by an unknown attacker. It was simply too much.

Two weeks later Jack received a call from Emily Townsend, Ford Carr's executive secretary. She advised Jack that he was to meet Mr. Carr in the executive office in Chester City at 9:00 a.m. the following morning. When Jack hung up the phone, he surmised that this would be the meeting about the new opportunity for him that Buzz Cutter had mentioned.

Jack arrived on schedule the next morning and was showed into Ford Carr's office. Not only was the office plush, it was the largest office that Jack had ever seen. Jack speculated it had the square footage of a small house.

This was only the second time in Jack's life that he met Ford face to face. As he studied Ford from his chair across the desk from him, he realized that Ford was a slim man of average height, with a full head of hair with some silver flecks in it, and a narrow face dominated by a large, full mustache.

Ford began, "Well, well. John Troop. John, good to see you again."

"Thank you. Good to see you again, sir."

"I understand that you are now engaged to be married?"

"I am, sir. Her name is Diana DeLeo. She's the receptionist at the Daily."

"So I've heard. Tell me, have you two set a date yet?"

"Almost. We're exploring possibilities for some time in October."

"I see. Yes, I see. That will be a very important event in your life, John. Your future. In fact, it is your future that I wish to discuss with you."

Jack was getting uncomfortable and fidgeted in his chair. That Ford continued to call him John was annoying the hell out of him. But he kept his mouth shut.

"That would be great, sir."

Ford started his pitch to Jack.

"Well good. Good. Yes, here's the thing John. You perhaps know that I own WFRX radio. Have for some time. It broadcasts right here from Chester City and has an extensive regional audience. It plays a lot of top 40 pop music, does some news and some sports. This format has gotten somewhat old. A survey that I paid for has ratings down 4.8 percent over the past year. And John, if ratings go down so does advertising income. I can't have that. So, to that point, I want to . . .

let's say, jazz up the programming. I am going to add another broadcast. A new show, so to speak."

Ford pauses drumming his fingertips on his large, polished desk.

"You may also be aware that I'm an activist in the Republican Party. I'm the chairman of the Shawnee County Republican Party and a major contributor to our candidates over the entire region."

He paused again, stroking his prominent mustache.

"I am aware of your standing in the GOP, sir. My father, Frank, is active in the Democratic Party."

"Ah yes, your father Frank. Frank Troop. Well anyway, what I'm leading into are my plans for a morning talk show. My vision is a call-in format with two hosts. Or co-hosts. One male and one female. One Democrat and one Republican. These co-hosts would field calls from listeners on both political and other current events."

He stopped again, staring at Jack and stroking the mustache.

"So, John, what do you think?" Jack had no idea what to think.

"Well sir, it sounds like a workable idea to me. Radio talk shows are growing in popularity."

"Workable? Hmm…yes, workable. Interesting choice of words John, but a good choice. I know how to make this project work. Now, would you be interested in helping me do it?"

"Of course I would sir. But…but I'm unsure how I could help."

"I'm coming to that. I just told you that I wanted co- hosts for the show. Yes? Now I've already got one real pro coming on board. Her name is Jean Lange. She hosts a similar morning show in Chicago. She's been doing it for a decade. She is now willing to work for me."

He smiled. "I can be very persuasive." He cracked a weak, crooked smile. "I can also pay her a hell of a lot more than she's been making. You know, that often helps." He chuckled.

"I'm sure it would, sir."

"So, I've already hired a conservative female host. Now I need the other co-host. Do you see it?"

"I think so."

"I'll clarify. You're a Democrat, right?"

"Yes, sir. It runs in the family."

Jack was now clear on where Ford was going with this conversation. He was excited.

"Well, since you are obviously a male, I have in mind to partner you with Jean as the Democrat co-host. Interested?"

"Sir, you bet I am," Jack replied with enthusiasm.

"Excellent. Excellent. You see John, Buzz sent me some tapes of your on-camera appearances from the news van. You speak articulately and intelligently. And it's also obvious that you can think fast on your feet. That will be a key asset needed for you to succeed in the radio talk-show business. You're young and not very experienced, but my hunch is that you can succeed in this business. You have my complete confidence."

Jack was breathing slowly, trying to keep calm.

"So, if you take this job, don't fuck it up." Ford grinned. The profanity startled Jack momentarily.

"Oh no, sir. I won't." Jack returned the smile.

"Good. Good. But here's the thing. A small fly in the soup, so to speak. I'm going to be rolling out this show in October." Jack's face sagged.

"Exactly. But until the show catches on, and it will, you've got to be focused and be here in the studio every day, busting your ass. Sorry, but you need to postpone the wedding. That is unless you wish to pass on this opportunity."

Jack was at a loss.

"Mr. Carr, please understand that I really want to do this. But, I also really want to marry Diana. She is the love of my life. I don't know what to tell you, or how to make such a choice."

Ford grinned again.

"Fair enough. So let me ask you, is that young lady worth waiting for? Maybe another six months?"

"Sure. She means everything to me."

"Perhaps I can help. I assume that she also has parents, brothers, sisters and other family planning on this October ceremony?"

"Yes, sir. It's a large family. Italian, you know."

"Okay, John. To start with, see if you can talk to Diana and her family. Tell her parents that if they can wait another six months for this wedding, I'll make a donation in her parent's name to any charity of their choice in the amount of $25,000. Now I know Dom. I know he is a rich man, but he'll be pleased with this gesture. I'll do the same for her brothers in the amount of $10,000. Now for you and Diana, I'll pay for a ten-day stay all-expenses-paid honeymoon to a destination of your choice. First class, five-star resort. I'll even kick in another $5,000 for the spending money that you won't really need. What the hell. Now you started out in this business selling ad space for the Morrisville News. Can you still sell? Could you sell a package like that?"

Jack was startled by his need to barter over his wedding date. But Ford's offer was generous.

"My God, sir, that's a lot of money."

Ford was tapping his desk again.

"John, John, John. I'll tell you what. I've pissed away more money than that before I have my morning coffee. I am a billionaire many times over." He let out a short laugh. "To tell you the truth, if I had a bigger pair of balls, I'd be a trillionaire." He resumed his laughing. "And, I would add, one hell of a stud."

At this Jack began laughing along with Ford. Jack was smart enough to stop laughing when Ford stopped. Ford then stood and extends his hand. The two men shook hands.

"Now today is Wednesday, right? Ah... I believe yes. So, let's say that you call Emily on Friday. Any time Friday. Tell her your decision. And also, I want Diana on board with this, too. Won't do for you to start married life with a pissed off wife."

"Yes, sir. I'll call Friday. And thank you so much. Thank you."

As Jack headed back to Scarsdale, he started thinking that Ford had given him no details about the job or his new salary. But what the hell, first he had to sell Diana and her family on the deal. He was confident that he could. Life was getting sweeter.

As Jack left Ford's office, Ford smiled. Jack Troop would take the offer. Of that he was sure. He would move to Chester City where Ford could keep a better eye on him. Keep him busy. Busy enough so that he wouldn't be interested in investigating his prized athlete Darnell Ducette. He wanted that to stop.

CHAPTER 29:
The Jack and Jill Show

At 7:00 a.m. on a Thursday morning *The Jack and Jill Show* aired on Ford Carr's radio station WFRX for the 100th time since it began the previous October.

Jack picked up a ringing phone.

"Good morning. My name is Pete and I have a question for Jack."

"Good morning, Pete. This is Jack. Hit me with it."

"I know you're a Democrat. So, at this stage of the President's administration, how would you rate his performance?"

"First Pete, allow me to say that the President is a fine, honorable man who has served his country well. As President, I would give him good marks for his handling of the breakup of the Soviet Union. The Americans with Disabilities Act is also a credit to his legacy as the leader of our nation. However, with that said, at this stage of his first term, there is much to be done that has not yet been addressed. I'd give him a solid C+ or perhaps a B- for his performance to date. Does that answer your question?"

"Yes, thank you." Another caller was on the line and Jill answered.

"Hello. My name is Cheryl and I have a question for Jill."

"Great. This is Jill. Go ahead and ask, Cheryl."

Cheryl said, "Does this President deserve re-election? After all, he did violate his no-new-taxes pledge. As a Republican, I find that reprehensible."

"I couldn't agree more with you Cheryl. When a politician makes a promise, it needs to be kept. If you can't keep it, don't make it. I think with the election coming up next year this will be a problem for him."

"Thank you, Jill."

The questions continued in this manner until 9:00 a.m., which was the sign off time.

Jack spoke, "Once again, I wish to thank all of our callers this morning. Our time is up but Jill and I will be back on the air at 7:00 a.m. tomorrow. I'm Jack Troop, signing off for the day."

"And I'm Jill Lange. But before I sign off, I wish to take this moment to thank all of our listeners, the people who every day call in with their questions and comments. I also thank our sponsors as we conclude the 100th episode of *The Jack and Jill Show*. Thank you and I'm out."

Jean Lange, under her employment agreement with Ford Carr, used Jill as her professional name. She got up from her chair as did Jack and they hugged each other. The show to date was an overwhelming success. They both headed for the conference room for a brief celebration, compliments of Ford Carr, who was again traveling outside the country. Ricky Jolly, president of Ford Carr Media, Inc., was the host. It was just after 9:00 a.m. but everyone attending already had a flute of champagne in their hand. Ricky signaled for silence and then began speaking.

"Everyone. Please listen up. I just wanted to pass on a message to you all from Ford. I'll read it: Thank you all very much for making *The Jack and Jill Show* the huge success that it has been from the beginning. It is going so well that plans are now in the works to take the show to a national audience. I intend to update you all on these plans as they develop. In the meantime, keep up the good work and always strive for even greater success. Now drink up and enjoy."

Everyone took a drink and then clapped.

"Cheers everyone. You all deserve it." Ricky started to mingle among the cast and crew, shaking hands as he moved through the small and crowded room. Jack shook hands with Ricky and the two men chatted briefly. Jack then said goodbye to Jill and left the building for the day. He needed to get back to Scarsdale. He had Friday off and would be marrying Diana on Saturday.

Jack had successfully sold Ford Carr's proposal to Diana and her family. After the wedding, they would fly to Hawaii and enjoy a ten-day honeymoon, all expenses paid by Ford. Ford had already paid the promised donations to the charities of choice for the members of the DeLeo family.

Jack and Diana were married Saturday at noon in the oldest Catholic Church in Scarsdale. While Jack was not a religious young man, he was continually awed by the beauty and elegant ceremonies of the Catholic Church. As Diana, escorted by her elegantly dressed father, walked down the carpeted center aisle, he thought his heart would burst. He was overwhelmed by the presence of his beautiful young bride. His parents had grown very fond of Diana and his father had told Jack on more than one occasion what a lucky young man he was to have earned the love of such an attractive and personable young woman.

After the wedding ceremony, the reception took place at Gino's Italian Restaurant in the banquet room. Diana's father had spared no expense to make both the wedding ceremony and the reception a memorable experience. The reception was attended by family and friends of both the bride and the groom. There were over a hundred attendees. Dom was paying for an open bar, so the alcohol flowed as the two bartenders on duty emptied fifth after a fifth of liquor, bottle after bottle of wine and filled countless mugs with ice cold beer. The buffet consisted of ten dishes—some were meat dishes and some were pasta dishes. Various salad and vegetable dishes were too numerous to count. Dessert consisted of a large chocolate wedding cake and assorted cannoli. Dom had also purchased six dozen bottles of quality champagne to go with all the various toasts that would take place during that evening.

It was after one o'clock in the morning when an exhausted Jack and Diana climbed into a limousine for the drive to Chester City, where they would take a plane to O'Hare Airport in Chicago later in the morning. From there they boarded an American Airlines flight on a DC-10 to Hawaii. After a ten-hour flight, they arrived on the island of Oahu. Tired and jet-lagged, they left the airport and checked into their hotel room. The plan was to spend two days in Oahu, visiting the famous beaches, trying their luck surfing after taking a lesson and then touring the battleship Arizona monument. When they reached the room, they were exhausted and gritty, so they stripped off their clothes and went naked together into a luxury shower with showerheads aimed to spray a body from every angle. Feeling clean and with their skin tingling, they leaped into the huge bed and enjoyed vigorous and passionate sex. When it was over, they held hands. Diana turned to Jack.

"Jack, I guess that was our first time as husband and wife. It felt great."

"It did, Di." He chuckled. "Can you believe we were actually too tired and too boozed up to give it a go last night?"

Diana also chuckled. "Let's face it, Jack. It wasn't going to work last night even if we had tried."

"True. So true."

"Well, we're on a six-hour time lag. It's dark back home. What do you say we go walk around some and see what there is to see?"

And they did. They easily found the gigantic swimming pool that was over an acre in size and had a bar and grill on an island in the middle of the pool. To get to it one had to swim out to it. Since it was past dinnertime back east, and since they were both hungry, they went back to their room, got into their swimwear and went for a swim then dinner and drinks. They fell asleep early that evening.

The next morning, they toured the Battleship Arizona Memorial. In the afternoon they took a surfing lesson, rented two surfboards and spent the afternoon attempting to surf the waves at Diamondhead.

The following morning, they decided to rent a helicopter that made a pass over Oahu and then traveled over the ocean to Maui, where Jack and Diana spent the next seven days of their honeymoon. The first day on Maui they rented a car and drove over to the Bay Course. They each rented a set of golf clubs and played eighteen holes of golf under the warm Pacific sky. They had been told that the Pacific sun was more intense than the sunlight back in the other forty-nine states. It turned out to be true, as both Jack and Diana left the course that afternoon too much on the red side of tan. They stayed in their room for the remainder of the day. They ordered from room service for dinner and a bottle of champagne. After dinner, they uncorked the champagne and watched some TV while lying on the bed. Both were stark naked. The remainder of the evening was all about more sex.

Over the remainder of their honeymoon, they rented another helicopter and flew over a couple of the volcanoes on the islands. They took a trip on the road to the tiny town of Hanna. This road was full of twists and turns and was cut into a coastal mountainside. As Jack drove the rented car both he and Diana could look down a thousand feet on the ocean below them. The road did not have a guardrail. The drive was about sixty miles and as both beautiful and frightening as any drive, one could make. Their hotel had put together a picnic lunch and some bottled water and a bottle of wine for their adventure. Hanna had a small hotel down on a black sand beach. The couple stopped there and inquired about the availability of a room. To their delight, there had just been a cancellation, so they decided to spend the night. They spent the day sunning themselves on the unusual black sand beach. Upon returning to their original hotel, they booked a boat to take them deep-sea fishing one day and whale watching the next. On their final day, they were tired and simply rested, however with a little sexual activity to keep life interesting.

The saying is that all good things must come to an end. Jack and Diana both promised each other that one day they would return to the islands. The Hawaiian Islands were just too magnificent and beautiful to visit only once in a lifetime. They returned to Chester City on a cool and rainy gray day. Jack had previously rented a small one-bedroom apartment in Chester City. The two of them began a life together in that tiny apartment. The reality of life together now began to settle in.

Diana had spent the entire 26 years of her life in Scarsdale. While the move to Chester City with her new husband was exciting, she felt sad and depressed. But life moves on. Things constantly change, and chances must be taken.

They spent a weekend in their new apartment together before Jack had to return to the show on Monday morning. Diana had to quit her job at the Scarsdale Daily. After Jack left for the WFRX studio, she began straightening things up around the house and by noon was feeling bored and lonely. It was nearly noon, so she sat down on a living room chair and turned the TV on. She channel surfed, but nothing interested her. She turned off the set, feeling so alone. Soon tears began flowing down her cheeks. Then she sobbed with her face buried in her hands.

CHAPTER 30:
Jean Lange

Jean Lange was born forty-three years ago in the small town of Indian Lakes, Minnesota. She was the third of five children born to Calvin Lange and Faith Ann Gale.

Calvin was a veteran of the Korean War and had seen much of the fiercest combat during that conflict. He was a reclusive man by nature and returned to his childhood home in northern Minnesota after the war. He was also a very resourceful man, having learned survival skills while in the war with the army rangers. His father had taught him how to work with wood, so after the war, he worked as a carpenter. Within a year he quit his job with the construction company and found whatever work he could as a self-employed handyman. When he didn't have a job to do, he started to build his own cabin in the woods five miles outside of the small town of Indian Lakes. The cabin had a basement dug deep into the ground and lined with re-enforced concrete. Over time he turned this basement into a fully stocked survival bunker with food, water, and weapons. When the bunker was completed, Calvin believed that he could survive for at least six months underground. The interior of the cabin was 750 square feet and the entire project took him two years to finish. It was just about impossible to do any building in those northern woods once winter arrived.

He initially made frequent trips into Indian Lakes in his old pickup truck for provisions, though he hunted and fished for meat. He had lived a solitary life until he met Faith Ann, who was working in the general store.

Faith Ann Gale was half Northern Sioux and half black. The obvious racial mixture made Faith Ann and her husband Calvin outcasts in Indian Lakes. From an early age, Faith Ann had been taught a variety of skills by her mother Hope. Hope taught her daughter sewing and knitting skills, how to cook basic meals, how to grow her own vegetables, how to never waste anything and how to survive on her own without depending on a man. Eventually, Faith Ann took a paying job in the town's general store. Of the variety of household goods available in the store, there was little that Faith Ann did not know how to use, so she became an effective salesperson when customers asked her how to questions. She bumped into Calvin at least once a week. He wasn't much of a talker, but he was struck by smiley and pretty Faith Ann. So, he would talk to her. He began going to the store more frequently, occasionally purchasing something, but usually just chatting with Faith Ann. He eventually asked her to go out with him. From that point on, the two developed a relationship until Faith Ann simply quit her job and went out to Calvin's cabin in the woods and stayed with him.

The two never married. They never felt the need to. Over time Faith Ann would have five children; two girls and three boys. All five of them took the last name of Lange. Both Calvin and Faith Ann taught children survival skills and how to be resourceful enough to get along by themselves without any assistance from anyone else. Calvin took the lead in instructing each of his children on skills with firearms, knives, and concealment. Jean was the best of Calvin's trainees. Faith Ann taught them the same skills that her mother had taught her. Even the three boys learned to cook and sew. None of the five Lange children would ever have to depend on another human being.

Jean was the smartest of the Lange children and did well at the Indian Lakes School. An excellent student, Jean had a thirst to learn and was an A student throughout her four years at Indian Lakes Senior High School. She attended the University of Minnesota majoring in communications. It was during her college experience that she learned to relax around people. By the time of her graduation, she was sociable but internally wary of deep human contact. She discovered sex and the fact that she liked it. But an emotional connection with a man was out of the question.

She could surrender herself to physical pleasure for brief periods of time, but trusting another human being was beyond her emotional tolerance.

She was able to secure a job in Minneapolis for a local TV station as a news writer. She did well and over the years had learned other parts of the business. She eventually became the morning weather girl. During this time, she began dating a young assistant. One weekend in mid-summer they drove eighty miles west of Minneapolis to a cabin by a small lake where they spent the weekend. Jean was mostly interested in the sex. But her partner turned out to like very rough sex. He raped and beat Jean, tied her up and put her in the trunk of his car. He dropped her in the woods ten miles outside of Minneapolis. When Jean returned to consciousness she had the skills to free herself. She was also pissed off that he had got the best of her. She returned to her job, much to the surprise of her attacker.

Jean ignored him for several weeks. Her attacker made sure to stay away from her, not really knowing how to handle the more than an awkward situation. Jean surprised him one day by asking him why he hadn't asked her out again.

"Wasn't I good enough?" she asked him. He replied that she had been plenty good, but he thought she was mad at him.

"Why would you think that?" she had replied.

"No reason," he responded.

He made another date with Jean. The two had dinner at a diner near Indian Lakes and then her date suggested another trip to the cabin where he had first assaulted her. Jean smiled and said,

"That would be wonderful, Al. Just like the last time." But Jean Lange made sure that this night was nothing like the last time. She told Al that she would stay in the car while he checked in and got a key to a cabin. Al parked the car outside of cabin 18. The two entered the dark room and Al turned to flip on the light switch. Jean held her hunting knife with an eight-inch blade in her left hand. As the light flicked on she plunged the knife into his right kidney. Al screamed as Jean pushed him to the old stained carpet. Blood gushed out onto the carpet. Al groaned with pain.

Jean only looked at him and said, "Die, you rotten mother fucker." She bent over and finished the job by slashing his throat.

She took a pair of plastic gloves from her coat pocket and stripped the bedspread and rolled Al up in it. Jean was much stronger than her size indicated. She waited for darkness and then dragged Al out to the car, popped the trunk and hefted his upper body over the edge of the trunk, then grabbed his legs and tossed them into the trunk. She got into the car and headed east, eventually coming to an old dirt road that led into a deeply wooded area. That was where she dumped him. She dug around in the soft earth with her knife until she got about an eight-inch deep shallow grave. She dragged Al into the grave and then covered him with old branches and foliage, which she had cut off some bushes with the knife. Work completed, she drove the car back toward St. Paul. She then wiped any possible fingerprints off the car surfaces that she had touched and parked the car in the lot of a local market. She walked through the dark of night some eight miles back to her apartment just outside the city.

The following morning, she showed up at work ready to go. She went through the day doing her job just like it was another day, which to her, it actually was. Al was not even a second thought. The supervisor went around several hours later asking if anyone had heard from Al. He was missing and hadn't called in.

When he had asked Jean if she had heard from him she shrugged and said, "No. Why would I?"

It was nearly a month before the body of Al Westwood would be found by the police. He had, however, been found much sooner by a variety of animals that inhabited the woods. All the employees where Al had worked were questioned but nobody had anything useful for them, including Jean Lange. About a month later she quit her job and went back home to spend some time with her parents.

Jean told both Calvin and Faith Ann that she would soon go to Chicago to see if she could find a job in the TV news business. Calvin was very concerned about the many dangers that life might present to her in a city like Chicago. Before she left, he equipped her with a 12-gauge pump shotgun, a .306 caliber deer rifle, and a Smith and Wesson .38 caliber revolver. Jean had buried the hunting knife deep in another wooded area and when her father asked her if she still had her knife, so she told him she had lost it, so Calvin gave her his knife telling her that he would get another one for himself.

Over the years Jean rose to the position of talk show host for a local radio station. She became an articulate spokesperson for the far-right philosophy. It was around this time that she was well enough known to garner the attention of Ford C. Carr.

She had met a man at a local tavern whom she became very attracted to physically. The man told her he was married but the two went to a local motel and engaged in sexual activity. It kept on happening once or twice a month for over a year. The man finally became afflicted with a bad case of a guilty conscience and broke off the relationship. She had become upset and asked him why. She would never tell his wife. She only wanted the occasional sex. He told her no more, in no uncertain terms. He said that he was still in love with his wife and that Jean wasn't really his type. This made Jean furious. She did not handle rejection well.

Jean began hanging out around the tavern where she had first met him. The man still drank there regularly and eventually Jean saw him leave with another woman. She followed the two to a sleazy motel located a dozen miles outside Chicago. In the early morning hours of that night, while it was still dark, a half dozen shots rang out, followed by the noise of a car speeding away from the motel. Police would later determine that both the man and the woman had been shot to death with a .38 caliber pistol. There were no witnesses, and no one had seen the car. The man had never told his wife of his affair with Jean Lange. Jean was never questioned.

However, she did feel that she needed to leave Chicago. As luck would have it, Ford Carr called her and offered her an opportunity to work at WFRX in Chester City. Jean met with Ford to go over the details and accepted the job. She would serve as the conservative co-host of a political talk show with a young male co-host named Jack Troop. She was advised that Jack was new to the talk show business, recently married, and in his twenties.

Her new employer was completely unaware of the dark side of her history. Jean Lange thought that her new situation with a young male co-host could prove interesting.

CHAPTER 31:

A Marriage in Crisis

Jack and Diana had just begun to settle into the joy of early married life, Darnell and Candy experienced something entirely different when they met down in the Florida Keys. The couple did enjoy five days of endless sunshine, fine food, and too much alcohol. But they merely went through the motions of being happily married. There was no physical contact between them other than a few chaste kisses and a little uninspired sex. Any casual observer of the couple would notice the lack of touching and tenderness. When those five days ended, Darnell flew back to Washington to attend the spring practice sessions while Candy flew back to New York City. She had grown weary of her cheap, one-bedroom apartment and wanted something nicer. Since signing with the Lola Getz Agency, she completed enough modeling assignments to net over two million dollars. With more assignments in the works, she upgraded to a newly remodeled apartment in Manhattan's East Side. The apartment was a plush two bedroom and fully furnished. Candy was approaching celebrity status and she was thrilled with the idea that there were genuine celebrities living in the same building that she was living in. Some were actors, some were sports figures, some were TV personalities, and some were rich businessmen. The idea that she was now one of them filled her soul with happiness. She had made it big and superstar status was now achievable.

Within a few weeks, both of them had returned to their second home in the Living Greens complex. Three days after they had returned they were seen in front of their house by neighbors arguing loudly and vigorously. Finally, the police were called. The responding officers got them both to calm down and then left with the neighbors still outside talking and shaking their heads.

By late July, Darnell had flown back to Washington for the start of training camp and the pre-season games that would follow. He was excited about the upcoming season. His first season with the Red Knights had been spectacular and the national sports writers voted him NFL rookie of the year. The Red Knights' head coach Henry Coffee declared to the press that Darnell was easily the team's most valuable player. The team had gone to the playoffs last season but lost in the first round. Nevertheless, it was a successful season for the team and an outstanding start to Darnell's professional career. The only negatives in the last season were the two concussions Darnell had suffered. The injuries had caused him to miss three of the sixteen games played.

On the road called life, everyone tries to negotiate the twists and turns that confront them as best as they can. They take some steps forward and often take too many steps back.

In late August, Darnell was the starter for the first half of the Red Knights' final pre-season game against the New York Giants. Late in the first quarter of the game, Darnell dropped back to pass. His target was wide receiver Jackson Flowers, who was running a deep post pattern. Darnell was waiting for Jackson to be open when he was simultaneously hit by several Giants defensive linemen. He had held the football a second too long waiting for his receiver to get open. When he got hit, he collapsed and found himself on the bottom of the pile with a thousand pounds of humanity squashing him into the turf. He was unable to stand and needed assistance to help him to the sidelines. He would later be diagnosed with a torn ACL. Darnell would not be playing football that season. He was crushed both literally and figuratively.

Darnell still spent the season in Washington. He had surgery and spent the fall rehabbing and watching the team from the sidelines. By season's end, the Red Knights' had finished with a 5-11 record. There would be no playoff game for the Red Knights' and no accolades for Darnell. By January he was back in Living Greens where he spent the winter and continued to rehab his injured knee.

Candy spent the fall and winter seasons in her new apartment. She had regular modeling assignments, some in New York City and some traveling to a special location. Her face and her body began appearing with greater frequency on billboards, magazines, and TV. News clips showed her mingling at various functions with the most notable celebrities of the moment. Candy was eclipsing Darnell in celebrity status while Darnell stayed at home constantly rehabbing the injured knee.

Darnell was furious with her. Livid and pissed off beyond all reason. It had been a crushing year for Darnell and a fine one for Candy.

One afternoon in between assignments, Candy Champion sat alone in her Manhattan apartment listening to music and sipping a dry martini. She knew that she needed to end things with Darnell. She had several eligible men who were eager to get together with her. She had already had a sexual relationship with two of the several possibilities.

She thought back to the day the two were married. She remembered it as a happy day and after all, it happened not that long ago. But it was clearly over. What happened? She thought. After their wedding day and the passionate sex they had late that evening, no day had ever been as joyous. But after mixing herself a second martini it occurred to her that she had probably never been in love with Darnell. Oh sure, he was handsome, had a great body and was usually personable and even charming. But she had discovered a dark side to him.

She had discovered the times when Darnell went cold when his eyes became narrow slits that were precursors of danger, of violence, of the potential to destroy lives. It was never anything that she could put her finger on, never anything material, or anything of human substance, of skin and bone. It was only the times, and there were many in their brief marriage when she could see the darkness in him. It was when he went silent and cold she could almost hear the low and menacing growling of a wild animal. Like she could smell the scent of death on his skin.

Candy made every effort to avoid Darnell. Mercifully her work kept her away from him, but when they were together, no matter how often he flashed that big smile, she sensed his terrible anger with her. She had started to fear him and needed to be free of him. She needed a divorce. She resolved to call her attorney the following day. After a third martini, she fell asleep on the couch with music still playing softly through multiple speakers.

It had been a crushing year for Darnell. His marriage sucked. It had gone all to shit, he thought, as he sat in his favorite lounge chair in his home in the Living Greens. He was sipping a scotch. He knew he was ready for the upcoming season with the Red Knights. The ACL had mended, and his surgeon had told him to keep up with his exercise routine but not to push it. He would be fine by the time camp opened this coming July.

But what to do about Candy? The bitch! Who had he really married? Certainly not a loving and devoted wife. Certainly not a woman who would cater to his every need and love him and support him. Oh, hell no! He had married a competitor. He had married a career woman. But hell, she had never mentioned to him any desire to become a model. Sure, she was pretty enough. She was personable enough. But, shit, why had she never said anything about it to him? The bitch was simply devious. Conniving. She was now making the kind of money that he was. She was now getting the kind of publicity that he was. In fact, more than he was. She was upstaging him. Humbling him. Emasculating him.

He had married her because he thought she would be an asset to his career. He would have the beautiful and supporting wife. He would have his fame as a great football player. And of course, he would have a multi-million-dollar contract to continue playing football for years. He would be the envy of every male in America because after all, Darnell Ducette had it all. But oh no. That's not what he had at all. What he had was a stinking, rotten, backstabbing bitch. And he hated her. No, no. Not hated—it was more than that. Loathed her. Despised her. He wished she would simply disappear. She needed to be dead.

CHAPTER 32:
A Little Politics

The year 1992 was a momentous year in American politics, with the upcoming presidential election to be contested. The local representative from the congressional district that included Shawnee and several of the surrounding counties was a Republican named Nelson Summerhays. Congressman Summerhays had held two recent fundraisers and at each one Darnell had appeared, introducing the congressman and spoken some words on his behalf.

Jack Troop, who was still intrigued by the career of Darnell, had picked up on these speeches and resolved to get in touch with him. He was hoping to talk Darnell into calling into *The Jack and Jill Show*. Two days later they agreed that Darnell would call into the show at 8:00 a.m. on the coming Thursday morning.

On Thursday at 7:59 a.m. Jack began the introduction of Darnell.

"Now for all you listeners out there, we have a special guest to begin our 8:00 a.m. hour. He is the popular former quarterback from Stannard High, who led the Stallions to consecutive state titles, then later led the Chester City State Crusaders to a pair of conference titles and set several NCAA passing records. He is now the starting quarterback for the Washington Red Knights. Of course, he is Darnell Ducette, and I have him live on the phone at this very moment. Good morning, Darnell. Good to talk to you again."

"Good morning, Jack," replied Darnell cheerfully. "Happy to talk to you, too."

"Darnell, we have talked many times in the past, but I want to introduce you to my partner, Jill Lange."

"Hi, Darnell. I'm looking forward to our talk."

"Nice to speak to you today, Jill."

"Okay, Darnell. Jill will ask you the first question."

"Darnell, you have been seen on two occasions at fundraising functions for Congressman Nelson Summerhays. You have endorsed his candidacy. Yet it is my understanding that you have only recently registered with the Republican Party. What do you find appealing about the party and Congressman Summerhays?"

"Jill, that's an easy question. Nelson Summerhays will return to Congress and continue to fight for Republican values. Now the principal value of our party is the freedom for every man and woman to make their own way in this great country of ours. That means that our government needs to stay out of our way and leave a clear path for all citizens to strive and thrive. That is what America is all about."

"Darnell, I like your answer. That would be the beginning of one hell of a speech. Strive and thrive. Maybe you should be running for Congress."

Darnell laughed out loud.

"Hey, Jill, I'm a football player. At least for now. Maybe someday I'll give politics a shot. It would be a fit for the competitor in me."

"Do you support the re-election of the President?"

"Of course."

"Despite the fact that he broke the no-new-taxes pledge?"

"Well Jill, I do make a lot of money these days. That ain't no secret. So for me having to pay more taxes is kinda like taking a pay cut. You see what I'm saying. But you know, on the whole, his presidency has been pretty darn good. Especially how good he handled the breakup of the Soviet Union. They got a lot of nukes, you know."

"You're echoing my thoughts on the subject. Are you sure you're just a football player?" Jill laughed a little.

Darnell also chuckled. "Why, sure I am. A rich one, but just a player."

"Hey Darnell, it's Jack. Jill is my Republican co-host. But I'm the Democratic here. So let me hit you with a different kind of question."

"Have at it, man."

"Okay, you're a black man—"

Darnell interrupts. "Sure, last time I looked."

Jack had heard this line before and ignored it. "Right. So, take America's inner-city population. Mostly black. Lots of poverty, lots of drug use, lots of crime and too many broken and dysfunctional families. How does the Republican message address this situation?"

"Same as it addresses any problem. If government stays out of people's way, then people are free to figure their problems out and fix what's broke."

"But Darnell, they have been living under the conditions that I just described for decades. Isn't it possible that they don't know how to fix it? Don't they need help? Some form of Federal assistance?"

"Are you talking welfare, Jack?"

"Not necessarily. But go ahead and assume that. Then what's your answer?"

"Jack, welfare ain't no dignity for any kind of man. Don't you see that?"

"I see what you are saying, but I think you're over-simplifying the answer to a very complex problem. Much of humanity hasn't been self-reliant for a long time."

Darnell chuckled again, but the tone of his voice becomes became sharper. "Sure, Jack. A bunch of dumb niggers, right? Now, who's over-simplifying?"

Jill jumped back in. "Darnell, I'm with you. Welfare is a curse on human dignity."

Jack changed the subject, "Okay, Darnell. Fine. But how about we now move on to sports. You're a famous NFL quarterback. So, let's talk a little football for the audience. How is your rehab going?"

"It's going fine. I'm right on schedule to start game one."

"Now that's good news. What are your expectations for the Red Knights this coming season?"

Darnell let out a sigh.

"Oh man, that's hard to say. We were 5 and 11 last season, but I never played. So how good will we be when I'm back starting again? We're gonna be better for sure. But every season in pro ball, the lineup changes. Players come, players go. So, you see, I'm not sure what kind of team we'll have but I know it will be better."

"That makes sense."

"It does for sure."

Jack then opened up the questioning to the listening audience.

Another twenty minutes passed quickly. As 9:00 a.m. approached, Jack broke it off and thanked Darnell for speaking with them. He and Jill then signed off for the day. After the sign-off, Jill turned to Jack.

"Jack, I'm from Chicago. Chicago is home to stadiums full of professional athletes. There's quite a few smart pro athletes in that town. But that Darnell is as sharp as I've ever talked to."

"He is. Darnell was a freshman at Chester City State when I was a junior. I interviewed him several times. He's an extraordinary athlete and equally smart. He's got a future. And I noticed he has cleaned up his speech a good deal. He used to have more of a home- boy tongue."

"Well, I'm kind of ignorant when it comes to sports, but I know political talent when I see it. He has a future in politics. He's the one that should be running for Congress. He is way more impressive than that stuffed shirt Summerhays."

Jack laughed.

"Oh yeah. Most of us locals think that Nelson exists just to look good in a suit."

The following week Nelson Summerhays was scheduled to speak at the Stannard High School gym at seven in the evening. Ford Carr was to introduce the speakers, among them, were Darnell and, of course, Congressman Summerhays. Jack decided to attend.

The Stannard High gym looked like any other high school gym where school funding was an issue. A stack of drab looking bleachers lined the cinder block wall at the rear of the gym. All the walls could use fresh paint. The usual rows upon rows of crappy-assed, greasy and chipped metal chairs lined the gym floor like rows of tired soldiers. Jack was late, so he grabbed some standing room by a cinder block side wall lined with torn and greasy-looking gym mats. Jack thought, Why in the hell do we send our children to places like this?

Ford Carr was the first speaker and outlined the evening's events for the audience. Several speakers from local offices in Chester City and Shawnee County then followed one after the other, with a consistent series of uninspired drool about what they expected to accomplish if elected in the coming fall. Darnell then took the stage. He was to introduce Nelson Summerhays. He gave a shortened version of the 'strive and thrive' theme that he had discussed on *The Jack and Jill Show*. It was a strong speech and got people's attention. And it got the blood circulating again in their sore and tired butts. The blood stopped circulating again when Summerhays drawled on and on about his list of accomplishments and things he expected to further accomplish. It was a speech peppered with um's and ah's and you knows. Jack walked out after ten minutes of such junk.

CHAPTER 33:
A Tragic Day in May

The chill of the April spring began to fade into the warmth of an early May in New York City. Daffodils, tulips, and irises were in bloom and lilac bushes were budding with the promise of scenting the air with their intoxicating aroma.

Darnell was in his Living Greens home readying himself to fly to Washington, D.C., for spring practice, although he was not yet medically cleared for any strenuous physical activity. Candy had just wrapped up a magazine spread for a new line of lingerie. She planned to meet Darnell in their Georgetown condo in the next couple of days. Or so she thought.

A warm front from the south had moved into New York City during the night of May 9th. In the early morning hours, it was humid and foggy. A steady breeze stirred the warmth and the fog. The breeze carried the odor of the big city. There was the smell of exhaust fumes from thousands of cars, the smell of diesel from the trucks and buses and boats in the harbor, the smell of breakfast being prepared by thousands of ethnic restaurants, the scent of tens of thousands of women dabbing themselves with perfume while getting ready for work, the scent of the freshly pressed suits of thousands of businessmen also getting ready for work and finally the smell of the sea emanating from the harbor. The French doors to the balcony of Candy Champion's eighth floor apartment were wide open and the smell of the city permeated her apartment. The breeze billowed the drapes covering the doors. A dining room chair stood against the wrought iron railing of the balcony. Candy's bedroom door was wide open. The bed had been slept in, but Candy wasn't in it. The clock on the nightstand glowed with a yellow light. It said 4:53 a.m. Then it was 4:54, then 4:55, as it ticked on relentlessly.

Candy Champion had died five minutes ago. At 4:50 a.m., Candy, clad only in her nightgown, had fallen over the rail of her balcony eighty feet to the sidewalk below. She had five seconds to think about her fall or her life before the fall. But that hadn't mattered. She had been unconscious when she went over the railing. Her skull had cracked open like a ripe melon, oozing cranial fluid. Multiple bones were shattered and blood, tissue and body fluids leaked out and stained the grimy pavement where she lay. The tall blonde-haired, blue-eyed beauty of a young woman was now only recognizable as a smashed Barbie Doll leaking dark red human ooze.

Ivonne Delgado was hurrying down the sidewalk on her way to Domingo's Real Good Eats, the restaurant where she worked as a short order cook. She was not paying much attention to her steps and nearly walked into the seeping puddle of goo that was now Candy Champion. But she saw the body, stopped and then began shrieking as loudly as she could. She ran the next two blocks, screaming all the way to Domingo's. Ivonne managed to calm herself as she spoke to the owner, Domingo, who quickly phoned the police.

Officers Juan Torres and Casey O'Donnell got the call from the precinct dispatcher. Their shift would end at 6:00 a.m. and neither officer was happy to get the call to check on a dead body. They arrived at the scene at 5:32 a.m., the patrol car's flashing lights clearly illuminating Candy's splattered body.

Officer Torres said, "Shit," and then so did O'Donnell. They called it into headquarters and began to secure the scene.

By 7:15 a.m., it was known that the deceased woman had fallen from the balcony of apartment 817. The day clerk at the front desk had started at 6:00 a.m. The police had to let him through the barriers. He later advised them that the occupant of apartment 817 was a Ms. Candy Champion. News hounds quickly realized that this was supermodel Candy Champion. The police would not comment.

Back in Chester City, Jack and Jill were twenty minutes into the day's show when one of the assistants, May Webster, entered the broadcast booth and handed Jack a note. Jill was busy talking with a listener. Jack read the note, a newsflash out of New York City describing the early morning fall from the balcony of a woman who was tentatively identified as super-model Candy Champion. No further details were available. Over the remainder of the show, callers were questioning Jack and Jill about the latest news concerning the death of Candy.

Neither co-host could confirm or deny anything. By the show's end at 9:00 a.m., both Jack and Jill headed into the newsroom to gather whatever new information was coming in on the horrific story.

A message came in from Ford Carr requesting that both Jack and Jill refrain from any speculation about this incident and to await confirmable facts.

CHAPTER 34:
Detective D'Antonio

At 6:18 a.m., Detective Sergeant Lou D'Antonio arrived at the scene of Candy's death as news reporters were flocking to the scene like out of control homing pigeons. The newsboys were already putting reports out on the airways of a young, unidentified woman who had apparently plunged to her death from her apartment in Manhattan's Upper East Side. The instant speculation as to the cause of death was suicide, then an accident and finally, murder. This speculation spread like a California wild fire from New York City to the surrounding states and ultimately across the entire country.

Detective Lou D'Antonio was pissed off earlier that morning when he got the call concerning the dead body on the sidewalk. He had a sleepless night and he was tired, cranky and concerned about his health and what he would say to his wife Rose and to his superiors at the precinct.

The Detective was six days shy of his sixtieth birthday. He had served the city of New York for thirty-six years as an NYPD officer. He had spent his first five years as a beat cop and had then been promoted to detective third grade. Four years later he was a full detective and two years after was transferred to homicide investigation. For the past fifteen years he had been the precinct's leading homicide investigator. Lou knew that at this stage of his career that he was damn good at what he did. But with thirty-six years on the job he could put in his papers at any time that he felt the urge. The trouble was that he liked what he did and had no interest in retiring. However, Rose was

171

pushing him hard to retire. He had worked long and irregular hours during his career and Rose was interested in spending some quality time together. He understood that. He understood that but didn't really know how to pull the plug.

But then, at the advice of his family doctor, he had a colonoscopy done. For the past two months he had struggled physically with abdominal cramps, bloating and daily constipation. He finally went to see Dr. Sturgis who advised him that the situation could involve a serious problem and so the colonoscopy had been scheduled. It took an hour until the exam was completed and the doctor who administered the test was able to sit down with him and give him the results.

The cancer appeared to be aggressive and had started to spread into his internal organs. The doctor recommended that he immediately place himself under the care of an oncologist and handed him several cards of doctors that he would recommend without qualification. The news hit D'Antonio like a punch in the face. It reminded him of what boxer Mike Tyson had famously said: "Everybody has a plan until they get punched in the face." So true Iron Mike, thought D'Antonio. Now what? He went back to work and spent the afternoon at his desk in the precinct. He then went home and did his best to spend a normal evening with Rose. Rose had told him that she felt especially tired and went off to bed. Lou said he would be along shortly. But that didn't happen. Instead he spent most of the night relaxing in his lounge chair and sipping scotch. He had fallen asleep in his chair until the ringing of the phone summoned him in the early hours of the following morning.

Later that afternoon the investigation was under way and Darnell Ducette was notified of Candy's death. It was requested that he come to New York the next day as soon as possible to identify the body and talk with Detective Lou D'Antonio. By mid-afternoon Darnell had identified the body and was now sitting in a 14-by-14-foot room accompanied by his attorneys Fred Fenster and Dante DeStefano. The two attorneys and Darnell sat across a cheap wooden table from Detective D'Antonio in the pale green room with a cracked and peeling ceiling and a gray and gritty tiled floor.

D'Antonio looked first at Fred Fenster, a tall thin man obviously in his sixties with eyes set deeply in their sockets surrounded by cadaverous flesh. DeStefano was much shorter and fifty pounds overweight, with dark eyes and dark straight hair combed back and extending over the back of his shirt collar.

DeStefano placed a pad of paper, a pen and a tape recorder on the table. Lawyer Fenster was the first to speak.

"Good afternoon, Detective D'Antonio. I'm Fred Fenster and my associate on the left is Mr. Dante DeStefano. We are both employed by the Ford Carr Sports Management Company and are here to represent Mr. Ducette, who is under contract to the company."

"Fine. Unfortunately, I feel this meeting is necessary despite the timing," D'Antonio said. "I apologize to Mr. Ducette for the inconvenience so soon after the death of his spouse. This is already a very high-profile case and I feel that clarifying as many facts as soon as possible is necessary before it all gets mangled up in the crap the press often puts out."

Darnell and the attorneys all nodded in affirmation like a trio of puppets.

D'Antonio then proceeded to ask Darnell to state his full name, his wife's full name and then asked for the addresses of all three residences that the couple owned. He then reviewed Darnell and Candy's current employer information. Darnell responded appropriately with this information and the two lawyers maintained straight faces through the series of questions.

Lawyer Fenster spoke, "Ah Detective, before we get into any further questions, allow me to state for the record that it is our understanding that this is to be an informal inquiry into the facts of Ms. Champion's death. Correct?"

"That is correct, sir," said D'antonio.

Lawyer DeStefano chimed in, "Detective, we will, as you see, be recording this interview and I take it that you will be doing the same."

"Yes. If you have no more objections, now I will proceed."

Both lawyers nod their okay.

"Now as I see it, the death of Ms. Champion appears to be the result of a fall from her eighth-floor apartment; however, I will note that the M.E. has yet to do the autopsy. It is unclear whether she accidently fell or committed suicide. A third possibility is a homicide. The autopsy should help us determine which."

The statement drew a frown from Darnell.

"So, Mr. Ducette, was your wife depressed or upset in any way?"

"Well, Candy and I have spent a lot of time away from each other lately. She has to be in New York for her work and I play football in Washington. What time we have left we spend together. I can't say for sure that she was depressed or upset. But she was normally an upbeat person."

"Did she have enemies? Someone who might want to kill her?"

Fenster cut in, "Hold on, Darnell. Detective, is there a strong possibility that Ms. Champion was murdered?"

"That possibility is on the table."

"Okay, Detective. But proceed with caution. Mr. Ducette is voluntarily cooperating."

"I appreciate that. Mr. Ducette, have you been in your wife's apartment?"

Darnell paused and looked to Fenster who nodded to him. "Yes, I have. Maybe three, four, or five times."

"Okay. Are you familiar with the balcony?"

"Yeah, I guess. I mean I've been there."

"There is a wrought iron railing along that balcony. Is that correct?"

"Yeah, I think so."

"Well Mr. Ducette, that railing is 45 inches tall. In my mind it would be hard to accidently trip or fall over that railing. Would you agree?"

"I got no idea."

DeStefano jumped in. "Detective D'antonio, where is this line of questioning leading?"

"Mr. DeStefano, I'm merely trying to determine if any of the three possibilities regarding Ms. Champion's death can be ruled out or ruled in."

"Proceed, Detective."

"Alright, Mr. Ducette, back to the possible cause of death. To your knowledge, did your wife use or abuse drugs? Either legal or illegal drugs."

"Not to my knowledge."

"Did she ever act strange, like she was spaced out on drugs?"

Fenster interrupted. "Don't answer that. Detective, our client has just told you that he didn't think his wife used any illegal substance or substances. Please move on."

D'Antonio glared at Lawyer Fenster.

"Sure, sure. Well, Mr. Ducette, did you love your wife?"

Fenster jumped in again, "Don't answer that. Detective, the question is pointless."

"Really? It's actually the most relevant question that I've asked."

He opened the file folder that had been lying on the table.

"I have a police report here about a fight in a bar between Mr. Ducette and one Douglas G. Ward over your then girlfriend Candy Champion. I also have two reports here of incidences of loud domestic quarrels between you and your wife. One report states that some objects were thrown. Finally, a report of another quarrel at your home at Living Greens that took place out on the street in front of your home and witnessed by neighbors. Is this all factual?"

Again, DeStefano jumped in. "There can be no point to these questions."

"I'm just exploring their relationship. These reports indicate that your relationship, Mr. Ducette, with the deceased may not have been all that cozy. Don't you think?" He tapped the folder.

"We was just disagreeing over all these homes. I told Candy that I make enough money to support her. She didn't need to work and didn't need that apartment. That's all it was. We still loved each other." Darnell started to choke up a little, his emotions now becoming raw from the trauma of the day.

He composed himself. "All of this shit is just arguments. I didn't hit her or do nothing to her. She didn't hit me. Nothing happened."

D'Antonio jumped at this, "Objects were thrown and broken. Who threw them?"

Again, the lawyers stop the questioning. Darnell and the lawyers moved to the rear corner of the room for a whispered conversation and then returned to their seats.

"Candy did."

D'Antonio tented his fingertips and looked at Darnell then Fenster, then DeStefano.

"Well gentlemen. Here's the thing. Ms. Champion was a young, strong, and athletic woman. I can't picture her falling over the balcony rail accidently, unless, of course, she was drunk or drugged."

He paused and stroked his chin with his thumb and forefinger.

"In our search of the apartment, a suicide note was not found. You gentlemen may now surmise that I am skeptical of suicide or accidental death. Now the tox screen is still pending, so we will soon see what, if anything, was in her system that may have contributed to her death."

Fenster said, "We understand your reasoning. But it is speculation."

"Yes, it is, Mr. Fenster. That's why we gather facts. But you both already know that."

Fenster retorted, "Sounds like we're done here."

"Almost. I have one more area to explore."

"Very well. But please proceed quickly, Detective."

"Mr. Ducette, you have stated that you and your wife still loved each other. Correct?"

"Yeah."

"So please explain this to me. Why did you kill her?"

The two lawyers jumped to their feet shouting at Darnell not to answer the question.

Fenster yelled, "That is outrageous!"

"Why?" D'Antonio shot back. "Let him answer the question."

"Guys! I need to answer this or the Detective will think I'm guilty."

Darnell shook his pointer finger at the Detective.

"I did not kill my wife. I loved her. Period. Now, let's get the hell out of here," he said, looking at his lawyers.

D'Aantonio stretched out his big six-foot three-inch frame and chuckled.

"Why the panic guys? I was just asking. You all are a nervous bunch."

Darnell and the lawyers left the precinct headquarters. The two lawyers returned to Chester City in Ford Carr's private jet. Darnell took a luxury room in the city for the night. He returned to spring practice in Washington, D.C., the following morning.

CHAPTER 35:
ADA Kellerman

The following afternoon at 2:00 p.m. the bright sunlight was shining across the front steps of One Police Plaza in New York City. A microphone had been set up several feet away from the top step. Standing around it were city District Attorney Harrison Foxx, Assistant District Attorney Marcie Kellerman, and Detective Lou D'Antonio. Harrison Foxx was wearing a hand-tailored, summer weight, light gray suit with a white dress shirt with French cuffs and a pale blue tie. Marcie Kellerman was also nicely dressed in a pale blue women's business suit. Lou D'Antonios' suit was dark and obviously wrinkled. He wore a red tie, which was poorly knotted. His hair looked disheveled and he had obviously missed some spots on his face when he had shaved hastily earlier that morning. The detective had a seriously crappy night's sleep.

Assembled below were the men and women of the New York City press corps composed of members of the surrounding suburban communities. The press conference was being held in an attempt to toss some red meat to the pack of rabid wolves that was howling for information on the death of supermodel Candy Champion.

District Attorney Fox stepped up to the mike and began to speak.

"Ladies and gentlemen of the press...Ah...I..." The pack was still restless and noisy. "Okay! Please listen up! Please. I'm not going to shout over you people."

As Harrison Foxx patiently waited, the crowd soon settled down.

"I understand how anxious you all are for information concerning the death of Candy Champion. My team and I will try to give you what we can. With me today are ADA Marcie Kellerman and Detective Sergeant Lou D'Antonio. I believe you know them both."

Foxx gestured to Kellerman and D'antonio who were standing off to his left.

"You must first understand that this investigation is but a day old. The autopsy on the body of Ms. Champion has yet to be performed."

Foxx heard several shouts of why. He put out his hand in a stop gesture.

"All things take some time and there are some technicalities to overcome. For instance, the body of Ms. Champion is ah . . . well, in serious shape. But the autopsy is a priority and will soon be completed. The rest of the investigation is off to a vigorous start. I'm now going to turn the mike over to ADA Kellerman."

"Good morning, everyone. I will first make a statement and then both Detective Sergeant D'Antonio and I will answer a few questions. I will be the ADA assigned to this case and will be the prosecuting ADA if it is determined that a crime has been committed. Candy Champion died at the age of 25. Her death was apparently caused by an eight-story fall from the balcony of her apartment. I emphasize apparently. We don't know that for an absolute fact."

A shout of, "Why not?"

"Well, just to purely speculate, what if someone entered her apartment, murdered her and then tossed her off the balcony to cover up the murder. It's possible."

Another shout: "Is that what happened?"

"I don't know. Her death could be a homicide, a suicide or a freak accident. None of these possibilities have been ruled out as of yet. We only know that she died tragically. As District Attorney Foxx has already stated, we are only a day into the investigation. I am not yet up to speed on the details. Allow me to bring in Detective D'Antonio. He can shed some light as to the progress to date. Detective."

Sergeant D'Aantonio stepped beside Kellerman. He stood slump-shouldered to the mic.

Another shout: "Are there any suspects, Detective?"
D'antonio replied, "There would only be suspects if this is deemed to be a murder. We don't know that yet, as ADA Kellerman has just told you."

Another shout: "Ms. Champion was married to Darnell Ducette, quarterback for the Washington Red Knights. Have you talked to him yet?"

"Yes, I have. But only on a preliminary basis."

"What was discussed?"

"That is confidential for the time being."

"Is he a suspect?" someone yelled.

D'Aantonio snapped, "For the third time, there are no suspects or, for that matter, no persons-of-interest. Here's what I can tell you. Ms. Champion was found lying dead on the sidewalk below her apartment at approximately five o'clock yesterday morning. A citizen was on their way to work when that person saw the body. The police were called, and a patrol car responded several minutes later and secured the scene. I arrived on the scene just after 6:00 a.m. The investigation has been ongoing since that time."

"Who discovered the body?"

"We are not prepared to release that information at this time."

"What else have you learned?"

"No comment. We are not yet prepared to release any facts until more is known. As you all know, this is going to be a high-profile case and the NYPD, and the office of the District Attorney are going to treat it accordingly."

"Detective D'Antonio, can you give us anything about the status of the investigation. I mean what's been done so far, if anything?"

"Look, the crime scene is being thoroughly processed. The techs have gone over the sidewalk and have almost completed processing the apartment where Ms. Champion lived. I have a team interviewing every resident of that apartment building. An additional team is interviewing Ms. Champion's friends and co-workers. And, of course, the coroner's office will be processing the body very soon. Twenty-four hours into this mess, it's a good start. That's about all I've got for the time being."

D'Antonio looked wearily out at the mob of reporters. "Thank you," he said.

With that D'Antonio turned and walked up the steps to where Foxx and Kellerman stood and the three disappeared into the hallways of One Police Plaza.

Darnell stayed in New York City, paid for an upscale hotel room, and began making calls to members of his family, his friends, Candy's family and some of her friends. That task completed, he took a cab to a good restaurant and had an excellent steak dinner. He purchased a fine cigar, a pint of good scotch from a store the cab driver recommended and then returned to his room. It was a non-smoking room, but he lit up the cigar and poured some scotch into a crystal rocks glass. He then kicked back in a plush lounge chair and smiled. It had been a fine day. He puffed on the cigar and drank scotch for a couple of hours before going to bed. Darnell was a happy man.

A week later Candy Champion was buried in a family plot in Carrollton County just outside of Laureldale, the small town where she was born. The funeral was attended by a small group of family and friends. A light drizzle fell during the ceremony. Darnell conspicuously did not attend the event.

Since the completion of the interview with Darnell and his attorneys, Detective D'Antonio was busy pushing his squad hard to leave no stone unturned in the investigation of Candy's death. Everyone was working overtime. Teams of police officers were interviewing every resident in Candy's building and also talked to people she had worked with at the Lola Getz Agency, including Lola Getz. D'Antonio reviewed the autopsy results with the M.E. and assembled his detectives to review the results of the investigation which included the crime scene analysis of Candy's apartment and the sidewalk she had landed on. D'Antonio reviewed all of this with ADA Kellerman.

Detective D'Antonio received authorization to travel to Chester City to speak with Candy's friends and family. He did this while Darnell was attending spring practice in Washington, D.C.

Four days had passed since the Detective had received his diagnosis of colon cancer. He had yet to call one of the recommended oncologists, had yet to talk to his wife Rose and had yet to inform his superiors that he may need an extended leave of absence to deal with his medical issues. He also had yet to get a decent night's sleep. The precinct's leading homicide investigator had no idea how to handle this problem. He knew, however, that the clock was ticking on him. Tick. Tick. Tick.

CHAPTER 36:

Darnell's Second Meeting with the Police

A week after Darnell had started spring training, he received a call from the New York City police requesting he meet with Detective D'Antonio for further questioning. Darnell called Ford Carr and Ford again dispatched his team of lawyers to meet with Darnell and represent him.

Darnell, his attorneys, and D'Antonio all sat at the same table and placed their tape recorders and file folders on the table.

D'Aantonio opened by saying, "Good afternoon, gentlemen."

Darnell and the attorneys all nodded to the Detective. None of the three men felt that Detective D'Antonio looked anything like the man they had talked to at the first meeting. He looked older and tired.

"First let me say that the investigation into Ms. Champion's death has proceeded rapidly. We have made this investigation a priority. The abundance of newly discovered information has prompted the need for this meeting. There are things that require clarification. Now, before I proceed, I will read Mr. Ducette his Miranda rights. He obviously has you two gentlemen here to represent him, but I will follow departmental procedure."

Lawyer Fenster said, "So your investigation has reached this point?"

"It has." Fenster and DeStefano both nodded and D'Antonio read Darnell his constitutional rights.

"Now, Mr. Ducette, your wife fell from her balcony just before 5:00 a.m. on the morning of May 9th. I need you to account for your time from midnight until 6:00 a.m. that morning."

Fenster jumped in, "Detective, we need to consult."

The lawyers and Darnell walked to the far corner of the room, whispering to each other for a minute.

Darnell answered, "No problem. That's easy. My friend and security manager, Marcus Wayne, was at my home in Living Greens in Shawnee County. We were watching a baseball game and playing cards until around 2:00 o'clock in the morning. We didn't wake up until maybe ten or eleven in the morning."

"What teams were playing?"

"The Cubs and the Dodgers. From the West Coast. It went extra innings. Dodgers won six to five in twelve innings. No way could I be in New York City before five in the morning. Check it out."

"We certainly will. How long have you known Mr. Wayne?"

"Since we was kids."

"Okay. How can I reach him Mr. Ducette?" Darnell reached into his pocket and pulled out a business card with Marcus' name and phone number. D'Antonio scrutinized it a moment then pocketed the card.

The Detective then pulled a picture from the folder in front of him and handed it to Darnell.

"Do you recognize this man?"

Darnell was looking at a picture of a fairly large man dressed in jeans and wearing a hooded sweatshirt. His cap was pulled down over his face and the hood covered the cap, obscuring the view of the back of the man's head and neck. The man was also wearing gloves.

"Nah," said Darnell. "I can't tell nothing about him."

"Yeah," D'Aantonio remarked, "I can't even tell whether he's black or white." He shook his head.

"As I'm sure you know, a clerk occupies the front desk from 6:00 a.m. to midnight. After midnight the lobby is locked and you need a key card to enter. This man entered the building at 4:07. Just under one hour from Ms. Champion's death. He used a key card. Do you have such a card, Mr. Ducette?"

Fenster exclaimed, "No! No! We need another consultation, Detective." The three again retreated to the corner and had another whispered conversation before returning to the table.

"Yes," said Darnell.

"Now, once you take the elevator to the eighth floor and go to number 817, you would have to open the door, assuming no one would let you into the apartment."

D'Antonio paused and the lawyers frowned.

"Yeah, sure," Darnell responded.

"I have been advised that in this building it takes one key for the door lock and two more keys for each of the deadbolts. Is that correct?"

Darnell just shrugged.

"And you have all three keys. Correct, Mr. Ducette?"

"Yes."

"Then to access Ms. Champion's apartment when no one is on duty at the front desk, it takes three keys and a key card. We located another set of keys in the bedroom, which would obviously belong to Ms. Champion. Mr. Ducette, are you aware of any other sets of these keys?"

"None to my knowledge."

Fenster chimed in, "Detective, I don't like where you are going with this line of questioning."

"I don't blame you. Here's the deal, gentlemen. Ms. Champion's apartment was not broken into. Ms. Champion either opened the door to someone she probably knew, or someone else had keys. If there wasn't another unknown set of keys, then Mr. Ducette has the only other set of keys. Now Mr. Ducette, did your wife open that door for you in the early morning of the ninth?"

Fenster tried to jump in again, but Darnell said, "No" loudly. "I was with Marcus Wayne. I told you that!"

D'antonio's face brightened with a big smile.

"So you did. Guess I forgot." D'Antonio pointed at the picture of the unknown man.

"Here's another thing Mr. Ducette. We have questioned every person in the building. None of them recognize this man either. On the night of May 9th, only eleven people entered the building after midnight. Nine of them entered between midnight and two in the morning. One entered around two-thirty. Then we have our pal here coming in just after four."

D'Antonio paused and looked at Darnell and the two lawyers.

He again pointed at the picture.

"Gentlemen, whoever the hell this guy is, he's a murderer. I believe he killed Ms. Champion."

"Hold on! Hold on!" Fenster screamed.

"And how do you know that, Detective?"

"It's simple, Mr. Fenster. This man has a key card and he was able to open Ms. Champion's door. He had all four keys. Ms. Champion's keys were on her bedside table. The only other known set of keys belongs to Mr. Ducette. You can deduce that I think my mystery man sits across the table from me."

D'Antonio then smiled as the other three men in the room yelled at him.

It was Darnell that finally said to D'Antonio that he had no proof.

D'Antonio was still smiling while he replied, "I'll ask you again, Mr. Ducette, who else might have another set of keys? For Christ's sake man, it takes four keys. How many sets of four keys can there possibly be out there?"

Darnell laughed.

"I told you I don't know about any other sets of keys. That don't mean that Candy didn't give a friend or two a set. But hell, I wasn't anywhere near her apartment. I was back home. You ask Marcus."

"I will. And soon."

Both of Darnell's lawyers launch into logical reasons as to why D'Antonio was merely speculating. D'Antonio sat and listened to the lawyers patiently until they concluded their thoughts. He remained silent for sixty or seventy seconds before speaking again.

"What you gentlemen say may well have some validity, but I will present you with an undeniable fact regarding this case. It involves Ms. Champion's fall from the balcony. Had she jumped or fallen accidentally, her forward momentum would have propelled her body so that it would have landed further out on the sidewalk, or maybe even hit the street. That is simple physics. But she fell straight down. Her body landed directly below the balcony. Gentlemen, she was dropped from that balcony. Someone picked her up and dropped her. She may have been unconscious or dead when dropped. Now, Ms. Champion physically was a big, young woman. Whoever dropped her was most likely a fairly large and strong man. You know, like a professional athlete."

D'Antonio stopped talking, looked at the three men sitting across from him and grinned.

Fenster replied evenly, "That's still speculation."

"Baloney, Mr. Fenster. That's science."

"Detective," Fenster retorted "This meeting is solving nothing and I believe I'm going to terminate it."

"Suit yourself, Mr. Fenster, but I'll leave you with another thought. I am convinced our mystery man in that picture got into Ms. Champion's apartment and murdered her. In his haste to leave after dropping her from the balcony, he forgot to lock the door. You see there is crime everywhere in this city. New Yorker's keep their doors locked. That would be especially true if you rented an expensive apartment with two deadbolts on it for security. The killer screwed up."

Lawyer Fenster stood, followed by DeStefano and Darnell. Darnell took an extra moment to glare at Detective D'Antonio. The Detective noticed and locked eyes with Darnell. Finally, the three men left and D'Antonio sat there alone with a few thoughts.

The bastard did it. I know it. D'Antonio had gotten most of what he wanted out of the interview. He had tipped his hand with some of the information that he had given the three men and yes, some of it was speculative. But he knew that he had watched Darnell as he reacted and, in some cases, failed to react to what D'Aantonio had said. D'Antonio had played Darnell to a degree and he realized that Darnell was smart. He had bitten on some of the information but had remained poker-faced on the other stuff. He was one cool customer. He had killed his wife coldly and then dumped her over that railing like a sack of garbage.

He shook his head. He knew that he lacked sufficient hard facts to prove the case. But he couldn't take what he had to ADA Kellerman yet. He needed to push his team harder to get more. Dammit!

And then there was the damn cancer thing. It had been over a week and he had yet to act. The doctor had told him that it was critical to saving his life that he received treatment immediately. And yet he couldn't. He was working his case and slowly killing himself at the same time. My God!

CHAPTER 37:
D'Antonio Meets with Marcus Wayne

After the lawyers and Darnell left, Detective D'Antonio dialed the number for Marcus Wayne. After several tries, he spoke to Marcus and set up an interview with him the following afternoon at Darnell's home in Living Greens. He had decided he would bring a photo of the man in dark clothes to show it to Marcus and see what would happen.

The chief of the New York City PD had authorized Detective D'Antonio to take a commercial aircraft to Chester City and then rent a car while he stayed there overnight.

With a reluctance that he didn't understand, he called the office of Dr. Marc Garvey and scheduled an appointment with him for the following week. The doctor had been advised that Detective D'Antonio may call and explained the urgency of beginning treatment. D'Antonio had chosen him because his office was the closest to his home—no other reason. Now he needed to talk to Rose. Here he was at this stage of his life, an expert homicide detective very adept at interrogating murderers, but without a clue as to how to talk to his own wife of forty years about his cancer diagnosis.

D'Antonio began the conversation with Marcus Wayne at 1:22 in the afternoon.

"Mr. Wayne, it is my understanding after talking to Mr. Ducette that he is currently your employer. Is that correct?"

"I do security work for him."

"Okay. I understand that you two have known each other for a long time."

"Yeah. I been knowin' Darnell since we was kids. Went to school together. Then we went to Chester City State together. So you could kinda say we like brothers now. Know what I'm sayin'?"

"I believe I do. Now tell me, Mr. Wayne, how many times have you visited the
Manhattan apartment of Ms. Champion?"

"You mean that fancy new place of hers? Cause I ain't never been there."

"Then how do you know it's fancy?"

"Darnell told me."

"I thought that on the night of May 9th you drove him to New York City."

"What?" Marcus exclaimed. "Someone tell you that?"

"No."

"Well, it's bullshit."

D'Antonio reached into his pocket and pulled out the picture of the man in dark clothing taken in the lobby of the apartment building.

"You're a big guy. You play any football?"

"Sure. With Darnell in high school and at Chester City State."

D'Aantonio placed the picture in front of Marcus. "Here's the picture of a pretty large man. Is that you?"

"Don't think so. He looks too short. I'm six, six."

"Is Mr. Ducette smaller than you?"

"Yeah. Darnell, he six two maybe three."

D'Antonio pointed to the picture. "Is that Mr. Ducette?"

Marcus looked at the picture once more and grimaced. "I don't know. Can't tell who it is."

"Is that man about Mr. Ducette's size?"

"Hard to say. He's all slouched over." D'antonio retrieved the picture.

"Mr. Wayne, what if I told you that every person living in the apartment building where Ms. Champion lived was interviewed by the New York City police?"

Marcus shrugged. "Sounds like a lot of work," he said.

D'Antonio chuckled. "Oh, it was. But it was worth it. You see the deal here is that several of these people say they saw a large black man in the building on two or maybe three occasions. So, I'll ask you again. How many times have you been there?"

Marcus chuckled briefly. "Got to be a whole bunch of large black men in a place like New York City. You know? But I ain't never been there."

"What if I told you that several of those people identified you as having been in the building?"

"I'd say that's bullshit. Ain't never been there. Ain't you hearin' me?"

"Where were you on May 9th?"

"Right here in this house. With Darnell. He lets me room here."

"Did Mr. Ducette tell you to say that?"

"Darnell don't tell me what to say. You axt and I told you. May 9th wasn't that long ago. I just remember is all."

"Anyone else with you two?"

"No. Jus' us."

"And what were you two doing?"

"Playin' some cards and watchin' a ball game. Dodgers and Cubs. It was a late game coming from L.A."

"What was the final score?"

"Dodgers won it six to five."

"I thought you'd say that. Did Mr. Ducette tell you to say that?"

"No. That's what happened. Check it out if you want."

"I already did. Okay, Mr. Wayne, I think I'm done here for the time being, but please keep yourself available. I may have other questions later."

Marcus said, "I ain't goin' nowhere man."

"Well, thank you for seeing me."

He drove the rental car back to the airport for the flight back to New York.

The following week Detective Lou D'Antonio met with his oncologist. The doctor showed him multiple pictures from the colonoscopy. The pictures showed two cancer nodules in his colon. From those two malignant nodules, the cancer had metastasized. The doctor explained to the detective that the spreading of the cancer indicated aggressive cells and that an equally aggressive program of chemotherapy needed to be started immediately, if not sooner. D'Antonio groaned and shook his head.

"Dammit, how can this be happening?" The doctor had no concrete answers but emphasized the importance of beginning treatment. D'Antonio asked some of the usual questions: will I lose my hair, will I feel sick, will I feel tired, and could I continue working?

The answer to the first three questions were probably and the answer to the fourth question was no. Due to the mental and physical stress of his job, he would need to get as much rest as possible to allow his body to fight the cancer.

D'Antonio nodded and asked when he should get started. The doctor replied that he could get him started later that week. Lou said no. Not enough time to talk to Rose and inform his Captain. He made an appointment for later the following week to get the process started.

CHAPTER 38:
D'antonio and ADA Kellerman Speak

Lou D'Antonio had just completed his second trip to Chester City. On this trip, he spent two days speaking to Candy's friends, parents and other relatives living in the area. When he returned to New York City, he headed to his office to check any messages. The one that caught his eye was from ADA Kellerman who wanted to meet with him in her office at 10:30 a.m. the next morning. D'Antonio double checked his schedule and then called Kellerman, leaving her a message that he would be there at that time.

He was sitting across from Marcie Kellerman the next morning. The investigation was just two weeks old and D.A. Foxx, as well as the media, was pressuring her for more information.

Kellerman sighed, "Detective, I am now under some pressure from multiple sources on the Candy Champion investigation. I need everything you've got."

D'Aantonio also sighed and said, "Roughly it's like this. We don't have a single eyewitness. Nor do we have a confession. The physical evidence is solid but proves nothing. Other evidence is circumstantial. If you can get a jury to buy the preponderance of the evidence argument, it's worth a shot. But any defense attorney worth a damn could blow it all away."

"Detective, if I take this to trial, Mr. Ducette will have every top lawyer and forensic expert in the country on his team. He can afford it. I'd be facing some seriously heavy artillery. But, what the hell, lay it out for me, Detective."

D'Antonio cleared his throat and replied, "Fine. I've ruled out a suicide and accidental death. I believe it's a homicide. I further believe that Mr. Ducette committed the act."

He handed ADA Kellerman three pictures. One of the unknown man that he had given to Darnell, one of Darnell's face, and one full body shot of Darnell in regular clothing.

Kellerman looked at the photos and then looked at D'Antonio with her eyebrows raised.

D'Antonio pointed to the picture of the mystery man and said, "That man entered the apartment building at 4:07 a.m. in the early morning of May 9th. He had a key card that would give him entrance to the building. I believe he then went to the eighth floor and walked quietly to room 817—Ms. Champion's room. The cameras on that floor are inoperable so I can't prove this. I also believe that this man had the other three keys—"

"Three keys?" questioned Kellerman.

"One for the door and one for each of two deadbolts."

"Proceed, Detective."

"He then entered the apartment. Now let me stop there, Ms. Kellerman. The picture of the unknown man was shown to everyone residing in the building. No one recognized him."

"Not surprising, Detective. I couldn't tell you if he is black or white."

"Neither could any of the residents. I had my team go back to the residents and show the other two pictures. At first, they weren't told who he was. Only about 30 percent of these people knew him from the news and TV. Of those who recognized him without any prompting, only 22 said that they had seen him in the building at least once. My hunch here is that Ducette wasn't here much more than that."

"So?"

"Let me come back to that point."

This man is now in the apartment. I believe he is carrying a syringe filled with heroin"

"Excuse me, Detective. Another question. This unknown man. If he is in fact Mr. Ducette, how did he get to New York City?"

"Yes. Yes. I was going to get to that later. But I can only guess. There are no records of any airline flights, trains, taxi services, rental cars, or anything that we could locate that brought Mr. Ducette to New

York. My guess is he drove. If he did, I can't find any evidence that he used any of the parking garages in the area. Could be that someone drove him. Like his friend Marcus Wayne. But I can't shake their alibi. If I'm right, then Wayne or someone else knows Ducette did it."

Kellerman just nods.

"Let's see now. Our assailant is now inside the apartment with a loaded syringe. He now moves toward her bedroom and opens the door, or maybe it's already open. Who knows? I think Ms. Champion is sleeping on her back or on her right side. That's a guess. But Ducette sticks the syringe in her upper left arm and shoots her up. She probably wakened, but Ducette could easily subdue her. She is now out cold either way. Maybe even dead. Anyway, he puts the syringe in her right hand to get her prints on it. He also gets out a baggie with the heroin and puts her prints on that. He leaves both in plain sight on the dining room table and goes over to the balcony and opens the French doors."

Kellerman interrupted. "You certainly have a vision of this murder Detective."

"Ms. Kellerman, it's what all this circumstantial evidence tells me. I'd testify to anything I've said so far."

"Good. Please proceed."

"The next thing our boy does is grab one of the dining room chairs and moves it out to the balcony and places it by the iron railing. Now, a couple of quick points. We believe that Mr. Ducette has been in the apartment once or twice before. His fingerprints are in the two bedrooms, the bathroom, the living room, and the dining and kitchen areas. They are also on the dining room chair on the balcony. So are Ms. Champion's. No other prints are on the chair. Finally, Mr. Ducette's prints appear in only one place on that balcony. They are the prints of his two hands holding the railing. You know, like he'd just dumped her body over the rail and placed his hands on the rail as he watched it fall to the pavement."

Kellerman jumped in. "Detective, if he'd been in the apartment once or twice before, he could have just been standing there looking out at the scenery. That's what any defense attorney would say."

"Yeah. I know. But I like my version better."

"Now back to the bedroom where he returns and picks up Ms. Champion's limp body and goes back to the balcony where he simply drops her over the railing. It's now time for him to hustle out of there."

"Return to the heroin thing again Detective. How do you know what you told me is true?"

"I asked the M.E. to check the body for needle marks. The body was a mess, but he took a shot at it. He believes he found one mark in her upper left arm. He's 90 percent sure. He found no other marks and he did look at the bottom of her feet and behind her knee joints."

"Where the junkies try to hide the tracks?"

"Exactly."

"So that's why you think that she wasn't using? That this wasn't a drug overdose with a bad accident?"

"Yes, plus the fact that my team talked to her employer, her makeup artist, her wardrobe stylist, and her photographer. Any of those people would have noticed either needle tracks or screwball behavior."

Kellerman nodded again. "Go on," she prompted.

"Our guy now is in a hurry to get out of that apartment and out of the building. I think he listens through the door for any noise in the hallway. He then opens the door and sees no one, so he shuts the door and exits the building as quickly as possible. But, big mistake. He forgets to re-lock the door and throw the deadbolts. With all the crime in this city, what resident forgets to do that?"

Kellerman shook her head. "I see," she says. D'Antonio then put out his hands in a palms-up gesture.

"Then, I guess he leaves town. By car, I also guess. That's my theory."

"Can I assume that you asked her co-workers, friends, and family if she was depressed or suicidal?"

"We did. Absolutely everyone we talked to said that she was upbeat and enjoying her life and was looking ahead to her future. Some said that she was thinking of divorcing Mr. Ducette."

"Well, I'm not sure what to think. It is not a solid case. I just don't know. I'm inclined to dump it on District Attorney Foxx. See if he thinks it's worth a shot."

"I understand," replied D'Antonio. The Detective then left, expecting the answer he had received. If he was the prosecutor he knew that he'd give it a shot.

Kellerman sat in her chair and sighed deeply. "Well shit."

Later that evening Marcie Kellerman was relaxing at home sipping a glass of red wine. Like most New York City ADA's, she was always busy and was reviewing the files of current cases. Her phone rang.

"Good evening. ADA Kellerman speaking."

"Good evening, Ms. Kellerman. My name is Mitch and I wish to speak to you briefly. I apologize for interrupting your evening."

"I don't believe I know you, sir. How did you get my number?"

"Well, let's just say I have my sources."

"No. I'm going to hang up."

"Please don't. What I have to say will interest you."

"I doubt it. But I'll give you one minute."

"It is my understanding that you would dearly love to start up your own law practice. Am I correct?"

Marcie stuttered, "W—Why . . . Why, yes. Wait, who told you that?"

"My sources."

"What damn sources? Who the hell are you?"

"I'm a money man. I can make your dreams come true. That is, for a small favor."

"Oh sure, and what favor would that be?"

"You talk to Harry Foxx. Convince him that there is no provable case against Mr. Ducette in the death of his wife. Convince him that the death was accidental. Eliminate any open murder investigation."

"What the hell? Who are you?"

Mitch said pleasantly, "How much startup money would you need to open your practice? Say two hundred thousand? Would that work?"

Marcie paused, breathing deeply, heart pumping, and her body shaking with nervous excitement.

"Ms. Kellerman?"

"Ah . . . that would be enough. Is this a joke? Who are you?"

"This is not a sting operation, Ms. Kellerman. It is a business proposition. You perform the favor that I described and then you get the money. It will be wired to you in a Cayman Islands account in your name. I will give you the number of the account. No one will know and you will then be able to pursue your dream. It's really that simple."

"Okay. Let's say I'm interested. How do I know that I can trust you?"

"Frankly, you don't. But Ms. Kellerman, you make your living reading people. Witnesses, criminals, and jurors. Trust your gut. My gut tells me that you believe me. That you want this to happen. I will call you first thing in the morning. Inform me of your decision. If you comply, the money will be in your account in one hour."

"I am your dream maker. You will soon have full control of your life. Please believe me."

The phone clicked off.

Marcie put the phone down and stared at it. This Mitch guy said, "I will call you first thing in the morning," giving her the night to think about it. But why would she care? She had so much to lose. Or did she? Then she started thinking. Thinking about her life, her accomplishments. She was now forty-two years old. She had been hired by the New York City District Attorney's office right out of the Columbia University law school at the age of twenty-two. Twenty years later, she was now the lead homicide prosecutor for the city. She had accomplished much. And then she laughed a hollow laugh.

Yeah sure, she thought. You accomplished a lot and have absolutely nothing to show for it. You live in a rented, seven hundred square foot apartment in Queens' that is costing you two thousand dollars a month. You don't own a car because you couldn't afford to keep one in the city. So you travel by subway, bus or taxi or sometimes, you walk. You own some reasonably expensive business suits and some decent jewelry, a pair of diamond earrings, a string of pearls and an expensive watch. You have nothing to show for your achievements but your status in life.

She had also worked hard for the past twenty years. She had no meaningful relationships and was still unmarried. Not that this surprised her. She was relatively tall at five feet and eight inches but was thin at 122 pounds. She knew that she wasn't a particularly attractive woman. And it was true that she loved the idea of having her own law practice and owning her own home. Perhaps in Connecticut, out in the suburbs somewhere. Hm...

Could this offer be on the level? She was not a risk taker, but could she give this a shot? Risk everything for her dream? Oh hell, risk what? Status? You own nothing, Marcie. Not a damn thing. But you can sleep on it. This Mitch guy said that he would call you in the morning. Think it through then, dummy.

Marcie Kellerman spent a sleepless night tossing and turning over and over again in her bed. At a little after five o'clock in the morning, she gave up. She got out of bed, slipped on her robe and walked over to her kitchen where she started a pot of coffee. By 5:30 a.m. she turned on the early morning news and began sipping her first cup of coffee, wondering if the phone would truly ring later that morning. And if it did, and if it was this Mitch guy, what would she say to his offer? Yes or no. Yes or no. My God.

Deep in thought and paying no attention to the news broadcast on the TV, the thought struck her that this could actually be a negotiation. Why not ask for more money? But how much more? She became lost in thought about the question of whether or not there was in fact even more money on the table than Mitch's original two hundred thousand dollar offer.

She glanced at the clock. It was now 6:30 a.m. She went back to the kitchen for more coffee. Then she thought and sipped and thought and sipped. She looked again at the clock. Ten minutes after seven. Would the phone ring soon? She was still thinking about more money and realized what she was going to say to this Mitch guy. That is if he really did call.

It was 7:20 when the phone rang. Decision time.

Marcie Kellerman stared at her phone. Three rings. A fourth. She took a deep breath and picked up her phone.

"This is ADA Marcie Kellerman speaking," she said. "Good morning, Ms. Kellerman."

She recognized the voice. It was him. This was for real. "Mitch?" she inquired.

"Yes, Ms. Kellerman, this is Mitch. I have called to ask you for your decision per last evening's discussion."

Marcie took the plunge.

"My answer is yes, Mr. Mitch. However, there is an issue." She paused for several seconds trying to relax. Her heartbeat had quickened.

"And your issue is what, Ms. Kellerman?"

Here it goes.

"The money Mr. Mitch. It's not enough. To get what I want, I need three hundred thousand."

A low-pitched chuckle emanated from the phone.

"Well now!" His tone was a loud burst.

"So, you have accepted the essence of this offer. You wish to negotiate. Very well. How about 175? And don't push it."

"Be serious."

Another chuckle.

"Oh hell, Ms. Kellerman. I was hoping for a little more fun than that. I can go to two hundred and fifty thousand. No more." Marcie replied, "That's acceptable, Mr. Mitch."

"Excellent." He recited the account number.

"The money will be there in one hour. In return, you must convince DA Foxx not to prosecute Mr. Ducette and further convince him that it would make sense to rule the death of Ms. Champion as accidental. I would advise you not to spend your money until you have completed your part of the deal. There are consequences for failure. You do understand that I assume?"

"Yes, I do. You don't have to worry."

"Very well. Game on, Ms. Kellerman. Good day."

CHAPTER 39:
Darnell and Politics

It was now June and the 1992 presidential election campaigns were gathering force like a hurricane moving westward across the warm waters of the South Atlantic Ocean.

Ford Carr had called Darnell. He knew Darnell had a couple months of downtime between now and late July. The Democratic candidate Bill Clinton was ahead of the President George H. W. Bush in the polls and Ford explained to Darnell that he wanted to add more fuel into the campaign and fire up local anti-Democratic sentiment. He also wanted to add some zest into the campaign of Nelson Summerhays, a lackluster candidate at best. He described to Darnell a series of three bus tours that he expected to make through the Congressman's district to promote the Congressman's candidacy and to beat up on the reputation of the Democratic nominee, who Ford viewed as the Devil's spawn.

In the couple of appearances, he had made earlier in the year on behalf of Congressman Summerhays, Darnell discovered that he enjoyed the crowds and the political spotlight. In fact, he felt the competitive aspects of politics were not dissimilar to football. He also knew he was a better speaker than the galactically boring Congressman. And so, Darnell agreed to the tour.

By late June Darnell, Ford Carr, and the Congressman, along with two busloads of staff, hit the campaign trail. The first trip covered Shawnee County, the largest county by population in the district. This first trip would include a concert, a barbeque, and some sporting contests. The Congressman, Ford, and Darnell would deliver speeches after the events while the two busloads of staffers would canvass neighborhoods distributing pamphlets and campaign buttons and talking to potential voters. The second bus trip covered Holmes and Carrollton Counties with scheduled events very similar to the Shawnee County trip. Of course, more speeches were delivered. The final bus trip covered the southernmost counties in the district, Colton and Maynard.

By the end of the tour, Darnell had written and re-written his stump speech, which was an extension of the 'strive and thrive' speech he had delivered earlier in the year. He had given the speech over and over again to cheering crowds who greeted him with shattering applause. On a warm July evening, Darnell concluded his final speech of the tour.

Darnell pointed to the crowd.

"You all deserve to be rewarded for your hard work. You all deserve to run your businesses freely as free men under our Constitution. Free from burdensome and senseless regulations, free from stifling taxation, and free from the mindless bureaucracy of a government that does not hear you. You deserve the freedom to strive and to do your best. It is in this environment and only this environment that you will thrive and believe me, you all deserve to thrive. Thank you. God bless America."

As Darnell was preparing for a new football season in late July, Jack and Jill were getting ready to start broadcasting their show to a national audience. The show was to go live in October, a month before the general election.

With *The Jack and Jill Show* going national in the fall, Jack started experiencing some stress. Did he have what it takes to talk to a national audience? Or was he just a local, small market type of broadcaster? Time would tell, but he couldn't help feeling apprehensive. Barney's Tavern was located a couple of miles from the broadcasting studio and Jack began stopping at Barney's after work for two chilled vodkas. Soon it became three and later on four.

Jack did not see the trouble headed his way.

CHAPTER 40:
Jack and Jill

Jack and Jill talked often when they weren't on the air. She was aware of his daily trips to Barney's to relax and relieve some of the daily stress. The callers to the show were becoming increasingly hostile. Conservatives hated the Democratic nominee and liberals thought of the Republican incumbent as an old stuffed shirt. Jack was more than ready for his regular break at Barney's. Then Jill walked into his office.

"Hey, Jack. You heading over to Barney's soon?"

"Yeah, I am. What's up?"

"Oh, I was just hoping that I could join you. I could use a drink or two myself." Jack had invited her to come along before and she had always declined. He wondered, why now? Then he thought, what does it matter?

"Sure thing. Are you ready?"

"You bet I am." Ten minutes later they were seated at the bar. The daytime bartender, Mick, asked Jack if he was having his usual. Jill said that she would have the same and Jack told Mick to put hers on his tab. Jill stopped him.

"Oh no, you don't Jack. Mick, I'm Jack's partner on the show. This is my treat. My name is Jill." Mick smiled at Jill and looked at Jack. Jack nodded an okay.

"It's only fair. I make more money than you."

Jack mustered a quick laugh.

"I know, I know. Ford told me about that when he hired me. It's okay. I'm the rookie in this business and you're the seasoned veteran."

"Well yes, but I'm not too seasoned."

Jack chuckled again and said, "Of course not. Perhaps just a pinch of salt and pepper."

Jill smiled at Jack and put her hand on his. He glanced at her hand and his heart began to race. The touching was too familiar, and it made him nervous, but also put him on alert. Something didn't feel right.

A cat and mouse game of inane banter kept up for over forty- five minutes. By then they had each had three quick drinks.

Jack looked very deliberately at his watch.

"Hey, sorry. But I got to get going. Diana will be home by now. Thanks for the drinks."

"My pleasure. Thanks for allowing me to join you. See you in the morning."

Jack left Barney's as Jill ordered a fourth drink.

Jack went to Barney's, as was his habit, for the next several days. Jill did not ask to come along. But on the following Monday, she did. They continued to meet at Barney's every day that week. They had their drinks, two or three and then went their separate ways. The next week Jill did not go. The following Monday she asked to accompany him again. From that time to the November election Jack and Jill went to Barney's together every day. During the entire month of October, the political dialogue became increasingly more heated. There were now occasions when both Jack and Jill had to cut callers off because of the bombast and profanity of their language.

The Democrat Bill Clinton won the election in November and became the 42nd President of the United States. Congressman Nelson Summerhays won another term in Congress.

Darnell Ducette was having a stellar season with the Red Knights. The team had a six and two record after the first eight games. Darnell got a concussion in game nine of the season and the team lost it by a touchdown.

A week after the election Jack and Jill sat next to each other at the bar in Barney's

Jill said, "God, Jack, I'm brain dead after a week of post-election anger. Such venom. I've been through election rancor before but never at this level. What's wrong with people?"

Jill reached out again and put her hand on his. It was a gesture that she had been making with greater frequency. It made Jack uncomfortable and he had now realized that Jill was becoming far too familiar with him while at Barney's.

"Yeah, I feel the same way. If it's this bad tomorrow how should we play it? Tone down our responses or say the hell with it and throw more fuel on the fire?"

Jill kept squeezing Jack's hand and then rubbed it. She leaned into him smiling.

"Let's just play it by ear. I mean Jack, isn't that the way life goes? Don't you just go with what feels right and run with it?"

Not the message Jack wanted. He was becoming upset. She knew that he was a married man and still deeply in love with Diana. But maybe this was just some innocent flirting? No. Flirting is never innocent. Should he push her away? And what about their work relationship? That would suffer but it was the only relationship that interested him about Jill. What to do?

Jill had ordered another drink. Jack declined. Jack then said,

"Sorry Jill, but I need to get going.

"Nonsense. Jack, we have a lot to talk about." She gave Jack's hand another squeeze and then slide it off the bar and gently placed it on her crossed leg. Jack looked curiously at his hand resting on the exposed flesh of her leg just above the knee. She flashed a big smile.

"How's that, Jack?"

He quickly moved his hand and allowed it to rest on the bar top.

"What's wrong? Maybe you need to just relax. Chill a bit."

She now leaned fully into him and whispers,

"Jack, there are parts of me that feel even better. Would you like to touch them?" She put a hand on Jack's thigh.

"Cut it out, Jill. You know that I'm a happily married man. So just stop it. Please!"

Jack reached down and removed her hand from his leg.

"Of course I know. You can have your Diana from time to time and you can have me, too. It's okay with me." She flashed a pretty smile.

She was not unattractive, but she was no Diana.

"Tell you what Jill. I don't think I want to play this game anymore. I'm going to leave."

"Just what the hell is wrong with you? You owe me an explanation.

"No, I don't. You're coming on to me and I'm not interested. I'm married. I told you that. Whatever game you want to play it's not going to be with me. So please, forget about it." Jack placed several twenties on the bar and prepared to leave.

Jill stared at Jack, her brows knitting and an angry glare in her eyes, her mouth slightly open like a wounded animal bearing its fangs.

She snarled at him, "You bastard."

Jack was standing, turning for the exit but stopped and turned toward her.

"Me?"

"You coax me over here week after week. You encourage me to come with you. You wanted me and now what, you suddenly just dump me? Like I'm an old sack of shit! Well now! I'll be damned if I'll put up with that by some little dick like you, Jack Troop."

Jill was very loud. The people at the tables turned toward the bar. Mick the bartender became concerned.

"Miss. Jill," Mick said. "You need to calm down. Please. I'll get you a drink on the house."

Jill gave Mick a quick look. Then she looked back at Jack.

"Just go, Jack, I'll deal with you later. Thank you, Mick. Another drink would be great."

Jack left and drove home. His nerves were on edge as he parked his car curbside and walked to the front door of his apartment. He entered and said hello to Diana, who was sitting on her chair and listening to the TV news.

"Hey Di, would you like a drink. I'm going to have one."

"Yes, I would. Thanks, honey."

"Well thanks for the drink, Mick," said Jean Lange as she stood to leave. As she turned toward the front exit her eyes had become hard and glaring, and her heart had turned to stone. She allowed her eyes to scan the dining room, back and forth, back and forth. People had turned their heads. Turned to watch her leave. The crazy woman who had yelled at the young man she had been sitting with. Jean felt like she could read their thoughts. Oh my, she is so much older than that young man. Why did she yell at him? Obviously, she embarrassed him. Well now, who could blame him? What a bitch.

Jean Lange knew what they were thinking, but she walked out of Barney's with her eyes focused on the exit and her head high. Fuck these people, she thought. You all just think you are better than me but you're not. And fuck Jack Troop; time to teach you a lesson you little shit. Jean knew his address. Knew where he lived. It was only a twelve or fifteen-minute drive. Payback time!

Jean entered her car and placed her handbag on the passenger's seat. She reached into the bag and extracted her .38 Smith and Wesson revolver. She turned the safety off. She then started the car and headed over to Jack Troop's address. It was now dark. She could deliver her message and not be seen.

When she got within two blocks of Jack's apartment, she put her headlights on dim and started driving the car slowly up the block. House by house she crept forward. No other cars were moving along the street. She realized it was dark enough that she couldn't read the house numbers, so when she came to the beginning of the block Jack lived on, she hit the high beams and read off a house number. She then dimmed the lights again and started counting upwards house by house until she arrived in front of the Troop residence, stopped and cut the lights completely. She reached over and picked up the revolver with her right hand and lowered the driver's side window. She aimed the gun at the Troop's front door and then took her two- handed grip. She slowed her breathing like her father Calvin had taught her many years ago. Breathe; breathe slowly, in and out, in and out. She squeezed the trigger.

CRACK!

The first bullet slammed into the front door.

CRACK!

The second shattered the front window and lodged into the rear wall of the living room. Both Jack and Diana shrieked and dropped to the floor. CRACK! CRACK!

Two more bullets hit the front door. Lights on the car still off, Jean Lange drove quietly away. Jack and Diana lay on the living room carpet shaking. After nearly two minutes, hearing no other shots, Jack crawled over to the desk in the living room and picked up the phone and called the police.

Ten minutes later a police cruiser arrived with two patrol officers. The officers took both Jack and Diana's description of what had happened and noted the bullet holes, the broken window and the bullet lodged in the rear living room wall. The officers requested help to process the crime scene. Neighbors were out in the street, despite the November cold.

Both went to bed early that evening after the police had left. Neither had eaten supper and neither had any appetite. Both were restless.

Jack had loaded his gun and placed it on his nightstand before trying to sleep. He and Diana had managed to drape an old blanket over the shattered window to keep out the cold.

He finally drifted into a light and restless sleep. Diana couldn't sleep at all and stayed awake until the early hours of the morning. She was asleep on the couch when Jack came downstairs to eat a quick breakfast. She heard him moving around the kitchen. She got up off of the couch and padded into the kitchen. Jack was sipping black coffee and eating cold cereal with half of a banana sliced into it. Diana poured some coffee for herself and sat down with her husband.

"Jack," she began. "Do you have any idea what happened last night?"

"Other than some jerk shot at us? Not really, but I could speculate."

"Okay. Please do."

"I've been awake off and on all night. I gave it some thought. You realize that I am a talk radio host. Of a political talk show. I'm a controversial personality to some people. Maybe some whack job got pissed at me and took a few pot shots."

"Really?"

"Di, I'm kind of fuzzy in the head and the truth is that I don't know what to think. Maybe it was just some random idiot. Who knows?"

"Well, all I know is that now I'm scared. You're going to work, and I've got to sit here worrying about when the next shot is coming."

Jack takes took a sip of coffee and put his spoon down.

"Look, honey, I've got a show to do this morning. I've got to get going in a minute. Go on and get out of here for a day. Maybe a couple of days. Go to Scarsdale and visit your parents. Please. It's a good idea. Don't worry about me."

Diana chuckled.

"How could I not worry about you? But I like your idea. I'm going to clean up and go visit Mom for the day. I'll get back around the time you get home. How's that?"

"It's a plan." Jack bent over to Diana and gave her a firm hug and a long kiss. "It's gonna be fine." Jack was full of apprehension about confronting Jill that morning. As it turned out, she had called off for the next two days, telling the station manager that she wouldn't be back until Monday. Dale Updegraff, the station manager, was pissed and informed Jack that the show was his for the next two days. Jack was fine with it. He was actually relieved.

On Monday morning Jack drove into the studio worried about what would happen when Jill arrived. What would he say to her? He didn't have long to wait. Jill opened the door to his office, shut it loudly and walked up to Jack, standing directly behind his back. Jack froze.

Jill said in a cold voice, "Well Jack . . ."

He turned to face her and stood up. She stared directly at him, her voice still cold as ice. A chill went through Jack from the top of his head to the pit of his stomach. He realized that this woman was a creature that he didn't really know or understand.

"How are we going to do this show together now that I completely despise you?"

"I have no idea. Carry on as usual?" Jack knew his response sounded lame.

"That's what I thought. So I'll tell you. We will both behave like the professionals that we are. And that will be it. No more friendly chit-chat, no drinks together, and no . . . well, no nothing. Got it?"

"Fine."

"And Jack. Just so you know. No man ever turns me down. Never. Not ever. I want to make you pay for your behavior, believe me."

"My behavior? That's crap, Jill. You came on to me knowing that I wasn't at all interested. Don't you stand there and try to rewrite the script."

She laughed at him. "You are so pathetic."

Jack didn't feel pathetic. But he did wonder how he had gotten himself into this predicament.

The show carried on over the next couple weeks. However, it quickly became lackluster since the two co-hosts quit interacting with each other. The show lost its zest and the audience began losing enthusiasm. It quickly became clear to Ford Carr that something was wrong between his two co-hosts.

CHAPTER 41:
Jack and Ford Carr Speak

Thanksgiving soon passed and *The Jack and Jill Show* dragged on as the ratings began their inevitable decline. That week the entire Shawnee County region was greeted by the first snow storm of the year. Jack made his way into the studio on a frosty Wednesday morning with six inches of new snowfall on the ground. Jill had not yet arrived, but Jack thought nothing of it. The relationship at this point was just as frosty as the new snow. As was his habit, Jack began immediately to prepare for the morning's broadcast. About a half hour before show time, Ford Carr walked into Jack's office, then shut and locked the door.

Ford said, "Morning, Jack. Listen up."

Jack turned toward Ford. He was waving a letter in his right hand. "This is from Jill." He handed it to Jack. "Read it. Please." It read:

> *To: Ford C. Carr*
> *Dear Sir:*
>
> *Effective today, December 1st, I resign my job as the co-host of The Jack and Jill Show. I cannot work with Jack Troop another moment longer. This decision is final.*

The letter was signed, Jean M. Lange.

"Mr. Carr, I don't know what to say."

"You don't? How about telling me just what the hell is going on?"

"Sir, I'm honestly not sure. It's probably a misunderstanding that she had concerning our personal relationship."

"Personal relationship? What the hell is that? Were you screwing her?"

"No, sir! Mr. Carr, over the past couple of months we were going up the street to Barney's Tavern together. We'd have some drinks and talk shop. It is my feeling that she was making more of this than it was. So I broke it off. To put it mildly, she got pissed off."

"So, no sex?"

"No. Mr. Carr, I am happily married to a very attractive young woman. I have no need to go elsewhere for sex. You've met her. I would not wreck our relationship for Jean Lange or any other woman." Ford looked at Jack skeptically, then shrugged.

"Jean is an attractive woman, you know."

"Mr. Carr, sir, you've met Diana and you know Jean Lange. Believe me when I tell you that Jean Lange is no Diana."

"Well, good point. So you're saying, no bullshit now, that you had no physical interest in Jill?"

"None. Under the circumstances, why would I want to, oh say… put my banana in another fruit bowl? Speaking metaphorically that is." Ford laughed at this.

"Okay Jack, you've made your case. But now that the show has gone national, you're going to have to carry the ball until I can replace Jill. You might wish to tell that young wife of yours that you will probably be working some serious overtime during the holiday season. Sorry. Not a good Christmas present for either of you."

"Oh, I'll manage, sir. So will Diana. We're a team."

"Good. Good." Ford Carr was correct. Without Jill, Jack did have to carry the show. He found himself working twelve-hour days, seven days a week, and coming home to Diana completely exhausted. He'd eat dinner with her and then they'd hug and kiss before Jack went off to bed. Their active sex life suffered greatly. Jack would leave the house around five in the morning and get home between six and seven each evening. That routine ground on day after day through a somewhat dismal Christmas.

Three days after Christmas Ford Carr again entered Jack's office before the morning broadcast.

"Good morning, Jack."

"Good morning, sir."

Jack turned toward him.

"Jack, I got some welcome news for you. I have hired Jill's replacement." Jack's face lit up brighter than the Christmas tree he had just taken down.

"Great! That's wonderful, sir. Can I assume that you have a few details for me?"

"You can. Jack, I have hired, shall I say, a more mature woman as your co-host. She is a Republican and can fill in Jill's old role as the antagonist to your point of view. For over the past twenty years she has been a speechwriter for Republican candidates and has appeared on TV from time to time as a political talking head. She is much older than you and is less bombastic than Jill but very knowledgeable. Her name is Laura Ringold. Have you heard of her?"

Jack rubbed his jaw and spoke, "I think her name rings a bell."

"Good. Now she won't be starting until late January, so you'll still have to keep busting your butt. Sorry."

"I've made it this far, sir. I can finish it."

"Excellent. I am going to arrange a meeting with you and Laura shortly before she starts and then leave for my annual trip to Europe for a few months."

"That's fine sir." Jack thought, how nice for you, and then inwardly groaned.

Jack, Ford, and Laura Ringold met in late January. Jack realized that Laura was around sixty years old, give or take a couple years. He thought to himself that he wouldn't have the problems with Laura that he had with Jill. Thank God. Ford and his two co-hosts chatted together for half an hour and then Ford left to prepare for his overseas vacation. Laura and Jack talked for a couple hours and had lunch together. On Tuesday, February 2nd, 1993, the new show, now called *America Speaks*, began at 7:00 a.m. that morning.

Jean Lange was a survivor. She had never forgotten the lessons her parents Calvin and Faith Ann had taught her throughout her childhood and into her early adulthood. During her time off when working she had thoroughly explored Shawnee County. She was delighted to discover the Piney Woods campground and resort located in the northeast tip of the county.

The resort was bordered by the Shawnee River on its northwestern perimeter and the Clark County line on its northeastern and southern perimeter. There was a boat dock on the river. The resort featured a man-made lake located in the heart of the property. It had a boat dock and a sandy beach. Two water slides were located in the shallow water of the lake.

The lake was named Piney Woods Lake, which was ringed by small clusters of rental cabins. There were also rental cabins near the Shawnee River. The resort featured a large clubhouse with games available on rainy days. There were video games, pinball games, and several pool tables and ping-pong tables. There was also a seating area where one could watch multiple TV sets. A snack bar was open during the summer season.

Jean knew that the cabins were easy to rent during the winter months, so she rented a cabin on a month-to-month basis. Her cabin was a small but comfortable one bedroom and one-bathroom unit. Other than the bedroom and bathroom the entire cabin was open space. Living, dining and kitchen space constituted the remainder of the layout. Simple, but very livable. Jean moved out of her small apartment. The apartment had come furnished, so all Jean had to do was to take her clothing and personal possessions with her.

She spent the winter at the Piney Woods Lake doing some fishing and some hiking, just relaxing . . . and working on a plan to kill Jack Troop. That was now her sole purpose in life. She had killed two men who had wronged her before. She would have no problem killing again. Jean believed in payback but had no idea that she had no heart and no soul.

CHAPTER 42:
Clete Chambers

Clete Chambers could be easily described as the classic loser. He was twenty-three years old and still lived with his parents. He had no marketable work skills. Clete had dropped out of high school in his senior year and had managed to get a part-time job at a local Dairy Queen in Chester City. He worked twenty hours a week either flipping burgers or building ice cream cones and making milkshakes. He was paid minimum wage. His future was dim, but he wasn't so dumb that he didn't know it. Mostly, he just didn't care.

He was average height and weight, with unkempt brown hair and brown eyes. Clete was awkward socially and never made friends while attending school. He had no distinguishing physical features or any odd mannerisms. He was one of the millions of human beings that looked unremarkable, that were, in fact, unremarkable, and that no other human being ever paid the slightest attention to except some members of his family.

Clete had a younger sister, Megan, who was in her junior year at Chester City State University majoring in mathematics. Megan was an A student and never did understand her brother's lack of desire to achieve. Their older brother Chuck had already graduated from Chester City State and was now working for the accounting firm of Foster and Weinberger located in downtown Chester City. In his brief time at Foster and Weinberger Chuck had been promoted once and had received two raises. Chuck's goal was to move up the ladder and secure a management position. From there he wanted to start his own firm.

Clete was the family failure. His parents, Martin and Judith, never failed to remind him of this at every opportunity. They had ranted at him without mercy when he had dropped out of school. It had required parental consent, which Martin and Judith never gave. Clete kept refusing to go back to school and was finally considered truant. That brought in the police and Martin and Judith just couldn't have that, so they ultimately gave their consent. His sister, Megan now paid little attention to him. He didn't even aspire to try for a full-time position at the Dairy Queen. He liked having time for himself. Throughout their childhood, his big brother Chuck was always willing to play games with him and had encouraged him to always do his best. Chuck had never uttered a cross word to him or berated him in any way. In Clete's mind, Chuck was more than a brother—he was his best friend.

While at Chester City State, in addition to majoring in accounting, Chuck was the starting quarterback for the university's football team, until an unexplained accident had injured him too severely to ever play football again. Chuck had fallen down a flight of stairs in the university's athletic dorm. Chuck had told just about everybody who would listen that he had been deliberately pushed down the flight of stairs. Over the past several years, Chuck had talked to Clete about this more than anyone else. He had told Clete that he believed it was Darnell Ducette who had pushed him. After all, once Chuck had been injured, it was Darnell who had been elevated to the position of starting quarterback. Clete believed his older brother without qualification. He was loyal to Chuck without any reservations.

Clete became obsessed with finding a way to get even with Darnell for ruining Chuck's life, but he could not figure out a good way to accomplish the deed. With increasing frequency Chuck, now a bitter young man would tell Clete that someone should just shoot the legs out from under Darnell. Then, like Chuck, he would never be able to play football again. It was this kind of talk that finally triggered in Clete's mind the beginnings of a plan.

As a child, Clete realized that there was one thing that he did extremely well. Since he was eight years old, Clete's father Martin had taken his youngest son on hunting trips. Father and son hunted everything. They hunted waterfowl and turkeys. They hunted deer each and every deer season without fail. By age ten, Clete shot his first deer and had not failed to shoot a deer for over a dozen years now. At age fifteen his Dad took him upstate to hunt black bear. Clete shot and killed a 370-pound black bear on his first time out. By then he knew that he had been born with a steady hand and sharp eyes. He could hit anything that he aimed at. Thinking logically, why couldn't he shoot the knees out from under Darnell Ducette? He knew he sure as hell could. It was only a question of getting close enough to Darnell to take the shot.

It would be that thought that would occupy Clete's mind as the weather became colder and colder as winter deepened over Shawnee County. He would find a way to shoot Darnell's knee up so badly that he would never be able to play football ever again. He would be just like his brother Chuck. Darnell would cease to be a hot-shot pro-football player and become an ordinary person, just like Chuck. He would have a limp, just like Chuck. The revenge would be so sweet. He would make it happen. But he didn't yet know exactly how.

CHAPTER 43:
The Threat

Jack had stopped going to Barney's after work and instead decided he would come straight home and have his drinks. The plus side to this change of habits was that Diana would be home and he would have some extra time each day to be with her. There also would never be any of his co-workers asking to accompany him to Barney's. It was a cold day in January when he arrived home in the late afternoon, greeted his wife with a hug and a kiss, and then poured his first chilled vodka. Diana also wanted one and they both sat down at the kitchen table to chat.

"Oh honey, here is your mail." Diana placed two envelopes in front of Jack and waved another in her hand. "This one is also addressed to you but there is no return address."

"Oh? Let me see it." It was indeed a plain white envelope. Jack opened it. Diana watched him, equally curious. It was a short message to Jack, only six words. It said:

JUST REMEMBER, JACK. NEVER. NOT EVER.

It was not signed, but Jack knew who wrote it. It was Jean. She had previously said those exact words to him in a low and threatening voice. The letter meant only one thing. The original threat was not an idle one. A quick chill went through him. He remembered the cool cruelty in her voice.

Diana saw the look on Jack's face.

"Jack, what is it?"

What to say to her? Jack wondered if he should tell the whole story or try to lie his way out of this mess. "Jack?"

She placed her hand on her husband's arm. Jack handed her the letter. Diana stared at the letter and furrowed her eyebrows.

"Jack, I don't understand." Jack expelled a long breath.

"Di, it's from Jean. Jean Lange, from the show."

"Oh . . . but Jack, I thought she quit the show." Her hand was still on Jack's arm and he reached over and covered her hand with his. He gave her hand an affectionate squeeze.

Jack began, "I guess I need to explain things." Jack plunged into the story of how he got into the habit of
having drinks at Barney's and then Jean accompanying him on a regular basis. He described Jean's flirting and then her overt offer of sex at her place.

Diana, the emotional woman that she was, screamed, "Jack! What! What the hell!"

He implored her to relax.

"Relax? Relax hell! You fucked her?"

"Diana! No. Please just listen." Diana glared at him and stood up from the table.

"Listen. That night. The night where four shots hit the house. You remember?"

"How could I not? Now answer me! Were you with her?"

"No. No, honey. Please just listen to me. That was the night she said those words to me. I had told her that I had no interest in her at all. Which, by the way, was about the fourth time I had said that to her."

He told her he believed it was Jean who fired the shots, but he didn't want to alarm her that evening, so he just decided to ignore the entire incident.

"Di, my concern was trying not to offend her. Obviously, that didn't work."

"Perhaps you should have been more concerned about offending me! How in God's name could you have allowed yourself to get into such a situation?"

Jack just hung his head. "I know. I know. But Di. Really. Nothing ever happened. I had no interest in anything happening. None. Please believe me."

Diana sighs.

"Okay, Jack. I believe you. But sometimes you are so damn stupid. And naïve."

"Guilty on both counts honey. But always, always, Di, I will come home to you and no one else. I was so stupid. Please."

Diana smiled, leaned over to Jack, and kissed him on the lips.

"Okay. But listen to me, Jack. That letter. That letter is a threat. She's back and looking to harm you."

"I know. We should contact the police again."

The following afternoon they both met with Detective Billy Washburn and explained the situation to him. The detective said there was little he could do. If the letter was a threat, it was an implied threat. Nothing specific.

Jean Lange was sure that by now Jack Troop had received her letter. Both he and that prissy little Italian bitch that he had married knew she would come for them. It was only a question of when.

Well, today was the when she had decided. But she wouldn't kill either one of them. She wanted to terrorize them first. Make them afraid every day of their lives until she finally killed Jack Troop and may even the bitch he had married.

It was a dark, black, winter evening. The wind blew the clouds around, keeping the moon partially obscured. There was not much available light that evening. Just the deep black and unseeable sky and the relentless cold. The darkness matched the darkness in Jean's heart. She had put on her warmest clothing and her heaviest winter coat. Her .38 revolver was cleaned and fully loaded. Jean also carried a small pouch with extra ammunition, although she did not expect to need it. But like her father always told her, be prepared, Jean. Always be prepared for anything.

She fired up her car and headed out of the resort area to make the drive to Chester City and the apartment where the Troop's lived. Time for a little fun and games.

For the second time, Jean drove her car slowly toward the Troop residence. Once again, when she reached the stop sign, which was her signal Jack's home was on this block. She dimmed the lights and moved slowly down the street. It was late in the evening and no cars were moving and the lights in some of the houses were already off for the night. She pulled up in front of Jack's apartment and lifted the gun from the passenger's seat. The lights were still on in the Troop home and so were the lights of his next-door neighbor. She stuck the gun out of the driver's side window and fired.

CRACK.

The first shot went through the window. The same window that she had shot through the last time.

CRACK! CRACK!

Two more shots into the front door.

CRACK! CRACK! CRACK!

Three shots randomly into the front siding. Nothing going on yet. She didn't hear any sirens. Nobody could be seen at the front windows looking out. But Jack and Diana Troop had to be awake. Perhaps they were hugging the floor. Good.

Then the neighbor's door opened and a man poked his head out to look. Jean had rejected the empty cylinder and put in a fresh fully loaded cylinder.

Let's terrorize the neighborhood, she thought.

CRACK! CRACK!

Two shots at the neighbor. She had deliberately missed him. After all, she had no beef with the man. The neighbor ducked into his house as soon as the first shot hit the siding above the door. The second shot hit the door as the man closed it.

CRACK! CRACK!

Two more shots into the Troop house.

CRACK! CRACK!

Two shots into another neighbor's front door. Jean dropped the gun on the passenger seat and hit the gas, lights still dimmed. The sound of sirens could be heard in the distance.

By the time three police cars arrived on the scene, Jean Lange was long gone, having made a turn that would connect her to the road back to the resort. She kept her foot on the accelerator knowing that a BOLO would go out looking for the shooter. That would probably mean roadblocks, so time mattered. She made it back to her rented cabin without incident. Nobody had seen more than a dark car with one shooter behind the wheel. Nobody got a plate number. Jean Lange had gotten away cleanly, just as she had expected she would. She was confident she had frightened the shit out of the entire neighborhood. The thought brought a crooked smile to her face.

CHAPTER 44:
Detective Billy Washburn

Detective first grade Billy Washburn had earned his new rank just ten days ago. He was young for a detective first grade, just thirty-three years old. It was the feeling that Billy was destined for a captaincy before the age of fifty. Billy was a good-looking guy. A bit over six feet and a muscular one hundred and ninety pounds, he had a thick head of dark brown hair combed straight back and held in place by lots of gel. Billy was single and dated various young women on a regular basis. Other than his job all Billy did was date and hit the gym.

On the evening that Jean Lange shot up the houses on Heritage Street, Billy was the lead detective on duty. He got the call from the 911 operator just after 9:30 on that dark, cold evening. He was advised that three patrol cars were now on the scene and the officers responding had already determined that no civilians were killed or wounded.

Heritage Street was in a predominantly white, middle-class neighborhood in the southwestern part of Chester City. Billy put on his winter coat and drove his unmarked car over to Heritage Street, arriving about fifteen minutes after he had received the call. Upon exiting his vehicle, the Sergeant in charge hurried over to him to give him the preliminary report. The other officers were busy securing the crime scene.

"Sergeant Elmore," Billy began, "what have you got for me?" The Sergeant glanced at his notes.

"Well, we have determined that no one has been injured. It appears that minor damage was done to three homes. Mostly from bullets going into the siding, doors, and windows of the homes involved."

"Anything on the shooter or shooters?"

"Not much, Detective. Witnesses are reporting they observed a car stopped on the street in front of house number 44. Most of the witnesses agree that it was a dark colored vehicle, but no one could be specific about the exact color. Most of them agree that there was one shooter in the vehicle. No one could supply a description. We put a BOLO out for a dark colored sedan with a single driver. That's not much but it's what we got."

"Okay," the detective replied. "So, the houses that took the shots are numbers, 43, 44 and 46. Is that correct?"

"Yes, sir."

"And the shots were fired from the vehicle stopped in the street? No other shooter or shooters?"

"I don't know if we know that for sure. But witnesses didn't see anyone else."

"But that doesn't mean there wasn't."

"Yes, sir."

Washburn glanced out at the street. He pointed. "Is that about where the car was?"

"Yes, sir." Washburn took several steps out into the street.

"I don't see any casings, Sergeant. What's up with that?"

"Simple. We didn't find any."

"Could the shooter have fired with his hand still inside the car?"

"Well, we got one witness, Mr. Townsend, that says he saw the shooter with his arm stuck out the window. He said that he saw the gun."

"If we believe that, then the casings would be on the pavement. But the shooter didn't stop to pick up casings. No time for that. So, the weapon was a revolver. That how you see it, Sergeant?"

"Yes, sir."

Billy Washburn stopped talking and scanned the area, noting the relationship of one house to another and then looking to the opposite side of the street and noticed homes of similar construction.

Most of the homes were older but not in disrepair. Basic cars in the driveways. No Lincoln's, Cadillac's, or any remotely upscale.

Sedans and economy cars, some relatively new, but most were older, all looking reasonably well maintained. A solid middle-class block.

As Billy studied the area a van pulled up and parked in the middle of the street. The crime area was blocked off from traffic coming or going by police cruisers. Four crime scene technicians exited the van, all carrying various equipment.

"Sergeant, make sure the crime scene boys processed the three houses both on the interior and exterior. I wanted all the bullets that were fired. We stay until we have them. Does anyone know how many shots were fired?"

Sergeant Elmore chuckled. "Sir, the witnesses place the number anywhere from five to twenty. I got other wits that say the number was a lot. Period. But I got one wit that says it was twelve and he's one hundred percent positive."

"What's his name?"

"Jack Troop sir. He and his wife rent the bottom floor in number 44."

"Jack Troop? I know that name from somewhere I think."

"He hosts a political talk show. It's on morning radio. He also mentioned your name. Said he and his wife talked with you about receiving a threatening letter. Said that you said the threat was implied at best. Nothing you could act on."

Washburn rubbed his right temple. "Yeah. Yeah, I remember now. Okay. He in the house?"

"Yes, sir."

"I'm going to talk to him first. You and your men carry on for now."

"Yes, sir."

Washburn strode up the walk of house number 44 and knocked. He heard a woman say come in.

He entered. Both the woman and the man stood.

"Good evening. I'm Detective Billy Washburn and I have been assigned to your case."

Both Jack and Diana nodded.

Diana said, "Yes, my husband and I have spoken to you before. Last December. Do you remember?"

"Yes, Mrs. Troop, I do. It was about a threat. In a letter. Now tell me please, do you still have that letter?"

"I do. Shall I get it for you, Detective?"

"Please."

Diana went to the desk in the rear of the living area while Jack motioned for him to take a seat. Diana handed him the letter. Washburn had put his plastic gloves on and accepted the letter, touching it on its extreme outer edges. He read it again, studying it briefly.

"Mr. Troop, you told me this was a threat. I can't remember who you think it came from."

Diana jumped in.

"The bitch. Jean . . ."

"Jean. Jean Lange," Jack said.

"Yes, yes," Washburn replied. "Now I remember. She was your co-host. You had a relationship with her."

"No," Jack replied sharply. "We were co-workers only. Any relationship was one that she had assumed. There was no reality there."

"So, her assumption of a relationship caused her to be angry enough to take a few shots at you?"

"Correct. She fired four shots at my house that first time. This time she fired twelve."

"Twelve? You're certain?"

"Yes."

"Please explain that to me, Mr. Troop. What makes you so certain?"

"Well Detective, it was the sequencing of the shots. She fired the first shot. She paused and then shot twice more. Then another pause, followed by three more shots. All at my house. Then there was another pause. Maybe fifteen seconds. I think she ejected the cylinder of a six-shot revolver and then inserted another loaded cylinder and started firing again. She fired in two-shot bursts. First to my neighbor on my left, then to my neighbor across the street and finally two more into my house. In all, eight shots into my house and two into each of my neighbors. I guarantee that your techs will recover twelve slugs."

"We'll see, Mr. Troop. Can you describe Jean Lange for me?"

"Sure." And Jack proceeded to do just that.

"Okay. Can you describe her car?"

"Yes. It's a black Chevy Impala. I'm not sure of the year but it's fairly new, maybe two or three years old."

"Thank you."

Billy Washburn had written everything down. He then thanked the Troops and went to each of the neighbors whose houses had been shot at and interviewed them, but didn't get as much information as he had received from Jack and Diana Troop.

Jean Lange was certainly a serious suspect and for now, the only suspect. He knew, however, that he had much work yet to do.

CHAPTER 45:
The Shootings

While Clete was busy plotting his revenge against Darnell, Darnell was flying high. But while flying high is an exhilarating experience, it always carries the risk of a crash landing. By early December, the death of his wife Candy Champion had been ruled an accidental death. Darnell had smiled when he got the news. Darnell was now free and clear and still flying high.

The Red Knights, under Darnell's leadership and outstanding playmaking, was 12-3, going into their final game of the season against the New York Giants. They won the game despite Darnell sustaining a mild concussion early in the final quarter. The Red Knights won the division and Darnell led the team to a win in the first playoff game. They were scheduled to face the Wolves from the central division of the NFC North. Darnell left the game at the end of the half with a torn pectoral muscle. They lost the game by two points. However, he still won the NFL MVP award, having led the league in passing yards, completions, and touchdowns. Despite losing to the Wolves in the second playoff game, Darnell was still gaining altitude.

After the surgery, while Darnell was rehabbing the pectoral muscle tear, he was anticipating a large new contract that would be negotiated by his agent Ricky Jolly with the Red Knights' management staff. He was back home at Living Greens, a widower and dating a new young white woman.

☘ ☘ ☘

In late January, Clete started following Darnell's comings and goings from his home at Living Greens, trying to formulate a plan to shoot him.

☘ ☘ ☘

During this time period, Jack ignored any possible threat from Jean and moved on with his work life with his new partner Laura.

☘ ☘ ☘

However, since Jean's letter, Jack began carrying his gun again, something he had stopped doing after he left Scarsdale. Both he and Diana viewed Jean Lange as a very real threat.

Ford had remodeled the broadcast studio, adding enough space to accommodate an audience for two hundred people. The morning news was reviewed each day when the show began and afterward, the daily guest was introduced. Both Jack and Laura would interview the guest and then the guest would take questions from the live audience.

Laura was new to the business of entertaining on a daily talk show. It was on Jack's shoulders to carry the show. He was the star of *America Speaks* and quickly discovered he loved the role. He came into the studio each morning ready and excited to entertain and enlighten his audience. He felt he had found his calling in life. He liked the daily task of educating his audience on the critical affairs that mattered in the world. He couldn't imagine that anything would ever again change for the worst. But it is the lack of foresight that is often a curse to the young.

☘ ☘ ☘

Clete Chambers had long known that he was not the sharpest tool in the shed. But that never bothered him much. He asked his brother Chuck if he knew where Darnell lived. Chuck had told him that Darnell had a multi-million-dollar home in the Living Greens community where he lived when he wasn't playing football. Chuck also told his brother that it was a gated, secure community patrolled by private guards. He drove over there one afternoon after he finished his shift at the Dairy Queen. He parked across the street and spent several hours watching people come and go in their nice shiny cars. He figured Darnell would own a car like that. Darnell was also black. Clete didn't think that a rich white community would have a whole lot of black people living there so he began going to Living Greens every day after work looking for a black man in a nice car to exit the front gates. This was good thinking on Clete's part, as there were no other black residents in the entire community. After three days, he believed his patience had been rewarded. A black man with a blonde woman in the passenger seat left the community in a shiny Porsche. Clete started his old sedan and followed them. He was proud of himself for figuring this much out.

He followed Darnell for about eight miles when the Porsche turned into a restaurant called the Always Prime Steakhouse. Clete turned in behind them.

Darnell parked the car in the front of the lot by the restaurant and entered, accompanied by his blonde girlfriend. Clete had parked toward the rear of the lot. Clete sat for an hour and a half until Darnell and the girlfriend left and got into the Porsche. Clete fired up his car and again followed as the Porsche left the lot.

It was mid-winter and dark by now. Clete had more difficulty following but kept up with the Porsche as it headed north. About fifteen miles later the Porsche entered the parking lot of a nightclub called Dewey's. This time Clete had a long wait before Darnell and the blonde left the club. He even nodded off briefly and panicked when he thought he might have lost them. But the Porsche was still parked, and Darnell and his companion got in the vehicle some four hours after they had entered. Clete again started his car and followed them back to Living Greens.

Clete now began using all of his free time to watch the comings and goings of cars entering and leaving Living Greens. He had purchased a camera and was taking pictures but his focus remained on the Porsche. When it left, he followed. He discovered the Porsche often left around mid-morning with Darnell driving without the girl. Routine errands were run—buying groceries, stopping at the bank, and picking up the dry cleaning among them.

It took a couple of weeks before Clete realized that the black man he had been following wasn't Darnell. He was a larger man with long hair. Clete had no idea who the man was, or how he figured into the picture. He further realized that the driver of the Porsche while on these morning errands was sometimes Darnell and at other times the big man.

The one consistency that Clete finally seized upon was that each week on a Friday or Saturday night, Darnell and the woman went out to the Always Prime Steakhouse and then on to Dewey's. He believed that he could count on this pattern of behavior. If he were to succeed in shooting Darnell, it would have to be at the steakhouse or the club. He decided to check out both locations in the daylight and figure out the best spot to shoot his prey. He was becoming excited as the plan to shoot Darnell began to take shape in his somewhat feeble brain.

A couple of weeks before Clete finalized his plan, he entered Dewey's and sat at the bar, drinking a beer while watching how Darnell and the blonde white woman interacted. Clete knew that there had always been talk about big shot Darnell always dating pretty white women. Being close to his target stimulated his desire to get on with the shooting.

⁓⁓⁓ ⁓⁓⁓ ⁓⁓⁓

It was dusk on the night of March 25th. The air was cold and crisp. The sky was clear with a visible half-moon. There was a wisp of a breeze.

It was a busy Friday night at Bill's Barbeque on the east side of Chester City. Jean Lange eyed the new Ford sedan that was parked between fifty and sixty yards away. She crouched behind a car near the wooded area at the far end of the parking lot. She was dressed in a black sweat suit with a dark blue ski cap over her head so that only cold, blue eyes showed through the slits. In her right hand was a .38 caliber Smith and Wesson revolver.

Jack had felt good that night. He had managed to finish up the tasks he needed to complete a couple of hours early. The couple had gotten into the habit of going to Bill's Barbeque for ribs on Friday evenings. Sometimes they would also go to a club for drinks and dancing. That Friday, March 25th, they had just finished their rib platters and were drinking the last of their wine. Jack paid the check

227

and they both headed to the coatroom and then left the restaurant, eager for the coming evening of music and dancing. A deep purple sky dotted with a few stars now hugged this section of planet Earth.

Clete had spent the day cleaning his deer rifle and getting ready to head over to the Always Prime Steakhouse where he would ambush Darnell and mess him up good, just like Darnell had done to his brother. He wouldn't kill him. Just shoot off a kneecap. Clete thought if he did that, the bastard would never play football again. Just like Chuck. Everything would be even by night's end. Sweet revenge was about to happen.

Clete also realized that he might go to prison. He believed that he would probably get caught. After all, how could he outsmart the entire Chester City police department? He'd get maybe ten, twelve, or fifteen years. Live in a small cell with a bed, sink, and toilet. Not much different from the room he lived in now. Maybe they would make him work at some crap job. Hell, he already had one of those. He'd eat shitty food. But Mom couldn't cook worth a damn anyway. Prison life would probably be boring. But other than this night, his life was boring anyway. In stark reality, everything would be pretty much the same. Nothing at all to risk. His life was nothing but an empty room in an empty world. A prison cell would merely be a change of address. Just do it, Clete, he thought.

On the evening of March 25th, Clete sat in his car waiting for the Porsche to appear. Just after 5:00 p.m. it did. Darnell had the girl with him. Hot damn, the hunt was on.

☼ ☼ ☼

Jean, who had been waiting patiently, now spotted Jack and Diana as they exited the restaurant.

As Jack and Diana walked over to their car, neither of them saw the black-clad figure back by the woods some fifty yards away. They were thinking of the pleasant evening ahead and totally unaware of the danger that lurked just yards away. As they reached their car, Jack noticed the black-clad person walking steadily toward them with the right arm extended.

☼ ☼ ☼

Before Clete had left for the Always Prime Steakhouse, it occurred to him that when Darnell and the girl returned to the Porsche from the restaurant, it wouldn't take long for them to enter the car. He realized he needed to slow them down to get a clear shot when they were outside of the vehicle. To accomplish this, he brought along his hunting knife. It had a thick eight-inch blade that Clete kept honed razor sharp. Once Darnell and his girlfriend Lily Rainwater went into the restaurant, Clete got out of his car and walked quickly over to the Porsche. He admired the sleek vehicle briefly but quickly took the knife and squatted down by the rear of the driver's side. He plunged the knife into the tire. He then pulled down on the knife to widen the gash. He heard the air hissing out of the tire, looked around and then walked back to his car. The tire soon flattened. Darnell would now have to go to the rear of his car and assess the damage. That would slow down his entrance into the Porsche. He would have plenty of time then to put a couple of bullets into Darnell's knee.

⁂

At first, Jack didn't understand. But then he saw the gun and immediately cursed himself again for leaving his gun in the car. He had gotten careless.

Jack hollered, "Diana! Gun! Gun! Get down!"

Diana looked over at Jack not comprehending the danger.

"Get down now! Now!" A shot rang out and hit the pavement about three feet in front of him and then ricocheted past him, striking the rear end of a car that was parked in the next row of cars.

Diana dropped to the pavement.

Diana yelled, "Jack, are you alright?"

"Yes! Yes! Stay down!" Jack opened the car door and dove over the driver's seat reached for the glove compartment and pulled out his .380 automatic. He started to push himself out of the car in order to return fire.

Another shot.

The bullet struck him in his right foot. He screamed out.

"Jack! Oh my God! Jack!" Diana began running to Jack's side of the car. Another shot followed by another. Diana felt a disturbance in the air as a bullet whizzed by her temple. The second shot hit her in the forearm just below the elbow. She dropped to the pavement again, screaming.

Another shot.

It missed Jack and struck the brickwork of the restaurant, just above the sidewalk. People in the building were up and moving, having already heard the previous shots.

Another shot.

It caught Jack in his right butt cheek. People were now streaming out of the restaurant, making the shooter stop and start to back away. The sound of sirens could be heard in the distance. A couple cars with would-be-patrons had entered the parking lot and stopped. The people in the vehicles could see the shooter and could see Jack and Diana lying on the pavement writhing in pain. The shooter fired a last shot toward the crowd in order to slow them down.

⁂

Jack had dropped to the pavement and had the presence of mind to roll on his back, lift his head, and point his gun in the general direction of the shooter. He began pulling the trigger as blood from his wounds began to stain the pavement.

With the tire of the Porsche flat as a pancake, Clete only had to wait. A little over an hour later, the sunset. Darnell and the blonde left the steakhouse and were heading over to the disabled Porsche. Clete picked the deer rifle off the passenger seat and quietly opened the driver's side door. The window of the car was all the way down. Clete stood outside the car, using the frame of the opened window to steady his rifle. He kept the rifle trained on Darnell as he moved to the car.

Darnell noticed the flat tire. He said shit and casually walked to the rear of the Porsche. He turned away from Clete, bending down and looking at the tire.

⁂

He said shit again. Clete was now perfectly sighted in on Darnell's left knee. A loud shot. A bullet crashed into Darnell's left leg about two inches above the knee. Shit, Clete thought and re-sighted the rifle. He immediately squeezed off two quick shots, both of which tore into the knee joint. Darnell howled with pain, now down on the asphalt of the parking lot.

Hot damn, Clete thought.

Then, for good measure, he put another shot into Darnell's left shoulder.

Darnell lay on the pavement dizzy with pain. Blood from his knee and shoulder gushed onto the pavement. His blonde companion was afraid but anxious and started to stand. She had hidden behind the rear bumper of the car. When her head and shoulders appeared above the rear of the car, Clete promptly put a bullet in her left shoulder. The hell with Darnell's bitch, he decided.

Clete then hopped up into the driver's seat of his car, tossed the deer rifle into the rear seat, and fired up the engine of the old car.

※ ※ ※

With the mounting commotion around the barbeque restaurant and Jack returning fire, the shooter turned and ran back near the wooded area. Her car was parked there. She went to enter it but then thought better of it and instead moved into the wooded area, found concealment, and waited to see what would happen.

Jack laid on the pavement, groaning and bleeding and going into the first stage of shock. Diana crawled around to where her husband was laying and tried to comfort him, not knowing what to do to help him. An ambulance drove into the parking lot along with several police cruisers. Diana jumped up on her feet and began hollering for the ambulance while clutching her bleeding forearm with her opposite hand.

※ ※ ※

Clete pulled slowly out of his parking space and turned onto the exit path from the steakhouse. He turned right, away from his direct route home and slowly headed up the road as emergency vehicles and police cars swarmed over the scene of the shooting. Darnell and his girlfriend were barely conscious when help arrived.

Clete drove several miles up the road, obeying the speed limit and then took a left turn, drove a couple more miles and then took another left. He pulled onto a dirt path and followed it for a couple hundred yards. He cut the engine and turned off the headlights. He got out of the car and went to the trunk and removed a tarp. He carefully wrapped the rifle in the tarp and tied it tightly. He took a breath and walked slowly toward a group of rocks and boulders with the rifle held between his left arm and body. He located a small gap between several of the larger rocks and slid the rifle into the opening. Once the gun was hidden, he returned to his car. Lights on low, he returned to the back road and then followed it, moving slowly until it connected with the main road a couple miles below the steakhouse entrance. The traffic was moderate. No cop cars were in sight. He eased the car onto the road and gradually accelerated to the speed limit and headed back home. He was relaxed and smiling all the way. He had taken vengeance for his brother Chuck. He had never been happier.

The Chester City Chronicle reported the next morning that radio talk show host Jack Troop and his wife Diana had both been shot and wounded by an unknown assailant last night. But the biggest feature was that star NFL quarterback Darnell Ducette and his girlfriend had also been attacked and shot by an unknown assailant also. The police had no suspects, no leads. There was speculation that maybe one shooter wounded both couples, but the timing was not right for that to be possible. The spokesman for the Chester City PD stated for the record that these were distinctly different and separate incidences occurring at nearly the same time at night. Coincidence or some kind of coordinated attack? No one knew. But what was known, was that it had been one helluva night for sure. It was after all a…well…

SON OF A BITCH.

The investigations of the two shootings would fall to Detective Billy Washburn. That Jack Troop had been shot and wounded somehow had not surprised him. In the case of quarterback and sports celebrity Darnell Ducette

and his girlfriend, he knew the investigation had better be by the book, with absolutely no screw-ups.

He planned to interview all four as soon as the doctors for each patient cleared it.

CHAPTER 46:
Recuperation

The gunshot wound to Jack's right butt cheek was not severe and was easily repaired surgically. The bullet had entered just below the hip joint and passed through the muscle and fatty tissue, exiting just at his butt crack. The bullet to the right foot was a much bigger problem. It had hit his heel and passed through the heel from right to left. As the bullet passed it shattered the heel bone. Both large and small pieces of shattered bone had been removed, leaving very little bone to support the foot well enough to walk on. The general surgeon consulted with an orthopedic surgeon and both doctors agreed that in order for Jack to walk on it again, it had to heal first. After it had thoroughly healed, the orthopedic surgeon could attach an implant to take the place of the lost bone tissue. It wouldn't be perfect, and Jack would probably have a limp for the remainder of his life, but he would be a fully functional human again considering his current lifestyle. He spent ten days in the hospital before being released. A surgery to insert the implant was scheduled for early June.

Detective Billy Washburn had arranged a joint interview at the hospital with both Jack and Diana.

Upon entering the room, he said, "Mr. Troop. Mrs. Troop. I'd like to spend a little time with you today and get your take on the shooting."

Jack was starting his fourth day in the hospital and Diana had joined him for the interview.

"So please," Billy began, "describe to me what you saw."

Jack started, "Well we both left Bill's Barbeque together and began walking toward our car."

"Where exactly was it parked?"

"Around the middle of the lot. About fifty yards from the woods." Jack looked at Diana.

Diana echoed, "Yes Detective. That would be correct."

Jack continued, "I saw a person moving toward us. My impression was that this person came out of the edge of the woods and began advancing slowly toward us."

Billy nodded.

Diana chimed in, "Jack, don't forget the right arm. It was extended out. Toward us."

"Yes, that's true." He paused. "This person was dressed to remain unseen. Dark clothing, either black or dark blue. Definitely wearing one of those ski masks—the ones with the holes for the eyes and nose."

"Then what?"

"I realized at that point that this shooter had a gun held in the extended arm. It was pointed at us."

"What kind of a gun? Any idea?"

Jack paused again. "My hunch is a revolver, but that's kind of a guess."

"Mrs. Troop?"

Diana just shook her head. "I honestly didn't see the gun, Detective. Jack started yelling gun, gun and then yelled for me to get down. I did and then heard the first shot."

"Yeah. That one hit the pavement in front of me."

Diana said, "Yes. That's correct. I was ducking down at the time. I was very scared. I think Jack was still standing." Billy turned toward Jack.

"I was still standing. I was concerned for Diana. I had a .380 automatic in the glove compartment. I made a big mistake. I should have carried it. I do have a conceal carry permit." Billy Washburn was nodding as Jack spoke.

"Anyway, I opened the car door. Sort of dove over the driver's seat. My gun was in the glove compartment and I got it."

Diana jumped into the narrative.

"The shooter fired a third time and almost hit me in the head. I could feel the bullet pass by my ear. I had stood up when Jack screamed, and I was going to go to him but then a shot hit my forearm." Diana held up the bandaged forearm as if the Detective couldn't see it.

"It just grazed the bone Detective and went through the soft tissue. No major damage."

Washburn grinned and said, "Well, that is good news, Mrs. Troop."

"Yeah," Jack said. "But the shooter fired a fifth time, and it caught me in the ass, which was hanging out the door. Just imagine being shot in the ass. It's humiliating."

"I can think of worse," Billy replied wryly. Jack snickered at the remark.

"Anyway, another shot was fired. I believe it went over both of us."

Diana said, "Yes. I think it went out toward the restaurant."

"I dropped to the pavement and then rolled over on my back and looked back toward the shooter. I just started firing in that direction and the shooter turned and retreated."

"Yes," said Diana, "I saw the shooter run back toward the wooded area."

Washburn kept scribbling into his notebook.

"Would either of you have any idea who the shooter might be?" Diana, her dark brown eyes flashing, practically shouted, "Oh hell yes! It was the god-damn stinking bitch that Jack worked with. It was Jill. Jill Lange. She's the one you want."

"Ah, Detective. Her first name is actually Jean. Jean Lange."

"Well now. That's interesting but perhaps not surprising," Washburn replied. "You see after the ambulances took you both away to the hospital we began interviewing people from the restaurant. Some had looked out the windows when they heard the shots. Others had come out of the restaurant to see what was going on.

"None of them saw much of the shooter. They all say that the shooter ran off toward the wooded area. But the gist of your story is pretty much confirmed by the eyewitnesses. By the time we had finished interviewing witnesses, one of the uniforms hollered out that there was still a car parked back by the woods. The registration was in the glove box. It was registered to Jean M. Lange. Bingo." Washburn grinned. Jack and Diana smiled. Got the bitch.

Jack spent another twenty minutes discussing his relationship with Jean and the possible motive for the shooting. Diana mentioned the note that was sent to Jack by mail again—the one with no forwarding address. Washburn said that he hadn't forgotten.

He thanked them for their time and left.

After Jack was released he went home to rest and recover. The time period for his recovery was flexible but would be at least six weeks. During this time span, Laura Ringold would soldier on with the show by herself. While her task was difficult, the extra work and responsibility only accelerated the rate in which she learned the business. By the time Jack returned to the show he had a seasoned partner.

Jack's butt had healed but still retained some soreness. His foot had healed as well but was sore. Jack's surgery to put the implant in was several weeks away. For those weeks Jack had an orthopedic boot and he used a cane.

Darnell's girlfriend's wound was not serious. The bullet had penetrated the soft tissue of her upper arm and continued on through. The bone had not been hit. Her wound was cleaned and stitched up, and she was given something to help her sleep and rest.

Darnell's circumstance was different. The wound to his shoulder was more serious than Lily's but was easily patched up. However, his left leg was severely injured. The first shot caught Darnell just below the knee but hit bone and shattered it. The two shots directly to his knee were even more devastating. The entire kneecap splintered and the connecting tissues were in shreds. Major blood vessels had virtually exploded. None of the emergency surgeons were equipped with the training to deal with a knee injury this serious. A prominent orthopedic surgeon in the area who specialized in joint repair was called in to consult. After he had examined the knee, he saw no acceptable way to repair it. He believed the lower leg would have to be amputated. Darnell's leg was wrapped, and he was made comfortable so he could sleep until morning. When he awoke the next morning, he was advised of his predicament. Darnell, upon hearing the news, simply froze. He froze mentally. He froze physically. He was asked questions but couldn't speak. He finally closed his eyes and remained motionless. He fell asleep for several hours and soon one of his doctors was summoned. Darnell was awakened, and the doctor advised him it was urgent that the leg came off. The risk of sepsis was growing. Darnell was silent, but he did give a head bob, nodding his consent.

The operation was performed that evening. Lily Rainwater waited while the surgery was completed and cried on and off for several hours ignoring her own wound.

In June, Jack Troop had his surgery to put the heel implant into his right foot. The surgery was successful. Jack was instructed to stay off the foot for a full month after being released from the hospital. Compliance with this instruction resulted in Jack's absence from the show for the month. After that, he worked the show for several weeks from a wheelchair.

CHAPTER 47:
Clete Chambers' Undoing

Clete Chambers knew that he wasn't smart but was feeling more confident after several days passed without being arrested. More days passed. Still no cops knocking at the door with an arrest warrant. As the spring warmed to early summer, Clete remained in the clear. He was still working at the Dairy Queen and the arrival of warmer weather produced bigger crowds and overtime. Clete didn't mind since he needed the money. It also helped keep his mind off the probability of a knock at the front door by the police.

As summer passed and September arrived Clete was still a free man and now beginning to believe that he had pulled it off. He had outsmarted the cops. It was at that point he decided that he could go back to the rock pile to get his rifle. After all, hunting season would soon begin.

Several evenings later he pulled his old car off the road and drove back down the rutted dirt path to the rock pile. He was somewhat nervous and started to sweat profusely. What if the cops were waiting for him? He turned his low beams off and parked the car about seventy yards from the rock pile. He sat in the dark for a while trying to let his nerves calm. It was what you did before you shot a rifle. Deep breath. In and then out. In and then out. Calm. Stay calm.

Now relaxed, he exited his car and walked slowly toward the rock pile. He went directly to the small cavern between the rocks where he had stashed the hunting rifle. He reached in. Felt around. Nothing. He tried again. Still nothing. It was gone. He started to sweat, panic setting in. Did the cops have it? No. If they did he would have been arrested by now. Okay, look around again. Maybe you got the wrong spot. He canvassed the entire rock pile but came up empty.

He realized the gun should have been where he had first looked. What the hell? It didn't just up and walk away. Someone had found it. That was the only explanation. But who? Who would have been messing around in a rock pile and accidentally found his rifle? Or did the police get a lead and find it? But no, again he would have already been arrested. Puzzled and confused about his missing rifle, Clete could think of no other option than to go back home and forget about it. He drove back home and went to his room. He soon fell asleep. Nothing he could do about it one way or another.

Strange things happen. As it would turn out, two boys both aged eleven had been playing with squirt guns on the rock pile. They were playing soldiers. One dropped his squirt gun into the gap where the rifle was hidden. In the child's search for the water pistol, he discovered the rifle. He and his friend decided to take the rifle home with them. Joey, who had found the weapon, asked his parents if he could keep it. His father was a sportsman and knew a good deer rifle when he saw one. He knew it belonged to someone and thought it strange that this quality deer rifle would be hidden between some rocks. Perhaps the gun was stolen. He and Joey took the weapon to the police who questioned the boy about where and how he discovered the rifle. Joey explained. The rifle had a serial number, which was checked. The gun was registered to Cletus L. Chambers of Chester City. A routine ballistics test was made. The bullets fired from Clete's rifle ultimately matched those that hit Darnell and his girlfriend Lily. Case closed.

The knock on the door that Clete Chambers had feared came several days after the discovery of his missing rifle. He was arrested and charged with the attempted murder of Darnell Ducette and first-degree assault on Lily Rainwater. Clete now sat in jail day after boring day awaiting his future trial.

The trial of Clete Chambers took place in the late fall of that same year. Clete was represented by a public defender named Henry Frankel. Chester City ADA Claire Rasmussen was the prosecuting attorney. During the trial, Prosecutor Rasmussen called forensics expert

Dean Dockerty to give the testimony linking the deer rifle to Clete and then the ballistics test linking the bullets that struck Darnell Ducette and Lily Rainwater to Clete's rifle. Clete's older brother Chuck was also called as a hostile witness. While Claire Rasmussen had to struggle with Chuck's reluctance to say anything that might harm his brother's cause, she eventually got him to admit he had told Clete countless times that it was Darnell Ducette who had pushed him down the third-floor stairs, causing the extensive injuries that kept Chuck from ever playing football again. A security guard at Living Greens testified that he saw Clete Chambers sitting in his car across from the entrance to the community at least six or seven times. Speculation was that he was waiting for Darnell, but the judge excluded this observation. The young boy Joey who found Clete's rifle testified as to where and when. The nook in the rock formation where the rifle had been hidden was only two miles from the Always Prime Steakhouse.

Attorney Henry Frankel didn't offer any defense and called no witnesses. Clete's parents did not testify on his behalf.

The trial lasted less than a day and the jury came back in forty minutes with a verdict of guilty as charged for the aggravated assault of Lily Rainwater and guilty as charged in the attempted murder of Darnell Ducette.

Clete was scheduled for sentencing in March of the following year.

Nearly one year after Clete shot Darnell and Lily, he received a sentence of five years in the case of Lily Rainwater and twenty years in the case of Darnell Ducette. The judge decreed the sentences were to be served consecutively, making the sentence twenty-five years.

Clete didn't blink at the sentence. His friend, his big brother Chuck, had been avenged. That bastard Ducette was short a bottom leg and was out of football. Fuck him, Clete thought and laughed out loud right in the middle of the courtroom.

CHAPTER 48:
Rayford Prison

Rayford Prison was built in the early 1930's when crime in the state was rampant. It had been decided the facility should be built somewhere near the state capital. After some searching, a large parcel of land was purchased twelve miles north of the capital on a long and wide sloping hill that was free of greenery except for grass, weeds and some shrubs. The prison was built on top of the hill and had enough square footage to accommodate a thousand inmates.

Rayford hill was sixty feet high but with some contouring, a large, flat area was created to build the needed square footage. The prison was constructed with steel and concrete and was a dull gray. The building was two stories high. The inner barrier was fifteen feet in height and built with a smooth ten-foot concrete wall, from which jutted five-foot steel poles that support the barbed wire that ringed this inner barrier. Ten feet out from the first wall, another wall of steel was built. This wall was also fifteen feet high and topped with the razor wire. The top three feet of the second fence was angled back toward the interior of the prison to make climbing it nearly impossible.

Rayford Prison had undergone some updates in the 1960's to comply with the more humane standards of prisoner treatment that had become somewhat popular but controversial at the time. Regardless of the updates, by the time Clete Chambers was checked in to begin serving his twenty-five-year sentence, Rayford was not the kind of place that anyone would want to spend a major portion of their life.

Ford Carr had called Mitch the Fixer shortly after Clete arrived at Rayford. Again, he was unaware that he was actually speaking to Gino DeLeo. Ford expressed his concern that Clete had shot a person that was a very important member of his organization. Ford told Mitch that Clete would probably be paroled long before the conclusion of his twenty-five-year sentence and was concerned that once he got out of prison, he may well seek revenge. Of course, Mitch knew Ford was referring to Darnell Ducette. The mission Ford wished Mitch to undertake was to make sure that Clete would be unable to shoot a rifle again whenever he got out of prison. Mitch advised Ford that fixing such a situation from inside Rayford prison might not be possible, but he'd see what he could arrange. That ended the conversation.

Gino then called the real Mitch and outlined his conversation with Ford Carr. Mitch had done two years at Rayford when he was nineteen. He had been convicted for a couple of breaking and entering jobs. Mitch knew the prison's layout and a few people inside. He told Gino he might be able to work something out, and then asked what kind of money Ford was willing to spend. Gino advised Mitch that he was told money was not an issue; he just find a way to do it.

Clete had been in Rayford for just over eight months. He lived in an eight-by-six cell that was furnished with a cot. On the cot was one skinny pillow, a grayish sheet that was probably older than he was and a worn-out wool blanket with two holes in it. The cell had a lidless and seatless toilet and a sink that only had cold water. Hot water was considered a potential weapon.

It was early on Friday evening just after supper. Supper was served at 4:30 sharp. After supper, the prisoners returned to their cells. Clete was in cell seventeen on block E of the main floor of the prison. He was scheduled for his weekly shower that night.

The guard on duty was Sergeant Packman. The Sergeant was into his twenty-second year as a guard and was forty-five years old. He was over six feet tall and weighed nearly two hundred and sixty pounds. About forty of those pounds were gut. The Sergeant was married with two teenage children and lived paycheck to paycheck. He and his family lived in an older home in downtown Rayford. His wife worked as a waitress at the Rayford Diner at the far end of town. The paycheck-to-paycheck existence was a constant strain on the family, and four years ago the Sergeant discovered there was money to be made by doing favors for prisoners or from people who wanted contact with prisoners.

Over a month ago Sergeant Packman met a stranger who called himself Mitch who was willing to pay for access to a prisoner named Clete Chambers. The Sergeant told Mitch such a thing was possible. Ultimately a deal was made, and the action would occur on that Friday evening in the shower stall where Clete was to wash up.

That evening, the Sergeant escorted Clete down to the shower. He then removed his baton from his belt as Clete began to take his three-minute shower. As Clete began washing another prisoner entered the shower stall quietly and rapped Clete firmly but not too firmly on the head with the Sergeant's baton. Once Clete was out cold, the other prisoner flipped him over on his back to better expose each of Clete's elbows. The man used the baton to pulverize each elbow joint. Once this was accomplished, he went about methodically snapping the finger joints on each hand. He then beat each hand with the baton. The entire assault was done in just over a minute. The Sergeant turned away from the stall and the prisoner tapped him over the head with the baton and dropped it by the unconscious Sergeant Packman. The prisoner then left the scene.

Later, Clete's family was advised of the incident and the prison warden invited Clete's parents to visit him in the hospital wing of the prison. The warden said the incident was now undergoing a thorough investigation.

The investigation went nowhere. Sergeant Packman was reprimanded and suspended without pay for one week. The attacker was never discovered.

Sergeant Packman looked at his suspension as a relaxing vacation. Mitch paid him twenty-five thousand dollars for his work, which was more than half the annual salary he made after twenty-two years on the job.

CHAPTER 49:
Darnell Runs for Congress

Darnell emerged from his surgery a bitter man. He spent time rehabbing his lower body to ready it for a prosthetic lower leg. He tried one prosthetic after another, looking for one that would be a good fit without being overly painful. When he settled on one he began learning what he could do when wearing it. Standing and walking were always painful after more than an hour. He discovered that it helped to use a cane. He was particularly bitter when he thought about his football career. He hadn't even had the chance to play out the final year of his contract. He also knew that his agent, Ricky Jolly, should have re-negotiated a new contract in his third season. He had the numbers. A contract for another four to five years in the 80-million-dollar range with 40 to 50 million guaranteed was very possible. But Ricky had waited. Darnell more than hated Ricky; he loathed him. He should have an extra 25 or 30 million in the bank instead of the 8.5 million that he currently had. A disability policy he had purchased with his rookie bonus now paid him one million per year. He was nothing like broke, but he knew Ricky's screw up had cost him.

Ford Carr had channeled Darnell's competitive instincts back toward politics. Now that he was a retired quarterback he had fully involved himself in this line of work and finally decided to run for office in the spring of the election year 1996. That spring he defeated the stogy, stuffy, and boring old Congressman Nelson Summerhays and was now running against his Democratic opponent for Congress, John J. Hayden.

The Ford C. Carr Convention Center was a large complex located on Market Street in the center of Chester City. It was a massive building that had cost over seven hundred million dollars to build. Ford had championed the project and financed a considerable portion of it. It featured two hundred and fifty guest rooms, twelve luxury suites, a conference and entertainment center that accommodated up to five thousand people, three restaurants, a sports bar, a full gym, an indoor and outdoor play area for children or adults, and two large swimming pools.

Eight days before the 1996 election, the conference room floor was jammed full of people. All seats were taken, and the standing room was shoulder to shoulder.

The people attending the Republican rally were eagerly awaiting an address from the former pro quarterback Darnell Ducette. Darnell was thoroughly embroiled in the election and currently held an eight-point lead over his Democratic opponent.

Five members of the Shawnee County Republican hierarchy had already spoken. The last of the speakers was Ford Carr ranting on the disasters that would befall America if the current president was given another four-year term. He finished his presentation with a rousing introduction of Darnell Ducette, the next congressman for the 21st district.

Darnell began his presentation at 9:40 p.m. and talked for nearly forty minutes.

At the end of his speech, Darnell pumped his right fist toward the ceiling of the convention center, acknowledging the cheers of the crowd engendered by his last statement. His speech had been energetic and magnetic. His forehead glistened with sweat. His pale blue dress shirt was also wet with perspiration. Most of the crowd was jumping up and down and waving signs as if some master puppeteer was tugging on five thousand strings. Darnell was flashing that big smile that had always been a part of his charm arsenal.

"Thank you. Thank you. Thank you."

He stood before the crowd using arm gestures to quiet the hyper-excited mob of humanity.

"Thank you very much. Now, please, I have just a couple more points that need to be made."

He paused a moment as he shifted his body weight to his right side. His left leg ached as always when he has been on his feet too long.

But he managed to shrug off the pain, the pain he had known since the shooting and the pain that he knew he must cope with for the remainder of his life.

"You see, folks, I am asking you all for your help. I am confident that you will support me with your votes and I greatly appreciate that. But I need more. I am asking you for more."

Another pause. The crowd was quiet and attentive. He scanned the room, looking left and then right. The crowd followed his gaze. He then raised his right hand, finger pointing to the right side of the room. He then moved his finger slowly across the room to the left side.

"I need all of you!" he shouted. "I need all of you to talk to your friends, your family members, your co-workers, and your neighbors. Talk to anyone about the fight that will culminate just eight days from now in the voting booths of our congressional district. We have endured four years of the socialist presidency of Bill Clinton and his wife Hillary. Talk about the need to defeat President Clinton. Talk about the need to vote for World War II hero Senator Bob Dole and repudiate the draft dodger, Bill Clinton. Talk about the need to maintain a Republican congress. There is much work that we Republicans have yet to finish. We need a conservative Republican to carry our message forward in the next Congress."

He paused again, holding his hands high. The audience was chanting, "More, more, more."

"Ask anyone you can to vote for Darnell Ducette. Make me your next congressman and reject the liberal policies of my opponent John Hayden."

The assembled crowd jumped to their feet yelling wildly. The decibel level of the shouting was ear-shattering. He again gestured for quiet.

"I want to close with a final thought, a thought that I always close with so you will tuck it away in your memories and never forget it. You must all strive. That means that you must all work your butts off to make a better life for yourselves and your children.

"You work! You sweat! You sacrifice! And the thing is that you can only achieve your potential when big government is off your back."

Again, he paused as the applause built.

"When high taxes are off your back." The noise level continued to rise.

"When government incompetence is off your back. Do you all get it? Do you all hear me?"

The crowd chanted, "Yes, yes, yes."

Darnell paused and was staring back at the thousands of eyes fixed on him, the locked eyes of the audience giving him an invisible energy that was like soul food to him.

"And what happens once we get rid of big government? When we discard it and put it curbside with the rest of the trash?"

Again, Darnell lifted his hands skyward.

"Now say it with me. We thrive! We thrive! We thrive!" The audience chanted with him.

"We thrive! We thrive!"

The chanting continued for nearly two minutes. Both the audience and Darnell were exhausted. But Darnell's exhaustion was also energizing him. It was just like a vigorous workout in the weight room.

"Thank you all. And remember to thrive with Darnell Ducette. God bless America!"

He stopped there and waved to the crowd. He stood near the podium for several minutes waving and enjoying the cheering. At last, slowly, very slowly, Darnell walked off the stage, visibly limping.

After Ford Carr had introduced Darnell he had left the stage and walked down some stairs to his front-row seat next to Ricky Jolly and some Shawnee County Republicans of note. He had stroked his Magnum P.I. mustache as Darnell stepped up to the podium. Like the rest of the audience, he was spellbound throughout the speech. Once Darnell had finished and left the stage the people slowly began to file out of the room. Ford poked Ricky in the ribcage and motioned for him to follow. They walked up to the stage and stopped, giving space between the departing crowd and themselves.

"Damn, Rick, do you have any idea how good that boy is?"

"Real good I'd say."

"Real good? Rick, my man, he's the best natural politician I've ever seen. And I've seen a bunch of them. He is more charismatic than Kennedy. He'll win this election. Easily."

Ricky quipped, "Is he that good? Seriously, Ford, this is his first election after all."

"Did you see how the crowd reacted to him? Did you watch him play the crowd? These people would anoint him, king, if they could. And here's the thing—I'm going to have the king in my pocket one of

these days. I'm going to have him there and he's even gonna like it."
Ricky just smiled. Ford smiled back.

Ricky said, "Ford, did you have to fix anything?"

Ford clapped Ricky on his shoulder.

"Ricky, I didn't have to fix a Goddamn thing. I've fixed a lot of things lately but Darnell isn't one of them."

"Yeah. I know. I guess you mean my screw up with Darnell's contract?"

"Well, Ricky. I can give anyone one free pass. But two . . . well."

Ford glowered at Ricky.

"Ricky, you just tried to get too cute. Darnell took that team to an 11 and 5 record and a trip to the playoffs. That was the time to strike. You should have pushed for a deal worthy of a top quarterback then and there. Instead, you wanted to wait. A couple of months later, that freaking kid goes and blows his knee off. No new contract and no future football career for Darnell. Big mistake. Remember, in every life, shit happens. But in every life, there is a time to strike. Success depends on recognizing that opportunity."

Ricky was standing slump-shouldered.

"But Ford, I couldn't foresee that damn kid shooting Darnell any more than you could foresee Darnell throwing his wife off her balcony."

"I don't know for a fact that he did that, do I? But either way, I had to fix that one. I want him in politics and I want to own his future. I couldn't let him just rot in a jail cell for the remainder of his life. Could I?"

"Of course not. But how did you manage it?"

"You know how. I used Mitch. Hey, I see Colin over there and I need to talk to him. Later."

Ford walked over toward Colin Grundy thinking that Ricky had cost him nearly five million dollars in commissions had he signed Darnell early to the kind of contract that he deserved. Ricky knew too much about Ford's business. He thought to himself that he needed to fix his Ricky situation, too.

CHAPTER 50:
Jack Troop's TV Show

Ford Carr was in one of his offices early on a cold and blustery morning the week after Thanksgiving. He had sent for Ms. Marlene again and had enjoyed a pleasant evening of sexual foreplay and then the sex itself. He had not requested Marlene's presence for the night, so he had paid her the normal five-thousand-dollar fee plus a twenty percent tip. Ms. Marlene left Ford's Living Greens mansion shortly before midnight. Ford had gotten six hours of uninterrupted sleep and awakened fresh and ready to get some business accomplished. His first task was a morning meeting with Jack Troop.

The 1996 election was past history and Ford was pleased Darnell had won his seat in the United States Congress. However, he was dismayed and pissed off that President Bill Clinton won a second term. Before he met with Jack Troop he needed to send some emails to various players in the Republican Party.

Jack arrived at the studio on that same a cold and blustery morning the week after Thanksgiving.

Darnell was be going to Congress in early January.

Jack got a cup of coffee and sat down at his desk. He wanted to start his day as he always did by going over yesterday's news. But the first thing he noticed was a note parked in the middle of this desk. The note commanded him to meet with Ford immediately after the show. Well hell, Jack thought. Something was up. But he set the note and his thoughts aside and began his preparation for the morning's broadcast.

Once the show ended, Jack obediently went directly to Ford's office. Ford's secretary escorted Jack into Ford's plush office. Ford was busy emailing but gestured for Jack to take a seat at his desk. He finally looked up at Jack and smiled at him. Jack thought that something was definitely up.

Jack smiled, "Good morning, sir."

"Yes, it is. Jack, I'm sure you're interested in why I needed to see you this morning. Well, here it is. Yesterday Laura came to me at day's end and resigned from her role on the show."

Jack was not prepared for this news and stared wide-eyed at Ford.

"She told me that while she likes the work, at her age, it proved to be too exhausting. She did say that she would stay on until the end of December to give me some time to find another replacement."

"I sure didn't see this coming. It's a real surprise."

"Well, not to me. I have actually been making plans for major changes for some time."

Jack inquired, "Such as, sir?"

"I think you're going to like them. I am actually counting on it."

"Yes, sir."

"Well, to start. I am taking you off *America Speaks*. That will become effective December first. Laura will carry on with it until the end of the month."

"Sir, do you mean I'm done?" Ford waved a hand at him in dismissal.

"Take it easy, Jack. Just hear me out." Jack nodded as his heartbeat escalates.

"Effective January first, Carson Sweeny will host the show, taking Laura's place." Ford leaned in toward Jack. "Have you heard of him?"

"Ah, I believe I have. Doesn't he have a talk show down south somewhere?"

Ford grinned.

"He does. A very popular one. It comes out of Nashville. He talks politics but he is also into country music. Nashville and all, you know. He usually has a guest star from the country music world to do a song or two. Carson plays guitar, sings and writes some of his own stuff. He's going to bring those skills here to Chester City. The show will become the *Carson Sweeny Show*."

Ford chuckled.

"I'm paying him a shitload of cash to do this. He's going to have artistic control of the show so I can eliminate a few people who currently do that. Jack, you will have no role in this show."

"So I'm completely out?"

Ford smiled. "Well yes. Out of the radio business, but you're going into the television business. How does that strike you?"

Jack was instantly speechless.

"Jack?"

"Ah, oh.... sorry, sir. I'm dumbfounded."

"You will be the star of your own TV talk show. No co-host. It will be all yours. I've been putting this project together for months and I was sure that you'd be excited about this opportunity. What do you think?"

Jack took a deep breath, exhaling slowly. A smile crossed his face.

"Mr. Carr, sir, you gambled right. I love the idea."

"I knew it. Now look, there's a lot of detail to cover here and I am already running late for another meeting. I have hired a director and he has already been busy hiring a support staff. His name is Slim Tallman. He's been doing this kind of thing for twenty-eight years. He's a pro."

"Sounds great sir. But what's—."

"I've set up a meeting tomorrow with you and Slim. He will give you all the details and answer your questions. Okay? Oh, and I almost forgot. You will be getting a healthy bump in pay. You can afford to upgrade your lifestyle. Tell that to Diana. Slim has all of this. Talk to him."

"Yes, sir." Ford stood and so Jack did, too, and the two men shook hands. Then Ford was off to his next meeting and Jack headed back to his office. His thoughts kept wandering back to the new opportunity. He was anxious to meet Slim Tallman.

How did the man get a name like that?

Jack simply had too much to think about. The thoughts bouncing between the twists, turns, and tunnels of gray matter sometimes were making sense and sometimes were taking form as blobs of utter nonsense. He hadn't been to Barney's Tavern for some time and on one of those mentally blurry impulses, he decided to sit at the bar and drink a chilled vodka or two.

He discovered that Mick, the daytime bartender, was still working there. Mick welcomed Jack and asked him if he was still drinking his usual. Jack nodded in the affirmative. Jack sat at the same barstool that he used to sit at. The bar at this time of day was still largely unoccupied. Jack finished his first vodka when a stranger entered and sat down two stools from Jack and ordered a draft beer.

CHAPTER 51:
Jack Meets Mitch

Typically, in a bar that only had a couple of patrons in it, people tended to sit away from others. Strangers stayed strangers until the bar filled up and then they were forced to sit side by side and would often talk to each other. Jack kept glancing at the stranger who sat just several feet from him even though he had virtually the entire seating area of the bar to choose from. Jack simply thought this was weird. Perhaps a violation of bar etiquette.

The stranger was probably six or seven inches taller than Jack and weighed fifty pounds or more than he did. His complexion seemed dark, but the bar was always kept dimly lit. His eyes were brown and his hair a light, sandy brown. He wore his hair long, just below his shirt collar and had it combed back with lots of gel. He wore wire-rimmed glasses and had an obvious scar on his left cheek. Jack decided that this guy was a little on the spooky side.

The stranger noticed Jack glancing at him off and on. He finally looked at Jack and said, "Good afternoon."

Jack turned toward the voice feeling mildly startled but unafraid. After he had been shot, he had never left the house without his gun and knife. He was prepared to use either but didn't think the current situation was threatening.

"Good afternoon," Jack replied and nodded.

Jack then turned away from the man as a signal that the conversation had ended. Instead, the stranger moved over and sat next to Jack.

"I need to speak to you."

Now the alarm bells started ringing in Jack's brain.

"I'm sure you don't. I don't know you. Please, leave me alone."

"You are Jack Troop, are you not?"

Jack froze. A chill went through his body. He had no idea who the hell this guy was, but he obviously knew who Jack was. He had gotten Jack's attention.

"Do I know you?" Jack asked. The nerves in his body were tingling.

"No."

"Okay. So how do you know me?"

"You work for Ford Carr. Yes?"

"Yeah. I do. Do you work for Ford?"

The stranger shrugged. "Sometimes. But not regularly."

"Okay. So, I haven't bumped into you in the workplace?"

"Correct."

"Look, enough of this crap. What's your name?"

"Mitch."

"No last name?"

"Not important."

"Mitch Not Important. That's an odd last name, Mitch." Mitch laughed a bit.

"Very funny, Jack. Didn't know that you had a sense of humor."

"Some people think so."

"Use Dingle. Mitch Dingle."

"Sure it is," Jack countered skeptically. "But Mitch Dingle it is." He swallowed some of the vodka from his second drink. Mitch was just sitting and sipping his beer. Jack got tired of waiting.

"Well, Mitch Dingle. Out with it. You're the guy that wants to talk to me and I don't know you. So for Christ's sake spit it out."

"Okay fine. It is just that I know that you have a problem. And I am a man who is in a position to fix it."

Jack sipped more of his vodka and Mitch drained his beer.

"I have lots of problems. But here's the deal. None of which are any of your fucking business. Get it."

"Oh Jack, that's harsh. But you are wrong." Jack sighed deeply.

"Then out with it. I am tired of this crap. What is it that you want from me?"

"A friend of yours has asked me to contact you. To see if I can help with this problem."

"Sure. Great. What damn problem would that be?"

"Why, Jean Lange, of course." Mitch signaled Mick for another beer and Jack drained his drink, also ordered another.

"Mitch, you have a creepy way of getting one's attention."

"Just one of my many talents."

Jack replied dumbly, "I see."

"Actually, I'm sure you don't. I earn a very lucrative existence by fixing things for people. I can fix all kinds of things." Jack took a sip of his fresh drink.

"Can I assume that you are not talking about things like broken light switches, flat tires, or overflowing toilets?" Mitch smiled.

"You can. Mostly, I work with people who have larger problems."

"And you do that how?"

"By any means necessary, of course."

"Of course. And you assume that I have a problem with Jean Lange."

"Yes, I do."

"And why would she be any further problem to me?"

"Jack, Jack. She shot you twice and shot your wife once. Doesn't that qualify as a problem?"

"Perhaps. But she's disappeared. The cops can't find her. Nobody has been able to. She's been out of sight for nearly nine months."

"Well, you see, Jack, I can fix the problem because I know exactly where she is. I've talked to her."

"Oh, sure you did, pal."

"Honest. You see, I'm the guy who arranged for her disappearance." Jack was incredulous and stared at Mitch with his mouth open.

"That's crap. Man, I simply don't believe you and you are now annoying the hell out of me."

"Jean is from Chicago. Let's just say that there are people of influence in that town that use my services from time to time. Jean knows some of these people."

"She called one of them. That person called me. Then I made her disappear. Like magic."

"Yeah right."

"Fair enough. I had her face changed. Plastic surgery, you know. Her hair color and hairstyle was changed. She lost some weight. Her name has been changed. She has new identity information. She has a new line of work. And presto, she vanished. Jack, I swear to you that if she was sitting beside you, you would not know her."

"Okay. That's possible. But why is she a problem for me or my wife?"

"Because she still wants to kill you."

"Still? What for?"

"She's just a nasty vindictive bitch Jack. Surely you understand."

"Maybe. Explain, please."

"She'd still like to kill you and you wouldn't recognize her. She could walk right up to you and blow your balls off. Get it?" SON OF A BITCH!

"Are you really expecting me to believe all this bullshit?"

"Suit yourself. But you should know that I could neutralize Jean before she gets around to killing you. And remember, life is now getting pretty sweet for you. A new job assignment with more money. Perhaps that new house you've wanted. Think about it."

"This entire conversation feels like a fantasy. Neutralize her. What does that mean? You'd kill her?"

"You're getting irrational Jack. I wouldn't have to kill her. Just relax."

"So what would it take to neutralize her? I assume that I'd have to empty my bank account, right? Or am I missing something? And if I didn't want to do that, I could tell you to go to hell. Then what? Would you kill me? I am armed."

"Armed huh. Well, well. Nice to know. But Jack, neutralize doesn't mean that she has to die, only that she has to fear my warning to her more than her desire to kill you. It's that simple."

"Do you mean that she'll listen to you?"

"Meaning that and the fact that she would understand the consequences of defying me and the consequences to her parents, friends, and her bastard child. People tend to fear more for their loved ones than they do for themselves. It's a good thing to know."

"So. You are a serious badass."

Mitch laughed briefly. "You have no idea."

"But I have to pay you to make it happen. You are not a charitable organization?"

"Correct."

"And if I take a pass on your little fantasy?"

"Simple Jack. Then I take a walk. I just didn't make the sale. No big deal. I don't have anything against you, after all. I'm not a threat to you; in fact, I do business with some rich men that you know."

"Really?"

"Sure. One is your father-in-law. Good enough?"

"Jesus!"

Mitch got off the bar stool and dropped a couple extra twenties on the bar.

"Please get Jack what he wants and keep the rest. Good day to you, Jack. Call me if you change your mind."

"I don't know your number."

"Ask Dom. See you around."

Jack ordered another drink.

CHAPTER 52:
A Serious Conversation

Jack watched Mitch as he walked slowly and deliberately out the front door. He wondered if the guy was for real or perhaps just an extremely good bull shitter. Mitch had climbed off the barstool leaving a lot of excess money on the bar for Mick. Jack went to his car and lowered the window to get cold air moving through the car. He hoped it would help him sober up some before he got home to the apartment. Even driving slowly, Jack got home in less than twenty minutes. He kept thinking to himself that he had drank too much vodka again. Why did he do that? He had cut his alcohol consumption down significantly since he had been shot, but as usual, every time he encountered a stressful situation, he returned to his old habit. Controlling the impulse was becoming a problem. Did he need help? No, he thought. He should be able to handle this. He should be able to toughen his resolve.

He opened the front door and entered the apartment. Diana was sitting on the couch watching the TV. She frowned at Jack as he entered. Jack knew right away that she knew where he had been.

"You were drinking over at Barney's again, weren't you," she said.

It was a statement, not a question. Not a good way to start the conversation Jack wanted to have with her. He made a palms-up gesture, indicating both a yes answer and at the same time an act of submission.

"This needs to stop, Jack."

"I know, I know, I know. I'm sorry, Di. I screwed up." Jack said it in a subdued voice, not at all happy with himself.

He had much that he wanted to talk to Diana about but his brain was still fuzzy from the effects of the alcohol. Jack slumped down on the couch next to her and sighed.

"Please Di. I messed up but there are a lot of things that I want to talk to you about."

"What is it, Jack?"

"How about a little later? Anything ready to eat?"

"I've been keeping it warm." They both ate supper with no further conversation. They watched mindless TV after supper and then both decided it was time to go to bed. Once in the bedroom, they began undressing. As they got down to their naked bodies the spark that was always there ignited. They moved toward each other, hugging and then kissing, both becoming fully aroused in a minute. They rolled onto the bed and began pleasing each other eagerly and with the knowledge that each knew what the other wanted.

After the sex, they lay on the bed side by side. They were breathing deeply and waiting for their heartbeats to slow.

"Jack," Diana began as she turned her head toward him, "You said you had something you needed to tell me. Then we had dinner and then we, ah, did this. What did you want to tell me?"

Jack rolled toward Diana and placed his hand on her hip. He moved his hand over her belly, below her navel, and then up to one of her breasts and then the other.

Diana purred.

"Are you starting something again, Jack?"

Jack grinned. "I'm tempted."

Diana grinned back. "That felt so good before. You can do it again if you wish."

"Well, there are two things. One is a good thing and the other is . . . well, I'm not sure."

"Out with it." There was concern in her voice.

"You sure you don't want to do the other thing?" He was feeling his penis stirring again.

Diana noticed and said coyly, "Perhaps it can wait a little. You are obviously ready for me again."

She reached to him and fondled his erect penis. Jack groaned with her touch.

"I sure am, honey." And he rolled over onto her.

After they had finished for the second time they both rested quietly.

Jack finally said, "I suppose I should say what I have to say." Diana nodded.

"Let me start with the good news. Ford has been busy putting a TV talk show together. I'm now off *America Speaks*. . .Diana turned toward him, her face etched with concern.

"But . . . I will be the sole host of a new TV talk show. A huge raise comes with the change."

"Oh my God. That's wonderful. You mean you are getting your own TV show? My God. So maybe we can afford a new house. We both know that we now need at least one more bedroom."

"We'll think ahead. We'll get a three-bedroom home," he said smiling.

Diana melted into his arms, giving him a passionate, sloppy kiss on the lips.

They had recently learned that Diana was eight weeks pregnant and had celebrated the event with a fine steak dinner and a bottle of red wine. Diana was somewhat disappointed that as a mother to be she had to abstain from the wine although she took a single sip while toasting the future of the unborn child.

"This is just great, Jack. It's a game changer. Just imagine, we have a child on the way and we'll be buying our first home. And you—you will be a famous TV star. It will be so wonderful." Diana was obviously effusive with joy. "And Christmas is coming! God, I'm so happy."

Diana was very Italian. When she is happy she is very happy and when she is pissed off she is very pissed off.

Jack hated the idea of spoiling Diana's moments of joy by bringing up the mysterious appearance of Mitch and the possibility of Jean Lange out there in the shadow world with murder in her heart and Jack in her sights.

"So when does the show start?" She was so happy and bouncy.

"Di, I don't have any details at all. I have a meeting tomorrow with the new director. He is going to go over things with me."

"Oh."

"Ford says he's a real pro. Been in the business for twenty-eight years. He will be my immediate supervisor."

"Well fine, I guess." Her emotional high was crashing. "Don't worry. I can make this work."

Diana smiled. "I know you can." Jack paused.

"But honey, I've got to get to the bad news."

"Sure you do. And just when I was in such a good mood." "Sorry, Di. I went to Barney's in a good mood. To think about things. The baby and the house and then the new job opportunity. I was only going to drink a vodka or two. Honestly. But then there was this guy sitting at the bar two seats away from me. He slid down next to me. He told me his name is Mitch, Mitch Dingle. He called me Jack, Jack Troop. He already knew my name."

"Mitch Dingle? Odd. Do you know him?"

"No. That's the point. He knew my name, but I've never seen this guy before."

The smile on Diana's face now disappeared.

"Well, what did he want?"

"He said that he wanted to help me with my problem."

"Problem? What problem?" inquired Diana.

"Exactly what I thought. He claims that I have a problem that he can fix. He calls himself a fixer. It's how he earns a living. By fixing things. So he says."

"Jack, what problem do you have that needs fixing?"

Jack started to stammer. He could barely spit it out.

"It's Jean . . . ah, you know . . . Jean—"

"Lange! Jean Lange! Nobody even knows where the hell she is."

"Yeah, I know. But this Mitch guy says that he does."

"He what?"

"Knows where she is. He said he helped her disappear." Diana was wide-eyed and sucking in deep gulps of air.

"Oh bullshit, Jack! The cops can't even find her. "

"Like I said, he says that he helped her disappear. Changed her identity. Plastic surgery, new hairstyle, new everything. He told me that I wouldn't recognize her if she was sitting next to me. I... I can't believe this."

"I don't know if I believe it either. I'm not sure he's credible. He could well be some con artist just after whatever money he thinks I can pay him."

Diana was up and pacing around the bedroom floor while slipping on her robe. Initially, Jack couldn't help following her still naked body until the robe spoiled his view.

"But here's the ugly part. He says that she still wants to kill me."

Diana yelled, "Oh shit! Shit! Shit! Shit! What should we do? Call the police?"

She was in an obvious panic.

"I know, I know. Di, please calm down. Easy. Easy. Please. Take it easy."

Diana sighed. "Sure, easy. Right. Sure, Jack."

"Hey, remember, Jean Lange has been out of our lives for a while. Would she really come back now? Is she that crazy?"

"Are there degrees of crazy? I think crazy is crazy Jack. She scares me. What if you talked to Ford? Tell him that you may be in danger. "

"I was thinking just that Di. But I'll tell you, this Mitch guy says that he's done work for Ford and . . . and here's the zinger Di. He said that he has also done work for your father . . ."

"So he has done things for Ford and my father? Fixing things? As in kill people," she asked.

"Not necessarily. He says that the trick is to make a person fear him more than they fear trying to do harm to someone that they wish to harm."

"So he's maybe a hit man, or something else?"

"He said that he made Jean Lange disappear. Anything else is an assumption."

"Are we in trouble here, Jack?"

"I wish I knew. I need to talk to Ford and to your father. We have to know more about this man."

Jack had his initial meeting with Slim Tallman the following afternoon. He stood up from his chair as Jack entered the office. He offered Jack his hand and the two men shook. As he sat down Jack couldn't help but stare at the appearance of the man. He was easily six-six or six-seven. Definitely a tall man. Yet his appearance was skeletal. He could not have weighed more than a hundred and sixty or a hundred and seventy pounds. His bones were covered by pale skin lined with large blue veins. Tall and slim. Jack was still looking at him as he began speaking.

"Yes, I know. My appearance usually startles people. I'm Slim Tallman and I am a tall man and a slim man. Slim is an obvious nickname. My first name is Ralph. Ralph Tallman. Tallman is my given surname. Just to satisfy your curiosity, I have a genetic disease. My body metabolizes food at the speed of light so to speak. I can't get fat and I struggle to eat enough to maintain my puny body weight as it is. I consume at least ten thousand calories a day. I have to eat constantly. My desk drawers are loaded with high-calorie junk food. So that is the reason for what you see. So there it is. Now let's put my problem to bed. When I meet new people in the organization I always try to get my medical problem out of the way. We will not discuss it again. Fair?"

Jack nodded.

"So let's get down to business. "He began to lay out the details of the job to Jack.

Their conversation lasted into the early evening. It continued the following morning, much of the time devoted to Jack asking questions and Slim answering them. He told Jack that he had hired a coach that would go over the things that he should and should not do. The most important thing Jack had to learn was proper conduct in front of a TV camera. He was told the camera captures everything. For instance, he should never scratch or touch his groin or rear end and not to pick his nose or ears. Doing things like that and he would make a clown of himself. With that thought planted in Jack's mind, Slim Tallman adjourned the meeting.

CHAPTER 53:
Christmas with the DeLeo's

Since Jack and Diana had been married, they rotated holiday gatherings between the homes of their parents. This year it was Thanksgiving with the Troop family and Christmas with the DeLeo family. Next year the opposite would occur.

Jack and Diana were getting ready to leave for the DeLeo home in Scarsdale when Diana told Jack she needed to speak to him.

"Jack, I need to tell you something before we go. You will be asked to go to my father's office along with my three brothers. This is a custom in our family. Since you will soon be the father of my parent's seventh grandchild, you will have a new status in our family. You will be one of us."

Jack interrupted, "I always thought that they liked me well enough. Even if I am a Democrat."

She grinned at this.

"They do like you. But they'll now see you more like you were born a DeLeo. It is a deeper bonding between you and the rest of the family. And they will make you an offer."

"What offer? What do you mean, Di? Are we doing the Godfather movie?"

"No, nothing like that. But I can't be absolutely sure. This conversation never involves the women in the family. Only the men. But you will know it when you hear it."

"Sounds a bit mysterious."

"Perhaps. But please treat this like a solemn occasion. No jokes. Show them the respect that you always show them. Everything will be fine."

"Jesus Di, this makes me kind of nervous. It's that important?"

"Yes, it is."

"I see. But I'll still need to talk to Dom about Mitch."

"Then let's get going."

The DeLeo family members were all mingling before sitting down for Christmas dinner. Jack and Diana had driven from Chester City and were the last to arrive. They began making their rounds somewhat late. They first chatted with Diana's brother Lou and his wife Kate.

Di's youngest brother Gino came over and hugged both Diana and Jack. Gino was about six one and around two hundred and five pounds. He was obviously very fit. His bride of two months also greeted Jack and Diana warmly. Her name was Samantha and she was called Sam. Like most newlyweds, they were very much into casual touching of each other as newlyweds are prone to do.

After chatting with Gino and Sam they went over to Nick, the oldest of the DeLeo children. Nick was about Gino's height and weight but he didn't have Gino's muscular build. Nick, like Gino, was a ruggedly handsome man. His wife, Reena, was a tall, statuesque blue-eyed blonde. The couple had a thirteen-year-old son and two daughters aged eleven and eight.

The adults were all sipping red wine and talking about family, business and other conversational odds and ends.

Finally, it was time to sit down for Christmas dinner. Dom said a long grace and a chorus of Amen's were uttered around the table. It took nearly two hours to eat the traditional Italian dinner, which was washed down with bottles of wine. The women, including Diana, finally rose from the table and began to gather in the living room. The men, including Jack, left the table and were moving about the spacious house.

Jack found himself standing near the entrance to the kitchen watching two maids clean the table. He felt a hand on his shoulder and turned to see Nick standing beside him. He smiled at Jack and told him that Dom and his brothers wished to speak to him in Dom's office. Jack nodded. This was it.

He turned and followed Nick into Dom's spacious and elegant office.

Dom's office had a dark, heavy, masculine look to it. The rear wall was lined with bookshelves containing maybe a thousand volumes or more. The paneling on the other three walls was of a dark, exotic oiled wood with dark red leather accents. Dom was standing over at the bar that was built into the right-side wall. He leisurely pours two fingers of brandy into each of five, fine crystal glasses. Dom motioned for Jack and his sons to take a glass. They then went to Dom's desk. Dom sat in his elegant chair and Jack and the sons sat in the four soft chairs arranged in front of the desk. A humidor and gold lighter sat on the desk and Dom gestured for all to take cigars after he had first taken one.

Brandy in hand, Dom spoke. "Please. Everyone. Enjoy a fine Cuban cigar with your brandy as we talk. But first, a toast."

He paused.

"Today, on this Christmas day, we have all enjoyed a fine dinner prepared by our women. We have enjoyed the company of our women and our children. We give thanks for the beauty of our women and the youth and energy of our children. We are all hard- working men who take pride and happiness in providing for our families. This is all as it should be. Finally, we give thanks for the newest member of our family, Jack Troop, husband to our Diana. This coming year she will give birth to my seventh grandchild. This is truly a wonderful thing. We drink a toast to all of these blessings."

They all clinked glasses and took a generous swallow of the brandy.

Dom and his sons lit the cigars, smoking and sipping brandy. Jack didn't smoke.

Dom noticed Jack without a cigar.

"Jack, Jack. Go on. Take a cigar. I know you don't smoke but this is an occasion. Yes? Please, smoke."

"Mr. DeLeo, sir, I don't . . ."

"Yes. Yes. Yes. But, I insist. Now please." Jack took a cigar, was coached by Nick on how to properly light it, then took a puff and blew it out. The four DeLeo's smiled.

"It is excellent, yes?" Jack held the cigar out and flashed a big smile. The DeLeo men all laugh.

Dom was not an especially large man. He was close to six feet tall but slim, around a hundred and sixty pounds. He had snow-white hair with touches of silver at the sides. Flecks of pinkish flesh showed through the thinning white hair on the top of his head. He also sported a small silver mustache above his upper lip. He was sartorially dressed as always. Dom's presence was always elegant but commanding. When Dom said something, one stopped and listened.

Dom took a couple puffs on the cigar and took a drink.

"Well, Jack, you have become family. A husband to my daughter, a brother to my sons. And soon to be the father of my next grandchild. This is a fine thing."

Dom puffed the cigar and drank some more. He practically glowed.

"So on this occasion, I think it is now time to give you some information about the DeLeo family business. But, what I am about to tell you is only for you to know. You are to tell no one else. Understand?"

Jack nodded. "But sir, you really don't have to tell me."

Dom frowned and replied sharply, "Of course I don't. I don't have to do shit that I don't want to do. But I choose to do this. You will please listen."

He glared at Jack who realized he had just screwed up. "Yes, sir. I'm sorry. I understand."

"Good. Jack, you already know that I am a banker. You know that Nick is an accountant and Lou runs the body shops. And then there is Gino, who helps us out when we have problems that need fixing."

Jack was listening intently, sipping brandy and puffing away on the fat Cuban cigar. Dom's phrase "problems that need fixing" stuck in Jack's mind.

"But this does not tell the whole story. There are fifteen Scarsdale National Bank branches. There are fifteen DeLeo Accounting and Money Management offices and there are twenty- three AAA Auto Body shops. I also own many properties."

Jack nodded again.

"I own all of this. These businesses are incorporated under DeLeo Enterprises, Inc. One of these days it will all pass to Sophia and my four children. But not too soon. I am but 71 years old."

He laughed at his little joke.

267

"So you see, I am a very rich man. My sons prosper by working for me, as could you. How would you like to be a part of this? I can bring you into the business. I could pay you much more than you are currently being paid."

"Mr. DeLeo, that is very generous of you. But you must realize that I know nothing about the banking business or accounting or auto-body work. What would I do?"

"I want to grow my business even more. I need a media man; someone who can get the DeLeo name out in the public eye. You work in the media. You have experience with newspapers and radio."

"All that is true, but I'm not an ad man."

Dom pointed to Jack. "You are a smart young man. You would learn quickly."

"Well, yes . . . it's something that I want to do . . . but I have to tell you. I've just been asked to—well, I've just been asked to host a TV talk show."

"Is it Ford Carr who has made you this offer?"

"Yes, it was."

Dom made a dismissive gesture. "I know Ford Carr. I could speak to him."

"Yes you could, sir. But I am very interested in his offer." Dom was sitting at his desk with his hands laying palms down on the surface. He brought them up to his chin and tented his fingers.

"I see. But you haven't heard mine. Do as you must, but please keep in mind that you are family and I can do better for you. Think hard about this. Think very hard. "

He was not smiling.

"Okay. So we are done here with our business."

"Oh, Mr. DeLeo, may I ask you something?"

"Certainly."

"I have a question on an entirely different subject."

"Very well. But first I want some more brandy. Anyone else?" Gino retrieved the bottle from the bar and refilling Dom's glass and doing the same for Nick, Lou and himself. Jack declined.

"Mr. DeLeo, I was recently at Barney's Tavern in Chester City. It's near the broadcast studio." Dom nodded.

"A man that I've never seen before walked over and sat down next to me. He called himself Mitch. Mitch Dingle. He told me that he could help me with a problem."

Every pair of DeLeo eyes was focused on Jack.

"He was referring to my problem with Jean Lange. The woman who shot me and shot at Diana. Mitch told me that he could neutralize her."

Jack paused and looked at Dom and his sons.

"He told me that he has worked for you in the past."

"Mitch, um, yes, I know this man."

"Good. So, should I believe what he told me?"

Dom didn't answer immediately and then slapped his hand on the desk.

"Tell you what, Jack. I'll get in touch with Mitch. We'll get things settled. So neither you nor my daughter needs to worry about Jean Lange. I will help you out."

"Great. I would sure appreciate that, sir."

"No problem. You are now family. But Jack, I would request a favor of you in return. A small thing. To be done in your spare time. Help me with the expansion of my business, just as I explained earlier. I know that you can do this. Is this satisfactory?"

Jack hesitated and replied, "Of course."

"Excellent. Then, we are done here, yes? Since we have resolved some things, would you please rejoin Diana? My sons and I have something else to discuss. It will be just a few minutes."

"Okay, sir. Thank you." Jack left Dom's office, more than happy to be out of there.

Dom asked, "Gino, has Mitch taken care of this Jean Lange thing?"

"Yes, Dad. Jean Lange is cooperating with Mitch. He made her understand the consequences of doing otherwise."

"Fine. Now, I think we should test young Jack once again. What is your opinion?"

All of the DeLeo sons agreed with their father. Dom nodded and finished his brandy.

"Gino, get Mitch on our boy Jack again. We will put him to a more interesting test." The meeting ended.

CHAPTER 54:
Ricky Jolly's Fate

By January Ricky Jolly was in a full state of panic. Ford Carr had basically ignored him since the close of the election season in November. A few days before Christmas Ricky received a memo bearing Fords' signature. The memo instructed Ricky to remove himself from the management duties of the Ford Carr Sports Management Company. Those responsibilities were to be turned over to the company vice president. Ricky was then to carry on with his other duties until further notice. Ricky was highly distressed at the way he had been demoted, knowing well that it was Ford's style to do his dirty work face to face. Not even giving Ricky the courtesy of a meeting told Ricky that Ford didn't give a damn about him anymore. Happy New Year Rick.

The new president of the Sports Management Company was an incredibly tall black woman with an equally incredible name of Ima Pirate. Ima pronounced her last name pi-Rate. She was six feet two inches tall. Her hair was short and done in cornrows, each row with a color of the rainbow. In each ear, there were ten studs and she wore six chains of gold and silver around her long, slim neck. She also sported a ring on each of her fingers, but not the thumbs. She always wore dresses that covered her from neck to ankles and were sleeveless and multi-colored. When Ford hired her, he was initially shocked by her appearance but quickly discovered that she had the intelligence and drive to become a great executive in his organization.

She was not yet thirty years of age and doubled the number of clients that Ricky had signed since her hiring, many of them women or minority sports personalities.

Employees of the sports management company sensed that Ricky's job might be in jeopardy soon after Ima assumed her duties as vice president. Deep down, Ricky sensed that also. The truth was that Ricky had always been in over his head and probably achieved the position he occupied because he was Ford's nephew. Ricky began drinking heavily. He had no idea how to manage this predicament.

Ricky's work situation was compounded by his personal life. He was recently divorced for the second time. He had three children from his two marriages and now had two alimony payments and three child support payments. In addition, Ricky had gotten addicted to the high life. He craved the best of everything and now his income would soon be insufficient to meet his financial obligations and live his lifestyle of choice. He started borrowing money to make these payments. At first, it was from the banks. Soon his credit reached his limit and he turned to men in the underworld for money. He began juggling payments to two different loan sharks and quit paying the banks. He was in too deep at this point.

Ford may as well have shot him in the head.

On a mid-week night in March, Ricky sat on a barstool at a tavern in the center of Chester City downing tumbler after tumbler of fine scotch whiskey that he couldn't afford to be drinking. While Ricky drank, a silver-haired man with blue eyes was sitting in the rear of the room observing Ricky and sipping a cola. Ricky had had too much to drink to notice the man watching him.

The man was Gino DeLeo. Gino was in disguise, but Ricky had never met him and wouldn't know him with or without it. Ford Carr had hired Mitch to take care of his Ricky problem. What Ford didn't know was that Gino frequently substituted as Mitch. In reality, it would be Gino disguised as Mitch who would solve Ford's Ricky problem

Gino had been following Ricky around for a week and anticipated that tonight he would be able to earn the second half of the hundred-thousand-dollar fee Ford had agreed to pay him.

Gino had met the real Mitch over a decade ago. He recruited Mitch to assist the DeLeo family when they had unusual problems that needed special fixing. Over the years Gino became the family's contact man with Mitch. Over those same years, the idea occurred to Gino that he could assume the role of Mitch to clients not in the realm of the DeLeo family's interests. He explained this to Mitch and Mitch had no problem with Gino using his name. Of course, both men knew that Mitch wasn't Mitch. Mitch was just a professional name. No member of Gino's family was aware that he was moonlighting as Mitch.

Gino reflected on all of this as he watched Ricky climb off the barstool and pay his bar tab. He believed that by the time this night was over, he was going to make nearly three million dollars in his career as a fixer. Gino left the tavern slightly behind Ricky and followed him to his home at 880 Archibald Street. He watched Ricky as he staggered up the walk to his front door and keyed the lock. Gino waited and prepared for what was to follow.

The following morning Ricky did not come into his office. Nor did he call in.

Nobody, including Ima Pirate, thought much about the missing Ricky throughout the busy day. The following morning Ricky was again a no-show. Again, there was no call in. But now Ima Pirate became moderately alarmed. She had Ricky's secretary call his home number. There was no answer so Ima told the secretary to call every half hour. By the end of the day, there was still no response from Ricky and Ima called Ford Carr. Ford told her to call the police, which Ima did.

Chester City uniformed officers went to Ricky's house and knocked repeatedly on the front door, then tried the back door. The doors were locked. Ricky's car was in the driveway. The officers walked around the house again peeping through the lower floor windows. Nothing stirred. The officers called police headquarters and notified their superiors of the situation. Ultimately the situation was passed on to Captain Warren Sunderberg who then called Ford Carr. Ford told the Captain that he wanted the house checked out. Period. Ford was used to getting what he wanted.

Two patrol cars arrived at Ricky's house with Sergeant Jeff Shipley in charge. They kicked open the front door and one team went to check the rooms on the lower floor as Sergeant Shippley went to check the upstairs and another officer in the basement. Shipley detected a foul odor as he headed up the stairs. Shipley had been on the force for fifteen years and knew the smell of decaying human flesh and body fluids immediately. The scent emanated from the master bedroom. He entered the room reluctantly and saw Ricky lying peacefully dead on his bed clad only in his underwear. A half a bottle of scotch and an empty tumbler sat on the nightstand along with a sheet of paper. The pillow that Ricky's head lay on was stained brown with more ooze discoloring the sheets. His right hand held a pistol that was pointed at his right temple. There was a gaping black hole in the temple where the bullet had entered. A few insects were around the wound.

Sergeant Shipley went to the nightstand and looked at the piece of paper. It was a note. It said:

I quit. Enough is enough.

It was unsigned. Shipley called Detective Mike Russo.

"Russo here."

"Detective, this is Sergeant Shipley. I am currently at the residence of Mr. Richard Jolly at 880 Archibald Street."

"Okay Sergeant. What have you got?"

"I've got a dead body here sir. It's probably Richard Jolly but we don't know that for a fact. He's lying on his bed. He's been dead for two or three days. The body smells."

"Any obvious cause of death?"

"Yeah. A gunshot. One shot to the right temple with a thirty- eight revolver. The weapon is in his hand. Could be a suicide. There is a note on the nightstand."

"Can you read it without touching it?"

"Yes. It says, 'I quit. Enough is enough.'"

"That's it?"

"Yes, sir."

"Is it signed?"

"No sir, it's not."

"Okay, Shipley. You know the drill. Secure the scene like a potential crime scene. Call the crime scene team. I'm on my way."

"Got it."

CHAPTER 55:
Another Broken Neck

The *Jack Troop Show* had an audience of about two hundred people each day. Jack always began the show by walking out on stage toward the audience and uttering the scripted line, "Good morning to you all. Welcome to another interesting and informative two hours of the *Jack Troop Show*." The audience was then prompted to applaud. At this point, Jack would walk back towards the set where an attractive, young blonde woman sat on stage left. Her name was Sandra Stallworth and she would read the hottest news clips from the last 24-hour news cycle. Jack triggered her reading by saying, "Sandy, please, tell us what's new in the news." She would say thank you, then start reading the various news stories. On this particular morning, one of the stories would include the death by hanging of a black man named Mayfield Pugh.

When Sandy finished Jack would introduce the day's guest. Jack would interview the day's guest for about twelve to fifteen minutes depending on how much material merited coverage and on how famous or newsworthy the guest was. After Jack's questions, the guest took ten minutes of questioning from the audience. Jack would thank the guest who would then exit stage right. From that point on, Jack fielded questions from the audience on just about any topic an audience member wished to discuss. Jack would then sign off for the day saying, "Sorry, we're out of time for today, but tomorrow I will return with another guest who affects the world around us. I'm Jack Troop. I wish everyone a happy and productive day."

During the first week of the show, Jack interviewed Ford Carr on the state of the national Republican Party. Then it was Chester City mayor Eliot Abraham on developmental plans for the future of the city, followed by county commissioner Ralph Adelson, state senator Mark Warfield, and state representative Colten Berger. It had been an exciting opening week for Jack and his enthusiasm for the show was boundless. Slim Tallman informed him on Thursday that he would be interviewing two nationally known guests next week.

After the show ended, Jack went back to his office to review the news items used that day on his computer. The item that had hit the national news was a picture of the body of Mayfield Pugh dangling from the window of an old apartment building, hanging from a sheet that had been tied around his neck. The name Mayfield Pugh meant nothing to Jack, but Mayfield's face did. Jack knew him as Chimp. No way could he not recognize the large ears on the little man.

As soon as he saw the picture of the dead Chimp Jack buzzed his secretary and asked her to connect him to the Detective in charge of the Mayfield Pugh case in Cleveland, Ohio. Fifteen minutes later his secretary informed him that she had Detective Andrew Lewis of the Cleveland, Ohio police department on the phone. Jack picked up.

"Good afternoon Detective Lewis. This is Jack Troop from the *Jack Troop Show* in Chester City. Thank you for talking to me."

"No problem. But Mr. Troop I'm really busy, so how is it that I can help you?"

"Detective, Mayfield Pugh lived in Chester City most of his life. His death is a hot story in this news area. I am the host of a TV news program and I'm hoping that you can provide me with some information that I can pass on locally."

Lewis said flatly, "Well, I assume you read the story published by the Cleveland Plain Dealer?"

"Yes. Mayfield was hung from his apartment window on 448 Stevens Street in Cleveland. A bed sheet was used to hang him but it has been determined that someone broke his neck and then hung him to make it look like a suicide."

"That is correct. Whoever snapped Mr. Pugh's neck was a seriously strong guy."

"I see. Do you have any suspects?"

"I'm not at liberty to say one way or another."

"Got it. So you don't have a suspect at this point."

"I didn't say that."

"I used to be a crime reporter. I know what you meant."

"Look, Mr. Troop. We have information that Mr. Pugh was a professional informant. He traded information. Perhaps he pissed off someone who didn't like what Pugh gave him. Would you know anything about his activities?"

"Yes, he was an informant. Hell, I even paid him a number of years ago for some very useful information."

"Well now. Could you fill me in?"

"Sure." Jack then laid out the information Chimp gave Marcus Wayne to give to him concerning the money that helped pay for the upgrades on George Ducette's West Buchanan Street home and for the Living Greens home purchase. He explained the information he received from Chimp regarding Willie's likely involvement in the death of his mother Estelle.

"That's very interesting, Mr. Troop. But tell me. The name Ducette. George Ducette. Is he any relation to Darnell Ducette, quarterback for the Washington Red Knights?"

"George is Darnell's father."

"Well, well. That's interesting. Now this Marcus Wayne guy. Is he anything to Darnell Ducette?"

"Ah, yes. They're best friends. They played football together in high school and college. Marcus is employed by Darnell to handle his security matters."

"Wouldn't Marcus have told Darnell what he knew about his brother's involvement in his mother's death?"

"I would think so, but I'm speculating here."

"Well, to be frank, I don't have a suspect here. Our speculation is gang activity. But I can see a possible motive for Darnell Ducette to get rid of Mr. Pugh and the same goes for Marcus Wayne."

"That's sure possible. Listen, Detective, try calling Detective Mike Russo in Chester City. He can provide you with information about both men."

"Okay. Thank you. Now I gotta go."

"Please call me if anything develops."

"Well, I'll think about it." Lewis hung up.

CHAPTER 56:
Jack Talks to Detective Russo

Jack's brain was spinning now. Another broken neck death, all of them having a solid connection to the life of Congressman Darnell Ducette. Jack had a mental list of them all: first Estelle Ducette, then Tawney Johnson, Willie Ducette, and Chimp. Of course, there was also the death of his wife Candy Champion whose fall from her eighth story balcony broke her neck and most of the other bones in her body. Then there was Chuck Chambers, Brent Reedy, and Doug Ward.

Jack decided that he needed to run all of this by Detective Mike Russo. He wanted a cop's perspective. He called Detective Russo several times that day with no luck.

Jack did the *Jack Troop Show* the following morning. By late afternoon he was ready to knock off for the day when his secretary put a call through to him.

Russo said, "Hello, Jack Troop please."

"This is Jack. Detective Russo?"

"Yes. But I'm awfully busy, Troop. What's up?"

"I need to talk to you."

"About what?"

"Broken necks. Some shattered kneecaps. Interested?"

"I said I was busy. I don't know that I have the time to indulge your curiosity. Can it wait?"

"I guess it could, but it's 5:30. You hungry? Thirsty?"

"Yeah, maybe. I guess I'm thirsty for sure."

"How about you and I take a break? You know Barney's Tavern?"

"Oh, hell yeah."

"Great. Want to meet me there? I'm buying."

"Well, that settles it, Troop. See you in fifteen?"

"Got it."

Jack and Detective Russo arrived at almost the same time. Business at Barney's was picking up but the two men managed to get a table in the rear of the dining area. When the waitress arrived, Russo ordered a Bud draft and a shot of Dewar's scotch. Jack ordered his chilled vodka. When the drinks arrived they both ordered bacon cheeseburgers.

Russo slammed his scotch and then chased it with half the mug of beer. Jack only sipped the vodka.

"So Troop, you want to talk about broken necks."

"I do."

"Okay. Ball's in your court." Russo then drained the rest of the beer.

Jack pointed at the empty glasses. "Another round?"

"Damn right."

Jack signaled to the waitress.

"Well now. Let's go back in time. Estelle Ducette and Tawney Johnson." Russo arched his brows.

"Yeah. I remember both of them. Darnell Ducette's mom and his girlfriend. Two women, two broken necks. Both with Ducette in the picture."

"Coincidence?"

"Nah, bullshit."

"Let's go to Willie Ducette. He was found face down in a swamp in Scarsdale. Cause of death was another broken neck."

"Sure. I talked to Sergeant Giamati about that one. Ducette's little brother. Giamati was thinking gang hit. Gave me the reasons why it could be that way. But I think those bangers like to shoot each other. I don't see a broken neck in their M.O. I see Ducette again. Maybe a beef with his brother. I think he's a stone-cold killer. A sociopath. I know it but I can't prove it."

"Well I got some information from an informant, he—"

"He who?"

"Let's just say a confidential informant for now." Russo nodded. His next round of drinks had arrived and he was already halfway through both. Jack was still nursing his first vodka.

"Let's say he claims that Willie fixed a rug at the top of the stairs in the Ducette home. Loosened it up so that Darnell would trip over it and take a header down the stairs. But instead, it was Estelle who took the header." Russo shrugged.

"Troop, there's no way to know if that's what happened. Hell, it could be nothing more than an accident. And Willie can't tell you nothing. Ducette sure won't implicate himself. So you're down to your informant. Come on, who is he?"

Jack smiled.

"He's dead. He died from a broken neck. He was found hanging from his bedroom window in Cleveland, Ohio."

Jack slid a copy of the newspaper article over to Russo. Russo read while Jack continued to sip his drink.

"Shit."

He looked at Jack.

"Dead end here again, Troop. Who's to know? Everything turns into a dead end." The cheeseburgers arrive along with another round of drinks. Both men ate silently. Jack finally slid another piece of paper to Russo with the name and number of Detective Lewis in Cleveland.

"Okay. I'll call him."

"Good."

"But Troop I still see multiple broken necks." Russo paused and drank some beer.

"All of the victims have a direct link to Ducette. This is no coincidence. I'm telling you."

Russo tapped his ample belly, which was pushed up against the table.

"My gut tells me this." He smiled. "And it's a big gut."

Jack chuckled at this.

"Detective, I agree with you. But you also have to keep in mind the death of Darnell's wife, Candy. She took a fall off her eighth-floor balcony. It broke her neck and other bones in her body. The detective in charge of the case, Lou D'Antonio, believes that Darnell is her murderer, but the ADA in charge of the case refused to give it to the grand jury."

"What?"

"According to D'Antonio, she just chickened out. You know how things work in any district attorney's office. Prosecutors make their living by winning cases. If they don't think they have a slam- dunk win, they don't go after it. Hell, Detective, you would know better than I. Am I right?"

"Well, mostly."

"So okay, she backed off. And the thing is that D'Antonio felt that the chances of getting a conviction were about fifty-fifty. But this ADA just shelved it."

"That's crap. Any ADA worth a damn would go after that case. Ducette is a celebrity athlete. Up and coming ADA's love to nail big shots like that. It would make the national news. It would make her career."

"Yeah, one would think. But it didn't happen."

Russo held out his right hand and rubbed his thumb and forefinger together. "Money. I just know it. That ADA got paid off. Maybe also the DA."

"You think so?"

"I'm telling you. In a big case like that any ADA would go after it. I've worked with prosecutors for over thirty years and most live for a conviction that would make the front page of the news."

"That's interesting. Now get this. I'm told that within one year she left the DA's office and opened her own practice in Connecticut."

"Well, well, well. That does it for me. She either got paid off or threatened or both. Hey Troop, maybe I can tell you something."

"Okay, fire away."

"I got an email from a friend. He's a cop at the state capital. He told me that a guy who's in Rayford got the shit beat out of him. Got his two arms broken and every finger in each hand."

"Jesus."

"Yeah. But you'll recognize the name. Clete Chambers. Ring a bell?"

"Oh yeah. Damn, more broken bones. Darnell again."

"Could be, but I wouldn't have a clue about how he worked it. The guy was in Rayford. Arranging that kind of beating wouldn't be easy. But hell, Ducette would sure as hell be holding a grudge."

"He would. I should look into it."

"Good. Troop, I gotta run. See you." Jack was thinking he did need to look into it. Perhaps a visit to Rayford. Jack was also thinking he needed to visit Marcie Kellerman as soon as possible.

Jack ordered another drink. He realized Russo was a good man who had been beaten down over the years by his job, yet had nothing to show for it other than two failed marriages, a large gut, and a liver the size of a sockeye salmon. He sipped his final drink and stands then headed for the exit.

A large portion of the *Jack Troop Show* was devoted to news and politics. After Jack left he decided that it was well past time he starts to pursue in detail the career of Congressman Darnell Ducette. With all the broken necks and broken lives, the trail of mayhem was just too obvious to ignore. Perhaps the legal system was too complex to put the accumulation of broken bodies together into a pattern of violent crime, but Jack thought that as a newsman, maybe he could. He was, after all, not bound by the rules of the legal system. As Detective Russo had insisted, there was just too much to be labeled coincidence.

CHAPTER 57:
Jack Speaks with Slim Tallman

The following day, after the broadcast, Jack arranged a meeting with Slim Tallman. In their short time working together they had achieved a relationship of mutual respect.

"Jack, I gather something's on your mind."

Jack leaned in toward Slim and began his pitch.

"Sir, I'm interested in doing a major story on Congressman Darnell Ducette. It will cover a large portion of his life in depth. It would require multiple broadcasts to complete."

"To what purpose? What's your angle?"

"I have followed Darnell's career since he was a star quarterback at Stannard High School. I interviewed him frequently when we both attended Chester City State University. He became an All-American quarterback and I was a journalism major. Later Darnell became the starting quarterback for the Washington Red Knights and had a short career. He was shot multiple times in the knee and his lower leg had to be amputated. Now he is our Congressman and is not even thirty years old."

Jack paused.

Slim watched him intensely as Jack wet his lips and continued.

"Darnell's life, to this point, looks to be a life of one success after another. And that is actually true. But boss, his life has been stained by a bloody and peculiar trail of dead and broken bodies.

"First, there was his mother Estelle Ducette. Then there was his seventeen-year-old girlfriend Tawney Johnson. Then his brother

Willie, and then a young black man nicknamed Chimp. All died prematurely. All from broken necks. But most importantly, there was his wife, supermodel Candy Champion. She died from a fall from her eighth-floor apartment balcony. Five violent deaths. All involving broken bones."

"Jesus, Jack. I read about the Candy Champion death."

"I recently had a conversation with Chester City Detective Mike Russo about all of this. He is sure that a chain of similar deaths like this cannot be a coincidence. I concur. We need to air this kind of story."

"Well, I would agree that we are talking about a lot of deaths from broken necks, all of them occurring on the same life path that Darnell has followed. It's very strange. Now this information was known when the Congressman was campaigning for office. Correct?"

"Yes."

"So no mud thrown stuck to the wall?"

"Very little mud got thrown. Darnell is a beloved celebrity in Shawnee County and the surrounding counties."

Slim tapped his fingers on the desk.

"Boss, Darnell smells of success, but my hunch is that he's rotting on the inside."

"Explain."

"If he is involved in these deaths then he will have to spend the remainder of his life defending his image from the cold facts. That would eat at a man. But if Darnell is the sociopath that I believe him to be, then he feels nothing. And if he feels nothing, then more bodies will follow. If we, the media, don't put it out there, we will become the unwilling witnesses and an enabler to the continued path of human destruction that he has been on most of his adult life. Frankly Boss, I think I messed up here. I should have been on this years ago."

"Shit, Jack. That's kind of spooky."

"I think this man has been hiding his true self since he was a kid. He can't hide forever. I want to expose him for what he is."

"Alright. What do you want from me?"

"For starters, a few days away from the show and an expense allowance. I need to do some more research."

"I can authorize that. However, I am going to have to clear this kind of story with Ford. There would certainly be liability issues involved."

Jack smiled a half smile. He knew that Darnell was Ford's pet project in the world of politics. He knew Ford saw Darnell as a possible future candidate for president of the United States. The first black president. Getting this story through Ford was Jack's biggest challenge.

CHAPTER 58:
Chuck's Second Broken Bone

Gino DeLeo was sitting alone at a rear table in an Italian restaurant called A Taste of Italy. He was eating pasta and sipping an expensive glass of Chianti. He was in no hurry as he was waiting for night to fall. It was mid-February and it had already been a rainy day, the sky painted by dark gray clouds. The evening held the promise of a deep and inky darkness. That was perfect as far as Gino was concerned. He had some dark and ugly work to do and the cover of a dark and cloudy sky would make his job easier.

Gino was working as Mitch tonight. Ford Carr had once again called him and assumed, as per usual, that Gino was Mitch. Ford described the task and suggested the price he was willing to pay. Gino accepted. Tonight, as Gino finished his meal, he was disguised as Mitch. When he left the restaurant, he would put on a black overcoat, a black winter hat, and black gloves.

His destination was a red brick building that housed the offices of Foster and Weinberger Accounting Services. Gino carried an eighteen-inch section of lead pipe concealed under his overcoat. His walk was nearly six blocks from the restaurant to the accounting firm where Chuck Chambers worked as an account executive. Gino felt invigorated by the crisp fresh air as he strolled evenly and with purpose to his destination. Just before he reached the building Gino paused and looked around. Cars were moving on the streets but traffic was not overly heavy. He had passed several other walkers.

Everything seemed normal. He then picked up his pace and walked to the employee parking lot in the rear. He ducked down between two cars in the lot. He would wait for his prey, the man who would be exiting the offices of the accounting firm through the back door any minute now. The man walked with a pronounced limp.

Chuck Chambers emerged from the building and headed over to his car, completely unaware that he was, for the second time in his life, about to be the victim of a man who wanted to hurt him badly. Chuck had walked with a limp since he was pushed down the stairway of the athletic dorm at Chester City State University during his junior year. He now used a cane for assistance. He had a busy day and was looking forward to returning to his Chester City apartment and kick back on his overstuffed chair. Lorraine, known as Rainey, his wife of just over a year now, was a good cook and he was looking forward to something hot and tasty.

Gino spotted Chuck as he neared his brand-new Lexus sedan. He gripped the eighteen-inch section of lead pipe in his right hand. Chuck reached his car and began fishing for his keys to open the vehicle. Chuck's back was turned to Gino, who moved from his hiding spot, quietly and quickly toward Chuck. When Chuck opened the car door he sensed the presence of someone behind him. But like many years ago when he approached the stairway in the athletic dorm at the university to head downstairs, his survival instinct was just seconds too slow.

Gino raised the pipe and gave Chuck a light tap on the skull that knocked him cold. He examined Chuck. The skin on his skull was slightly broken and Chuck was breathing normally. He would live. But not comfortably. Gino rolled Chuck over and examined his good knee.

Well sorry, Chuck, he thought. Nothing personal. I just have a living to earn. He took the pipe, raised it up, and smashed it into the good knee. He then repeated the blow, and then a third strike. The knee became bloody pulp. That would do. Gino shook his head and stood up. It was still early evening and he had some time to get a few drinks after a job accomplished.

Jack worked late after his meeting with Slim Tallman. He would be taking a flight to Connecticut the following morning. When he finished, Jack hurried home to be with Diana for a while. She was in the final two months of her pregnancy and Jack wanted to eat supper with her and chat about their future together. They would soon be settling on a new home they had purchased earlier and the baby was due in April. It was an exciting time for the young couple.

CHAPTER 59:
Marcie Kellerman

Jack took an early morning flight to Hartford, Connecticut. His research staff had located the address of Marcie Kellerman's law practice and her home address. It was early in the work week, so Jack decided to try her business address first.

Jack entered the small office of Marcie Kellerman shortly before noon and was greeted by an attractive and very young receptionist.

"Good morning, miss. My name is Jack Troop and I am hoping that it will be possible to speak with Ms. Marcie Kellerman." Jack handed her his card. He received a hundred-watt light bulb smile from the young woman.

She gushed, "Oh my God. Jack Troop. Jack Troop from the TV show? I've seen your show. Wow. This is so cool."

Jack returned her smile. "Thank you. But is it possible that Ms. Kellerman is available?"

She put her hand to her mouth. "Oh! I'm sorry. Ms. Kellerman is on leave. She is recovering from an injury. Mr. Quinton is taking her place for the time being. I can see if he's available."

"Ah, no. My business is with Ms. Kellerman. Is she at home?"

"Oh, I really can't say."

"Well, if I may ask, what happened to her?"

"She broke her leg. She's now recovering."

"Okay, thanks for your help." Jack left the building and headed for the residence of Marcie Kellerman. He located her home at 44 North Broadmore Street and parked curbside in front of a well-kept but small Cape Cod home with taupe colored siding and forest green faux shutters. He walked up to the door and rang the bell. Thirty seconds later the door was opened by a small, dark-skinned, dark-haired Hispanic woman of middle age.

"Good day. My name is Jack Troop. I'm here to see Ms. Marcie Kellerman."

A voice from within the house called out, "Who is it, Delores?"

"He says his name is Mr. Jack Troop," Delores said.

"What does he want?"

Jack explained to Delores that he wished to speak to Ms. Kellerman about a case she had worked on while still an ADA in New York City.

Delores repeated this to Marcie Kellerman.

The figure of Marcie Kellerman soon appeared in the hallway. She was casually dressed and sat in a wheelchair. Jack's initial impression was that she was fairly tall despite her sitting in a wheelchair. She was obviously thin. Her left leg was perfectly normal. But her right leg was beyond broken. It was missing. The stump that was her upper right leg was heavily bandaged.

Jack spoke over Delores, "Ms. Kellerman, I apologize for disturbing you at this time. My name is Jack Troop. I am the host of a morning TV talk show that focuses on politics, current news, and celebrities. I'd like to talk to you in that regard. If, of course, you feel up to it."

Marcie was frowning at Jack, looking at him intently. Her face was as thin as her body and lines around her eyes and the corners of her lips made her look older than she was.

"Well, Mr. Troop, I'm obviously not feeling well. Perhaps some other time."

Her voice was weak as her lips appeared to quiver as she spoke.

Jack shrugged and replied, "Sure. I could come back, but please understand that I will come back. So maybe it might be better to have our discussion and get past it now. That is if you wish."

He felt guilty about pushing her but shrugged it off. She muttered something to herself.

"Very well. Please be brief." She waved him into the house, backing the wheelchair into the living room. She motioned for Jack to sit in a chair near her. No refreshments were offered. She was obviously irritated, but also curious.

"Well, what is it?"

"Ms. Kellerman. I host the *Jack Troop Show*. Do you know it?"

"No. Why? Should I?"

"It doesn't matter. I want to talk to you about a case that you worked on back when you were ADA Kellerman of the New York City district attorney's office. This case was in the national news."

She scrunched her face into a deep frown. "Yes?"

"The case was never sent to the grand jury. It involved the quarterback of the Washington Red Knights Darnell Ducette and his wife Candy Champion. I'm sure you remember it."

Her hand immediately went to her mouth. Her eyes squeezed shut and a tear rolled down her cheek. Jack was confused but continued.

"Darnell Ducette was investigated as a suspect in the murder of Candy Champion. The case never went to the grand jury. I was wondering why you never went forward with the case."

Marcie was still wiping tears from her face. Her look was not a friendly one. There was fright in her eyes. "Who . . . who sent you here? Who do you work for?"

She was shrill but there was still a quiver in her voice. She clasped her hands together, her eyes wide open. She started to shake. Jack realized that she was afraid of him.

"Ms. Kellerman, please, relax. I'm only here to talk. You have nothing to be afraid of."

She stared at Jack without speaking, but muscles in her body were quivering.

Jack continued in a calm, quiet voice, "Relax, please. I'm here for information. Nothing else."

"Ducette. Darnell Ducette. Do you work for him?" Marcie continued to shake and started to sweat. She was clearly losing her composure.

"I work for a TV news station. I am working on a story concerning Congressman Ducette's life. That's all."

Marcie pointed to her missing leg. Her tone of voice was accusatory. "Did you do this to me? Are you responsible?"

"My God, no." Jack realized that he spoke to her in too loud of a voice. "I'm sorry. I have no idea what happened to you."

"So who do you work for?"

"For Mr. Ford C. Carr, who owns the TV station."

"Did he pay you to do this to me?" Again, she pointed to the leg.

"Please, Ms. Kellerman. I am not involved in any way."

Marcie screeched, "Oh bullshit! Bullshit!! Bullshit!! I was attacked. You came to my house. With a club. You pushed me down and then beat me on my leg with that club. My knee was destroyed. They had to amputate."

"Please, please, Ms. Kellerman, please calm down. I didn't hurt you. I'm a TV talk show host."

Delores chimed in, "Ms. Kellerman. I see this man. He is on TV. On a show. It is true."

Marcie looked at Delores and then back at Jack. She blinked and then her entire body slumped. More tears dripped down her cheeks. She shrugged her shoulders.

"I'm sorry. I'm overwrought. The doctor gave me medication but they don't seem to help much."

"Perhaps I should leave."

"Mr. Troop, it was only a month ago when the man who did this came to my house. I didn't know him. But he hurt me badly. He took my leg. They had to. . ."

She started sobbing again, this time without control.

Jack knew that he should leave, but he felt compelled to stay. Perhaps he could still learn something. Jack completed her thought, "Amputate? Amputate your lower right leg? I'm very sorry for you."

"He said this was a warning to me not to talk. But why would I? I could go to prison for taking that money." She started to calm down again.

"Are you saying you took a bribe? A bribe not to prosecute Darnell Ducette. Is that it?"

Marcie huffed, "You know I did. You gave it to me."

"And you told no one?"

"Goddammit, no! That money bought me my dream. My own law practice. It was something I wanted my entire adult life. Why would I tell anyone that?" She was now hyperventilating.

"Just relax, Ms. Kellerman. I won't harm you. It's okay. Please." Jack started to feel like a jerk. He was pushing a mentally fragile woman way too far. He stood and prepared to leave. He had gotten what he came for.

Marcie then screamed.

"Don't hurt me! Not again! No! No! Please!"

"Delores. Call 911. Ms. Kellerman needs help. Now please!"

The paramedics arrived in about ten minutes and quickly gave her an injection to settle her down. They then took her to a local hospital for evaluation.

Jack left the home of Marcie Kellerman. He had spotted a bar and grill on the way to her home and this time decided to stop there since he was hungry and stressed out. He entered the tavern and sat at the bar. He ordered a double vodka on the rocks and a burger. After finishing the vodka, he ordered another and made a call to Slim Tallman to advise him that he wouldn't make it in for the show tomorrow but would be there the following day. He made another call to Diana and advised her that he would be home sometime tomorrow. A final call was made to the Hartford police department to see if he could speak to the detective in charge of the Marcie Kellerman case. Jack was advised that the case was an investigation in progress but that he might be able to talk to Detective Samuel Snowden sometime tomorrow.

As things turned out, that didn't happen, so Jack reluctantly flew back to Chester City the next afternoon.

CHAPTER 60:
April Troop

On the return flight to Chester City Jack had time to consider what had befallen Marcie Kellerman. She had made it clear to him that she had taken a considerable bribe not to pursue the prosecution of Darnell. Jack was unsure how much money was needed to set up a new law practice and purchase a new home, but he knew it was well into six figures.

It was also obvious it was Darnell who had the most to gain by her failure to prosecute, so he suspected the money had come from him. After all, he could afford it. However, Darnell was Ford Carr's pet project, which caused Jack to believe that Ford Carr could just as logically have funded the bribe. But what was the motive behind the vicious assault on Marcie Kellerman? Had she gotten cold feet? Did she want to turn herself in? Or did she get greedy and try to extort even more money from Darnell?

Regardless of motivation, who had committed the assault? Jack couldn't see Darnell doing it in person. Had he hired a pro? Maybe. Jack knew Ford Carr had the resources to locate a professional. Dom had told him Ford had used Mitch the fixer on more than one occasion. Mitch was a distinct possibility.

Jack was back in Chester City in the late afternoon and went directly to his office. Back at his desk, he got Marcie Kellerman off of his mind and started going through the news clips from the past couple of days. He was not far into the list when an article from the Chester City Chronicle caught his attention. The article was titled, *Chambers'*

Brothers Assaulted. He read through it once quickly and shook his head and went to the break room for a cup of coffee. He returned to his desk and read the article again slowly, absorbing every word.

Holy shit, he thought. What's going on here? Both Chuck and Clete Chambers had received injuries. The assault on Chuck Chambers may well have been the second time he had been assaulted in his life. That is, if you believe that he was pushed down the dormitory stairs at Chester City State. His second assault involved a shattered right knee. That was just like Marcie Kellerman. According to the news article, Chuck's brother Clete had received two shattered elbows and both of his hands had been pulverized to the extent that his lower arms had been amputated. He was waiting for prosthetic lower arms. Jack felt that this couldn't be a coincidence. The Chambers brothers had been punished. Hell, Clete would never shoot a rifle again. And just as that thought hit him, he knew why. In Clete's case that was exactly it. Clete would never shoot anyone again and that sure as hell included Darnell and Lily. As Jack mentally chewed on the situation he remembered that years ago, both Brent Reedy and Douglas Ward had also been attacked by an unknown assailant, who had shattered their knees with a blunt object. Damn!

Jack set his thoughts aside and went home that evening. He took the last day of February off to deal with a big event in his personal life. At ten o'clock that morning, Jack and Diana sat in a conference room of Gaines Realty Agency. They spent the next hour signing settlement forms and writing out multiple checks necessary to purchase their new home. Everything went smoothly and the couple then drove to their newly purchased home. It was located in the Sunny Acres development on the eastern outskirts of Chester City. Sunny Acres was under a cold slate gray sky on that day.

Since this was their first real house, Jack and Diana decided to play newlyweds. Jack carried Diana over the threshold along with the growing baby only about six weeks away from birth. The couple's new address was 37 Sunnyview Drive.

They spent several hours going over each room in the house and mentally placing furniture in various locations in each room. The bedroom they had selected as the nursery received the most attention. Diana was especially gushing over what must go where. Of course, the task of furnishing this room was still to come. It also occurred to Jack that the new 2,200 square foot home had put him nearly two hundred thirty thousand dollars in debt.

While the two were discussing all of this the van pulled up in front of the house with their furniture and possessions from their apartment. The men unloaded the truck and placed the furniture at Diana's directions. Then it was done. They had a home. They both cleaned themselves up and went to an expensive restaurant for an excellent steak dinner. They returned home tired and sleepy and settled into bed for a long night's sleep.

The following weeks passed quickly. Jack was busy with the new show during the day and then came home at night to help Diana with the seemingly endless unpacking of cardboard boxes, some of which was discarded. The process produced a shopping list of new items that needed to be purchased. This made Diana happy and Jack worry about the shrinking status of his checkbook. As the due date for the baby approached Diana found herself constantly tired. More work for Jack to take care of.

At the end of March, Diana attended a baby shower and brought home a van-load of baby paraphernalia that needed to be unloaded and put in the nursery. Jack happily attended to the task. Diana had also returned home with two substantial checks from each set of soon-to-be grandparents. This helped soothe Jack's growing money anxieties.

Another two weeks passed with the Troop's baby still rollicking around and kicking in its mother's womb. On April 14th, Diana had an appointment with her OB/GYN physician who advised Diana that the baby would come any day now, but that if it didn't, they would induce labor to keep the infant from growing too big. The prediction proved accurate. The very next day Diana called Jack and told him to hurry home— her labor had started. When Jack got home he grabbed the bag that had already been pre-packed and he and Diana headed for the Chester City Hospital. A girl was born to Jack and Diana Troop in the predawn hours of April 16th. She was named April Sophia Clara Troop. April for her birth month and Sophia and Clara to honor her two grandmothers. She weighed just under seven pounds.

Diana and young April came home two days later. Jack and Diana were both exhausted. But Diana was able to rest during the day when young April slept. Jack was in awe of his young daughter and was always excited to hold her. He now had two girls in his life to love. He was so happy, so excited that he couldn't think or control the overwhelming emotions he felt.

April Troop was the third grandchild of Frank and Clara Troop and the seventh grandchild of Dom and Sophia DeLeo. Both little April's parents and grandparents were overjoyed with her presence.

CHAPTER 61:
Jack Meets Chuck Chambers

Chuck Chambers had been a bitter young man since his fall down a flight of stairs. He was the starting quarterback of the football team with young Darnell Ducette as his very talented backup. Among the coaches and team players, it was no secret that Darnell thought he was the better quarterback and should be starting.

The infamous fall down those stairs left Chuck Chambers with a compound fracture in his left leg, a torn MCL and ACL of the same leg, and a broken right arm. He was unconscious when the paramedics had arrived. After his surgery and during his recovery, Chuck had no memory of the fall.

As he sat in a wheelchair in his apartment waiting for the arrival of Jack Troop, he still had no memory of that event. Yet he had spent his life telling anyone who would listen that Darnell Ducette pushed him down those stairs. Chuck particularly told this story to his younger brother Clete. He told it to Clete over and over again. Clete had always believed Chuck and Clete was eventually motivated to shoot Darnell in the knee and his girlfriend Lily in the arm.

He heard a knock at his door.

"Come in," he shouted. Jack Troop opened the door and entered the living room of the apartment. He shut the door.

"Good afternoon, Mr. Chambers. How are you today?"

"How do you think I am, Troop? Just look at me."

Jack saw a young man sitting in a wheelchair. He was unshaven and his dark hair was a mess. He wore an old t-shirt with a few obvious food stains on it. He also wore a pair of blue shorts. There was no left lower leg sticking out from the shorts. Only a thick layer of bandages. The right knee was full of old surgical scars.

"Please sit down. That is if you want to. You could obviously stand since you have two good legs."

Jack sighed. He was not prepared for the depth of the young man's bitterness. He ignored the comment and took a seat next to Chuck.

"Mr. Chambers, I will confess that I'm very curious about the cause of your latest injury. I am also aware that your brother previously suffered an even more grievous injury while in Rayford Prison. I have an interview scheduled with him next week. Can you fill me in?"

"It's simple, Troop. It's Ducette again. It's payback."

"For what?"

"There is not a doubt in my mind that Ducette blames me because my brother shot him. Then he took revenge on my brother."

"Okay. And he did that how? I'm sure that you're aware that Darnell uses a cane and has a prosthetic on his right leg."

"Shit, Troop, come on. He paid someone."

"Okay, who?"

"How the hell do I know? I never saw the guy that attacked me and the cops couldn't come up with a single suspect."

"Let's go back to college. You're the starting quarterback, you're backup was Darnell. It is no secret that you blame him for pushing you down a flight of stairs. Yet you never saw him. To this day you have no memory of that event. So why have you spent all these years blaming Darnell?"

"You're defending him!" Chuck shouted.

"No, no. Hardly. But I am saying that your accusation has always been pure speculation. You are guessing. The police questioned Darnell, questioned your teammates and questioned the coaching staff. They questioned your friends and your girlfriend, Cindy. They came up with nothing. Zip. Zilch. Nada. Your fall was ruled an accident. Aren't those the facts?"

"Screw the facts!" he shouted again. "Look, Troop, Ducette thought he should have my job. So he got me out of his way. It's that simple."

Jack said nothing but sat and again looked at Chuck Chambers up and down.

Finally, he said, "You know Chuck, yours is a sad story and believe it or not, I suspect that you are probably right. But your anger, your bitterness, is getting you nowhere in life. I'd think about that if I were in your position."

"Troop, I don't need your pity or your two-cent psycho-babble." Jack shrugged.

"Tell me about this most recent attack Chuck."

"Not much to tell. I finished up for the day and left my office and walked over to my car. It's a new Lexus. Is it possible to drive without a foot? Anyway, that's it. Somebody hit me from behind. Knocked me cold. After I was out I guess he pulverized my knee. Obviously, my lower leg had to be taken off. I'm sitting here now waiting for it to heal and then the doctors will fit me for a prosthetic leg. The cops have no suspects. Ducette has an ironclad alibi. He was at a political event. A hundred people saw him there."

"Yeah, I talked to the Detective on the case. He's frustrated because he can't come up with a lead."

"Yeah, sucks doesn't it. I've been assaulted twice in my lifetime. Shit Troop, I'm thirty-one years old and I'm already a freaking cripple. Nice life, huh?"

"I'm told that you were recently promoted to account manager. You're moving on up. Look at it that way. The assaults are merely bumps in the road."

"Easy for you to say."

"No, not really. I've hit a few rough spots and I suspect that there will be others. Life ain't always fair, Chuck."

"Like I said, Troop, easy for you to say."

Jack stood. "Well, good luck to you." And then he left.

CHAPTER 62:
Jack and Mitch Again

Jack was sitting on his favorite barstool. He hadn't gotten a lot out of his interview with Chuck Chambers and he realized that it was happy hour at Barney's, so he decided to have some drinks and pass out some cigars. He had given Mick the bartender a cigar and who in turn gave him a chilled tumbler of vodka with a lemon twist on the house. A couple of the waitresses congratulated Jack on the birth of April.

As the baby banter settled down, a man entered the tavern and sat down next to Jack. This startled Jack as there were over a dozen empty barstools besides the one next to him.

"So Jack, how have you been?" Jack stared hard at the man whose voice sounded familiar but he couldn't place the face.

"Do I know you, pal?"

"Sure you do. We've met here before."

"Sorry. I can't place you."

"Well it has been a few months and my appearance was quite different from what you're now seeing. Does that help? Come on. You'll get it," Mitch quipped.

Jack looked the man over. Tall and dressed in a leather coat, blue jeans, and a Kangol cap on a bushy head of hair. He had a gray mustache and a small chin beard and wore sunglasses.

Jack shrugged and said, "Perhaps it's the sunglasses." The man removed the sunglasses and allowed Jack to look him over.

SON OF A BITCH!

"Mitch, right?"

Mitch smiled. "Very good, Jack."

"Mitch Dingle?"

"Exactly." And just as quickly as he said "exactly" the joy that Jack had been feeling turned into darkness.

"You suddenly look a little pale, Jack. Not getting enough sun?" Jack didn't reply.

"Well, no matter. So tell me something. Have you heard from Jean Lange again?"

"She sent a letter," Jack replied peevishly. "It was a threat but not an explicit one."

"Damnit! Then I'll have another talk with her."

"Sure, sure. Try again. Feel free, by all means."

"Jack, Jack, Jack. You should be grateful."

"If you say. Wait a minute. Just why in the hell are you here anyway?"

"Ah, I should get to the point. Indeed. Well, the simple answer is that I can make some money for you. That should be useful to you with a big fat new home mortgage and a new baby girl. Yes?"

"I guess news travels fast," Jack said, still annoyed. Mitch grinned. "Mitch, could you just leave me and my family alone?"

"Actually, I can't. The gentleman employing me has a proposition that I am required to explain to you."

"Shit. Not interested."

"Nonsense. Listen for a minute. Then make up your mind."

"You're wasting your time."

"My client is a wealthy man."

"How nice for the son of a bitch."

Mitch said sharply, "Quit being an asshole and listen." Jack just stared at him.

"My client needs information either written or oral. He's looking for an edge. Something that he can use to tilt negotiations in his favor."

"Who is this client?"

"Confidential."

"I knew you'd say that. Doesn't matter anyway. Mr. Carr signs my paychecks. I won't knowingly cause him any harm. Besides, I could lose my job. And my self-respect."

"The job pays one hundred thousand dollars."

"Nice. But I'm not interested."

"Fine. I can go to two hundred thousand." Jack arched his brows.

"Wow. Can you go higher?"

"I can go to two fifty but that's the limit. It's damn generous."

"Yes, it is. It's tempting."

"I would think it would be." Jack paused.

"So you'll take it?" prompted Mitch.

"Tell you what. Stuff it, pal."

Mitch shrugged and then smirked. "I told my client that you wouldn't do it. I was right. Congratulations. You passed the test."

"What test? What the fuck is going on here?"

"Not important. See you around sometime."

"I hope not."

Mitch was laughing as he left Barney's.

SON OF A BITCH!

CHAPTER 63:
Jack Interviews Clete Chambers

Rayford was a town populated by fewer than thirty-five hundred people. It was located three miles south of Rayford State Prison and about eight miles north of the state capital. Jack Troop had never been to Rayford before and had also never been to the state prison. When he entered the small town, he thought it somewhat odd that even in his days as a crime reporter in Scarsdale he had never had to make this trip. He started out from his home that morning and drove leisurely but steadily the one hundred and eight miles to Rayford. It was lunchtime by then and Jack was hungry. When he reached the town's mini business district he spotted a tavern on his left. The sign above the door painted in large red letters read: Doodle's Tavern, Come on in for food and beverages. So Jack did, intrigued by the name of the place. He made a quick right, parking between angled white lines in the business district.

The interior of the tavern was dark and small. The bar accommodated sixteen people and there was seating for another two-dozen. Jack sat at a corner stool at the bar and ordered a cheeseburger and a double vodka chilled. After he ordered he asked the bartender,

"Please, I'm new in town and curious as to why the place is called Doodle's Tavern?"

The bartender, a large but overweight man who was probably about fifty years old replied, "Because I own it." He stuck out his hand. "I'm Harold Doodle."

Jack shook his hand as the man introduced himself. "Honestly," he continued, "no bullshit."

Jack replied, "Jack Troop. Nice to meet you, sir."

Harold Doodle nodded and then went about his business. Jack ate his cheeseburger and washed it down with another double vodka. He paid his check and left an appropriate tip.

As he got up off the stool and started to leave, Harold Doodle called out to him, "Hey, Mr. Troop." He was holding the tip money Jack had left "Here. Take this with you. You don't need to tip the owner. I'm doing just fine."

Jack reached out and took the offered cash.

Both men exchanged farewells. Jack drove the three miles to Rayford State Prison and then went through what he thought was a tedious check-in procedure. However, he understood the need for identification verification and precautions when civilians were scheduled for face-to-face visitations with inmates.

A half-hour later Jack was ushered into a conference room. Clete Chambers was seated with his back to Jack as he entered the room, who then walked to his side of the table and sat opposite the prisoner who had shot Darnell Ducette's left knee to shreds, shot him again in the left shoulder, and put a bullet in Lily Rainwater's arm.

"Hello. Mr. Troop?"

Jack didn't immediately respond. He was struck by the sight of a young man sitting opposite him with only the top half of each of his two arms. His prison uniform was short-sleeved and the stump of each elbow was covered by a white tube with Velcro straps that kept each sleeve secured to each arm. Jack noticed that Clete's legs were shackled and that both chairs and the table were bolted to the floor. Nothing else was in the room.

"Good afternoon, Mr. Chambers. Nice to meet with you."

"Clete," he responded.

"Fair enough. Call me, Jack" Both men smiled at each other.

"You're a news person?"

"I currently host a national TV talk show that predominantly deals with news and current events. I am interested in talking to you about the shooting of Darnell Ducette."

"Sure. But what does pre . . . domni . . . nantly mean?"

"Ah, it means mostly. Mostly news and current events," Jack replied, somewhat startled by the limited vocabulary of Clete.

"Oh. Okay."

"So Clete, how did this start? Why did you want to shoot Darnell Ducette?"

"He hurt my brother Chuck. Chuck and me are best buddies, you know. I just had to get him back for what he did, you know?" "Sure I do. But exactly what did Darnell do to your brother?"

"Geez. I thought everyone knew that. He pushed Chuck down the stairs. Chuck hurt his leg bad, you know. So he couldn't play football no more, you know."

"Okay, but how do you know that Darnell pushed him?"

"That's silly, Jack. Chuck told me, you know. Like maybe a million times."

"But Clete— "

"Ah . . . Jack, could you help me? Could you come over here a minute? I got an itch on my nose I can't scratch."

He flapped his two upper arm stumps at Jack.

Jack got up and scratched Clete's nose. Instinctively he wanted to wash his hands but there was no sink so he carried on.

"Thanks, Jack. I'm always having to have people help me with dumb stuff. I can't dress myself. I can't feed myself. I mean, geez, I can't even wipe my ass. I feel bad somebody's gotta do it."

Jack only nodded.

"Clete," Jack began again, "how did Chuck know?"

"Chuck saw him. He told me."

"Chuck was unconscious. He has no memory of the assault to this day."

"Chuck is my friend. He told me he saw him, you know."

"Sure. So, you decided to get even with Darnell. How did you figure all that out?"

"Jack, I know I'm not so smart. But there is one thing that I can really do good. I can shoot. I been hunting since I was little. I can shoot what I aim at. Honest."

"I believe you. So, you decided to shoot Darnell. How did you find him? How did you know where to ambush him?"

"Oh, Chuck told me where he lived. So I would go over there and watch. They won't let you in, you know. So I sat in my car and watched. I looked for a black man driving a nice car. I didn't think there would be a whole lot of black men living in that place."

Jack chuckled at that. Clete could reason things out.

"How did you pick the Always Prime Steakhouse as the place to shoot him?

"I always followed him when he went out. On Fridays or Saturdays, he would always go out with some girl. They always went to that steakhouse and then later they went to a club. I figured he would be easier to shoot at the steakhouse. Jack, what does ambush mean?"

"It means to get someone from a hiding place."

"Oh, good. That's what I did."

"Please explain, Clete."

"Well, first thing I got outta my car and took my knife. I cut a hole in his tire so he would have to stop and change it. That would give me time to shoot him. That's what happened. Him and his girlfriend came out and went to his car. He saw the flat tire and went to the trunk. I leaned my rifle on the window of my car and sighted him in. It was an easy shot. I hit him above the left knee. I aimed too high. So I dropped it down a couple inches and shot him twice through the knee. I knew that would cripple him. Just like Chuck."

"But you also shot him in the shoulder."

"Yeah. I guess that was mean but I was really pissed off about what he did to Chuck."

"Fine. So why would you shoot his girlfriend?"

"Because. She was his girlfriend, you know. That makes her as bad as him, right?"

Jack said nothing to that.

"Let me ask you this, Clete. Are you aware that your brother was attacked again? That he also lost his whole lower leg."

"Yeah, Dad told me when he came to visit. After I got hurt. Darnell did that, too. Dad told me."

"And how does your Dad know that."

"Easy. He told me. He wouldn't lie to me. He used to be mean to me, but he wouldn't lie. I'm his son, you know.

Jack shook his head and replied, "I see."

"Dad is suing Darnell. And the prison. He told me, you know."

"No, but thanks for telling me. Well, Clete, I appreciate your time. Thank you for talking to me, but now I've got a long drive home."

"Oh, are we done?" Jack stood to leave.

"Yes, we are."

"Oh. But Jack, could you do me one more favor?"

"Sure, if I can."

"You already did once. Could you scratch my nose again? Same place."

Jack groaned and then scratched the young man's nose. He left the prison as fast as he could get out of there. The road home led back through Rayford and this time Doodle's Tavern was on the right-hand side. It was after five o'clock as Jack pulled into a parking place near the tavern.

Thank God it's happy hour, Jack thought to himself. What a depressing place. What a shitty draw that young man had gotten from the deck of cards that is often symbolic of human life.

CHAPTER 64:
Jack's Rift with Ford Carr

Throughout the summer Jack Troop spent a considerable amount of time organizing everything he knew about Darnell Ducette into a comprehensive narrative, from Darnell's high school football career to his current political career as a sitting United States congressman. Once the project was completed he presented the information to Slim Tallman, who promised to evaluate it and then consult with Jack in several weeks. Jack was skeptical about what the term several weeks meant. Sure enough, the several weeks morphed into two whole summer months. By late summer Jack met with Slim and discussed the information that he had laid out. Slim was very concerned with issues of libel and slander. Jack pushed back on this concern, telling Slim that the information was completely factual and non-speculative. Jack explained that in his opinion, one couldn't lose a lawsuit for telling the truth. Jack also emphasized that this was a compelling story and would surely increase ratings. In the end Slim didn't commit to allowing Jack to air the story, telling him he would run the story by Ford Carr. Jack knew Ford would only drag things out further. That thought discouraged Jack. At last, in mid- November, before Thanksgiving, Jack was able to meet with Ford Carr on a warmish, sunny day.

Jack found himself once again sitting in a chair in front of Ford's massive desk. Ford looked at Jack, his expression neutral. Jack wasn't sure how to read him.

"Jack, good afternoon."

"Hello, sir. Good afternoon to you."

"Jack, I'm not sure how to say this. I mean, this is interesting material. I hadn't realized that Darnell is . . . uh, shall I say, remotely connected with people who have had some misfortune befall them." He paused and cleared his throat, stroking his mustache.

"Is it your theory that he is somehow implicated in these...these . . . well, misfortunes?"

"Perhaps, sir. But you must keep in mind that my presentation is non-speculative and lays out the facts in a timetable that can be substantiated."

Ford was listening intently to Jack while continuing to stroke his mustache.

"Well, Jack. Ah . . . wouldn't we be assaulting the congressman's character by presenting this information without absolving him of any blame?"

"Sir, we don't know that he's blameless. Nor do we know if he was directly involved in any of this. But everything in my narrative is a matter of public record. I've detailed and sequenced each event and explained Darnell's connection to each one. It is painfully obvious that an awful lot of human tragedy has littered the path of the congressman's life to date. It's damn hard to ignore. Don't you think?"

Ford said tonelessly, "Perhaps. But Jack, there is nothing in your work that suggests anything more than mere coincidence. Right?"

"Yes, sir, if you believe in multiple coincidences. I can tell you that Detective Mike Russo of the Chester City police department doesn't believe in them."

"You discussed this with the Detective?" Ford stated sharply. He began drumming his fingertips on the large desk. "Don't you see slander or libel issues here?"

"Sir, facts are neither." Ford slapped the desktop with his right hand.

"Well, that may be. But Jack, I have to exercise caution here. I am a billionaire many times over. Unscrupulous people are always after my money. Why hell, the congressman could file a suit against me merely hoping for a cash settlement. You must realize that I am at risk here. So your story is going to be given to my legal department. After all, I pay those S.O.B's a ton of money to watch out for my ass."

"Sure, sir. But that will take more time. I've already waited since early summer."

"Who gives a shit about time? This story will still be there. The hell with time! I want my butt covered. The lawyers will see to it. Period!" Ford's face was beet red with anger. Jack exhaled. He knew he had lost.

"Okay, sir. Fine . . ." Jack took a deep breath and fired back as he stood, "But that's a chicken-shit decision . . . Sir." He turned and walked out the door with Ford standing behind his desk, scowling at his back.

As Jack left the building he wondered if he had just kissed his job goodbye.

CHAPTER 65:
Happenings

As it turned out, Jack Troop didn't get fired. His show continued to be a huge success, the ratings were high and the show was making Ford lots of money. Ford was no longer a big fan of Jack, but he had yet to lose his appetite for money.

Jack continued to press Slim Tallman to meet with Ford and get permission to run his story on Darnell Ducette. Slim continued to waffle. Jack's frustration was morphing into intolerance.

As the Troop family entered the year 1998, Jack still stayed with the show. He was being paid well, but any communication from Ford now came through Slim Tallman.

1998 was another mid-term election year. Darnell and his fellow Republicans had been busy attempting to impeach the President. By the fall, Darnell was busy campaigning against state senator Elizabeth Hammerstein.

He defeated her easily and returned to Congress for another two years.

There was still no decision about Jack's piece on Darnell. It had been on hold, being evaluated or being re-evaluated, for way over a year. Diana was the one who finally opened Jack's eyes to the simple reality. She and Jack were talking over dinner one evening with Jack grumbling over his inability to present his story on Darnell.

Diana put down her fork, finished chewing and looked at him as he completed his rant over the big stall that was holding up the airing of his story. Airing this story on national television had reached the point of obsession with Jack.

"Jack, listen to me!"

Jack looked up from his dinner plate and met her eyes.

"Ford Carr is not going to let you put that story on the air to a national audience. Period. You are deluding yourself. I spoke to Dad last week about this. He said that Ford believes he has Darnell in his pocket. He is a young, rising political star. Dad told me that he will run against Senator Mary Higgins for her seat in the United States Senate in 2000."

"Your father knows this for sure?"

"Ford and my father are well acquainted with each other. They have done business together. My father is not as rich as Ford but he is a man of considerable influence. In this case, he knows what he is talking about."

"Well sure, Di, I guess I sort of knew that."

"Good. Then kindly move on, for Christ's sake."

"I don't think I can. This is my story and it's a good one. I want it to air." Diana forked some more dinner into her mouth as she started shaking her head. "This is a dead issue, Jack. Ford is not going to destroy his prize congressman. If Ford owns him, then one day he'll be in a position to do favors for Ford. Favors that could net Ford millions. Don't you see that?"

Jack's mouth dropped open.

"You know this?"

"Yes, because Dad knows this. You really have no idea just how powerful my father really is." Jack sighed.

"So what should I do?"

"Maybe you should talk to Dad. He might have an idea or two."

"Okay. Maybe I will."

But Jack didn't; he chose to soldier on with the Carr organization. Jack had put in a lot of time and energy with Carr and, despite the rift between them, he retained a sense of loyalty to the man who had given him his first job and then opportunity after opportunity to move up in the world of journalism. He had come a long way from an apprenticeship at the Morrisville News to a crime reporter in Scarsdale, to his appearances in the crime van, to talk radio, and now the host of a nationally broadcasted TV talk show. Jack continued on and settled down into life with Diana and April.

CHAPTER 66:
Clinton Troop

The year 2000 was ushered in with great enthusiasm by people all over the world. It was the beginning of a new millennium and a new century. Some had great optimism for the coming years, some had predicted the end of the world, and many were sure that the world's computer networks would crash because of something called Y2K. Of course, nothing happened and the world continued on. Not a big surprise.

Later that year Clinton Jack Troop was born. Keeping with the Troop family tradition, he was named after a democratic president. In this case, the president was still in office for another twenty days. So the couple decided to name the baby Clinton Jack Troop. Of course, George W. Bush was elected president that fall and would take office on January 20th of 2001. By that time, Jack was pre-occupied with leaving the Ford Carr Media network to pursue other opportunities. After several years of doing his show, he had achieved national recognition. He received calls on a regular basis from networks across the country inquiring into his interest in coming on board with them. He had accepted none of their offers. He still wanted to air the Darnell Ducette story using multiple episodes.

Darnell Ducette was elected to the United States Senate that year, defeating incumbent Senator Mary Higgins by more than six points. Dom DeLeo had been right two years ago. Jack continued to follow the senator's career, adding more information to the saga of Darnell Ducette.

Marcie Kellerman had continued to decline mentally over the past years and had to finally abandon her law practice. By the time the new president was sworn into office, Marcie's residence was a psychiatric hospital located just west of Hartford.

Marcus Wayne was still employed by Darnell. He spent his days taking care of the house at Living Greens and smoking dope.

In the spring of 2001, Darnell's father George was working in a flower bed in front of his home in Living Greens. He was completely disabled and retired now, finding a new passion in his rose bushes. George was mulching his precious roses when he had a massive heart attack and died among those thorny, aromatic bushes that he loved.

Darnell's brother Lamar had graduated from college with an engineering degree and now worked in Silicon Valley in the tech industry. Lamar had become a wiz with computer programs and computer design and, unknown to his employers, was a master at computer hacking.

Darnell's sister Juliet was finishing her senior year at Chester City State. She was set to graduate with honors and pursue an MBA degree.

On September 11th of 2001, America was attacked by a group of Muslim terrorists. A commercial airline jet was flown into the north tower and another into the south tower of the World Trade Center. Another airliner was flown into the Pentagon in Washington, D.C. A fourth hijacked jet crashed into a field in rural Pennsylvania. Its intended target was the White House. After the attacks, the people of the United States became edgy, concerned about their safety and the safety of their families. Making America safe would become the hot political topic for years to follow. Senator Ducette became a leading advocate for legislation to make America safe again.

Jack Troop continued to seek other employment opportunities. That summer Jack and Diana, along with April and Clinton, were attending a barbeque at the DeLeo home in Scarsdale. After the meal was finished, Jack was asked to meet with Dom and the DeLeo men in Dom's office. Of course, Jack had done this before, but as usual, did not know the subject matter that would be discussed. Jack was not prepared for the surprise.

CHAPTER 67:
The Real DeLeo's

In the middle of the week in the afternoon of a lazy late summer day, Nick DeLeo phoned his sister Diana. After a few minutes of catching up on things going on within the family, Nick asked Diana if she would like to come to Scarsdale that weekend. Diana said most likely, but she would talk to Jack. Nick replied that the purpose for the visit was that Dom wanted to speak to Jack privately. He suggested that they all sit down for a family lunch and then the men would meet with Jack. Nick gave her a time. She would call Nick if Jack had to work.

After the Saturday lunch, Jack and the DeLeo men headed for Dom's office. They took their customary seats in front of Dom's desk. The brandy was poured and the cigars lighted. Jack didn't take one. Dom had just taken a generous swallow of his brandy and smiled with satisfaction. He began the meeting.

"This is an excellent brandy, yes?" Jack and the sons all nodded in affirmation.

"Well, we need to talk." He paused and puffed twice on the cigar.

"Actually, Jack, most of this concerns you." Jack sat up straighter in his chair, his eyes on Dom.

"Diana mentioned that you may be seeking other employment."

"Yes, I am. I have been for a couple of years but nothing has come up that has interested me or would sufficiently compensate me."

"Diana told me that you have a news story that Ford Carr has been unwilling to have you broadcast."

"That's true, sir."

"For these past few years, I have not been able to help you out in the area of employment. But I now may be in a position to fix your problem."

Jack inwardly cringed at the word 'fix.' Dom puffed the cigar. He was enjoying himself.

"So you have a choice to make. I think this will be an easy one for you."

Dom had Jack's undivided attention. Dom pointed at Jack with his cigar.

"Number one: you continue on with Ford Carr as you have been. But now . . ." He began waving the smoking cigar at Jack. "Now you have the opportunity to break with Ford. You, of course, realize that my business holdings are vast. But, I have never given the media business a try. I have recently had the opportunity to buy a cable TV network myself. The network competes with Ford Carr for market share. I . . . well, I believe this opportunity will be a chance to poke Ford in the eye."

He paused to drink his brandy.

"My new company will be called DeLeo TV. DLTV. It will have a two-hour afternoon talk show involving current news and politics. It is my thinking that you should host the show. I will, of course, pay you substantially more than Ford is paying you. I will also have no problem broadcasting your story concerning Senator Ducette. I don't like that nigger bastard. If he is Ford's ox, let's gore him. Breaking this story about a murderous senator will make our ratings soar. What do you think? This is your second choice. It should be easy. Yes?" Jack was speechless. He was dumbstruck by the offer and had cringed at Dom's word choice.

"Ah, sir...may I have a cigar?" Jack stammered.

"Of course."

Jack took one and lit it as he had been instructed to do in past meetings. Dom looked amused.

"So, is it that you have become a smoker, Jack?"

"No, sir. I'm celebrating." Jack drank a couple healthy swallows of brandy.

"Celebrating what?" The three sons were watching Jack and their father intently as they, too, sipped their brandy.

"Why, my new job. What else?" All five men laughed out loud and drained their glasses. Gino went to the bar to fetch the bottle and poured more in every glass.

"Very good, Jack. I am so happy for you and Diana. You have given me two beautiful grandchildren and now you accept my offer to join the family business. Your name is Troop, but you are very much a DeLeo."

He paused, now turning very serious.

"So now, I must speak of serious things. First, I must confess that your loyalty to this family has been tested in the past. Do you remember a man named Mitch?"

Jack nodded.

"He once asked you to betray Ford Carr. To spy on him and give that information to Mitch, who would pass it on to his employer. I paid Mitch to tempt you. I was happy that you would not betray the man who paid you. It shows the character of the man you are. Of the man who I was sure you were. But . . ." He waved the cigar. "But I had to be certain. I have enemies. I must be sure that one of them is not a member of my own family. It is my wish that you understand this simple thing."

Jack nodded affirmatively, not sure he understood any of their mysterious behavior at all.

"Good, good. Now, from this point forward, anything else that I tell you must remain between my three sons and us. You will never speak of this to anyone but us. And that includes Diana or the children. Never. This is to be kept among DeLeo men. My sons and I consider you family, so you must understand that the business of grown men must not be discussed with the women. The women and children do not need to worry about DeLeo business. That is the job of grown men. You understand?"

"Yes, sir." But Jack understood none of this. Was this some ancient Italian code of behavior?

"I have already told you that I own the Scarsdale National Bank, that I own many AAA body shops, that I own accounting firms and a small chain of pharmacies. I also own many rental homes and business properties. I have just told you of my purchase of the DeLeo TV Cable Company. My holdings are vast. I am a rich old man, but not too old to run my business."

He chuckled and then quickly turned serious again.

"You now know that I employ Mitch the fixer."

Jack nodded in acknowledgment.

As Dom said this, Gino smiled. Neither Dom nor his two brothers knew Gino had also been working as a fixer disguised as and using the name Mitch. There were, in fact, two Mitch's. The real Mitch had simply been given too much of that kind of work too often, and as he had aged, he found he increasingly wanted to get away from it. Besides, Mitch had made plenty of money and lost his youthful desire to accumulate vast wealth. He already had over three million dollars.

Dom continued, "A man of my wealth needs such a person. I have problems and I have enemies. I have also had to fix the problems of wealthier men in the business world. Like Ford Carr. For example, years ago I fixed Ford's problem with ADA Marcie Kellerman of New York City. Had Ducette been prosecuted, he might never have become Ford's personal senator. Ford wished to take revenge on the Chambers' brothers for what was done to Ducette. I had Mitch fix it. That was not so long ago.

"Then there were the lawsuits against the senator back in his younger days. Mitch fixed them by persuading the Reedy and the Ward families to drop them. Ford wanted to get rid of Mr. Richard Jolly. Mitch again. And of course, you know that Mitch fixed your situation with Jean Lange, who, by the way, is alive and well. She now helps me fix other types of problems. She has many useful skills.

"Now Mitch had fixed many other problems for other men. Most have wealth so they can pay. But, understand this. It is most important. Ford Carr has no idea that I know he has had all of these things done. When he calls for Mitch, he believes he is speaking to Mitch. He does not know that it is Gino he speaks to. It is Gino who runs Mitch. In this way, I always have an advantage over Ford. Ford may be a richer man than I am, but I hold that which can destroy him and his business empire. The same is true with the other rich men Mitch has fixed problems for. When I am gone, it is Nick who will hold this information. So you see, Jack, you may feel free to join my sons and me in our business endeavors. Run DLTV for me without fear. We DeLeo's can bury Ford Carr and his black lackey at any time it suits our purpose."

Jack's head was spinning.

SON OF A BITCH!

The meeting progressed to more brandy and family small talk. After another hour, the five men were nicely buzzed and exited the office to return to their wives, children, and grandchildren. Soon after dark, Jack and Diana headed back to Chester City. Diana drove. Jack was in no shape to do so.

CHAPTER 68:
Jack and Darnell's Next Conversation

Jack awakened the following morning feeling that his body was as dried out like a sponge that had been microwaved on high for about an hour. His head felt fuzzy and his tongue felt like it had been stuffed into a cruddy old sock. It was a Saturday morning. He was glad he had drunk all that brandy Friday evening. It helped him to sleep. He had needed to sleep. To forget. To forget about the problem that he now faced in his young life. Had he not had all that brandy, he would have been up all night worrying about his current predicament.

Last night he had committed to working for Dom at his new cable TV station. He knew that he had to stick with that decision. And hell, it was surely time to leave Ford Carr. The hell of it was that Dom was not just a wealthy businessman; he was a thug and a murderer. He had facilitated crimes committed on behalf of Ford Carr. Crimes committed for a price. Some involved killing, some involved assault. Now he knew the true nature of the DeLeo business. Gino was responsible for hiring Mitch the fixer. Fixer was a family euphemism for murder and mayhem. My God. Gino was also a murderer. Gino's brothers Nick and Lou were surely complicit. But his former employer Ford Carr was exactly what Jack's father had warned him about a dozen years ago. Ford hired killers to fix things that angered or upset him. Ford and Dom were both cold-blooded killers. He would quit working for one and begin working for the other. Damn, damn, damn.

Jack quit the Ford Carr Media Company the following week. Diana's father made a lump sum payment to Ford to buy out his contract with Ford Carr Media. When Jack met with Ford, he was called every foul name in the dictionary, and as much as accused of treason. Jack tried to explain the decision was not personal and he would be going to work for the family. It made no difference. Ford ordered Jack out of his office, hollering obscenities at him on his way out the front door and promising Jack that he would even the score. Fuck him, Jack thought. But then, he also thought, so was Dom. Ah hell, Dom he would have to hug.

Officially Jack's new employer was DLTV. DLTV broadcasted from Chester City, with the studio located on the northeast side of the city. Dom would be paying Jack a seven- figure salary to start. His new show aired at 4:00 each weekday afternoon and was called America As It Is. Jack was to report the most unusual and dramatic stories over each 24-hour news cycle that shaped and affected everyday life in America. The format excited Jack.

Dom had recruited a large and talented research staff to search nationwide for the stories. The staff was the true meat and potatoes of the show, and Jack was to be the sizzle. There would be the story of the day that was to occupy the bulk of the first hour of the show. The second hour would briefly repeat the story of the day and then go into other minor events, with the last half hour of the show left for Jack to field questions from the studio audience.

Dom had also hired Pauline Goodfellow. She would occupy a supporting role and serve as a backup host to Jack. She was young, bright, and attractive. When Jack first met her the danger signals flashed through his brain. Keep it purely professional, he told himself. No more Jean Lange screw-ups.

After two months, the ratings for *America As It Is* were climbing at warp speed. Jack knew that the show was on its way to become a hit in the late afternoon time slot, and that drove him to do better and better each day. Dom and his sons were happy with the increasing popularity of the show. Jack was satisfied that his decision to leave Ford Carr had been the right one. Dom and his sons were family, after all. Diana's family. Flawed as they were, they were no more flawed than Ford Carr.

It was soon after the show was becoming an obvious hit that Jack took a call from Senator Darnell Ducette. Darnell requested a meeting with Jack at his home in Living Greens. Congress was in its summer recess. He met with Darnell on a Tuesday afternoon.

Darnell had a table ready with some fruit and cheese on it. An ice bucket and with a bottle of vodka and a bottle of scotch and two tumblers sat on the table.

Both Jack and Darnell were seated in plush chairs on each side of the table. Darnell popped a couple of grapes in his mouth and poured himself two fingers of scotch. He gestured for Jack to help himself. Jack took a cube of sharp cheddar and poured two fingers of vodka over some ice.

Darnell sipped his scotch, put the glass down, and began rubbing his temples.

Jack noticed this and spoke, "Senator, are you alright?"

"I'm fine. Damn headaches. I get them a lot lately. And you can call me Darnell. Okay, Jack?"

"Sure it is. We haven't talked for some time, Darnell. What's up?" Darnell grimaced. Jack noticed.

"Perhaps it would be better to talk when you're feeling better."

"No, no. I don't know when that will be."

"So what do you wish to talk about?"

"Me."

"You? Okay, what about you?"

"Well, if I remember right, you always did want me to talk more about myself. Now I'm ready. Look, Jack, you're the one person I know that has sort of followed my life since I was playing football at Stannard High."

Jack nodded and took a swallow of the vodka.

"Here is the simple truth. I need someone to tell the story of my life."

"You mean like a biography?"

"Yeah that's it. A biography."

Darnell downed the remainder of scotch and poured another.

"I'm not sure that I understand. Why now?"

"We've been talking to each other on and off over the years now—since our college days at Chester City State. Right? You know a lot about me and about my family. Right?"

"Yes and yes."

"And you're a TV news guy now. Kind of like a reporter. Right?"

"Yes."

"I can't think of anyone else who could do this. So I'm asking you to do it."

Jack let out a long sigh.

"You want me to write your biography?"

"Yeah. A book. A published book."

"I've never written a book. Only news stories. But, I probably could. Hell, I've been sitting on a documentary news story about your life for the past two years. I have a lot of information about your life Darnell. But, I would need to know a lot more."

"I can give you that."

"I've also got a new TV show. That takes up a good chunk of my time."

"I've seen the show. It's good. And I understand the time thing. I'm convinced you're the man for this project."

"Well, I don't know what to say. Could you begin supplying me with the information that I would need? Soon?"

"I'll tell you anything you want to know. The sooner the better."

"That would be great."

"When could you start?"

"Well, I'm not sure that I agreed to do this yet." Darnell frowned.

"What would it take? I got money." Jack waved him off.

"It's not money."

"Then what?"

"It's a project. I probably just need some time to think about taking it on. Are you in a hurry?" He looked Jack hard in the eye.

"Yes."

"What's the hurry then?" Darnell took a breath and exhaled. He rubbed his temples again, swallowing more scotch.

"It's about time. Jack, to tell the truth, time is something I ain't got a lot of."

Jack just stared at Darnell.

"I got me a problem, Jack."

Jack kept staring.

"These headaches. I told you I get a lot of them. They're only getting worse. Went to the doctor a few months back. Then to a neurosurgeon. They did a CAT scan on my brain. I got me a big old fat brain tumor. He said the cancer might have been caused in part because of all the hits to the head I got playing football. Who knows? But shit, it's there. And the doctor said it's inoperable. Gave me six or eight months to live. There you have it."

"Jesus Christ, Darnell. Nothing can be done?" He shook his head, then rubbed his temples again. "I don't know what to say."

"Nothing you can say. Except yes. Do the book. Please."

Jack drank some vodka.

"Okay. I'll do it."

"Thank you, Jack. Thank you." Jack noticed something that he has never seen before. A tear from the corner of Darnell's left eye rolled down his cheek. He didn't move to wipe it away.

Jack wondered if there had always been something more to the cold, calculating man he thought he had always known.

"You know . . . I always thought I'd be a big star in the NFL. Make a shitload of money. Be famous. Then that little piss ant white boy goes and shoots my leg off. Shit. Football career over with. My dumbass agent doesn't get me a new contract in time. So here I am. No football career. But now I'm a senator. I'm an important man now. A powerful man. But all I ever really wanted was to play football. Funny how things work out."

Darnell paused and drank some more scotch.

"But maybe I deserved this. I've done some bad things in my life. Maybe it's payback . . . you know?"

"Oh?"

"Doesn't matter now."

He perked up, suddenly alert again.

"Here's the thing, Jack. I was counting on you agreeing to this. So I had my attorney draw up an agreement. A contract between you and me. You know, to tell my story."

"Hold on, Darnell. I'd need to look at that first. I need to run it by my own attorney."

"Of course."

"I would also want some information on the . . . well, the misfortunes that have happened to people involved in your life."

"You mean the bad shit. I knew you'd want that. I'll tell you everything."

"Good."

"All that stuff is in the contract. You'll like it."

"Okay. I'll get my attorney on it." Jack opened his wallet and pulled out a business card with his attorney's contact information and handed it to Darnell.

"Okay."

They shook hands and Jack left the house. Darnell poured himself more scotch. He sat drinking scotch until he passed out.

CHAPTER 69:
Revelations

Contracts were soon finalized as Jack agreed to write Darnell's story. Darnell agreed to the full disclosure of any information Jack requested. The book would not be released until after Darnell's death, which Jack didn't believe would be an issue. Jack would receive two hundred thousand dollars to write the book, but the proceeds from sales would go into Darnell's estate for the benefit of his wife, Lily.

They met again at Darnell's home in Living Greens in the late afternoon. The ice bucket, the scotch, the vodka, and two tumblers were on a cart by the desk in Darnell's office. He fixed the drinks for both of them.

"Afternoon, Jack. I guess you got some tough questions for me today. Don't worry. I'm more than ready."

"I'm glad to hear that, Darnell, because I'm going to do some serious muckraking. I already have many of the details of your life put together in a timeline. I need to eliminate the speculation about what happened to some people who are either dead or were seriously injured while being a part of your life."

"I know Jack. And I'll give you what you want. Under the circumstances, I got nothing to hide."

"Good. Let's get into it. I'll start with your mom, Estelle. Although I'm reasonably sure of the answer to this question I'm going to ask it for the record. Were you involved in her death?

"I was not."

"I received information from your friend Marcus who got it from a guy called Chimp. According to Marcus, your brother Willie told him that he was trying to mess you up by loosening that rug at the top of the stairs. Apparently, you were always the first one up to use the bathroom and Willie thought that you would slip on the rug and fall down the stairs and injure yourself. Perhaps so severely that your future as a football player would be jeopardized. To be clear, Chimp told that to Marcus and Marcus repeated it to me. I have taken the word of both men on those details. Your thoughts?"

"Yeah. I know. I heard that story. It was Mom that got caught in Willie's trap. You know, with all the pills Mom was taking and all the alcohol she drank, she could have just lost her balance. It's hard to say. I just don't know about that one. But Jack, I can tell you this. We all loved Mom. I never saw another nicer, kinder, or more loving person than Mom. I think it was more an accident than anything."

"I agree. And that's the way I intend to use this information in your biography. My intention is to portray your mom as a kind and caring person."

"That would be fair. Thank you."

"Alright. I'm going to follow my timeline in order. That brings up Tawney Johnson. The second broken-neck death. It was ruled an accident. I'm not so sure."

Darnell smiled and drank some of his scotch. He then explained to Jack how the accident was set up between Marcus and him. It was to look like an accident, but an accident designed to kill Tawney.

Darnell concluded, "So when I crashed the car into that embankment, it was either me or Marcus who was to reach over to Tawney and snap her neck."

"Who was it?"

Darnell chuckled and said, "Who do you think?"

"You."

"Shit, man. Yeah, it was me. I'm way quicker than Marcus, you know."

"You murdered her."

"Yeah man. I had to."

"But why? Why did she need to die? Damn Darnell, she was still just a kid."

Darnell's eyes closed for several seconds, as he appeared to be thinking.

"I know, so was I. But to me she was kind of a silly little bitch. Nice looking. Good sex, but damn she got herself pregnant—"

"Didn't you have something to do with that?"

"Yeah. But she told me she was on the pill. She lied to me. Dammit, Jack, she shouldn't have done that. Why would she do that?"

"And that's why you killed her? Because she lied to you?"

"Kinda yes and kinda no. I was eighteen years old at that time. Think about that. I had a career in the NFL on my mind. I knew I could be an NFL quarterback. Shit, almost everyone knew that. I did not need a stupid white bitch with a kid to get in the way of my career. I just couldn't have that, could I? Don't you see that? I had no room in my life for a wife or a kid. I've always known that anyone who got in my way, well shit, I've already told you how I felt about people like that."

"That's it?"

"Yeah, that's it! Shit, Jack, I was going to be a college freshman. I had four years of football and four years of trying to graduate. She woulda been in my way. I killed her and then she wasn't in my way. Simple as that. Simple, right? Don't you see?"

"Frankly, no, Darnell. But you and I are different people. So let's move on to Willie. Another broken neck. First there . . ."

"Look. I killed Willie, too. You already know that." Jack exhaled deeply.

"I kind of thought so. How did that go down?"

"Marcus told me about Willie doin' that rug. I saw it as him hurting Mom. Marcus also told me Willie said that I was the target of his little scheme. I never liked Willie much anyway. You already know that. Hell, when I was just a little kid I had my own bedroom. Then Willie came along and I had to bunk with him. Even as a kid I hated that. Hated him for getting into my space. I mean, shit, he pissed me off since I was little, pissed me off while he was alive, and pissed me off for the last time when he did what he did to Mom."

"I called him and told him that I wanted to talk to him. He told me to meet up with him in the Roonies. I drove into the Roonies one night and picked him up. Near some old boarded up houses. He got into my car. Willie was always a dumb shit."

Darnell laughed as he said that. "He was shuttin' the car door when I leaned over and grabbed his head and twisted. He had turned his back to me and that gave me my chance. Snapped the dumb fucker's neck. Just that quick. At that point in my life, I didn't have to hate him anymore. He was dead. Nobody hates a dead man. Am I right?"

"Really?" Jack questioned.

"Then what?"

"I just took a nice, long, easy drive out to Scarsdale with Willie laying there in the front seat. I dumped his sorry ass in that swamp they got outside of town. Case closed. Nothing more to say. He deserved what he got."

Jack just shook his head.

"Well Darnell, I always thought you murdered Willie. Now I know for sure."

"Like I just said. He pissed me off for the last time. I got tired of his stupid shit, man."

"Now how about Chimp? He got himself hung from his apartment window in Cleveland. Did you do that one?"

"That's another kind of yes and kind of no."

"That's not an answer, Darnell. You can't have it both ways." Darnell shrugged and smiled.

"Well, I always thought that Chimp should have told me himself what Willie had said about the rug and how he was trying to get me hurt. It made me mad. And Jack, I usually stay mad when people start screwing with my life. So I kind of suggested to Marcus that I thought it would be real cool if that little shithead was hanged from his window. Marcus ain't the brightest star in the sky, you know, but he is receptive to suggestions. I guess he liked my idea. Marcus killed him, I guess. I never did ask him if he did it but I led him in that direction. Piece of cake, man."

Jack kicked back in his chair, drink in hand took a couple big gulps while looking at Darnell.

"This is some heavy shit, Darnell."

Darnell spreads his hands palms up.

"You're the guy who wanted to know, Jack."

"Yeah, I did. But do you really want the world to know who you truly are?"

Jack took another gulp of vodka.

"I don't remember ever caring what people thought about me, Jack. This book, by contract, ain't getting published 'till I'm dead. Why would I give a shit when I'm dead and buried six feet under? I would take a bet from my grave that this will be a best seller. Lily will get the money, along with the rest of my estate. That's all that matters to me at this point. Get it? I mean the whole point of the book is to make some money that will go to Lily. It's her that I'm doin' this for."

Jack sighed. "Well, let's get to Candy. The cops see you as the killer but could never prove it. And, of course, ADA Kellerman never pushed to put the case before the grand jury. She took a bribe instead."

"I know. I got Ford Carr to handle that problem. I needed the case to be ruled accidental, otherwise, it would have stayed open forever. I needed it to be closed. Ford's money did the trick."

"So you murdered her?"

"Bitch was crampin' my style, man. Taking away the headlines that I should have been getting. Making more money than me. I was the man of the family. Don't you understand? Does your wife Diana show you up? I'd bet not. It wasn't proper for her to show me up. She might as well have cut my balls off. I couldn't have that. No man could. No man, not even you, Jack."

"So you killed her?"

"Damn right I did. I thought I had it figured out pretty good, but I did fuck it up some. That detective had it right. There were only two sets of keys to Candy's place and I had one of them. Like a dumb shit, I forgot to lock up the front door after I tossed her over the balcony. I was obviously the killer, but I got lucky."

"So you killed her because she was . . . well, upstaging you?"

"Hell yes! She was disrespecting me. I can't put up with that from my own wife. How could I? Jack, she deserved what she got. Surely you can see that."

"Damn," Jack muttered quietly.

"Put it this way. Lily don't treat me like that. She's not as pretty as Candy but she is the better woman. That's why I want the book sales to go to her, along with the rest of my money."

"Okay. Another question. Did you push Chuck Chambers down that flight of stairs?"

"You know I did. Again, the guy was in my way. I was, by far, the better quarterback. Remember once when I told you that I was going somewhere in life and nobody was going to get in my way? He was in my way. Period. I took care of it and then he wasn't in my way anymore."

"I assume you know that Chuck was recently attacked a second time? Your handiwork?"

"Yeah, but I asked for Ford to take care of it. For setting his brother on me."

"So it would be logical for me to assume you had Clete taken care of too."

"Oh, hell yeah. I asked Ford to do them both."

"Well, you sure didn't lie to me when you told me that you took care of people who stood in your way. But I didn't take you literally."

"I also told you that I am a serious guy, too."

"But I guess you didn't plan on Chuck Chambers' brother Clete shooting your leg off?"

Darnell shook his head. "My mistake. No way to plan on gettin' shot at by a piss ant white kid with a rifle."

"Life is full of bullets that you have to dodge, Darnell. Some of us just get lucky, and some of us duck and get hit anyway. That's how it is."

Darnell laughed. "Yeah, I guess you're right. Just like a brain tumor. I didn't see that one either. Once again, shit happens. Trouble is, I don't know how to break a tumor's neck. Jack, does a tumor have a neck?"

Jack shook his head. "Damned if I know, Darnell." Jack stood and told Darnell that he had enough for one day.

"I'll be in touch if I need more. Take care."

"I'll be here, Jack. At least for a little while."

Jack headed for the front door as Darnell reached for the scotch bottle.

CHAPTER 70:
Road's End

In the seemingly endless weeks that followed Jack's meeting with Darnell, he spent his time doing the *America As It Is* show and working on the book about Darnell's life. He had gathered all the information that he needed and was now in the process of writing. During his evenings he occupied himself spending quality time with Diana and the children. Things were settling down into normal life.

One Saturday evening, after eating supper with his family, Jack's cell phone buzzed. He answered it promptly.

"Hello."

Detective Russo said, "Hello. Is this Jack Troop?"

"Yes. Who's calling, please?"

"Mike Russo. From the Chester City PD. You remember me, don't you?"

"Of course, Detective. How are you?"

"I'm fine. But listen here. I got a murder-suicide on my hands. It would appear that the murderer left a note for you." He paused. "It's addressed to Jack Troop. How about that?"

Jack paused, confused. "A note to me? Who wrote it?"

"Troop, are you free by any chance? I'll let you read it."

"I sure as hell am curious, Detective. I've just finished eating supper with my family so I'll clean up and change then head your way. Where are you at?"

"No need for formalities; just hop in your car and get on over here. I'm at the Living Greens. The home of Senator Darnell Ducette. Got it?"

"Darnell? I'm on my way."

"I'll leave word with the cop at the front gate."

When Jack arrived at Darnell's home at Living Greens, Detective Russo was waiting for him at the front door.

"One minute. Just to be sure, you've seen crime scenes before?"

"Yes."

"Okay, then. Come on in."

Jack and Russo walked through the hallway leading into the living area. It was spacious with a high ceiling. On the right side of the room was a stairway that led to the upstairs rooms. The open hallway at the top of the stairs ran mostly to the left side of the house. A thick solid banister guarded the edge of the hallway from the floor below.

Jack's eyes took in the scene. Several crime scene techs were still processing the area near two bodies. Both Marcus Wayne and Darnell Ducette were hanging from the banister, ropes tied to their necks, bodies dangling above the floor below. Jack breathed slowly in and out several times, calming himself. The body of Marcus had a gunshot wound in the center of his chest. No visible sign of violence could be seen on Darnell. A .38 caliber revolver was lying on the floor below the two hanging men. Both bodies were in the early stages of decay; body fluids had started to drip from each corpse to the floor. Reddish-brown ooze stained the beige carpet. The eyes of both men bulged in their sockets and their tongues had flopped over the lower lips of their open mouths.

Jack spoke through clenched jaws. "Jesus Christ, Detective. What a hell of a picture that is."

"Amen to that. It's not very pretty. I'm thinking murder-suicide here. The senator shoots the other man in the chest and then hangs him. He then hangs himself. Here's the note. It explains everything. But you knew the guy. I'd like your take on it."

"Sure." Russo handed Jack the note.

To Jack Troop:

Hey man, I took care of Marcus. He was a bad guy. I always knew that he would do what I asked him to do. I shot him and then hanged him. Simple justice.

As for me, maybe I'm a bad guy, too. Maybe not. But I always said that I'd live life my way. I decided to die under those same terms. I hanged myself. No sense waiting on a brain tumor to do the job.

Remember that I told you I kind of liked the hangings in those old western movies? I figured hanging myself would be nice and quick.

Remember, we have an agreement. Get the book published. Maybe I'll run into you someday in another world. Ha. Not. I don't believe that shit.

-Darnell

Jack finished the note and looked at Russo.

"I read over it several times. What it says is what the scene looks like. Murder-suicide."

Russo gave Jack a hard look and said, "Now what's this shit about some agreement?"

Jack knew Russo had been waiting to ask.

"I agreed to write his biography. I am under contract and can't publish the book until after his death. He revealed some things to me. Those things will be in the book. You will find them interesting."

"Really? Things I need to know? Anything that would close some cases?"

"Yes."

"Explain."

"I can't."

"Are you going to tell me what happened?"

Jack grinned. "Detective, when the book is published, I'll give you the first copy. I'll even autograph it. It has all the dirt on his life. It will definitely clear up a few cases for you."

Russo nodded. "Okay, Troop. I'm too tired to argue with you and don't really feel like charging you with obstruction of justice on unsolved cases. I can wait."

Jack nodded and said, "Thanks."

Both men left. Marcus and Darnell still dangled above the living room floor. As Jack reached the doorway he turned and took a final look at Darnell Ducette hanging from the banister. He knew that he was looking at the final scene for his book about Darnell, one he decided to title *The Hanging Man: the Life Story of Senator Darnell Ducette.*

CHAPTER 71:
Surprise

On a warm day in summer, Jack, Diana, and their two young children were attending a family picnic at the DeLeo home in Scarsdale. During the course of the afternoon, Gino came up to Jack, tapped him on the shoulder and asked to speak to him briefly. The two men separated themselves from the others so they could talk in private. Gino explained to Jack that now that he was working for the DeLeo's, he was not to forget that if a serious problem came up, to come to him. If a problem needed to be fixed, Gino would fix it.

Jack faked a smile and told Gino he would remember. The conversion soured the rest of the afternoon for Jack, reminding him of the fixes Dom had described previously. Jack still felt uncomfortable working for a family that was comfortable using thuggery as a business plan.

Two hours later the Jack Troop family was headed back to their home in Chester City in Troop's new Cadillac. Jack was quiet but also distracted. His wife noticed this.

"You are being awfully quiet, Jack," she prodded.

"Oh. Yeah, I guess. Things on my mind."

Diana laughed a short laugh.

"Was it your private conversation with Gino?"

Jack glanced at her. She was so damn perceptive.

"Yes. I guess I should tell you something. Something about some . . . ah, some of the business decisions that Dom or your brothers have made."

"Oh? Such as?"

"Well, unpleasant decisions. Ah, Di, I'm not sure how to explain this to you. Maybe I shouldn't. I was told not to."

Diana replied, half scolding, "Jack, Jack, Jack. Of course, you can't. But don't worry about it. You're talking about Mitch the fixer. I know about him. In fact, so does Mom. We've known for many years. Both Mom and I have accepted it, but we don't approve of it."

"Well damn. I . . . I don't know what to say, Di." He glanced at his wife.

Diana winked at him.

SON OF A BITCH!

ABOUT THE AUTHOR

Dan is originally from Columbus, Ohio, but has also lived in Long Island, N.Y., Alexandria, V.A., and Lancaster County, P.A. As a child, Dan enjoyed reading comic books and always wanted to write his own adventure story.

Dan graduated from Marietta College in Ohio in 1968, majoring in English and History, and later worked as a teacher, in retail management and also as a life and health insurance salesman. Dan frequently contributes to his local newspaper by writing editorials and has had 93 editorials published.

Dan lives with his wife, Pat, in Pennsylvania, and has two grown sons and five grandchildren.

Broken Bones is his first novel.

Dan's email address is DanBetz@ptd.net

Melissa, thank you for your support. Happy reading.

Daniel Oliver Betz, III

338